BETWEEN

Wendy Glassby

Lily El\en *Publishing*

ABN 82 215 570 029

Lily Ellen Publishing is an independent publisher whose address can be found below.

First published in Australia in 2021 by Lily Ellen Publishing
P O Box 3043 Shelley Western Australia 6148 Australia
lilyellenpublishing.com

Typeset in Adobe Garamond Pro
Cover design and layout by Cathie Glassby
Cover photo: TheRoadProvides/Shutterstock.com
Edited by Ilsa Sharp, Professional member Institute of Professional Editors (Australia)
Printing and distribution through Ingram Spark www.ingramspark.com

A catalogue record for this book is available from the National Library of Australia

ISBN 978 0 64883410 6

lilyellenpublishing.com

DEDICATION

For Ben, may he rest in peace, for his children and their children, and for Ben's extended family and friends, especially Aunty Coba and cousin Michael. For all whose hearts still linger in the politically ever-changing islands to Australia's north, both familiar and alien as they may be.

FOREWORD

Sean Dorney AM MBE CSM FAIIA

When Wendy Glassby sent me an early draft of this intriguing novel, she had tentatively titled it, "Bitter Sweet Aibika". Those of us who have spent a lot of time in Papua New Guinea know this leafy vegetable, Aibika, quite well. Indeed, my wife Pauline, who is from the Manus Province in PNG, grows it here in our garden in Brisbane where it does particularly well during the summer months. We often eat it boiled in coconut juice with fish and rice. Wendy describes it well in this passage: "Ah, aibika, your peppery aroma. Its deep green leaves makes us exPNG people feel homesick. For her, it's the contrast between the sweet pepper of the young leaves and bitter bite of the old. As in life, there are sweet times and bitter times and you need to know only how to make the most of what you have."

Eventually, Wendy chose a different title, "Between", which has a more universal meaning especially to those who never resided in Australia's former colony. The Chinese and mixed-race families of Rabaul which she writes about are caught forever between cultures feeling never fully accepted by, first, their German then their Australian colonial masters and, later, by the indigenous people of Papua New Guinea following independence in 1975.

The story is told through the voices of several generations of mostly female members of the one extended Malay\Chinese\mixed race family. And, despite the fact that the story leaps about back and forth, again and again, over decades and decades, it works. The family gets torn apart by volcanic eruptions, the Japanese occupation of Rabaul during World War II and, crucially, PNG's Independence when some believe they have no alternative but to flee PNG to Australia.

The two main population centres that provide the locations for much of the tale – Rabaul and Brisbane – are places that I know very well. I live in Brisbane and although I never lived permanently in Rabaul I often visited it when I was the ABC Correspondent in PNG. I spent quite a bit of time there during the 1994 volcanic eruptions and my reports actually get a mention when the family in Brisbane watch the ABC television news "with before-and-after shots of Chinatown, the part of town buried the deepest".

This novel is a thoroughly good read and, importantly, tells the story of a community that has given an extra richness to both countries – Australia and Papua New Guinea.

Sean Dorney OA AM MBE CSM FAIIA

Mr Dorney's extensive career of Australian journalist, foreign correspondent, and writer, covered the Pacific with a particular focus on Papua New Guinea. Mr Dorney was the Pacific and PNG Correspondent of the Australian Broadcasting Corporation on and off from 1975 to 2014.

NOTE TO READER

This story revolves around the human need for recognition. It is also a celebration of human diversity. Thus, there is a need to explain the use of terms that might be read as pejorative or racist: 'Chinese and Mixed Race', for example. This is an identifying name accepted and adopted by members of a group who by and large are descendants of non-western expatriates not only from southern China but other regions as well. From early in the twentieth century, individuals found their way to the remote settlement of Rabaul in search of work and for a variety of reasons did not return to homelands. Over time, an inclusive and blended culture has emerged, sufficiently developed to be transported when many of the group migrated. The use of capital letters identifies the phrase 'Chinese and Mixed Race' as an accepted if unofficial name for a diverse and otherwise unnamed social group and differentiates it from other terms such as 'mixed race' or the Tok Pisin word 'hapcas', both of which categorise individuals by visible markers of an individual's ancestry.

Another point that needs clarifying is the terms used to represent locations and populations in a story that spans more than a century. In the late nineteenth and early twentieth centuries, the region surrounding the Bismarck Sea, in which the town of Rabaul is located, was known as 'New Guinea' or 'German New Guinea'. When the narrative covers this era, I use both of these terms for the region and 'New Guineans' for the indigenous tribal population. Later, in the narrative when covering the period under Australian control, I use the terms 'Territory' and 'Territories' to describe the separated and combined mandated territories of New Guinea and Papua and again 'New Guineans' for the population. When the narrative reaches the period following Independence, I use the terms 'Papua New Guinea', 'PNG' and the Tok Pisin word 'Niugini' for the nation and the Tok Pisin name of 'Niugineans' for its population.

A glossary of Tok Pisin and other words and phrases can be found towards the back of this book.

wai na yu go?

wai na yu go
tru tumas mi laik dai
dispela pen i wok long
kilim mi wansait
maus bilong mi pas
na nek bilong mi sore stret
mi karai dei na nait
tasol aiwara i kam daun nating
yu lewa bilong mi
wai na yu go

peles yu go long en
em i long wei stret
sapos mi go long
maunten mi no nap long
lukim yu
wai yu go
aiye wai na yu go
yu brukim lewa bilong mi
taim yu lusim mi na yu go

Why have you left?

Why have you left
It's true I want to die
The pain
is killing me
My mouth is heavy
I am sore to the throat
I weep
teardrops fill my days and nights
my sweetheart
why have you left

The place you have left for
is too far
if I reached
the highest of mountaintops
I would not find you there
why have you left
Oh lover, why have you left
you have broken my heart
by leaving me behind

(Kalupio, Gwendolyn. 2003.
Meanjin 62(3):198–199.)

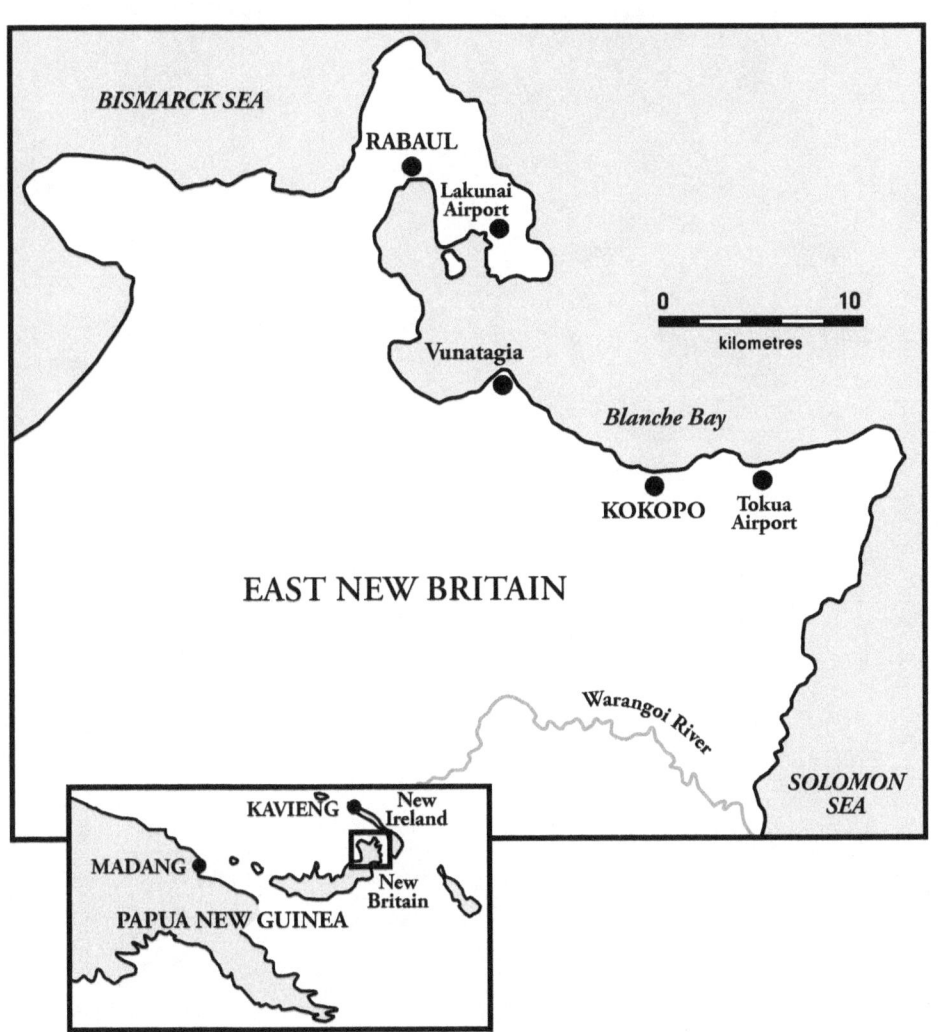

CONTENTS

PROLOGUE

1

KAVIENG, NEW IRELAND PROVINCE, PAPUA NEW GUINEA
Late 2010

The room is plain. It contains only essentials. Exactly as a hotel in a remote Papua New Guinea town needs to be. It's not a resort. It isn't designed to entice poolside lingering. Its aim is merely to provide single-night sleeping facilities for people travelling to or from other places. A dying woman requires only a bed, water to sip, and her own contemplations. These are what this room offers me, and now I must wait.

Time is beyond my jurisdiction, nor can I identify what's authentic and what's imagined. I'm tempted to assume this means I'm on the path to the place where my ancestors are waiting. And yet, I am not so far gone that I can allow myself to concede this is truly not at all about temptations, nor about paths and desires, but more about my impatience. Because I wish for a truncated journey to the holy place, I have convinced myself that if I can hear my grandmother's voice my aspirations will be met, and that soon I will be with my grandmother.

As I wait in my plain room, I call to her.

'Nenek, Granny, I am here.'

Only I can hear my words. They echo in my head. My voice has lost its worldly power.

§

Nenek is the Malay word for a grandmother. My grandmother Koti Pereira is or, I should say was, of Malay heritage. She says she was born on the island of Ambon. Today that's part of Indonesia. Over sixty years on and I still hurt from losing her.

I'm a grandmother too. Two of my three sons have children, but they don't call me Nenek. I insist they use the Cantonese term 'Ah Ma'.

I have my reasons.

To hear Nenek's voice will offer me hope. Yet, despite my declining state, I can still recognise my journey has a long way to go and even if I can hear my grandmother call 'Ria', as I believe I can, I know it's an hallucination.

Only Nenek uses the name Ria. Everyone else calls me Maria, Maria Seeto. Except for Stephen. My 'One-true-love' has another name for me.

Again, I convince myself I hear her – 'Ria' – and my plain room is replaced by a scenery scattered with primitive and tumbledown shacks. In front of me are fallen palms and bomb craters scarring the earth. I'm six or seven and I know this place. It's where I was born and where I lived most of my life. It's on another island, across the Bismarck Sea from Kavieng where my body lies.

I'm 'Home', and my hometown Rabaul is a Japanese military town, and once more I am the child Ria, full of curiosity.

'Nenek, where's my little brother Henry?'

'You mustn't fret, child. Your papa tru is keeping Henry safe.'

Her words terrify me. I fear for Henry. Yes, the man everyone calls David Seeto, or Seeto Wei, is our real father, but he's also a stranger. Papa has not visited us since Henry was born five years ago. Who presents the bigger menace to Henry: his father or the Japanese soldiers? Granny and I sell vegetables to the soldiers every day. Our papa is a shadow.

More questions.

'Where's Mumma, Nenek? Daddy-George is not here either, so where's my stepfather? Why have they both left me?'

Grandmother pats my head. This is all I need to be reassured. For a moment I forget to worry. Then I remember. She still hasn't told me where everyone has gone.

She and I are beneath a lean-to constructed of palm fronds and bamboo, open to the world and the weather on two sides. It's our wartime home. There are holes in the roof. As it rains often in Rabaul, I have mapped those holes in my mind. Each night when the gaps are no longer visible against the dark sky, I use my memory of them to choose a suitable place on the ground on which to spread my mat bed. However, avoiding drips does not necessarily ensure sleep. With two open sides, our wartime home may as well sit astride a main thoroughfare. Both the long-term residents and the invaders are restless.

'The outcome of the war worries everyone,' my grandmother says. 'Walking at night makes them feel better.'

The hum of muted voices, the padding of soft footsteps, and the flickering shadows the walkers create as they pass each lamplit hut inhibits my sleep. As I lie awake, I imagine I'm back in Nenek's real home, the one underneath the Mango tree, the one we had to leave. Soldiers need a place to live. Nenek and I pass our home every day on our way to the village gardens to collect taro to sell. I resist looking. There are always soldiers sitting on Nenek's verandah. I hear them laughing and I smell the smoke of their cigarettes. If I look, they will see my angry eyes and I've heard the stories.

Nenek picks up a ladle from the table and moves closer to a fire ablaze in a firepit positioned on one of the open sides. I hear it plop as it's dropped into a pot propped across the centre of the fire and I watch as she gives our evening meal a stir. As she bends over, the glow of the flames transforms the dark skin of her face and arms, washing one half of her body with a rosy hue and creating a luscious contrast between front and back. I can't drag my eyes away. My grandmother's beautiful and unique. I don't look like her. I'm coffee; she's ebony. There's a white cloth wrapped high on her head, as always. When she steps away from the fire and straightens, she appears even taller than normal. No one else, except Mumma, is that tall. From her white headdress to her feet, she's like no one else I know. Words tumble out of my mouth. I hear myself asking her why her clothes are unlike anyone else's in Rabaul. She takes a moment to answer.

'To remind me I'm Malay. Remembering who I am helps me understand the world.'

Sixty-eight years later, as I wait in my hotel room, I see, as if it's happening now, Nenek's tall thin body returning to the fire to continue her stirring. Her body's swaying to a tune she's humming. I want to hum along too but I don't recall the tune.

Did I ever know it? Instead, I tap my fingers on the hotel sheets stretched across my aging body. My waiting-room has become dark; as I dream, night has overtaken day. A flash of white startles me. I know what I'm seeing. It's a miracle that can only have begun on my grandmother's face. Her smile has traversed through the years and it's pulling me back to 'The War', back to my place beneath the lean-to, and there I see it again as it flies across to me from near the fire where my grandmother is still dancing. She looks happy.

Then her body bends at the waist and her head turns toward me. Her eyes are wide. I know she's sending me a silent but clear message.

'You see? Life's good. Be kind to yourself.'

I wish for more light. Only in sun-like brightness is it possible to look deep into eyes that are as dark as a starless night. In my grandmother's eyes is where I ache to be. That's where I'll find my answers.

The older, dying Maria reminds herself of the distinctiveness of those dark eyes set in a dark face while younger Maria only sees how they contrast with her own blue eyes and cinnamon-toned skin. Younger Maria wonders, can this tall dark woman truly be her grandmother? Nenek's hair, long, heavy and black. Hers, short, brown and frizzy. The seven-year-old looks around and sees the other children waiting for whatever is in Nenek's pot tonight. Legs sprawl in front or behind or under, as they sit on a circle of woven mats spread on the ground around Nenek's fire and wait. Grandmother takes care of these children.

'They are my children until their parents come for them after "The War".'

Young Maria doesn't believe her grandmother's words. Those parents won't be coming back. People are dying in 'The War'. Does this mean she too is yet another orphan? Is she another child waiting for parents who are never coming back? Is she a sister waiting for a brother who won't come home? Does this mean Nenek's not her real grandmother?

'Nenek, please tell me. If I'm your granddaughter, why don't I look like you?'

'Oh, my little Ria. You worry so much. I'm blessed with two grandchildren. Neither looks like me and yet they're mine and they're beautiful.'

Her grandmother's response provides no satisfaction for young Ria, nor for the older Maria whose time for resolving her lifetime of doubts is running out. Decades have passed between 'The War' and the moment of approaching death. For dying Maria there's nothing left but to face the truth. She's dying and yet she's still the child everyone forgives for asking awkward questions. As it has always been for that confused child, forgiveness is of no help. Nor has she found any satisfactory answers. The questions asked under the lean-to linger.

'Am I the Ria that others see me as being? Am I the Ria that Nenek tells me I am? Or am I the person no one can see but me? About that person, the one inside, I can only see bits and pieces. That one lives in a deep private place. Why can't someone tell me the truth? If I see myself as different from others, those differences must be obvious to everyone: differences between me and my grandmother, me and my mumma, me and my father, and even between me and my brother.'

It's the differences between her and her brother that nag at her. If Henry's absence during the war years is because he 'looks Chinese, and the Japanese hate Chinese', as Mumma and Nenek tell her, then why did that trait miss her? In her heart, she knows she's a good Chinese girl. She has followed all the rules her father delivered when he still acted like a father and visited her. She learnt to speak Cantonese; she follows Chinese ways and she wholeheartedly believes in Chinese values. Tears well as she recalls the time before her father abandoned her, when he delivered occasional encouragement to her.

'A girl like you Maria, who doesn't look like a Chinese girl, must show you are Chinese in other ways. Follow what I have always told you, my Chinese daughter, and this will be so.'

She must have failed. No one sees her as Chinese.

Too easily the word 'misfit' comes to her and, with it, pain. Dying Maria sobs. A life lived as an oddity. To add to her puzzlement, there's her grandmother's strange story, told only once but never forgotten, woven throughout a lifetime into every other piece of evidence informing her of her nonconformity.

She loves Nenek's stories. The best ones describe Nenek's homeland, a tiny island far from Rabaul. Others are about Ria's grandfather, Datuk Josef, 'the love of Nenek's life, taken from her too soon'. Each tale leads to the one about how Nenek happened to find herself in Rabaul; each explains how Nenek fits within this town of many. But this singular one is disappointing.

She remembers the day the story slipped out. She remembers Nenek's mood. Later, as an adult she recognises that something was wrong. But for her younger self, sensing more and being compelled to accept what was given, only added to her confusion.

'Ria, when I was a young woman, I worked for your great-grandfather. You understand? Your mumma's grandfather. He was a rich and powerful German man. His wife was not German. She was born on the mainland of New Guinea. From near Madang. She was New Guinean.'

That's the beginning. And then comes the ending.

'The only good thing their son did was to give you your blue eyes and curly hair. You are special, Ria.'

There's no middle.

After she finishes that solitary telling, Nenek turns away, angry, and Ria knows she will never understand. Yet she doesn't give up. She has another question.

'So, Nenek, am I a Malay girl like you are? Or am I German? Or a woman of New Guinea? Or am I Chinese, as my father is?'

Nenek has a perfect answer.

'Oh, without doubt, Ria, you are a Rabaul woman. Rabaul is a town that belongs in the stories of many people. You, too, have many stories in you. You should not forget this, Ria. Always remember the stories because they'll explain to you who you are and how you became that person.'

Since that solitary moment of storytelling, from war into peace and never fully convinced of her Nenek's advice, she continued to ask the same question. Each time it was asked, Nenek would place her long thin fingers over the centre of her granddaughter's chest and tap them several times, beating out her answer.

'Ria, you are yourself. You're special. Many beliefs and customs come together inside you. Look into your heart. Know yourself. Carry this knowledge with you no matter where you go. Never forget who you are and what makes you, you.'

Nenek's repeated phrase of reassurance provided Ria comfort, even after the day Grandmother left her to go to a better place on high.

'Know yourself Ria.'

Even though Nenek's words echoed in Ria's mind throughout the passing years, the adult Maria knows she has failed. As she continues to wait for her final breaths, as she fluctuates between past and present, she permits herself one final indulgent moment of regret. The sorrow of failure seeps out of her.

'Too late now. Only in death will I escape my shame.'

§

I'm still waiting. How long must I linger?

At last I sense small changes. My body no longer listens to my mind's commands to make the movements required for continued living. My surrounds have lost permanence. My soul feels ready to leave my body. I can recognise that I'm no longer bound as I have been for over seventy years to the assumptions, allegiances and limitations of my physicality and my name Maria Seeto. There's a change in my demeanour. There's certainty in my thinking. I know who I am.

I'm the offshore breeze that ripples and whispers in the tall wild kunai grass; I'm the night wind that persuades one coconut to leave its brothers and sisters high in the palms; and I'm the pre-rain bluster that pulls the ripe frangipani blossom from the plump arms of its mother tree. I'm the dark ash cloud above the volcano; I'm the voice of the waves lapping on the grey pumice beach; and I'm the bite to the nostrils that comes with cooking together ginger, garlic, fish and taro. My heartbeat's the pulse of dragon drums on New Year's Day and the throb of village kundu in celebration. I'm here, there, nowhere; I'm past, present, future; I know everything and I forget everything.

What I understand at last is that Home is a location, a site linked by emotion to memory, and that's where I'm dying. But Home is a place far from where I live with my children and my grandchildren. That's the home in which I should be spending my last seconds of living, not here.

I wish to offer one reassurance to my dearest brother Henry, sobbing in a nearby hotel room, but it's impossible and too late. Normal speech has gone. Yes, I understand, Henry my dearest brother, how your heart aches. It's too cruel that after a lifetime of separation, you and I have had only weeks together. But soon we'll be together again. As you waited for me to come Home to you, I'll wait for you to join me in heaven. Please take your time. There's no need to hurry. Time isn't measured in the final resting place. Once you arrive, we'll be together throughout eternity. Nothing can ever separate us again. When it's your time, your family will be there in the clouds, waiting, with arms outstretched. First will be me and my darling Stephen, then our mumma Josefina and Daddy-George. Nenek Koti will tell you her stories, as grandmothers love to do. Even Datuk Josef will be there. Then you too will understand everything as I do.

2

BRISBANE, AUSTRALIA
December 2010

They tell her there are seven stages of grief. They tell her, each caring soul in their own particular style of consolation, using their own words not hers: 'Francine, your grandmother loved you. Through her eyes, you were the tops. You two, like peas in a pod. You both think the same,' they say, tapping their own head to demonstrate. 'You speak the same. Both bossy as. It'll take a long time. Let your mourning take its course. Don't rush it. Don't be ashamed to cry.'

She's finding it hard to deal.

She resists the concept that Ah Ma Maria is dead. That's stage one: shock.

Everyone who knew her grandmother also knew of her health problems but not one, especially not Francine, believed they were sufficiently critical to bring about her death. Francine wants to blame Gran's stupid decision to travel to Papua New Guinea. She wants to blame her grandmother for doing that alone, for not consulting anyone, for not checking out matters like health and difficulties. Francine has heard it's not so easy just to board a plane and go. Isn't law and order fragile in PNG? Did PNG's limited services mean Gran didn't receive the care she needed in good time? She's discovered being angry with a dead grandmother doesn't work even if she's in the angry phase of grieving.

Although anger is said to be stage three, that emotion arrived early and stayed. It arrived during the first phone call from PNG, when this so-called cousin of her father introduced himself as Ling. In real terms and under other circumstances, this should have been only a small issue. But her first response definitely was anger. How come she only hears about other Seetos, the PNG Seetos, as an outcome of Gran dying? She imagines some form

9

of conniving but for what reason? She hasn't a clue. So, this Ling's a son of Gran's brother Henry who, surprise, surprise, is also alive. Are there other sons and daughters, grandchildren? No answer. Henry's the one Gran went to visit. Somewhere during this part of the telephone conversation, she felt herself slip into denial. Ling may have 'said' that Gran didn't want them to go to PNG while she was ill and dying nor to attend her burial, but to Francine that didn't sound like something her grandmother would say. Gran wouldn't have been so cruel. She would have known how much her family would have wanted to be there. When Ling cautiously tried to clarify her grandmother's instructions by detailing them in his own words, she began to suspect a self-serving conspiracy. A free trip to Oz, maybe.

'Use my ticket and take your papa down to Brisbane. Reunite family. Tell Francine and Andrew and the others I want a big New Guinea-style party, mumu pig and the works. I want all the ex-PNG people to do what they always do when someone dies: sit there and pretend they remember, make up stories of how good life used to be, and let them make me into a good grandmother and mother when I'm not. They will discover soon enough I'm not who they think I am, so before that happens let them think good things of me.' Ling said he didn't know what she meant by this last part. Maybe delusional, he suggested.

All rubbish, in Francine's mind.

At that moment, if it had been physically possible, she would have gladly forced her mobile back through whatever cables and wires connected him to her across the Coral and Bismarck Seas and right into Ling's mouth. She needed him to stop talking. Everything he said hurt. A troubling thought had played in the back of her mind. Is her anger not with Ling but over the possibility that Ah Ma, as her grandmother likes to be called, had let this Ling take her place? Why didn't Gran call her? For the whole of her life, forever, as long as her memory could stretch, she had shared a tight bond with her grandmother. As she grew older, the confidences became more mature. She had spent considerable energy boasting to all and sundry about how 'Gran and I, we tell each other everything.' Yet, now, with the finality of death and opportunities lost, the untruth inside this declaration twists her grief into guilt. Had she told her grandmother everything? Hadn't she delayed telling Ah Ma the most important secret of her life? She couldn't explain why she had held off. Which was it: pride, shame, or fear? Whatever the reason, because of death, any prospect of sharing her secret with her grandmother has been ripped away from her. There's no going back and putting right. Death freezes everything at the moment of dying. The what-ifs and maybes are no longer redeemable. No longer are the ready excuses relevant: that the unexpected had happened, that she could have never predicted Gran to take herself on a secret trip, nor that Gran would die so far from home. She might convince herself that, had she been aware, she would have revealed her secret before Ah Ma left but this justification only magnifies her regret. Ling's articulation of Gran's instructions feels like a warped form of punishment. If only, then maybe... as if Gran knew her granddaughter was keeping secrets and hence had moved on to another confidante.

It's clear. Now. After the event. She tortures herself with an image in 3D of Ling and her grandmother, sitting side by side. There's a sharp edge to her imaginings. The site in which she pictures these fantasy conversations occurring is foreign to her. It's a place in another country, the name of which has been heard many times in conversation but about which her knowledge is limited. Like, let's face it, she hadn't known a thing about the rest of her family 'up there', and this has shocked her. Was she negligent? Or did no one talk about them? Yet that place for Ling is his home, neither foreign to him nor to Ah Ma. By admitting her grandmother's familiarity, Francine must also concede her lack of comprehension of Gran's love of her former homeland, a truth that is underscored by Gran's choice to risk health and body to make a clandestine return.

A sense of abandonment is raw inside her. She is the Jesuit priest in the movie 'In the Name of the Rose' shredding his own back with a knotted rope. These unfamiliar emotions undermine her sense of self. Has the view of her grandmother that she has held all the twenty years of her life been one-sided?

Back in the present and facing her needs for this day, her anger is evident but now it has taken the form of impatience. Her television is on. She's waiting for the weather report, placing too much importance on hearing it, but the news of the day is dragging. The stranger she has become since learning of Gran's death fills her with a desire to kick the television box in order to move the program forward. What's more, her need to know today's forecast is unreasonable and irrational, because she already knows what the forecast will be. Since November, a major part of the state of Queensland has experienced continuous and often drenching rain. There's already been some flooding and the potential for more is perfect fodder for the news crew cranking out scare headlines on the half-hour.

As expected, the reports have not changed and in her present mood, she lets the information dissipate. Figuring whether there is much truth in what is being said is beyond her. Nor has she found it in herself to spare any concern for those at risk. Is it a valid worry that the capacity of the Wivenhoe Dam has peaked or that a monsoonal trough coming in from the Coral Sea will bring more rain? Her internal dialogue spits out: 'Who cares? Brisbane has experienced many floods throughout her lifetime, but she has had only one grandmother die.' Her only interest is to assess whether the weather today will affect the delivery to Gran's home. There's a battle inside her head, between the delirium that claims a need to protect the goods and the sanity that faces the truth: wet or dry, damaging or not, the state of the weather and its effects on the cargo is not only not her worry but someone else's, and it's redundant: Gran's precious consignment has already survived a journey by sea from PNG.

Two weeks ago, the shipping company set the parameters. Someone has to be there to sign for the delivery; someone has to give directions. Because of her condition her father Andrew allowed her to choose the date for the delivery, but then he stepped in.

'Let me do this for you, Francie. Let me sign for it; let me be there to supervise its unloading. You need to look after yourself. No stress.'

She gave him permission and stood aside, so today he's the one there at Ah Ma's house. She scrolls through the warped logic of her father's offer. Uncle Daniel could have done the job. It's his home. He shares it with Gran. He would have been Johnny-on-the-spot, easy-peasy. But how could she refuse her father's generosity?

While her father awaits the mercy of the truck driver's schedule, she's spending the morning at her parents' home, a suburb or two away. Hours seem to drag. She has used the small worries of weather and damage to keep her mind busy and away from the larger issue that keeps crowding her thoughts, also involving the weather. Heavy rain might mean there's a need to store the goods inside the house and there's only one clear place: the centre of Gran's living room. She pretends her anxiety is centred on how this might impact upon the daily lives of Aunty Anna and Uncle Daniel and the boys who live there, but packed away behind this is a realisation that their inconvenience subtly applies pressure on her. If their home is to be restored to normal, then she must give prompt attention to whatever is being delivered. About that and the possibilities surrounding it, she sways between curiosity and fear. Gran's effort to ship this implies importance. What if this's Gran's personal stuff? She's scared. Shitless. Panicking, if she's truthful to herself. How will she cope? Already the tears are welling up inside her. Forget the Wivenhoe, this dam is about to break. The weight of responsibility falls on her. Because Gran addressed this to her. Can she live up to her grandmother's expectations?

Nothing feels right. She wants to spew. There's sweat on her forehead.

Then the phone rings. Her father.

'It's here, Francie. Waiting for you.'

When she arrives at the house, along the edge of the driveway beneath the spreading branches of Ah Ma's trees and bushes, there's a stack of rough timber. External protection, she decides. The outside crate. Her gut contracts. That means the contents are no longer shielded. Yeah, she thinks, Dad's been taking care of things, as he always does.

Inside, she finds her father seated on the sofa, his head supported by his arms, shoulders hunched, and his eyes fixed on a fabric-covered rectangle taking up a fair chunk of space on Gran's living room floor. Her heart aches for him. Has this task been too much? She's been selfish. She's forgotten all of this concerns his mother and must emphasise for him the reality of his loss. Perhaps, like her, he's trying to comprehend how a crate shipped to Brisbane could take on more importance than his mother's return. She bends over and hugs him. This provides her with a temporary distraction from what Gran would call 'the elephant in the room'. However, she reminds herself, trying to add steel to her resolve, this object she's ignoring is what today's about.

And there it is, an anonymous mass cloaked in crude blankets. Army Surplus, she likens them to, and imagines them being scratchy and coarse. If their purpose was to protect what lies beneath, then they appear to have done their job. There are no loose ends, no gaps to hint at what they cover.

'Dad, why didn't you lift these blankets?' She pauses, filled with doubt. 'Do you already know what's underneath?'

'No, I don't. But it has your name on it. It's yours. From your grandmother. Not mine to open.'

To show him there are no secrets between them, Francine lifts the coverings. Never would she have guessed what lay beneath: a beautiful chest made of rich, honey-blond timber, enhanced by carvings. She holds her breath at its beauty. It's clear there's history here. With the coverings removed, a clean medicinal aroma – camphor – fills the room and bites into her nose and eyes. She snorts and clenches her fist to rub her eyes. Her fingers are impatient to move to the next phase of the unveiling. Their excitement opposes the responses coming from her heart and her mind. Her fingers reach for what they need to do next, unclasp the latch and release the chest's lid. She feels the zing of the brass fastener on her fingertips and senses the tensing of the muscles of her forearms, as they prepare to take the weight of the lid. Her will, now convinced by the curiosity of her fingers and limbs, wants her to continue. Then her body stalls. She can neither resume the task nor return to a standing position. Bent and bowed, confused and distraught, her head drooping, she feels strands of her hair being lifted away from where they have fallen over her face. Still bent, she turns her head to one side. Her father's face is level with hers. His gaze locks with hers. His eyes are dark pools, almost unreadable, but what translates them into a display of concern for her are the wrinkles across his forehead, around his eyes and under his cheeks.

'Leave it go, Francie. Do it tomorrow, or another day.'

He eases her upward. Only after they are both standing upright, facing each other, does she realise she is crying and her father's face is destroyed.

PART 1
INDEPENDENCE

1

RABAUL, NEW BRITAIN, UNITED NATIONS MANDATED TERRITORIES OF PAPUA AND NEW GUINEA (TPNG) UNDER AUSTRALIAN GOVERNMENT ADMINISTRATION
September 1975

By Henry's reckoning this year, 1975, will be no exception to any preceding year. Days will turn into weeks, weeks into months, and another year will have come and gone. That's because he sees his world, the Gazelle Peninsula and the island of New Britain, as a still pond, disturbed only occasionally by nature. He prefers to push away the large facts. The first is that those acts of nature have at times been large, such as major volcanic eruptions, and the second, that over the past century the outside world has brought its politics and disagreements to the shores of his seemingly remote region. He pushes behind him the fact his own life was changed dramatically over the four years World War II consumed Rabaul, a painful thought he prefers to downplay, and his awareness that the very first conflict of World War I happened here at Bita Paka, not too far from his home village. That small but significant battle marked the end of Germany's twenty-five-years rule over the area and the beginning of Australia's curatorship of more than fifty years.

He rolls these thoughts through his head, shrugs his shoulders, and concedes that perhaps the most consistent aspect of the Gazelle Peninsula is the weather which varies little. The Peninsula is located a little over four degrees from the equator. This means there are no dry's, like on the mainland and the 'rainy season' is recognised only by a small increase in rainfall. Throughout the whole year the temperature hovers just over 30 degrees Centigrade accompanied by high humidity of just under 80%, and each day usually brings a mid-afternoon downpour. On the personal front, his social life is sufficient. It includes his wife and her family and his step-mother's family, both of whom live nearby, and his own kids. That's all he needs. He doesn't permit himself the indulgence to linger over the possibility that his birth family, should any of them still live, would most likely reside where they always have within a short drive from his home, conceding people in Rabaul rarely move from one house to another. He's not curious about where they are or how their lives have gone since he last saw them when he was four, or so he convinces himself. The exception is his father, Seeto Wei or David as the town people call him. He has irregularly come into and moved out of Henry's life and who Henry hopes might now be in Hell. Once he expressed this wish, Henry regrets his bitterness and reverses it. Despite his history with the man, he can't wholeheartedly damn him. As a Chinaman, he must uphold his respect for a father, no matter how much he dislikes the man.

Never, never does he permit himself to think about his sister, Maria, who he knows is still alive because with his own eyes he has seen her talking to his father, an act he sees as an ultimate betrayal by both. No, he affirms, never her.

So, back to his first stream of thought. Yes, despite and ignoring the current rumblings he hears every now and then, he expects for him 1975 will not be exceptional.

Henry packs those thoughts away to prepare himself for today's excursion into Rabaul. He throws himself into the driver's seat of his dilapidated ute. Already seated in the vehicle are his passengers. They watch him, holding in smiles, a routine they follow regularly, with each adopting a small role in the enactment. Henry's part is not to turn toward his audience. He keeps his eyes focused ahead staring, as his passengers expect him to, in an over-exaggerated manner through the steering wheel towards the bottom half of the dashboard. Certainly not a view that would aid driving. Seconds pass before the person closest to the passenger door, his daughter, passes him a cushion. He takes the offering and engages in large gestures to make himself comfortable on top of it by wriggling his bottom and stretching his neck. He needs this uplifting because Henry's short and the driver's seat's padding has disintegrated. He can't afford another vehicle. After more bouncing and wriggling, he turns towards his wife and daughter and smiles. He keeps his gaze on his passengers as his right hand reaches forward so his fingers can grasp the ignition key and turn it while each of his feet do their respective dance on the brake and clutch pedals. He drags his eyes off his passengers and looks through the rear window, all clear, and while his right hand grips the steering wheel, his left pushes the gearstick into reverse.

While one of his feet releases the clutch, the other presses the accelerator, and back they lurch.

They are on their way. Never quietly. Gear changing often involves the grinding of metal and the roar of the engine when the gear cogs fail to synchronise. It's as if the car is stuck in second gear. Whenever he takes his vehicle out from under the tarp to drive into town, he's aware of a strong possibility it might be the vehicle's last journey.

No one talks. Three sets of eyes focus upon the road ahead in a silent agreement that it's too hard to make words heard above the noise. No need for speech, anyway. Already agreed upon in last night's conversations around the fire are the reasons this trip is necessary and what each will do once they reach town. Same as always.

Henry's naturally a man of few words, but this silence is dangerous territory for him. The road is so familiar, the driving is almost automatic despite the noise, and with nothing to distract it, his mind's certain to wander in places he doesn't want it to go. On this trip, it's led to the hot topic of the moment. Independence. After years of speculation, the date's almost upon them. September 16. A Tuesday. Does it matter when it happens? He tells himself that no matter who's making the rules, the cock will still crow too early; the hens will still scratch up clouds of dust; the village dogs will still yawn and stretch around the fire of an evening; and the women will still work in the village gardens while their men fish and the old men will spend their days, rain or sun, sitting on driftwood, scratching their balls, their only sound phlegmy coughs, as they wait out their final years.

And yet, even he can't ignore the reality of Independence. Even he can't pretend he hasn't heard the rumours. Against his will, little rivulets of panic rise inside him. He hears the same ripples of apprehension in others' conversations. Fear of the unknown. Fear of change. Fear the good life is over. He keeps his personal fears at bay by holding fast to the fragile notion that the small consistencies of life in this town – the ones that have held his life stable through volcanic eruptions, war, and his own abandonment as a child – will resist any change of government. But that restlessness, the lingering spectre of yet-to-be answered questions around the ability of New Guineans to govern, casts a doubt over every matter, large or small. He clings to what he sees as the strong fabric of life and his reliance on his existence continuing as a 'still pond'. To him, that's all about doing the same thing in the same way, day after day, month after month, year after year. Yet he can't deny there's a little unravelling happening around the edges. Protruding from the corners of his mind, troubling notions prod at his resolve to ignore them, reminding him that denial is futile. In defiance, he reminds himself of who he is: he's Henry Seeto, a husband and a father – neither role being pre-planned, but when he thinks about how things are in his part of the world, perhaps for him a predictable future. Bro, or brus, in Tok Pisin – he might tell himself if it was his nature to do so but it isn't – he's a man who cannot live alone. He blames that on his family's desertion of him. With a partner comes children who require being cared for. And if he lets himself weigh up the pros and cons – but he would never do that – he'd admit that it's the realities and demands of both familial roles that ground him. They keep him from wandering into the parts of himself that know he's a lost man. Rather, he's a man who was once a lost boy and, in many ways, who still has not found himself. A man who sees himself as distanced from everything, belonging nowhere, never being recognised. In his heart he has never gotten over being discarded.

However, on this humid morning, Henry works hard to convince himself this is irrelevant to the grand scheme of life. From his perspective, he can reassure himself that life rolls on regardless, there are no ripples in his pond, and he's happy to recognise that on this seemingly ordinary day, as he and his passengers rumble into town, he can recognise evidence of continuity ahead of him. Here it is, yet another Saturday morning and following a long-held Rabaul tradition, the town markets are open for business. Same as always, whether or not he and his family attend. Reliably always the same.

He pulls into the kerb despite the 'No Parking' sign, and lets the engine idle as he watches his wife, Rachel, and his youngest child clamber out of the cab and lift the fruit and vegetables from the tray onto the ground. When they have finished, he pulls out, drives further up the street and parks. He strolls back towards the market.

Ah yes. The bung. The market. Gutpela ples long bung. Great place. One you can count on. He's happy doing and seeing the same-old things.

With so much on his mind, he's feeling much older than his thirty-seven years. He leans against a concrete brick wall, comforts himself by massaging his hairless scalp with both hands, and lets the sounds and the smells of the bung wash over him. The market services all the communities of Rabaul so he's able to immerse himself in the babble of many languages: Kuanua the local Tolai language mingling with Tok Pisin, Cantonese and English.

These diverse conversations reassure him. For him, they're yet another measure of stability.

Traders and their customers spill out from under the shaded area into the sun. The overriding aroma is of ripening and decaying fruit and the occasional tang of betel nut. A truck laden with villagers arrives. Men, women, and children jump from its tray to the ground and the truck roars away. Another takes its place. Babies sleep as they swing from colourful plaited string bilums suspended from their mothers' perspiring foreheads. Old men take ropes of tobacco and strips of newsprint from their palm-frond pouches and roll them into long lengths of smoking pleasure. Children with hair peroxide-bleached by their mothers scratch their heads and bottoms, their large eyes unable to move fast enough to take in everything. Men and women, already swaying from betel nut intoxication despite the early hour of the day, spit dialect at each other between their ruined red teeth and roar at each other's jokes. Fine pumice dust rises and settles, again and again, stomped on by hundreds of feet. Dust and noise: this is the bung, same as always.

He's distracted by a group of giggling pikininis. What seems to amuse them is the white masta and missus trying to beat down the price of a basket of tomatoes, their limited Pisin causing confusion. He hides his smile behind his hand. Not that he cares, but it'll be a hassle if the Europeans notice and include him in their battle. A scrawny old Chinaman at the next stall's faring better. He promises the seller he'll buy 'plenti moa laulaus' if the price is right but, despite his commitment, he walks away blank-faced with only three baskets of the red, shiny fruit, for a bargain price.

Henry's wife is setting up in the front row of tables. He watches as Rachel and his daughter unload the produce and organise the display. It's been months since they were here. They need cash. Rachel's hoping to sell her taro and bananas so they can buy a new cotton shirt and a laplap for him to wear at his number one son's, Ling's, wedding. He'll buy them from one of the trade stores, not in Chinatown but along Malaguna Road, where he always shops. He squats down and folds his laplap between his legs; not at all self-conscious he dresses more in the village style, rather than the way the Chinese or Mixed-Race people in Rabaul do. A small gesture that separates him from his own community, and yet he knows somewhere deep down he still searches for recognition.

By mid-afternoon Rachel has sold most of her produce. He takes the coins she gives him and leaves her with her Tolai wantoks, chatting and laughing in their shared language, and chewing on betel nut. Already he can see from her eyes she's falling under its spell. Often it would be him too, sitting there chewing and floating. Not today. He meanders along the street towards his favourite store. Past Seeto Brothers, past Leung's and Chan's, to Wong's. He wanders at a leisurely pace like other pedestrians. Maybe it's the heat, maybe it's the character of the people, but there seems no reason for haste or worry. He weaves around the gatherings at the front of each store. Men sit or squat upon the ground or stand on one leg, one foot tucked behind the standing leg's knee, a habit so common, it's invisible. They smoke long cigarettes or watch the crowd or talk to wantoks. Women and children watch the men and wait. What are they waiting for? Who can say? It's as if time to linger is endless. He has seen no Europeans, no Chinese, no Mixed Race. Where are they? Has something happened, something important, that he didn't hear about?

At Wong's, he finds the double doors are closed and is even more surprised to see huge padlocks securing them. He can't believe the store isn't open. It trades almost 24-hours a day, every day of the year, except maybe New Year when everyone stops for the dragon. He cups his hand to shield against the glare and peers into the store. It's difficult to see through the squares of the reinforcing mesh window protection and the dust-misted glazing, but in the dimness, he can see stock still standing on the shop floor.

Wah? Me no savy. He doesn't understand. How can this be?

He tries the next store. It's identical to its neighbour, except that the corrugated iron external wall is green not blue. This store also has its guardians watching and waiting. One Tolai man watches Henry as he moves to the door, and he's grinning.

What he's laughing at? Does he think the Chinaman is longlong trying to get into Wong's? The second he asks this of himself, he feels still more foolish than he may have appeared to the observant Tolai. He knows his uneasiness is unsettling him, making him forget what he has known all his life: for the Tolai, a grin is often a greeting. He turns back to the man and returns the smile.

Inside the shop, an elderly Chinese woman is serving. He speaks to her in Cantonese, tipping his head towards the closed store.

'Where's Mr. Wong? Not doing business today?'

The woman's eyes are empty. Does she understand Cantonese? Not all Rabaul Chinese can speak the dialect. Maybe he should speak in Pisin.

'Lo missus. masta Wong, he go where?'

The woman continues to stare at him. He sighs but does not break eye contact. After some minutes, the woman shrugs her shoulders.

'Yu been bush longtaim, mister? Masta Wong go to Australia longtaim now.'

'Masta Wong on holidays?'

'Nah, he go-finish.'

She looks down at the counter and watches her own hand as it shuffles across to tidy something not needing attention. The changes that cross her face shock him. The Chinese people he knows pride themselves on containing their emotions. He worries this is another sign he has missed something important. His wife tells him he lives in his own head too much. He doesn't listen or pay attention.

'Yu slack,' she berates him. 'You a man who walks in his sleep.'

Is she right? Did he miss the important things?

Moving away from the counter to the boxes that hold the packs of shirts, Henry rustles through cellophane packs and selects a white one in his size, then moves to the rack that holds the laplaps, chooses a floral one, returns to the counter, and passes over the coins without looking at the woman. She wraps his purchases. He takes the parcel and strides out of the store. When he looks back into the store, she's still watching him.

He'd heard the rumours, but he'd pushed the news aside as impossible or unbelievable. Olegeta toktru: it's happening, everyone's leaving. Maybe he's made a big mistake. But anger spurts inside him. No, it's everyone else who's making a mistake. Believing in false Australian promises. It's all gaimin. Lies. As it has always been. Too many years of being told Chinese and Mixed Race are not good enough. Too many years of being told, 'Yu pipel with parents or grandparents from other places need special permits to stay here.' Now passports come too late. And could someone please explain why we need these to stay in our home? Or why do we need them to visit Australia? This place's our home and this is Aussie territory. We would be just visiting the mother country. Pah. Too late. Anyway, some won't get the passports – people like him: those without paper proof of who they are and where they come from, beyond just a birth certificate that says a man was born in Rabaul. One thing he had heard was that even to stay or become citizens of Papua New Guinea, the new government might demand proof of a three-generational paternal link to the new nation. He shrugs his shoulders, noting the unlikelihood of anyone he knows meeting that criterion should such a restriction come into play. The mums provide the New Guinea link, not the dads.

He can only reach one conclusion. No one has ever wanted his people here, and no one wants to deal with the problems that arise from them still being here. To express his anger, Henry stomps his foot onto the ground then glances around to see who has noticed his tantrum. He doesn't like to draw attention to himself. But extending his ire further, he gathers together all those he imagines have gone south into one bunch of cowards: why doesn't everyone throw this bribery back in Australia's face? He knows the reason, but he doesn't want to admit it even if doing so reinforces his own arguments. And yet, despite his effort to compress his knowledge of the cause, he knows it's oozing out of his pores like sweat and invading his every thought. Fear. Everyone's afraid. What's ahead? If no one wants them, where can they go?

Henry waves his one free arm wide and flaps his hand. The smokers and loiterers pay him no attention. Right. That's it. He's decided. He'll be a citizen of the new nation, Papua New Guinea, because that's who he feels he is. Yet inside, deep down, he's worried there'll still be trouble for people like him, for Mixed Race and Chinese, even if they stay. The knot inside him grips tighter.

He's overwhelmed. There's too much to absorb. His thoughts have stalled. He's beyond trying to understand what he's seeing. He wanders around the town centre, his bundle of shopping tucked under his arm. His sweat pools around the package, but he ignores the discomfort. More closed stores. Is he seeing fewer familiar faces than usual? To lessen his panic, he reminds himself of the village in which he lives with Rachel and his children where he feels secure as a 'local'. There, he can forget his ancestors originated in other places. He walks and walks. Down Mango Avenue; up Kamarere; along Casuarina; around Ah Chee. The street signs are unnecessary. He has walked along these streets all his life: Mango, the big stores and the Palms Theatre; Kamarere, Chong Bros. and Wong's milk bar; Casuarina, its huge trees in straight rows either side, as it passes by Queen Elizabeth Park; and on Ah Chee, the sounds and smells of China. Written into his memory since he was a child are the experiences of noticing every missing piece of pavement along the pathways. Along the way, each aroma he smells in passing, and every sound he hears are almost as familiar to him as his children.

The familiarity hurts rather than reassures him. He can sense the potential of future loss. It would be unbearable not to be here. But what if – because his brown body says he's a Chinaman or, if he toktru, because he's Chinese and something else, so not Papua New Guinean – what if he has no choice but to go to Australia? He shudders to think of this possibility. He's certain that Australia doesn't like brown men; that Australia doesn't like mixed race people; that Australia doesn't like Chinese, so then what?

Enough's enough.

Again, the tightening inside his chest.

He can't shake one particular fear. How might he feel if they forced him to move long Australia? He's never been there, so he uses his limited knowledge of that country south of his homeland to imagine it. No bananas and pawpaw hanging off trees for him to pick. No taro growing in the ground waiting to be dug out. Would the fish be as plentiful as here, in this beautiful harbour? He knows no one. How would he get work? Here, he knows who to go to for a job. He smiles. It's rarely he needs a job here. Why would he? There's little need for money. There's always Rachel's vegetable garden for kaikai to feed his family and free fish from the sea, and little need for clothing – well, he reassures himself, his laplap and meri blouse for Rachel cost little and only for special occasions did they need new ones. He pats the parcel under his arm to emphasise the point.

These complications overwhelm him. Oh, Australia nogat ples for him. No. He's New Guinean. Born long New Guinea. Government might make a rule, but no kiap – no government official – no ken toktok long Henry Seeto, yu go long Australia. Nobody ken toktok yu no belong tispela ples. No one can say he doesn't belong long New Guinea just because his papa come long China. This is his place; here's where he belongs; this is Home.

He's back at the bung, wandering through the crowd, looking for Rachel. There's a fight starting up on the far side of the market. The men's voices are loud. The way they are talking warns him they are drunk. They're bickering about who has first rights to flirt with a particular meri. The woman is drunk too. The noise and the way such disturbances can escalate remind him of the big fear that creeps into any talk about Independence – payback. Even Aussies worry that once PNG gets to rule itself, there'll be retaliation.

He remembers, back – when was that? Late 'fifties maybe? When the Tolai decided they'd had enough of colonial rule. The Tolai called themselves the Mataungans, and their leader John Kaputin stood in front of the

New Guinea policemen and spoke, one New Guinean to another. He nods to himself.

Kaputin smart. Kaputin savy olegeta emi policemen were mainlanders and that meant they would not savy his Tolai language. Instead of talking in his own language, Kuanua, Kaputin he toktok Pisin. He tok: wonem laws and wonem property yupela polis protect? Nodding and approving of Kaputin's wisdom, Henry concedes. Even now, the property is either that of white men or wealthy Chinese. Still not the property of New Guineans, though it's soon supposed to be their country. Maybe all those leaving, like masta Wong and other hapcas familiis or whoever, maybe they all savy something he doesn't about the likelihood of payback. His chest muscles spasm once more. Until Kaputin, everyone thought New Guineans too easy-going to make trouble. Everyone hoped they'd forget the times trade stores and others had fleeced them by short-weighing products, overcharging or selling shoddy goods or treating them like idiots. Everyone knows about tribal payback, an eye for an eye, a wife for a wife. But after Kaputin, everyone wondered if New Guineans would forget Aussie law and revive tribal law. Tribal law includes payback. Everyone fears payback.

Henry sighs.

China face bilong emi bring him nuting but pain. Brought him pain when he had to leave his family because of the Japanese soldiers, when his first mumma said Japanese soldiers hate Chinese boys, and he's sure that now, with Independence coming, declaring himself as Chinese will bring him pain again. Time now to stop swinging like a pendulum, to stop being Chinese, to be only one kind of man: New Guinean, or perhaps he'll call himself a Niuginean, the Tok Pisin name that each citizen of the new nation of Papua New Guinea will call themselves.

With the matter of his citizenship resolved, Henry settles himself back into his localised and contained view, an internal hymn that reiterates a perspective that even the forthcoming big event of Independence can bring little change to the progress of the years ahead. 1975 will become 1976, and 1976 will become 1977, and so on. With an inward smile, he contemplates the notion that his only worry for the future might be whether he can find someone with a pig to sell. If he can find one, if all the pigs on the Gazelle Peninsula aren't already sold out, he'll cook one in a pit to celebrate the day Papua New Guinea is born. On September 16, he'll have a mighty mumu feast to look forward to.

2

RABAUL, EAST NEW BRITAIN PROVINCE, PAPUA NEW GUINEA
December 1975

As much as Maria might try, she can't ignore the facts. This town, Rabaul, her hometown, will never be the same. Perhaps not only because it's no longer under administration and now part of a new nation, but also because progress and change are unavoidable.

She doesn't like what's happening.

It's December, and PNG has been governing itself for three months. The past is behind her. No way to go back to those times, even if she had a wish to. Not all of the past is worth returning to, though some is so precious she wishes she could compact it and take it with her. And leaving is what she is doing, According to her husband, there's no choice but for the family to become Australians. Patrick's fear is that he will lose everything he has fought hard to gain.

'We Chinese fought hard for our properties and our businesses. Independence comes and deems everything worthless or we have to hand it over to the Niugineans.'

She doesn't want to leave. But what can she do? She is powerless. As she has always been. And voiceless. She likens herself to a fallen frangipani blossom blown here and there by the wind. She and the bloom have no control over destination or destiny.

Her head is bursting with questions. About why her community has become disposable; about how she and her family and friends have lost their claim to an identity, and much more. Her community, the Chinese and Mixed Race people of Rabaul, neither tribal nor western expats, have contributed to the region's development since German times, the era in which her grandmother came. Now, they must either become an Aussie and be a foreigner in PNG, or become Niuginean, an alien in the eyes of Australian border control. How will they be able to explain themselves? They're neither this nor that and have no connections to the countries their ancestors left. This place, this town, in their hearts, will always be their home.

She receives no answers because she asks no questions. Years of habit of not being listened to have silenced her. Not even her husband understands. He sees himself as Cantonese and that some time, any time he chooses, he can return to China. But those borders have been slammed shut by world events and historical changes. He's as lost as she is. When she attempts to talk to him about it, his answer is a shrug of his shoulders. He mutters, 'samting nuting'. Her ears hear this as, 'Only a woman like you, worth so little, could ask such stupid questions and therefore you deserve no answer.' From her perspective, his reaction has grown into a universal one.

But the loudest unasked and unanswerable question must surely be: 'Why? Why me?'

And now the moment has arrived: the soul-destroying, can't-delay instant that she has no words to describe. The pain inside her is unbearable. Her heart is being torn out. Again, she needs to shout out loud the words roaring around inside her. Why? Why me? All her life she has been a good Catholic girl, gone to the Fathers whenever she has needed to understand the complexities of life. So why no answers? Inside her, this crisis feels like the one she faced decades ago when she went to Father Gustav to find salvation. She needed help then because her life was being shredded, as it is now, though in that past moment she never told him why she had found herself bereft of hope. Nor did she tell him then why she had come to feel there was no place, not even in the Church, where she could be herself. Father Gustav did not require details. He had a ready answer. He took inspiration from Saint Benedict's 'Intention'. As Father recited Benedict's words, he assured her she would find a resolution in them. But she didn't. She never told the Reverend Father of his failure. Instead, she locked the confusion and pain inside. All that remains for her today is a sense of how she felt as she'd listened to Father's slow, careful words. She is certain that Father would not agree with her interpretations. Not as she understood him then, at the time of the telling, nor today, when she has recalled his consolation for another crisis.

Father's paraphrasing went like this: Home: the place where St. Benedict says we will find God and, once found, it's the place where one should remain.

This is her Home. She doesn't understand why God doesn't let her stay in her Home? Why has God forgotten her?

Maria's feet lead her up the aircraft boarding steps. There is a flapping in her chest. Like the wings of a copra beetle speared to the ground by village children. At the cabin entrance, she pauses, nostrils flared, and tells herself she must remember this moment. Last smells: sulphur, rotting vegetation, aviation fuel. The steward takes her boarding pass from her hand and repeats the words written on it. 'Maria Seeto. G4'.

Yes, her name is 'Maria Seeto' but Maria Seeto is no longer the person she has always been. What will the new Maria Seeto be like when she no longer lives in Rabaul?

She turns back, the air shimmers, and she gazes over the tarmac towards the terminal, the capital letters R A B A U L painted in red across its corrugated roof. At the gate, hands wave. Cautious. Sad. The ones who are staying. A surge of envy passes through her. She doesn't wave back. And there, to the right and bordering Lakunai airport, is the peak of The Mother draped in green, and the smaller, partly denuded, volcano Tavurvur with its wispy clouds hovering above its gaping mouth. It's as if these mountainous guardians of Rabaul can't believe she's leaving. Grief fills her. No hope of ever coming back. One last look at Home. Except it's no longer her home. Already it's Papua New Guinea and belongs to New Guineans. She glances back to the gate. Those there are still waving. Her heart softens.

It doesn't matter who is staying, like those at the gate, or who is going, as she is. Everyone's worried about what's ahead. Everyone's sad, lost, and homeless. Even if they stay. She places the blame on the United Nations who claim to speak for New Guineans. But they are speaking only for some, the tribal people, not for others, not for those who have lived here for many, many years and see this as their homeland. Like Nenek. Her grandmother, if she was still alive, couldn't go back to her little island in the Banda Sea. And for her, leaving means she can never visit the grave of Nenek or contemplate the sites where Mumma and Daddy-George are said to have died. She represses her sadness over her losses but, try as she may, she can't stop another realisation from sneaking in, one that compels her to look once more at the crowd by the gate, hoping to recognise a once-familiar face.

'Henry, are you there, little brother? You left me when you were only so high and never returned. If you change your mind and become my brother again, I'll be far away.'

She is certain he'll not leave. As sad as it may be, she'd like to imagine that he's at the gate, crying for his sister who's leaving. And deeper still, in the dark cave of exclusion, there's Stephen. Every day she has held onto the hope that by chance she'll see him, even if from afar. One glance will help her survive. But, now, there will be no chances. He can only live in her heart.

She knows, but resists, the reality. Niugineans have a new future in their new nation Niugini – their homeland. The Aussies can return to their country Australia – their homeland. But the remaining former-New Guineans can only be visitors in a country that shaped them. Perhaps they will call themselves Australians or Niuginean, but neither identity explains them. Their history will disappear. In a need to establish an authentic national one for the new nation, the history of a minority will be overwritten by the tribal journey to nationhood under Australia's curatorship. Thinking this, knowing this, makes it hard not to bellow. Instead, she lifts her chin in defiance.

She holds at bay her awareness that her family are ahead of her. They're already struggling up the DC3's steep aisle from the rear entry door. Each is pulling himself forward by grasping the corner of each seat in the rows ahead as they move upward towards their allocated places. First, there's her husband Patrick and then her sons – Andrew, Gabriel and Daniel – almost no longer boys but young men. She refuses to give in to her habit of mentally guiding their progress. Today they must find their own way. She enters the plane's cabin and begins her own ascent to her seat, puffing and panting in the effort. Overriding the demands the ascent makes upon her body is a fear building inside. This journey can only end with her becoming an empty shell, devoid of hope and a body without a soul.

3

BRISBANE, AUSTRALIA
January 1976

Weeks have passed since the five landed in Australia. As Maria didn't want to come to this country, today she doesn't want to be here in Brisbane in Patrick's uncle's car. She's certain this journey today can only bring her pain. For her husband, this outing's only about regaining his good standing in life by gaining assets here in Australia.

She sneaks a sidewards glance at Aunt Louisa sharing the back seat with her. Maria's ribs and arms are aching from being held tight for too long. She rubs them. Tiredness sweeps over her. Five in one bedroom means little sleep for anyone. She tries shutting her eyes, tries to take herself elsewhere by imagining herself in some other place. Nothing happens.

She needs to identify something – anything – that might fill the space inside. Lukim. Lukim samting. Kissim samting. She is searching for something to help her get through this nightmare. Is something out there, something that'll replace what's missing? She squints to focus as the world flashes by, but the contours of this strange city offer no meaning. She has left one place and still not arrived in the next, lost in the in-between.

She wants to pray. Or does she need to pray? She remembers her childhood and the nuns at Saint Joseph's Malay School reassuring her. They'd said: He'll accept all prayers, including those of sinners.

She doesn't believe God will listen to a Catholic who's lost her faith but, despite her doubts, silently she recites the scattered phrases she can recall.

Grant me O Lord a steady hand and watchful eye that no one shall be hurt as I pass by... Protect me and lead me safely to my destiny.

'What?'

Not just in her head. She's disturbed Aunt Louisa's catnap. She feels

Aunt's stare. But when she turns to look, Aunt is facing the window. Maria brushes her forehead with the back of her hand. A migraine. A cup of tea would be nice. The mood inside the car is oppressive. Her thoughts turn to the past. This is dangerous. Permitting her mind to turn backwards has brought about her isolation during this journey.

Uncle Michael's car hurtles on. She clings to the seat belt, body tense. The others are silent. It feels personal. The wind swirls in through the car window and dries tears she hadn't noticed. This twisting and turning, no wonder she's confused. A child who has lost grip of her mother's hand.

She wills herself to piece together the jigsaw of Brisbane, its suburbs confined and stretched by the twisting, turning river. She's lost count of how many bridges crossed. After each crossing, she's asked Uncle, 'Which river tispela?' Each time he answers 'same-same.'

The day's hot and Uncle's not-so-new station wagon is stifling. Her face is as stiff as Patrick's white shirts had felt when Samuel the haus boi back home had over-starched them. The car passes weathered timber Queenslanders high above the ground, tiny fibro cottages, and ancient stone buildings. Now older suburbs. Established gardens. Her head swivels to permit her eyes to keep those gardens in sight: foliage so mature, so green, they seem familiar. She wonders how long it has taken for this southern vegetation to establish itself. In the tropics, plants look like this after only a few weeks' growth. Plants go from pikinini to lapun grandpa in weeks. Perhaps they do here, too. But through this random thought, the distance between her Rabaul garden and herself amplifies the finality of separation.

Uncle's car passes new brick and timber buildings with well-ordered gardens and, now, newer developments. A Martian plain with timber skeletons of half-built structures standing out from the bare red soil. Not even a weed. What hope here?

The car comes to a standstill alongside a cluster of almost-completed buildings.

Patrick is first out. Keen. 'Humph.' he says, as if his presence deserves a special greeting when there's none. Maria watches as he plants his feet on the roadway, fists on hips. This, all his to grab. A piece of the new country. Land's the key to wealth. She's heard that lecture often.

With no clear alternative but to join the house-gazing trio, she opens the car door and swings her legs out so her feet can drop to the roadway. Heavily. Cautiously. She straightens her back and stands, arms dangling by her side like a puppet, with shoulders rounded and her back facing her companions. A way of punishing them, if they'd take notice – punishment for their enthusiasm to adopt a new life; for pushing her to settle; for not seeing her pain, or if they see, for treating it as 'samting nuting', as if her opinions are worthless. Besides, she doesn't want them to see her face. In case. She looks at what lies before her. Homes for the picking, yet none appeal. A desolate landscape, so bare, so hopeless, and so remote from the soft green she's spent a lifetime knowing. Not one building can override the memory of her little house in Rabaul, snug beneath the wide sheltering spread of mango and casuarina trees. She suppresses a whimper. Won't do if they hear.

What's this? Wonem tispela? Look. Lukim, Maria, you see? A liklik haus. There it is: small, inconspicuous, shy. Not up here on the hill, not showing off, not here where these three are looking, but down there, at the bottom of the street. Conservative and modest. Looking like a house she could live in.

That tiny house, not yet completed, its skeleton timber still bare in places, stands out from the others on offer because of its dainty porch-like verandah facing the street. A verandah's important. Nenek's house had a verandah. A verandah makes a house a home, her grandmother had whispered as she told her stories: 'kissim verandah long haus, na tispela haus ken kam long Home'. Maybe this verandah will make this house a place where she could stay for many years. Perfect for lots of children, or as Nenek would say 'ples bilong plenti pikinini.' For a family. For her perhaps a place to make a new beginning.

She imagines floorboards and pictures herself standing on them. The image grips her, carries her away from the spot in which her feet have stalled. Without a word to her companions, she meanders down the hill and mounts the timber steps. One, two, three. So small is the space it's more a porch than a verandah; from the top step, the doorknob is within reach of her fingers. She takes that last step onto the floorboards then turns towards the street and looks out as a captain might from his ship's bridge. Her head lifts and stays high. There's no protection on the porch. The brightness forces her eyes to squint, and this leads her to destructive thoughts, knowing full well that thinking of other places and other times drags her into a precarious mindset: this Brisbane sun's far too harsh, too bright. There's nothing here to stop the sun's harsh rays but... oh how well she remembers. Long Home sun not so bright; long Rabaul sun softer and gentler. Clouds, bushes, trees filter...

She drags her attention back to the vista before her. Builders' rubble, short ends of timber, globs of discarded concrete.

The others have followed. Her companions fix their eyes upon Maria. Do they think she has gone insane? Patrick wants this settled – he's scolded her several times, about her unreasonableness. Aunt and Uncle want their home back to themselves.

With Uncle, Aunt and Patrick alongside on the porch, it's crowded – but she doesn't care. She doesn't say a word nor does she look at the other three. She stands, her hands resting on the rail, eyes intent. The other three look to the place that seems to hold her attention and see only bare earth. It's only in her head. The future: she's older, surrounded by thick foliage, and she knows that this garden will have been planted and nurtured by her. Yes, this'll do. She turns and let her eyes speak to Patrick. He'll take care of the practical considerations. Already he's pulled the price list out of his pocket and is running his finger down the numbers. His brow furrows. He leans over and speaks in Cantonese to his uncle.

'This one's cheaper. Why, do you think?'

His uncle strokes his chin, his eyes scan the building without moving, and then his face brightens, as if he has become wise. Nodding his head, he replies in Cantonese, 'Not modern.'

Already she knows this house is hers – this verandah, which is a mere porch but never will she say so; a future garden; and a home for her family. Patrick won't worry about style if lack of it makes it cheap. Her husband nods his head, like a king to his subject. Aunt and Uncle smile. She can feel her body releasing, the corners of her mouth twitching. Not a home, she concedes, but a house.

PART 2
MARIA

1

BRISBANE, AUSTRALIA
October 2009

Thirty-four years of sun, rain, and wind have turned Maria's verandah a soft grey. This morning, dappled sunlight dances across its floorboards as Brisbane's south-easterly shakes the leafy bushes of the garden. A willy-wagtail is flitting through the vegetation, in and out, then stops to rest on the fence between a neighbour's property and Maria's. The energetic creature is dashing between the outer tips of the taller bushes, the bottle-brush and the lemon-scented tea tree, and then to the sturdier stems of the cut-leaf daisy and the guinea vine, with a purpose that seems obscure to Maria. Perhaps that's why she can't take her eyes away.

'Me likim yu, little bird. You are pretty and quick. Are you showing me how much you like my garden?'

It's a miracle anything grew in this patch of earth. It was the place into which she planted her anger. Her need to hit back propelled each downward plunge of the shovel or arc of the hoe. Into the soil she planted the pain of her loss. Bad karma, she had warned herself. Nothing will thrive in this bitter soil. She taps her temple, reminding herself of those times all those years ago, when it was only an imagined garden, when everyone else could see only bare soil scattered with construction rubble. She's certain this garden has saved her from madness. Hard work, daily, with head down, shoulders bowed, muscles straining to loosen and move the soil and then work in compost and manure to assist the drainage and lighten Brisbane's clay soil is how she survived those early years. By maintaining a focus on creating her fantasy, she could block out what she didn't want to face. There's been a price to pay for ignoring grief. Her internal pain hasn't lessened. Unexpressed and buried, it's formed a tight wad. She rubs her abdomen, sure she can feel it there, in her centre. Like a tumour.

These days, the garden requires less effort. It's almost self-sustaining. Sometimes her sons and their wives stand in for her with any heavy work such as replanting or mulching. Such good children. A smile creeps across her face, as she thinks about her grandchildren. Sometimes they need a little incentive to get them into the garden, like bribery with the food they love her to cook for them. Or last resort, a threatening glare from a parent. She titters. Once there, then they find it's all fun. Adults should never under-value the pleasure of playing with water, where spraying sometimes ends up on the garden but more often elsewhere, especially if a potential victim passes by. Oh, what it is to be young. She's too old for such high-spirited fun, more's the pity, and if she's honest also too old for gardening. Not enough energy. Too many aching bones. Too fat. Her joy these days is to sit and observe, such as now, when immersing herself in this bird's dance.

'Old age' provides her acceptable excuses to do just that. But when did that phase of life arrive? After some thinking on the matter, she decides the invasion of geriatrics is not dissimilar to that of tropical mildew, which begins by digging its black roots into crevices and cracks, almost impercep-tible in the early stages but, once visible, its grip is startling. Aging arrives via subtle attacks on perceptions of competences, both internal and exter-nal. A person wakes up one morning and discovers her legs aren't as eager to drag themselves over the edge of the bed; or a name of an acquaintance is there, on the periphery of recall, but not accessible; or there's a little hesitation in going about a chore that, until that moment, had been done without thought. At first these irksome occurrences are private and mostly ignorable. Then others notice and don't keep their observations to them-selves. All done under the banner of 'helping' or 'caring'. A head dipped down to ensure a presumed failing eyesight might lead to not being able to recognise a face unless close; words spoken at a higher volume to convey a clear message, usually something quite obvious and familiar; or a firm but gentle and uninvited hand placed under an elbow, in case of an assumed certainty of unsteadiness; and most humiliating is when opinions once valued are ignored as noise. All signs that if you don't think you are old, someone else does.

She can't ignore the passing of time, but still can wonder at it. Where has her life gone? Here she is, almost seventy-five and a widow six years. Patrick's passing seems like only yesterday. She indulges herself in a wry smile as she recalls that day. Cold but dry at least. Her three sons at the gravesite, heads bent, and dressed in their best, showing respect for a man who had now left this world. 'You got a bargain there, Patrick. Three dutiful sons.' The truth rips through her. Patrick's sons. 'If only you knew, Patrick.' Maybe he did? Maybe it suited him to accept his gifts.

A small tremor works its way up her skeleton to her jaw. Should she worry? Are twitches and shudders inevitable? There are good days and bad days. While she might fob it off as a symptom of aging, her critical self won't fully indulge in the 'old age' excuse. Age may account for some of her body's responses but not all. Her rationale tells her otherwise. It's not healthy to repress emotions. There's a war going on inside her, a conflict that has raged since she was twenty. Or, should she say, all her life? Her external form is resisting her inner will. No wonder her jaw aches or her chest spasms. As hard as she works at not giving anything away to the ones who care for her and watch her, in case she needs assistance, she also yields to practicalities. Truth will surface. The how and the when of the inevitable revelation adds a chilli-kick to her fear. If only she could bypass that fear. Then, she might word her explanations in a manner that her family might comprehend the prevailing influences of those past moments, the nuanced events and difficulties of decision-making in another era and under violently different circumstances. But the greater fear of the cost of any exposé, small or large, is too overwhelming. Fighting apprehension is a daily reality that is amplified by accepting there's never a guarantee about the length of life. Each new ache in her back or throb of her arthritic knee, every minor stumble as she walks along the street, every twinge or nerve spasm, every moment of forgetfulness or a high sugar test warns that Death is her stalker and when he catches her, if she hasn't offered her own version, her legacy to her family will be false elucidations from others and no one alive who knows the truth to challenge them. Either way, there will be a price for truth. Will her boys still love their mother? When they do know, and they will sometime or other, can they cope with learning her secrets? What will the truth about their grandmother do to her grandchildren? How will Francine react? Will her only granddaughter, her special girl, feel betrayed? Will she understand?

She clutches her chest. She should act. She really doesn't need convincing but, instead, she takes the easy way out and withdraws into a safe space. That space is to immerse herself in the recall of a vivid memory of a pivotal moment that represents the end of one life and the birth of another. An instant when she might have chosen a different path. By reliving it, she can pretend she's still free to decide.

It's once again late December 1975, and she's navigated the aisle and reached her allocated seat and has now squeezed her large body into a narrow aircraft seat. Bone-tired, her body allows itself to let go and slump. So weary is she, she has only a faint recognition that the plane is moving along the runway. Then comes the roar of its engines as they work to separate aircraft from ground to gain elevation. As if in a dream, her body rolls with the turn. Despite her resolve not to look again, her eyes slide to the window and watch the changing scenery below. A dip of the wing to the peaks of The Mother, The Daughter, and the baby volcano Matupit as the plane and its passengers swing in a tight circle, following as it must the flight path that will take them across the north-easterly tip of the island of New Britain towards the mainland to the next landing at Lae. She can't explain to herself why she chooses to re-live this moment on sleepless nights or instances, such as today. Perhaps it is to remind herself that somewhere soon after this moment she had made a decision to become the future Maria and maintain a silence. For that, there's a price.

Back on her verandah, she's standing upright, body erect and supported by a light grip on the rail. Yet, somehow, she's drifted in and out of consciousness. She calls it 'i na slip piksa' or awake dreaming. Another sign of aging? Maybe. More likely too much uninterrupted spare time. Or else it's avoidance of other things. A heavy wave of weariness floats down and wraps around her. She doesn't care if she's away for seconds or hours. She doesn't answer to anyone, a definite luxury for an advanced age. Besides, this is beyond her control.

Today, a loud blast of a car horn hauls her into the present.

She laughs. It's Andrew, playing his entry prelude. Her eldest presses hard on his horn. He's her favourite though she tries not to show it. Every time he comes to pick her up, he follows this routine. A joke, perhaps. Or a way to tease her, knowing she'd love to berate him. There he is, in his car by the kerb, and even her old eyes can see his grin. He's being dutiful, doing whatever he can to improve her life, even if it's only taking his mother to the supermarket. Whenever he has spare time, there he'll be, honking and waiting with his grin. She can count on him and his visits. And many more things.

'Hey, Mum. Let's get a coffee.'

She will never say no. He'd worry if she did.

He's out of the car now and standing beside her, his wicked grin lighting his face. He's playing with her. Such a cheeky boy. No, not a boy. A man heading towards old age, too. But to her, he's always that little two-year-old, who buried his head in the space between her shoulder and her breast. Does he remember? Was he too young? Or, is he happy to think she gave birth to him? He never says. Nor does she mention it.

As he fusses around her, she's giving him the same attention as earlier she had given to the willy-wagtail. She notices how his eyes never stay still. He spies her coat, and his left hand reaches out and grabs it by the collar while his right is picking up her handbag and transferring it to his left so his right hand is free to apply firm but gentle pressure to the small of her back, to steady her as she moves. He shuffles around to stand beside her and places his right hand on her elbow as they descend the stairs together.

'Okay, Mum, take it easy.'

Along the path, towards the street, they walk side by side. The outstretching branches of her shrubs caress their faces and chests as they pass. Andrew says, 'These need trimming.' She shakes her head. She imagines her garden is saying goodbye. By reaching out, the plants are whispering to her and her son: 'See you soon, Maria. We'll be waiting for you. And you, you sweet little boy, take care of your mumma.'

At the store, Andrew stops the car right out front, as close to the kerb as possible, then he jumps out and runs around so he can open her door. She knows she shouldn't, but she can't help but smile at this fifty-something guy running around like a schoolkid. She knows he's working hard to make life easier for her. It's his way to show he loves her. And she loves him for this. There's a bench to the side of the sliding doors. Andrew leads her towards it and helps her sit. As always, part of his ritual, he leans over, and with his face close to hers he says, 'Now don't go running off with some good-looking stranger, Mum, else I will be in heaps of trouble with the rest of the family.' He winks at her then runs off and disappears, hidden from sight by his car. She hears his door slam and watches as his car moves off, turning left and disappearing down a lane at the far side of the shopping centre. She knows this leads to the parking area.

From her spot on the bench, she watches shoppers as they pass by. Always looking, just in case. A lot of ex-PNG people live in the nearby suburbs and there's often someone to see and chat with. And it's as well she does because she catches sight of Teresa Leung. Teresa's eyes are looking down to the ground and a frown is spoiling her forehead. Maybe she is trying to decide what to cook for her family this evening. If she doesn't lift her eyes, Teresa might not see Maria sitting on the bench. Maria doesn't want to call out. That would make others look her way, and she doesn't like to draw attention to herself. She feels a little anxious. What if Teresa doesn't notice her? What should she do?

'Oh, hello there, Aunty Teresa. How are you?'

It's Andrew. He's walked right past his mother and is already giving Teresa a hug. Teresa's face lights up. Everyone loves her son.

'Mum's here, Aunty. We will have a coffee and then do a little grocery shopping. Do you want to join us?'

He gives Teresa no choice. His arm goes over her shoulder and he leads her towards the bench.

'Come on, Mum. I need that coffee.'

Andrew releases Teresa and reaches down to help his mother up. Together the three, with smiles on their faces, walk around the corner, past the entry to the supermarket, into the coffee shop and settle themselves into a booth.

'Lattes, ladies? As usual?'

Maria smiles and looks at her friend, thinking Teresa will, like her, be thinking, 'How lucky to have a son like this one. Thoughtful. Generous.'

Andrew doesn't wait for Teresa's answer. This is not a surprise encounter, more a regular one so often does it happen. But Andrew always acts as if he's surprised and pleased. It makes Teresa smile. 'She probably feels very special and we all like to feel like that,' Maria mentally notes. Andy's already heading towards the counter. Teresa begins to talk, but what Teresa has to say has nothing to do with Andrew or his earlier question. As she talks, Teresa is still smiling, but her voice sounds sad. And she doesn't move her gaze from Andrew's back as he moves away.

'Oh Maria, mi no happy. My sister, her husband. You know him, Benedict Chan – you remember? He went to school with us at St Joseph's – he's only got weeks to live. Cancer.'

Teresa's eyes look like they have too much water in them. She's not crying. 'Chinese women are too tough to cry,' thinks Maria. But it's obvious her resolve is crumbling. To hold herself strong, Teresa falls silent, lips tight, and she drags her eyes away from Andrew's back and onto her lap. Her fingers are twisting and twisting at a serviette, twisting it so tight it doesn't unwind when she at last drops it onto the table. Only then does she glance in Maria's direction, a glance, Maria decides, intended to monitor her friend's reactions. It's as if Teresa has rolled these worries around in her mind so often, she is no longer sure of what she has said out loud and what's just a thought in her head. Maria understands. It's the same for her. A wave of sorrow washes over her. Why are we like this?

Maria says nothing. What can she say? Sad, yes, but so many have cancer and she's almost run out of her supply of 'Sori tumuchia.' Of late, there has been a run on withdrawals of that Tok Pisin phrase. She thinks better of it and opens her mouth to say those words but then shuts it again. They seem to have lost their power, and she has nothing else to offer her friend. Silence and a nod of the head is all she has to give.

Teresa again looks towards Andrew, who remains at the counter chatting. The woman that works at this coffee shop is the granddaughter of someone from PNG. Like a cousin, Andrew would say. Not related by blood, but maybe she is? No one remembers the complex relationships of marriage and blood these days. But everyone with PNG connections are 'family', because they understand, because they remember, because they have all had the same experiences. Maria and her friend already know what's happening over at the counter. Andrew will, as always, be acting as if he's reluctant to make too much effort for the elderly females awaiting their lattes, inferring he's given up his valuable time and those two ladies take him for granted. He might say something like, 'Well, just taking the lapun meris out for coffee, earning brownie points.' Far from the truth. He's that person who will do whatever he can when he sees a need.

With her eyes still fixed on Andrew, Teresa leans over and whispers, 'Maria, don't you wish you could go home? Everyone's dying. We are spread far apart, some of us are here and some still there. My sister, she still in Lae. She worries she won't be able to be strong with no family nearby. My sister phones me, toktok a little and then she cry, cry, cry. She strong. But this, too much for her to handle on her own. It's killing me, too. She toktok: "Oh Teresa, it's all too hard. Not like before. Before, when you were all here, if someone dies or have bad troubles, people would come and cook and clean. Not just family. Anyone, everyone." But my sister, she doesn't have family in Lae; no one to cook her meals; no one to cry with; and no one to keep her strong. You remember, Maria? Oh, people so good to each other, even in the worst of times. And there's the family business. No one wants to buy businesses in PNG. Or can't afford to buy. She has no sons. What's she going to do? She is Niuginean citizen. Will she be able to migrate? Australia not so keen these days. We lose everything when we leave, but people who stay lose something, too.'

There's a long pause, and then Teresa's eyes come back to Maria.

'You know Maria, dangerous long home, these days. Security fences. Gangs.' She shudders and returns to watching Andrew. 'Children belong you and me, they happy long Australia. They not think much about home. They tingting mi longlong if mi tok about home. They laugh and tap their temples and roll their eyes, saying words like "This is madness, Mumma." Then they hug me, as if that makes it right, that I am stupid like a child. But, toktru, me sad. Miss it. Miss the old days. PNG not the same now. And that makes me sad too.'

Andrew leaves the counter, his eyes fixed upon the froth of the lattes, his lips tight with concentration, trying not to spill the coffees. Teresa straightens her back and lifts her face. Andrew dodges around a young man moving to replace him at the counter. He rolls his eyes for his audience of Teresa and Maria to see, as if to say 'Young people', and continues his journey towards them. As he places one cup in front of Teresa, her face has returned to normal. Her smile is back. Did that one-sided conversation ever happen?

Maria understands Teresa. Or at least she convinces herself she does. She and Teresa began school together, grew up only a few houses away from each other, and, if she dug deep enough, Maria would uncover Teresa's relationship to her, distant though it may be. Perhaps the connection is through marriages of one's cousin to another's, or one's great aunt or uncle to another's. It's the way of their community. Generations of their families living in one town, unable to move elsewhere. Some marry an Aussie or a local but it is likely a husband or wife will come from within the community, everyone related if not by blood then by marriage. In those times, privacy was hard to achieve and maintain. Maria knows this only too well. She suspects her greatest secrets aren't mysteries, even if not fully known or reported.

Although Andrew returns to the counter for his own drink, Teresa is now silent. She slumps back in the seat with shoulders drooping. This is a sign that the conversation will end here. Unless Teresa takes the initiative and begins it again at another time. In Maria's opinion it's likely that Teresa is already regretting she has picked the scab off this old wound. Teresa's right, though. Family don't understand. They don't remember how it used to be. To them life is how it is now, with the many advantages of living in Australia. They view their homeland as being how it appears in those horrible news reports, not like it used to be. Her boys were too young to take notice. How can they have the same ties? Oh yes, it had its problems back then. A colonial life is hard when you are the outsiders. Maria's fist goes to her chest, where her own little wad of locked-in pain lives. But being surrounded by like-minded people who shared the values of a blended culture is comforting. Some had plenty of reasons to carry into their new lives many resentments and unresolved issues. For Teresa, yes, she feels empathy but if she's honest, she'd admit she is also disdainful of her friend. Teresa is being foolish. Teresa should have more control. But, then, maybe this brother-in-law's cancer is Teresa's last straw. The two friends sip their lattes, and stare into the dwindling froth as if there's a message in there or a puzzle to resolve. They wait in silence for Andrew. He returns with his own hot drink, a cup of black tea with a slice of lemon, and a surprise. Andrew knows they both adore Chinese custard tarts, and he's bought three, even though he's well aware both Teresa and his mother are diabetic.

2

BRISBANE
2009

Another loud toot of the horn and Andrew is off.

Maria sighs. 'Back to work.' Andrew's gone to his job and she will return to her previous occupation, which was standing near the porch rail and gazing out through the vegetation towards the street. She ignores the cane chair behind her, intended for her use.

Her grandson worries about her. He once asked her, 'Ah Ma, why don't you sit on a chair? I got you one. Isn't it comfortable? Shall I find you a different one?'

How can she explain? This position, contrary as it may seem for a woman of her age and condition, feels natural. But she can't squash Nathaniel's effort.

'Thank you for your thoughtfulness, Nathaniel. But, you know, we old people do too much sitting. If I grow tired, your chair will be perfect.'

Perhaps the habit of standing began on that day, years ago, when this house was little more than a skeleton of a building. Who would have thought taking her position at the rail of an unfinished porch would bring her to see that her battle against the inevitable was futile and allow her to give her husband a nod of approval? Now that once unfinished building is her home. The constancy of adopting this pose has developed a meditative response in her. Move to the rail, grip it, and her thoughts slow. She can distance herself and reflect on past and present. Today, she's contemplating the layers beneath Teresa's one-sided conversation.

'Well, my goodness,' Maria can't help but smirk. 'Seems that it's not just me who keeps secrets from their children.'

But conceding this possibility does not offer her comfort. Her common sense tells her this is a certainty for many. People always have their little secrets and their private frustrations and resentments. That's human nature. Her community may have more than average, like others who have lived within a difficult environment such as a minority in a colonial state, or who are migrants and have left behind their families and their histories. But why is Teresa spilling now? Old age, too? Nostalgia, maybe? People do become sentimental as they age. Not her, she vows. After her outing she's feeling strong and young. It won't last but it's sufficient to encourage her to declare she's going to remain strong and to express her disdain for people like Teresa who can't control their thoughts. Is she harsh in her judgment? Yes. She is. She knows she is. And she knows she's lying about herself. She may not be broadcasting to all and sundry but she's weak inside. And that flaw in her character is no better than Teresa's need to spill out her worries today.

Maria can't erase the memory of Teresa's face, of reading the emotions that scrolled across it as she talked about her sister. Teresa's pain was visible. And what Teresa's face was saying cut right into Maria. That's how she feels inside. That's how she'd look if the situation was reversed. Perhaps she envies Teresa's willingness to talk. To talk about Henry and Stephen is impossible, too destructive, because one story would lead to another. A brief flicker of regret passes through her. She's let her friend down. Teresa found no answer within her conversation with a friend who should understand the helplessness of being confined to Australia when the family is suffering in PNG. Perhaps all Teresa needed was to hear herself say those words. Fears that are spoken about openly lose some of their power. Maybe Teresa is smarter than her unreliable friend.

If it wasn't for her fear of unravelling everything, of losing control, maybe… yet she knows her own reticence has gone too far. One part of her says it is well past time to make a start, tell Nenek Koti's stories, about how she came to be the first of the family to live in Rabaul. She's the only one still standing who can remember Nenek Koti's history. She chuckles at the irony of her use of the word 'standing' as she grips the rail. If by chance her brother is still alive, what would he remember? A five-year-old hasn't many memories, the age he was when they were separated. Now she has opened the same old wound, the seeping slash to her heart that Henry's failure to return home after the war and his non-contact since must have been deliberate. He would have been aware of who was leaving. Why didn't he make the effort in 1975? A tear wells in one eye. He's lost to her. Or she's lost to him.

'Come on stupid meri,' she prods herself. 'Start by telling Nenek's stories, then move on to Mumma's story, about how she met Daddy-George. But motivation flags when thoughts of Nenek and Mumma and Daddy-George lead to memories of Stephen. Stephen is interwoven into her life. Each event in her life is assessed against its importance in relation to Stephen. A red light flashes. All progress is halted. Opening her own personal Pandora's chest will destroy her family. But what if the truth comes out late? Won't that make the telling more destructive? On and on the argument between her conscience and her fear continues.

Maria's self-interrogation is gruelling. Her shoulders slump and her head drops. She can no longer hear the traffic passing in the street, or the children playing hopscotch along the footpath, or Mrs Solomon shouting to her husband Isaac who is, as always, working in his garden. With a clenched fist she pounds her chest.

'You a selfish meri. Everyone pays the price for you needing to hide your pain, for you keeping secrets.'

She's plummeting into remorse and self-degradation, unable to deny the inevitable and indisputable reckoning. Death. That's when a person's life takes on a different shape. Death brings an end to the manipulations and deceitfulness of the living. A static version of the deceased replaces the dynamic living form. The dead can't protect themselves. Any malicious gossiper can influence perceptions.

She wants to do what's right. But how can she get past her self-imposed blocks? Attempting to goad herself into action, she plays out in her mind her own death. She knows what to expect. Their community has traditions. Her family will choose her favourite dress. They'll choose her red floral shift. They will lay her body to rest in the undertaker's casket. Then one by one following a customary order of hierarchy, the ones she loves will pass by and say what they need or want to say. First Andrew her eldest, his wife Kathy, then Gabriel, her second-born, then Daniel and Anna, and then the grandchildren: Francine and her brother Lucas, then Jonas and Nathaniel. Each face loved by her. She imagines their tears, and her heart swells with love for each one. As she's dead, she won't be able to see or feel all this love. Then there will be the traditional PNG Wake. Family and friends close and distant will gather to 'pay respect'. She recalls her husband's. For days people turned up, stayed, shared food and talked. Conversations did not always stay with the deceased. Everyone fattens thin memories for the occasion; they banish unpleasant thoughts about the deceased, if for no other reason than to stave off bad karma for their own passing. Ex-PNG people are superstitious beings. It's not only a matter of celebrating a life ended but reconnecting the living, binding each to the other. She imagines, based on other Wakes she's attended, that on one evening, memories will be hard to find. Each will want to demonstrate a 'belonging', and eventually someone will ask a question that will lead to another and then to another.

'Can anyone remember what it was like in Rabaul?'

Maybe Andrew or Kathy or Anna will remember something, but it'll be small, and when pressed for more, perhaps about other family members such as grandparents they'll have nothing. Or maybe, a harder one might come from someone like Francine, always the inquisitive one.

'How did the Seetos come to be in PNG?'

The answer will be a guess, someone's uninformed opinion.

'Why did Grandma Maria and Grandfather Patrick leave?'

'What was our great-grandmother like? Do any of us look like her?'

And perhaps this might lead to thoughts about how a woman who looked like Maria Seeto might identify as Chinese.

'Why are Grandmother Maria's eyes blue?'

They will reach a conclusion, make assumptions, but there will be so few answers to too many questions. Grandma Maria, well, she didn't talk about her family but – she must have remembered? They will think and think, wonder and wonder, until the questions come to them: did Grandma have secrets? Was there something that stopped Grandma from talking? Did our family or Grandma do something shameful? And after some time, they will wonder how they can uncover this mystery. That's when the true shame of what Grandma Maria has done, or not done, will be there for all to see. But there will be others at this inquisition, someone like Teresa, who might remember something from the Rabaul gossip vine of their former lives. That person will concoct a version that will remain as the truth forever because there will be no one left to put the story right, because she, the deceased, is the only one who knows.

She does a quick audit: is there anyway Teresa knows about Stephen?

She is free-falling. Dark fear is gripping her. Then, somehow, wafting out to her at the rail from inside her home, the hullabaloo of everyday human interaction saves her. Through the fog she hears a female voice, distinct, decisive and direct; a voice that shows only a trace of evidence that its speaker once spoke another language and perhaps was born elsewhere. It's Anna. Maria gives credit. She loves Anna. She's so proud of her daughter-in-law. Anna learnt English at a school in Brisbane but as a child was a fluent speaker of not only the common language of PNG, Tok Pisin, but also her tribal dialect. It's her voice that has caught Maria's attention, as it rises above the whoosh, whoosh, whoosh of the washing machine and the grinding of its motor reverberating around the laundry. Maria, dragged back to the here and now, is smiling.

'Ah, yes, evidence of the benefits and disadvantages of sharing your home. Yes, having Daniel, Anna and the boys here in the house keeps you alive, ensures you live in today, not in the past as you are wont to do.'

They are all home from work and school. Did they come home while she was at the Mall or while she was dreaming? If the latter, she sighs in gratitude. No one interrupted her. Regardless of the circumstances, at this moment, her home is full again. And she loves it.

'Daniel, garbage please.'

The background sound is a crowd roaring and excited television commentary. The adult Daniel is watching a replay of the weekend's footy game. Then comes Daniel's reply: slow, half-hearted, ill-considered. She smiles. Her boy's playing with fire.

'Jon-as. Garbage please.'

Daniel's passing the buck to his son Jonas, playing a video game in one corner of the living room, as he does every afternoon after school. He'll have his headphones on so his game's battle roar can't interrupt his father's footy.

There's a pause. She pictures Daniel moving so he can release his son's ears from the earphones, and turn his son's face towards him, ensuring that Jonas can see his father's raised eyebrows. She pictures Jonas' face reflecting his shock at the interruption. Shock will turn into a teenage scowl.

Jonas's voice.

'Awww, Dad, but...'

Anna silences both. 'Daniel, kissim. Now. Take the garbage out before your mum gets back. Jonas, your bedroom needs tidying.'

Silence. This is better than TV. Laughter gurgles up her throat.

Daniel responds with a grunt. The sound of his footsteps marks his passage towards the back door. There's a whisper of some comment Anna makes to him as he passes her in the laundry, followed by Anna's wicked laughter, and then there's only the cheering footy crowd melding with the metallic music of the video game now released by the removal of the earphones. Jonas must have taken over the living room. She pictures Jonas stretching out, relaxed and sporting a victorious grin. Anna will check on her husband's journey, a huge grin on her face. Playful prodding. And there'll be no anger or resentment from Daniel. He's tried his luck and failed. In a few minutes he will wander back to the television and the footy, reining in Jonas, and life inside the house will resume as before, as Daniel awaits his next orders. He's nothing like his father – except in looks.

Meanwhile, inside, the drama continues. Anna offers a final reprimand to her non-compliant son.

'Jonas.'

The silence of obedience is loud.

Maria has a video running in her head, of her grandson Jonas slamming the remote control down but looking over his shoulder to make certain his mother didn't see him do it. Then, with shoulders hunched, he's heading towards his bedroom and to the chore he needs to do. She smiles. Boys, father and son – both trying their luck. It's well one's wife, the other's mother, is a strong woman.

She can't remain here at the rail much longer. Time to go inside, time to think of a meal, and see where the evening takes her. But, hungry not just for food, she lingers to drink in this evening's brilliant vista: the last hour of daylight; the sun painting the western sky a gold-streaked rose as its final rays form a halo along the top of the range; and one last glance across the broader vista of her private oasis, a panoramic view past the pawpaw, hibiscus, fig and mango trees. Peaceful. Calm.

Maria ignores her earlier self-directive and does not hurry to turn away from the rail and head for the front door of her home. When she does move indoors, she carries Teresa's sadness with her, an external symptom of her own internal pain. In her assessment, the weight that hangs over her is of a collective pain felt by each compulsory migrant.

She hears Daniel's voice, as if it's from afar, and yet he's less than two metres from her.

'Mum, dinner's ready.'

Nathaniel, her younger grandson, the worrier, stands beside his father and repeats his father's invitation in his own way, voice tremulous, as if he's aware that all is not as it should be.

'Grandma? Coming for dinner?'

Even as she sinks further into her mental fog, she can still recognise his concern for her: Grandma is acting strange. Though she can see she is causing concern, she isn't in control of herself. Her feet have a mind of their own. They are padding on their own journey. They carry her past her son and his son. A great need to close her eyes overtakes her. She tells herself she must maintain her dignity, must not stumble, as she gives in to her need for her bed and for sleep to clear her mind. No words of explanation does she offer those worried souls. She can't speak. Stumbling along, needing now and then to steady herself by pressing her hand against the wall, she heads down the central hallway, one step at a time.

Halfway along the hallway, though, she falters. It is impossible for her to pass the mirror that is hanging there. It's been there since the family moved into this house. As if in a dream, she turns and faces it. She nods at its dull, tired and blemished face and her own one stares back at her. She smiles. Her treasure. Her fingers trace its fading edges and the corners of her mouth pull upward. She claims it. Her mirror. First thing she ever bought herself. Meanwhile, Daniel, Anna and their sons are staring down the hall towards her. She senses their presence. They are worried. But her mind is working on a mission of its own. The mirror has her mesmerised. It's hers, this mirror. And as she reminds herself of the fifty years of ownership, she also can't ignore what arose out of its acquisition. Gaining the mirror arose out of losing Stephen. Sweet and sour.

Over fifty years on, the mirror to her eyes is still the bright shining new one she purchased in 1957. Its bevels are not the patchy dull ones of today but are still sparkling like diamonds in the light. Today's version is weary. As she is, a truth she ignores. Seeing it, though, reminds her of what rankles with her, even though decades have passed. Pah. The way her late husband had dismissed this mirror as a 'chattel' or, more often, as 'rubbish', an object not worthy of being packed to ship to Brisbane back in 1975. She lifts her nose and screws up her face to her dead husband, whether he is 'on high' or 'down below'. The latter is where she wishes him to be. 'Poof, Patrick.' That man needed to control everything. She had to obey his law. He would declare, like he was the Lord and Master, what she could or could not do. Even if she debated, most times he would win because she was too much a coward to stand against him. But not about the mirror. She smirks. He said 'Don't pack'; she pretended she hadn't heard him.

'Mister Bossman, you not control everything. I packed it anyway.'

When the crate arrived in Brisbane and the unpacking began, Patrick had watched her peel off the cloth protection and wipe the mirror over with a soft cloth. She asked her son Andrew to hang it on the wall, here, a place that had felt right. It had hung in the middle of Chong's store in Rabaul, before she bought it and here it is, in the middle of the hallway of their home. Patrick had nothing to say. Instead, he showed his ultimate disregard by raising one eyebrow and snorting. She's certain that from then until his death, the mirror was invisible to Patrick though he passed it multiple times every day.

And just as Patrick deemed the mirror useless, perhaps she too might concede, when it was placed into the mix of everything else necessary to start their new life in Australia and measured against the limits economics placed on the shipping volume allowable, then the mirror's practical value was not high. Patrick may have had a point. It didn't feed the family, nor offer comfort for sleeping, nor protection from rain and wind. Nor was it useful like, say, the heavy pots they brought from Rabaul, or the blue-and-white dinner service. But dollars and cents didn't come into any assessment of the worth of the mirror and thus it was beyond Patrick's capacity to calculate. Had Patrick an inkling of its importance to her and those other ways of valuing, he'd have smashed it. The story of the mirror is another of her many secrets. No one knows her secrets. No one knows what happened in 1957, to give the mirror its significance. For her the mirror is compensation for her loss.

She turned twenty-two in 1957, but her age, despite her still supposedly being in the era of golden youth, meant nothing to her. The glorious promises of 1952 and 1953, although hindered by the sad and soul-destroying events of 1954, somehow lingered through 1955 and 1956. Then came catastrophic 1957 when every hope was destroyed. By chance it was also the year she married Patrick. That made it easy for her to blame him for everything bad in her life. Yet she knows she would be lying to do so. Although Patrick played a role in her destiny, he was not the master. But she had to blame someone. And who else? God, maybe? Goodness knows she has blamed God for his lack of consideration for the many other difficult moments. Patrick's arrival had merely set off a chain of events but, she censures herself, 'Time to let your husband rest in peace, Maria. You know only too well that your ill-fortune began earlier, before you knew that Patrick and his sister would enter your life, and destroy your dreams.'

In those days Patrick preferred to be called Seeto Tak Tam.

'That name, "Patrick", too western,' the young Tak Tam grumbled. It took him a while to see that in a new home, perhaps a new name was also appropriate.

Tak Tam accompanied his sister Seeto Mei Yee on the long sea voyage from China to Rabaul. A wealthy businessman had contracted Mei Yee to marry one of his employees who, he told the marriage broker, showed promise for the future. As Tak Tam became Patrick Seeto and found a wife, if a reluctant one, of his own, he became much more than an escort to a bride-to-be. This unwilling wife came as a package deal. His businesses flourished by way of association and alliances that were a side benefits of agreeing to this marriage; he had sons to carry his name into the future; and unexpected respect from his adopted community. What he hadn't foreseen was his inability to return to his homeland for the same reason as his sister was forced to return, whether married or not. The siblings' polar opposite fates came via the Territories' rather difficult to understand immigration regulations of the time. Nor might Seeto Tak Tam have anticipated that in twenty or so years in the future, he'd become officially known as Patrick Seeto, a naturalised Australian, and be starting over again in another foreign land.

3

RABAUL, TPNG
1954

It's the Lunar New Year of the Wooden Horse. She had celebrated the coming new year along with crowds of Chinese, Mixed Race and Europeans. The Lion Dance is always an annual focal point in Rabaul. But this time the Lion could not dance outside her home because she was homeless, therefore she could not put her head into the beast's mouth to ensure her success in the coming year, as tradition demanded. Nor did she have money to fold into a shiny lucky red packet for the Lion, to encourage him to dance and jump and for him to devour, in order to ensure her good fortune. Perhaps these omissions are the reason the year isn't going well for her. She's in survival mode. To achieve this, to hold back the melancholy that threatens to overwhelm her and to retain within her the tiniest flicker of hope, she attempts to narrow her focus to the day-to-day chores of Loi Fook's trade store. Keep busy and lock out other thoughts. Chores must bind her mind: serving customers, sewing, unpacking stock, cleaning.

Tinkle, tinkle, tinkle. The door is being opened.

She lifts her eyes above the glow of the sewing machine lamp. Who is entering her dim world? Her father? Or maybe the store's owner? It'd be too much to ask for it to be Stephen. But, God willing, maybe today's the day.

No, not today. It's a customer. She rises from the sewing machine, blank-faced, and waits for him to speak.

'Me like emi tin pis.' The Tolai man has his silver coins ready. He exchanges them for a can of salmon. He's a regular.

Canned fish or bully beef are always popular. Either goes with boiled rice to make a nice meal. Perhaps also some bubbly water, made locally by a Chinese soft drink manufacturer. Sarsaparilla or ginger beer is her best seller. Often her clients only need a rope of trade tobacco and a sheet of an out-of-date newspaper. Rolled in the paper, the tabak becomes a long cigarette and then she might sell her customer matches or a lighter.

Only when she feels her muscles relax does she realise her relief – it was a customer and not the store's owner. Why does she trouble herself over Loi's visits? She reasons with herself: there's nothing more he can take from you. But deny as she may her fear of Loi, there is one important thing she can't ignore: Loi must never know about Stephen. Stephen works for Loi too. Denial of her relationship with Stephen, she has convinced herself, is her protection. But everything is dangerous. Loi's visits are neither regular nor verbal. His power over most of his employees, or in her opinion his slaves, is such that his physical presence tends to make them quake. Not a cruel man himself, Loi has others to do the dirty deeds. Like her father.

When Loi visits, she hears the same tinkling bell as she would for any visitor. But it's the silence that follows Loi's entry into the store that announces his presence. His steps are soft. His hands grasp each other behind his back and he bows his head as he strides across and around the store. He always ends at the counter, but never does he examine the till or the ledger. As if he wants to show that his presence is threat enough to halt any thievery or deception. And then he's gone, the door tinkling a farewell.

After each visit, she vows to herself: 'If Loi believes he can frighten me into obedience, he's mistaken.' He can intimidate only those with something to lose. Compared to the veiled threat of her father's visits, Loi's provide a break in the day's monotony. But one strange habit has her curious: the lingering minutes he spends staring into her face. Is he trying to read her mind? Her only precious possessions are those she keeps in her mind: memories of moments spent with Stephen. She protects those by working hard to think of other thoughts than those of her beloved.

Loi uses Stephen to manage a copra plantation. She has chosen the word 'uses' because Loi does not pay Stephen. He argues Stephen owes him a debt for his passage from China. That journey was a quarter of a century ago. With some irony she notes the price of the voyage must have been high. She has never been to Loi's plantation. But Stephen describes it as taking up the whole of one small island. She knows it is out there, somewhere far away, at least a day trip on a small inter-island ship. Her father David hates those trips. But, as Loi's second-in-charge, or his heir as he tells everyone he is, David must do what his boss/adoptive father doesn't do. Loi, or in practice,

David keeps Stephen reined-in. The pair permit Stephen the occasional visit to 'civilisation' but he never knows when that will be and that visit can, according to his managers, only serve a need of the plantation, not for any of Stephen's social needs or pleasures. That means Stephen can't forewarn her of his visit. All communication via the ship or from the plantation is via an open-channel radio-telephone. Stephen just turns up, maybe for an hour, or sometimes, thanks be to God, for a day, and once or twice in a year, even overnight. She despairs over the many factors that keep him away: storms that makes access to the plantation's jetty difficult; a change of schedule by the shipping company; Loi's or David's decision to cancel a trip to Rabaul; or some minor drama in plantation life that means Stephen must stay on the island.

Ah, but when Fate and Fortune come together, those rare days are glorious. The memories of them are what carry her forward through the drudgery and hopelessness of each day, each week, each month and each year of her day-to-day life. She replays them in her head, as she runs through the automaton of her daily routine: open the store early in the morning, cater to her customers' needs, supervise labourers to unload and pack deliveries, sew the multitude of seams that comprise Loi's stock of smocks and laplaps, and close up late after the day's trading. Somewhere in between she prepares herself a simple solitary meal, and later, she will fall onto her canvas camping bed in the back corner of the store with her only light the soft golden flickering glimmer of a kerosene lantern, softer, more comforting, than the store's industrial fluorescents.

On those days when the bell tinkles and there he is, a smile on his face, his eyes alight, and his arms outstretched, she's out of her chair, away from the sewing machine and running to him in a flash. For as long as they dare, they stand close to the entrance, embracing each other. Each time, she will take his hand and lead him to the cane chair on the opposite side of the worktable upon which her sewing machine stands, and talking, she will put the kettle on to make him a cup of tea. He sits and smiles and waits for her to finish talking. When the tea is ready, and she brings it to him, still smiling, he nods in thanks and sips. His eyes never move from watching her face. Oh, how that makes her feel loved. Loved as she has only ever felt loved when as a child, when all those who loved her filled Nenek's home. Stephen shows her someone does hear her, someone does see her, and someone does enjoy being with her. She's alive.

There are words already queuing, ready to spill. All the words she has no opportunity to utter during the weeks, sometimes months, between Stephen's visits, but that she works to keep contained until Stephen has spoken. As soon as she allows them their freedom, they fall out of her mouth like a waterfall. 'Oh Chun Yuen, did I talk you about…?' She uses his Chinese name and he listens to her funny little stories about her customers, the only world she knows, and laughs. He tells her about what has happened on his little island. Babies have been born to the wives of workers, a storm blew in and upturned the roof of the outdoor kitchen. He caught a large fish a few weeks ago that would feed himself and the families of his workers. His joy at sharing moves her to tears. She has never been to this island plantation but from Stephen's many hours of storytelling she can see it as if she were there. A long jetty reaches out into the Bismarck Sea. Small waves roll in along a short beach, its bright whiteness a surprise to her. Fine black volcanic pumice forms Rabaul's beaches, the only ones she knows. Around the jetty cluster thatched-grass workmen's huts and a small one room manager's cottage constructed of galvanised iron, with a push-out window and only doorways with no doors. The children of the workers spend their days following the masta around, no school to keep them otherwise busy. She can see the workers' wives and daughters sitting on straw mats and chewing buai, rocking babies or preparing food or plaiting coconut fronds, as the Tolai women do in Rabaul's marketplace. She sees Stephen joining the menfolk climbing aboard an ocean-going lakatoi or a canoe to go fishing after the day's work, to catch something for their families' dinners. In her head, she hears the voices of workers singing in dialect as they sit on the trailer behind a tractor and head out to collect coconuts. Her imagination paints herself there, in that modest home, and she is preparing the fish brought in from the sea for her and Stephen's meal, and afterwards, she and Stephen spending their evenings doing as they do here, in Loi's store: talking, laughing, and loving.

Here in the store during those precious visits, they spend whatever few hours he has available together in the circle of light thrown out by the sewing machine as she continues to do what she must each day: sew, sew, sew. She cannot let her production drop because Loi will notice. Darkness comes courtesy of Loi's miserly limitations. 'Yu no waste my money on kissim electric light all the time.' The darkness of the store is comforting. If she's honest, she'd say it feels less dangerous. Less chance of being noticed.

In Stephen's presence, she forgets the drag of the heavy fabric, callouses on her fingers, and her weary eyes. As the machine chugs its way along the seams and hems, they sit and talk. Around them, in the darkness, ropes of trade tabak dangle from a beam above a counter stacked high with boxes of cigarette lighters, and piles of discarded newspapers to accompany the ropes of tobacco. In the gloomy background, the many cartons of shirts and towels are no longer visible. Nor the mountain of bolts of coarse trade fabrics, the stacks of rice bags and cans of cooking oil, the wick lanterns sitting on timber crates, piles of hairy blankets in bright shades, mounds of folded laplaps, and the row of meri blouses, hanging off wire coat hangers suspended from the ceiling by a rope stretched between one wall and another. This is their private world. A different world from the one she lives in when Stephen is back on his plantation. His, she imagines, is noisy, but hers? Days, weeks, and sometimes months pass where all she hears are the requests of her customers. Excluding Stephen's visits, people only pass by her – the store's customers, Loi and her father – and the only words they share with her are those necessary for her to do for them whatever is necessary.

Stephen's visits as few and far between as they might be are all that sustains her in this terrible year. This year except for Stephen she is alone.

4

BRISBANE
2009

In those years she spent labouring in Loi's trade store, once or twice or maybe three times, Loi would take care of his own store for an afternoon. Perhaps these generous moments happened because he had won well at mah jong or, applying a more cynical tone to her reasoning, he'd ruined another family's life. With a flick of his wrist he would dismiss her for a few hours. Not wanting to risk Loi's change of heart, in five minutes she would be out of Chinatown, heading towards Kamerere Street, towards Chong's.

§

Three Chong brothers own and run the store. The families of all three work in the business: wives and children and grandchildren. In some ways her haste is laughable. She rushes from one store to go to another, but there's a marvellous difference between the two. Where Loi's trade store caters to New Guineans, Chong's offers its goods to Chinese and Mixed Race and also to Europeans whose smiles show their love of the surprises they would find there. Westerners can explore the mysterious and exotic east by visiting Chong's store to journey into the unknown without leaving Rabaul. At Chong's, Maria travels to another world and hides from the misery of her own. It's her sanctuary.

On her way to Chong's, the road is lined with stores. Inside of each are women hidden in their dark interiors, doing what she does, taking care of their family's store. As she passes, some call to her, lifting their heads from serving a customer or from the sewing machine. Out of some stores come the squeals and shrieks of children, playing among the stock, their games interrupted as they look to see to whom their mother is calling. 'Good day Aunty Maria,' she hears one child say. Not aunty by blood, but someone to whom they should show respect. Respect is a scarce commodity in her life. She basks in her moment of visibility. She smiles, and waves to the children without slackening her pace. Near the park, on Casuarina Avenue, sitting in the shade of a casuarina tree, are two women she recognises.

'Me lukim yu tupela' she calls out, and they laugh and carry on talking.

She's almost there, almost at Chong's store.

Chong's store is a deep cave filled with familiar and foreign treasures. On sale are large carved camphor-wood chests, like the one she inherited from Nenek, but they also stock matching carved sideboards, ivory ornaments for women's hair, and strings of cultured pearl and gold rings set with beautiful opals. For the Chinese, an opal symbolises truth and honesty. To receive an opal as a gift, one must be true of heart. She has always wanted an opal. And there are the embroidered satin cheongsams in brilliant shades, and their matching brocade slippers. Chong's also sells modern electrical appliances, ceramics from Germany, fine china from Japan, the latest British records, and grand gramophone players in polished wooden chests. Inside, the air is thick. Above the musty smell of bolts of silk, lace and brocade, there's camphor, candle wax, incense, shoe leather, the occasional bite of tiger balm and the cloying sweet scent of 4711 Eau de Cologne. Sneaking into these exotic aromas is a touch of the everyday: garlic and onion coming from the rear of the store where a meal is always being prepared.

Oh, how she misses Chong's. Chong's store and its exotic stock remind her of Nenek's chest, and thinking of Nenek's chest brings her around, again, to Stephen. She says a silent prayer to thank God for bringing Stephen back into Nenek's life. She'd known Stephen when she was a child, but there were many years of absence. After the war, when everyone else had gone, so many dead, Stephen returned from the far coast where he had served as a coast-watcher for the Australian forces. He turned up one day and knocked on Nenek's door, as if he hadn't been absent more than a day or two rather than years. Nenek loved Stephen, and in the years between the end of the war and Nenek's death, Stephen's work for Loi was in Rabaul so he'd often share meals with them. What lovely evenings they were. On Nenek's precious verandah of the house that had been Maria's home all her life, the three would sit together. One of them would lift the lid of Nenek's chest and extract an item and a story would follow.

§

First, folds of batik fabric.

'This come long Hollandia,' Nenek begins her tale about wandering through the markets in search of treasures during her short spell in the far-off western New Guinea town that really was called Numbay in the era that Nenek had lived there, and Jayapura now. A pearl comb for clasping hair and a matching string of artificial pearls; 'Oh, this was for my wedding to Josef.' Those words transform the Nenek sharing the verandah with them into a younger version, jet black hair pulled back on one side by a pearl comb and, plunging down almost the full length of her plum-red baju kurung, the matching string of pearls.

Ancient newspaper cuttings; drawings by Stephen of Nenek and Maria; a plaited band Nenek claims once belonged to Datuk Josef; and more. Each item with a story attached. Sometimes Stephen would add his tales to Nenek's. When it was one of his drawings that was extracted, he'd recall the moment a subject caught his eye and the essence of what he tried to capture in his drawings. On rare occasions, he'd talk about his wartime experiences and his Aussie friend who taught him to read and write in English and encouraged his art as they sat out the war and reported on passing ships through the straits.

Maria has no stories to share, but she believes herself blessed to be the listener. The story heard most often is Nenek's story.

§

'Tell us again, Nenek. Tell us your story. Please, Nenek,' she begs of her grandmother.

As always, Nenek begins her story with a hoot, 'Oh ho, Maria, if only you could see my little island. Our little island, he something people dream about. Blue water all around. Spikey mountains. You savy. They liklik volcanoes. Only tiny. Dutch ships, they come long our harbour. Dutchmen like em tumuch our cloves. Our papas and mamas toktok to us: you children no go long sailors. But young people, always the same. Take no notice of what parents talk. We sit in shadows, hiding, pretending we shy, but we listen well. Ho, ho, all a same you listen good long my story, Maria. Oh, so magical their stories. Other islands and other places. Cities of gold. Sultans in palaces. Jewels traded for spices. Storms that whip up mountains of waves and take them to some place they never been before. We listen and we learn.'

This story retold so regularly, as soon as the words tumble from Nenek's mouth to begin her migration story, a movie runs in Maria's head. She sees the six rowers, digging oars deep into the dark green of the ocean. In her mind-movie, their bodies appear similar in appearance to her grandmother's: tall, slender and dark Malay bodies. Perhaps this is not so strange, as she hasn't known many people who come from the same place as her grandmother, so she has only one person on which to model her characters. She sees the rowers: black skin shining with sweat, shoulders bowing, muscles rippling with each plunge of the oar. And, at last their destination, that town, the name of which Nenek whispers: 'Hollandia'. She pictures the rowers, imagines the relief they feel at the sight of their destination appearing on the horizon and, their six heads rising as one, oars suspended mid-air as each rower takes in the sight of this alien landscape. In her mind-movie, for a short time after the rowers have ceased rowing, their giant canoe continues to move forward as if the canoe itself is impatient to end this journey of weeks of resisting the weather and waves, of being pulled ashore and pushed out into the water again and again, one tiny island or atoll after another. The canoe slows almost to a standstill, and only then do the rowers' heads lift, and once again the rowers plunge in the oars and take them up. Plunged, taken up and plunged. In her imagination, the bow cuts through the small waves of the harbour and ahead, Hollandia, that seems familiar because its image is much the same as the only place she knows. As in Rabaul, buildings cling to the shoreline. In the background a ring of volcanoes. Unlike Rabaul, in the far distance beyond the Hollandia of her imagination, as described by her grandmother, 'The land goes on forever until it reaches tall mountains with their heads in clouds.'

'Tell us the rest, Nenek. About Hollandia and Grandpa Josef.'

'Ah, that man, so handsome, Maria. Josef Pereira. He kam long place where there were Sultans. He wok long the ships. He toktok me stories, he make me laugh, and we love each other so very much. Love. The reason I left my island: to find love. And me find it in Hollandia.' A deep sigh, always, and a sad pause.

'Josef and me, we marry and he like build me a house for our children, so he tok me: "Koti me need to get more work so we have money to buy a house. Long wharf they asking strong men to go work in Deutsch-

Neuguinea for German tobacco planters." Sad but me think Josef, he savy what best. We want children and for that we need money. Work not so plenty for people like us. Then me wait and wait but Josef, he no kam back. Can wait no more, so me pack our few belongings, take our savings and buy a ticket to go to this place Josef call Friedrich Wilhelmshafen. Me toktok myself, me make our home there, no different to making home for Josef and me in Hollandia, and off me go. When me get there, me come long house of boss of plantation, masta Schultz, na he tok me "Sorry, missus, your husband Josef get very sick na die pinis." Me cry plenty. Me toktok long masta Schultz, "masta, me no got money now." Masta Schultz, he givim me a job cleaning and cooking, and when masta Schultz kam long Rabaul, me come too.'

'And, Nenek, you missed the bit about your wedding chest?'

'Oh yes, Maria. So romantic. This how much your grandfather love his new wife: he work, work, work to buy something special. He givim this before he go long tobacco plantation. Precious is this chest. This chest come with me wherever me go. When mi die pinis, Maria, he yours.'

And that is how it came to be Maria's chest. Nenek died. Loi Fook claimed his right to his house, the one she lived in with Nenek, and her father bound her to Loi to work and live in his store. No money. No choice. Only Nenek's chest. Sometimes she hates that chest. After Nenek's death, there were many times she wished she could trade Nenek's glorious chest in order to have her grandmother's life extended.

Eventually, however, working for Loi, with so little money meant nothing special went into that chest, and even Stephen's artwork has become less and less. In Loi's trade store, the chest never came out from under a thick trade blanket. Circumstances meant the object that had once been central to her life became almost invisible. Anyway, she had no time for sitting and taking items out and telling their stories. That good life died with Nenek. But she did promise herself, God willing, there will be better times ahead.

One last tiny bud of a thought. As much as she loves Nenek's story about Josef, she has always struggled to accept Nenek might have exaggerated. If Datuk Josef died before Nenek moved to Rabaul, then how come Josefina, their daughter and her mother, was born in Rabaul? Her grandmother's story never changed, nor would she have ever challenged it. But a lie is a lie and Nenek has raised her to always tell the truth. Each time the story comes to its usual end, her fingers would twitch as they have always done when she senses something isn't right.

5

RABAUL, TPNG
1956

Maria's visits to Chong's ceased once she married. Her father delivered the news of her forthcoming marriage on her twenty-first birthday.

§

For her, the day of her birth is yet another ordinary day, like every other day. Rise in the morning, wash and dress, straighten her bed by stacking her pillows and folding her blanket, then prepare and consume her usual plain breakfast of congee. She moves on to opening the store and re-stocking shelves, sweeping the floor, and if no customers have visited, she moves to the sewing machine. She has no expectation that others will remember the importance or significance of the day. And what does it mean, anyway? Westerners think being twenty-one represents becoming an adult. She feels old. Westerners also believe that after twenty-one an individual may follow his or her own path in life. This is an unlikely future prospect for her. With a sigh, she gets on with the tedium of life, pushing all thoughts of freedom and a future to one side.

The working day is drawing to a close. The final seam of a bright red laplap under the machine needle is receiving her close attention when the little bell sounds its gentle warning. She doesn't look up, tells herself it's another customer, but these footsteps go beyond the front end of the store and enter the reserved space behind the counter. Ready to fire a short sharp sentence in Pisin to remind her customer that entering this space is taboo, she lifts her head to see it's not a customer. It's her father David.

Why is he smiling? David never smiles. Her mind warns her but her heart doesn't wholeheartedly agree. Despite the many times her father has hurt her, there's always a flickering hope of discovering him to be a good man underneath his public face. Her mind attempts to pinch out the flame in her heart by scrolling a list of disappointments and cruelties perpetrated by this man, and the concentration demanded of fear and optimism causes her hands to pause in its task of pushing the heavy red laplap fabric under foot of the sewing machine. Her feet cease to press and lift on the treadle. She's stalled, alert and waiting.

There's something odd about David's behaviour. Is it the over-bright sparkle of his eyes, or the uncharacteristic expression of joy playing over his face? What a rare and frightening sight. What can please him so? That can't be a smile?

And now her brain has caught up with her sight: this behaviour is familiar. The memory of when she's seen this before rushes in, startling and scaring her. Yes. David behaved in this manner on that day two year's earlier in 1954. The year of loss. He had knocked at the door of Nenek's home and she had opened it. There was her father. Nenek was dead, and she was alone and she needed comfort. So great was her need, she had ignored a voice in her head, which may have been the almost forgotten one of her mother whispering, 'Maria, expect nothing from this man.'

She should have listened to her mother's warning. No paternal condolences were delivered on that day. Only Seeto Wei, her father's Chinese name, acting as Loi's lieutenant by pronouncing in a grand tone of power: 'Grandma dead, agreement between Loi Fook and grandmother ends today.' What that deal between Loi Fook and her grandmother might have been was the least of her concerns. Of greater importance was the realisation that if a man feels nothing, perhaps he can't realise the damage his words might do. On that day he delivered news to her with a smile, convinced as he was that the news must be well-received.

'Yu so lucky, yu got a better place to live.'

Her first response was to wonder. What could he mean? Where could she go that would be better than Nenek's home with its verandah? Nothing could be better than the house in which she and her brother Henry had been born, where at one time their family of her mother and stepfather and brother and grandmother had been happy. That house featured in every phase of her life until this moment This is her home. This is Nenek's home.

Recalling that day almost undoes her. Tears well, and she fights them off.

She doesn't want to show him her weakness. Again, he begins.

'Oh, yu so, so lucky.'

And there's that phrase, a warning to her: it's a subtle predictor of disaster. In 1954, it led to a 'new' home that was Loi Fook's store, and to the life of a slave, unable to make choices of her own and to have no means to go elsewhere. Her father's excitement encourages him to blurt out his announcement.

'Yu soon become respectable Chinese wife. You look after your new husband's store. Loi say you a superb worker.'

Has all reason flown? Who in all of Rabaul would want her as a wife? Oh – a revolting possibility flashes into her comprehension – not some decrepit and reclusive 'bush' Chinaman that Loi or David owes money to, or from whom they want something? A less desirable possibility, for her something far worse, is a man with a need for a third or fourth wife, for sex only and, if that were possible, even fewer rights and hopes ahead for her. And, always, the one who benefits will be David. So, what will be in this for him? A sense of hopelessness fills her. What's the use of her arguing? She has no power; she has nowhere to run to; and she needs somewhere to sleep and eat if she is to survive. She prepares herself for her fate.

Her father teases her. He lets his words hang, aware of their impact, and then it comes to her. David knows hers and Stephen's secret. She's doomed.

'You savy my brother Stephen getting Chinese bride now?'

His eyes scan her face. He wants her to feel his victory, and she wants to retaliate, to shout against the ugly implication of incest, to challenge the lie that permitted Stephen's entry in the Territories. 'Stephen's not your brother.' She isn't willing to gift him that reaction.

Her ears are buzzing. David's words are now coming fast. He's excited but for her what he says no longer makes sense. She's losing the battle to control herself. Her emotions are boiling inside her filling her with a desire to shriek. She stands and wills her legs to keep her body straight and tall, her face to remain blank. At that moment, another Maria steps out of her body and looks back at the one seated at the machine, the Maria with one hand on the yet unfinished seam and the other suspended mid-air, one finger pointing upward. The externalised Maria looks with despair at the frozen expression on the living Maria's face, notes how her lips open in a silent gasp, and recognises the panicky rapid compression and expansion of her ribs. To the ethereal Maria, the words Seeto Wei is throwing at his daughter are perceptible as a string of exploding New Year fireworks sparking across the narrow space between father and daughter.

'My brother Stephen getting Chinese bride now,' he repeats for impact. Or is it for pleasure?

Punched in the gut, breathless Maria has no words, no response.

'Loi buyim a bride long China for Stephen. Name belong bride is Mei Yee. Also name Seeto. Good name, eh?'

A victorious grin emphasises the full stop of her father's declaration. The pause is short-lived.

'Her brother Tak Tam, he kam long New Guinea too. Emi take care of Mei Yee long voyage.'

And still it continues. He draws in a big breath. 'And he like marry yu. Loi says Stephen and Mei Yee makim plenti pikinini, become cheap labour for Loi's trade store. Bargain for Loi. And me think you and Tak Tam make plenty more pikinini that can work long my trade store. Bargain long me.'

And there it is: David's gain, her loss. She wills herself to remain in control. Her body ignores her and goes into spasms. She grits her teeth. Can't let him know he's won. But her mind rolls on and on. Why? Why? Why? Does she ask for much? Oh, where is her God? He has abandoned her.

The trade store, the hanging laplaps and meri blouses, the sacks of rice, her sewing machine with its little light still glowing, have disappeared. She can only see her father's smirking face. Time stretches, as if years have passed since her father entered Loi's store. The haze clears. Next comes a furious white anger. She thought the punishment was over, only to find there was more to endure.

'This man, respectable Chinese man. Yu very lucky. Yu should appreciate. This man he calls himself Seeto Tak Tam. You no need change your name. Yu still Maria Seeto. Gut name, eh?' Her father can't stop laughing at his own cleverness. She imagines a pool of blackness running out of her body. The death of hope. Inside her the rot has begun. She is dying. Soon death will appear on her face like a mask devoid of emotions, her body will turn into a machine, engaging in life without reason or ambition. Seeto Tak Tam, you'll be marrying a ghost. A dead woman.

A few weeks later she has her first conversation with Father Gustav about St Benedict and his 'Intention', but God and Father Gustav have no solutions, either.

6

BACK IN BRISBANE
October 2009

Maria works hard to bring herself back into the present but is failing.

'Where are you, stupid meri? Are you in the here and now? Ready for your family? Or are you staying in the past? Where nothing changes.'

She can't stop herself from sheltering in that place of regret and anger, though she knows there's only the same-old coconut to roll around and around, its soft inside hidden within a hard shell. Whether the flesh inside is nice and juicy or all dried up is unknowable until it's too late. Only after its shelled armour has been destroyed is it visible. No matter how often you re-live the past in your mind, the consequences can't change. How it is now is what you must live with. And yet still she regresses, even now. She is still permitting herself to wander back into the torturous past.

As fresh as if it were only yesterday, she remembers.

She's saved her meagre earnings from Loi by burying her coins in a small vegetable garden. Her intention had been to buy freedom. Loi's bind over Stephen was the cost of his fare from China, even though Stephen's voyage was never his choice. Only a boy snatched from the streets of his village to become a slave. Who snatched him? Seeto Wei or his employer? No matter who the kidnapper, Loi held the cost of the sea journey over Stephen's head and her father kept adding the cost of food and lodgings for every year since. Loi did not pay Stephen enough to reduce the debt, nor did he allow for the underpayment of wages. That would be too fair-minded. And beyond what a 'slave' should expect of his master. It was pointless to argue with a man who followed no rules but his own.

In 1957, with her dream shattered, freedom more unlikely than ever before, in what she feared might become her last independent act, she purchased the mirror, not realising at that moment what it would come to represent. There in Chong's deep and narrow store, halfway along on the right, the mirror she wanted. Now, as this old woman in Brisbane, she can picture it as if she were still there, in that store, lingering over the marvellous collection of items and breathing in the aromas.

She's there again. The windows of the store are high and protected from break-ins by welded mesh, and through them thin rays of sunlight struggle to illuminate dancing dust particles. An air of mystery pervades, as the dim light compels her eyes to wrinkle in order to see what she is seeking. On both sides, for the full length of the shop, runs glass display counters filled with surprising treasures. Stock hangs from rafters, is piled high behind and in front of the counters, fills the display cabinets and crowds the counter tops. Only a narrow passageway remains down the centre of the store. And yet, somehow and without hesitation, she locates the object she has chosen to replace her dream of a future with Stephen.

And here in Brisbane, almost fifty years later, her mirror also hangs halfway along a narrow space, the hallway that leads to bedrooms and bathroom, and again its position is a focal point. From anywhere in her home the mirror can be seen, though it's been there so long, no one but Maria notices it any more. For her, though, the sight of it brings the same response as when she first saw it hanging in Chong's. Her lips stretch upwards, as if she's smiling at her own image. Well she is smiling, but it's the same smile she uses to greet an old friend. As she gazes into the mirror her chest quivers, like the flutter of love she feels as she watches her sons. Looking at the mirror or her sons is an act of watching past and future being folded. About her sons, she remembers them as children, and within the man she glimpses the child once so dependent upon her, whose every achievement filled her with joy. The funny way Daniel twists his body before he moves or the way his hand always wipes his chin when he's thinking about something, habits he has kept since he was a babe in arms. Only she, his mother, will notice these things, and when she does, her heart swells with love. This man, who was once a boy, is hers. No one can take that from her. He's her child, no matter what age he is. As his mother, these little gestures, these exhibited mannerisms, are her privilege to recognise. And as this overwhelming love for a child, as these small, private, observations together fill a mother, memories of almost but never forgotten moments add texture and depth. A whisper of a recollection of the labour to bring that child into the world, the exertion and pain experienced, this, she tells herself, is the way one person measures the depth of loving.

Attached to the mirror are similar dualities. In its cloudy image and dulled bevels is proof she is still who she has always been. There's proof not only that at one time in her life she spent every bit of three years' hard savings on its purchase, but also that before she selected the mirror as the object upon which she would give that precious, hard-come-by money – the only money she'd ever had that she could spend as she wished – other wondrous and calamitous things had brought her to a point where such a choice had become possible. That too is a memory of love.

Oh, but back in 1957 she was wrong about Stephen, when she thought she'd never see him again. What a twist. Stephen's life did reappear in hers. Does she regret that? No. Never. Does the mirror remind her of the accidental gift that reunion delivered to her? Yes. Though she won't admit it. She's aware but dismisses the truth that she's never honest in her recall of those later events, preferring the fiction she tells herself, the one with her a mother and not someone who lies about how motherhood first approached her. Did she keep her secret to protect the child? Or to protect herself? The truth is too complicated, and, now, it's too late. Best to leave things be. True stories can only hurt.

The best memories, the ones about which she forgets no detail, will always be certain special days in the years spent in Loi Fook's trade store before her twenty-second birthday. Wouldn't it have been marvellous to talk about how it felt and smelt and how precious those times were to her? And yet how can you share this memory with her family? Could they ever understand? Only Stephen knew how much Chong's meant to her. Only Stephen knew what pain and trouble her father David brought to her. Only Stephen knew her, the real Maria.

She bites her lip, hoping the pain will jolt her back into today, where the reality remains: she is here in Brisbane and Stephen is no longer in her life and time is running out for her. No one lives forever. And, anyway, she chides herself, this is the way to madness. Thinking of Stephen, commemorating the losses incurred, is futile. She wipes some illicit tear-drops from her cheekbone, rebuking herself. 'What if someone saw? You'll worry your family.' She sighs, resigning herself to the reality of her life in which the past seems closer than the present. She must stop this. Either do something about the situation or let it go. Perhaps it is too complicated to talk about Stephen, but what of Nenek Koti and Datuk Josef, and your own mumma Josefina and Daddy-George? To her children and their children, these people are ghosts because of her silence. They could only live in everyone's minds if she had done what Nenek had instructed her to do, to remember the stories. No historian will ever find them. There are no documents or papers that prove their existence. No one else can tell their stories. Certainly not her brother, too young when he went from their lives, so only her.

From her place near the mirror she looks back to the living room. There they are, Daniel, Jonas and Nathaniel, like statues with eyes fixed upon her. She rebukes herself. 'Oh, come on stupid meri. Wake up. Get back to the real. You are frightening your family.'

'Be there in a minute, boys. No need to worry. Grandma, she lapun. Slow. But I'm coming.'

She doesn't even convince herself.

BETWEEN

PART 3
AUSTRALIA

1

QUEEN STREET SHOPPING PRECINCT, BRISBANE
November 2009

Maria has kept her secrets well. Her sons and their families believe she's like them, immersed in ordinary Australian life, happy in Brisbane. Those that are aware there were bad times back in their former home, maybe only Andrew and possibly Gabriel, believe she has, like they have, pushed all that behind her. For Andrew, her eldest, life is simple: there's work, there's family and there are exceptional special Mondays, like this one in which he waits to have lunch with his beautiful daughter.

It's somewhere around midday. The air shimmers across the city. The population has not yet fully immersed itself into the vibes of the approaching festive season and children are still at school. In a Queen Street Mall café in Brisbane's CBD, Andrew waits for his daughter, congratulating himself for being so clever. These rendezvous mean he need not compete for Francine's attention. When Francie comes to any of their family's homes, his mother Maria wins the contest. A quick look at his watch. It's only 11.50. Still too early. Francine won't get here until after 12.

Blue, red, yellow, green. Purple, pink, orange, white. Florals, checks, stripes and denim. He's picking up kaleidoscopic flashes from the passing mob. His job involves handling crowds. There are moments when dealing with the behaviours of the masses are annoying – their impatience, their rudeness, their self-centredness – but this is different. Here, on this one day, as the crowds rush by him while he sits and waits for his daughter, he's grabbing fragments of others' lives.

The waiter brings him the beer he ordered and leaves. Andrew reaches over, takes a firm grasp of the pot and lifts it to his mouth. His lips, already pouting, take that first long-drawn-out suck. A fine fuzz of froth tingles across the place where a moustache might grow – the sensation reminding him of the smoothness of his upper lip. Since puberty he's fancied himself with a moustache and furry sideburns. Fits with the other image he has of himself, the one where he's strumming his guitar, his friends/admirers seated at his feet, their adoring faces turned up to him, loving his music. Pop. He can almost hear the dream bubble burst, so he laughs at himself. Pop. Andrew Seeto, no rock star, but an ordinary Joe, whose particular specialty is being a son, a husband, and a father. He smiles at that. Good enough for him. It doesn't hurt to wish the impossible dream. But the moustache and sideburns would never happen. His lips roll inward and he sucks once more, and that automatic action of clearing the froth reminds him of the smoothness of his body. That's the only thing that makes him self-conscious about being Chinese. Ever see a hairy Chinaman? His kids always tease him. 'Dad, have you ever seen a rock-and-roll Chinaman? You got no need for sideburns and moustache.' He's always the man with the quick answer. His is: 'There's always a first time for everything, even a born-again hairless Roy Orbison.' To remind him of that dream, between the broken conversations wafting in from the passing population comes a sound so familiar he has almost overlooked it: the melodic words of 'She Believes in Me'. Ah, Kenny Rogers. Kenny is a favourite. Kenny's CDs have a permanent space in his car. He plays each one so often that his familial passengers always groan when they see him reach over to the glove box. To hear Kenny's voice coming from a nearby store, one of the many that line the mall, is the icing on the cake for him on this beautiful Brisbane day.

Another suck of his beer, then he runs his tongue along his upper lip and completes the clearance; this time his hoovering of the remaining dregs of the bitter but delicious residue is more efficient. He returns the pot to the table, studies the mall, the stores, the people passing by, and the others sitting at the nearby tables in the café. Fragments of conversation and bursts of laughter filter through to him.

This life – so, so good. Hard to believe this was a future life he once worried about. An unknown future that faced his family. Before migrating, around his former hometown, rumours and innuendo ran wild and played havoc with his imagination. The what-ifs? All dire. Nothing uplifting. And now this life is so familiar, so routine, but always, right from the first day, so different in so many ways, from the one he had left behind. Sure, that was years ago, over thirty perhaps. To calculate how many years is too much effort. For him, leaving that other life and coming into a new one was as if he was reborn. One Andrew before leaving, and another Andrew in Australia. No regrets, but it's kind of earth-shaking when he thinks about how things changed. Overnight, from a teenager with dreams and comforting familiarity, to an adult in a strange city, another world that operated at a whole different pace and with many sets of rules and priorities. One set of expectations left behind for an open-slather, anything-goes bundle. Hah, those teenage dreams: the one about becoming a rock star which everyone laughed at, may have been unlikely but then he didn't work at it, mostly a game of pretend. But the other one, the one he always thought impossible, like a miracle did happen. That was all about winning over the heart of one particular Aussie girl who also lived in Rabaul, a town in which many forms of social demarcations were in play. But he got that one right. Or did she pick him? Either way, he thanks God for his blessing. Amazing. A lottery-win. Who'd believe? At fifteen, a skinny-legged runt that still rode a push bike found his wife-to-be.

2

RABAUL, TPNG
1972

He's picturing himself back in Rabaul, when it was still the Territories of Papua and New Guinea. He's fifteen. His family live over near Sulphur Creek, in Chinatown. He comes to this side of town to attend the Catholic school, Sacred Heart, so it's easy to go to his mate's house on posh hill where the Aussie Admin people live. Where Kathy's family, the Cunninghams, live. Big houses, high off the ground. He's never been in Kathy's house but he knows what it's like inside because he's been to his mate John Watson's place, and the way John tells it, 'Been in one Admin house, you've been in them all.'

Sometimes, but not too often, he questions himself. How did he and John become friends? Didn't happen often, Aussies and Chinese or Mixed Race. Most of the Aussie kids went to boarding school in Australia. The few that didn't, stuck together. Did he set out to become John's friend because of where John lives and the nearness to Kathy's house? Or did John accept him as a friend because he's the guy who sees no differences in people? What does it matter who a person is or how he looks? Him and John, just great pals. Laugh at the same things, make the same dumb choices, like the same stuff.

Those Admin houses – like mansions to him, compared to his family's home which comprises a few rooms behind his dad's trade store. Admin-supplied homes are huge and open, looking out at the harbour like they own it. Guess they kind of do as the Admin are the bosses of everything. Inside John's house, even his furniture is big. Giant-sized rattan lounge suites with soft floral cushions. Hardly anything on the floor, except the stuff that should be there. In his own home, it's as if there's too many people and too little space. Tidy, but packed tight with all they own. Even stock from the trade store spills into the house. He's impressed by the empty spaces of John's house, but not sure it feels lived-in. John complains the same furniture is in every Admin house because it isn't each family's furniture or each family's house, but the Government's.

Kathy's family's house is out of his way, but he always rides past it on the way to John's and on his way home. He remembers one particular day, but that day could be any day because the same things happen so regularly. In his memory, he's on his old hand-me-down, fixed-up-with-odd-spare-parts-too-small bike that clanks and rattles, and he's riding past Kathy's house as he does every afternoon and doing stupid things to get her attention. Riding as slowly as he can without the bike falling over, or riding seated backwards on the handlebars. There've been times when his knees have collected asphalt from Kathy's street after falling off because his eyes are on the Cunningham house and not on the road ahead and so he's not watching for cars parked in the street.

Ah, Kathy: at first, she doesn't know him, because they don't go to the same school, yet she laughs at him, standing by the large louvred windows, looking down at him on the street. Later, some days, she'd move onto the porch and lean against the rail. He wonders, every day, every time passing her home, whether she thinks he's only a troublemaker from Chinatown, or perhaps someone just sent to entertain her and break her boredom?

3

BACK IN QUEEN STREET SHOPPING PRECINCT, BRISBANE
November 2009

She's here. Francine. He looks at his watch. Not too late. A good day if that's the measure.

'Hi there, Pops. Give us a hug.' Arms wide, a smile beaming across her face.

'Late as usual.'

'You haven't even looked at your watch. To you I am always late even if I'm early. I do it to make your life interesting.'

Her mouth quivers, as she suppresses her smile. She's teasing him.

'Not sure if "interesting" is the correct word, but there's no doubt you enhance my life. So, I'm waiting to hear what troubles and tribulations you have to share today, miss city-life-girl?'

'Started without me, eh?'

He follows her eyes to the empty beer glass. Now it's his turn to tease her.

'Needed Dutch courage to help me keep up with what's going on in your life.'

'Ooh, Dad. Anyone would think I live a terrible life, to hear you talk.'

'And don't you? What would you care to drink, young lady, or will we order food now, straight away, so we get time to eat it, because you will need to dash off, always in a hurry to go somewhere, do something? Today, I'm sure, is no exception.'

She rolls her eyes and says, 'Well...,' and laughs. He smiles.

'Wouldn't have you any other way. So, what's it to be today? Usual? Something different? I'm having my usual – barramundi and rice.'

'Dad, some things will never change.'

This time her whole face lights up with her grin, and he's reassured that she feels the same as he does. Same routine, every time they have lunch together. He waits while she skims the menu, knows she'll end up with the same thing. As always. He likes this is how it is between them, these funny little habits, symbols of a silent pact between them about the routine these luncheons follow. Different from how it is between them at family do's, which are hectic, with everyone wanting to gain her attention and him standing in the background and observing. She's the star of the family. Everyone's favourite.

She's looking at the menu, as if it's the first time she's read it, but he can see she's ready to order. Knows her so well. The thrill of his ability to recognise her behaviour swells his chest with pride. He puts his hand up. The child waiter comes over, ignores him but flirts with Francine while taking her order. He feels annoyed when the waiter continues to look at Francine while taking his order. Annoyed but proud. She is beautiful, his daughter. The waiter leaves, his eyes still on Francine.

'Bit young for you, isn't he?'

'Come off it, Dad. Just doing his job.'

He smiles. He watches her as she twists around her wrist a beaded bracelet, a band of several strands, each of a different shade. Her hand moves up to restore one thin strap of her top to its rightful place on her shoulder, and then she whips her head around, flicking her hair, as her hand moves onto her mobile, juggling its position on the table. Her eyes glance down. Messages? Then they flash around, checking out the passing parade of the Mall or other diners in the café. Restless. Aware. Conscious of others, while he has eyes only for her. Is she looking for someone she knows? Is she expecting someone? Meanwhile, she's talking nonstop, telling him about her week. Same prattle as he always hears. He's only half listening to the 'and then…'; 'but she said…'; and 'whatever.' Thinks he's trained himself to pick up on the important stuff, from the change of her expression or tone of voice.

But he realises his mind has slipped right away from her chatter when he hears his own voice.

'I hope you're not wearing that to Gran's next week.'

He sees his daughter's eyes drop and then flash up and glare at him. At first, he thought, oh, she has forgotten what she is wearing. But the stubborn tilt of her chin, the straight line of her lips, and her angry stare tell him she's ready to argue, defend her honour, so to speak. That look, that response, reminds him she's like his mother. The steeliness in her eyes makes him quiver. Must remember she's the child, he's the parent. She raises her brows and wiggles her shoulders, replicating, it seems to him, something he's seen on TV, a dance video maybe. The message is clear, but he's already committed to this line and, for pride's sake, can't withdraw.

'Ah, come on, Francine. Out of respect for your grandmother. A little less boob showing, please.'

She will not let him win. He waits for her offensive.

'You're old-fashioned, Dad. It's not Gran you're worrying about. And anyway, it's in. Look, everyone's wearing clothes like mine.'

With one braceleted wrist, she makes a wide sweep of the mall, its many boutiques on both sides, and the shoppers striding past, bags swinging. His eyes follow her arm, but he sees no one. Nor can he tell if those others she's gesturing at have low-cut dresses or barely-there attire with bits of belly showing, because he can't see past her palm – the one that's pointing out these 'in' styles – and what seems to be a blue-and-red outline drawn on it. He grabs her hand and makes a big show of pulling it up to his eyes.

'Francine.'

She's too clever for him. She raises one eyebrow, and her mouth turns up into a one-sided smile. Her indifference knocks the wind out of him.

'Oh, come on, Dad. Are you making a big deal over a small tattoo? You're being over-dramatic, aren't you? Everyone has tattoos, Dad. Anyway, I'm twenty. Not a kid anymore.'

He can't look her in the eye, feels powerless, so what's next? Tears are welling up and he has to work hard to hold them in. He would be humiliating himself if he lets them escape just because of her challenge. He reminds himself once more, who's the parent here? There's that alien again, the strange creature that his once cute and little girl has become. Not the first time he has felt this way. And he's sure it won't be the last. Now he feels weary.

Perhaps she understands him as little as he understands her. Something is being ripped out of him. But she lifts his hand, the one still gripping her palm, moves it towards his face, then turns her palm around so it strokes his cheeks. His hand falls away. He's lost to her. He can hear her saying, 'Only a tattoo, Dad,' and he permits himself to look at her.

'Only a tattoo.'

He forces himself to join in her soft laughter, but his sounds hollow, even to him. Yet he no longer feels as panicked. A little used maybe. Perhaps his girl's still in there. She knows what to do to get him back on her side.

The waiter comes with the food. She moves back onto her chair. Soon she's telling him the stories she seems to want to share with him: about her life at uni, her flatmates, some party she went to. There's his little girl back. He shuts out of his mind the low-cut neckline that he concedes isn't as low as he has implied it is. And the jeans that hang off her hips, and the gap he noticed, when she turned to go to her chair, between her top and the jeans. And that flash of flesh, not obscene and perhaps, yes, 'in style' but yet another sign that this person sitting opposite him, about whom he knows so much, is not anything like the one he has in his imagination. That glimpse drags him back to the tattoo and a sense he's seeing evidence of the ultimate act of rebellion against all previous generations and their rules and codes, their measures and restraints. He feels censured. Anger is curdling his gut, though he's resisting its call. He knows he's overreacting, but he feels slighted and also somehow tainted. He doesn't understand. Emotion settles back into the hidden spaces in which it hides until moments like these. Normal again, he sips his second glass of Light, tucks into his barramundi and smiles across at her.

Meal finished, he looks at his watch – time to go – but he's reluctant to move, feels as though they have together spoilt today's lunch, and he blames himself. He squeezes these luncheons between shifts at work, and they're precious to him. She has a half-smile on her face as if she too can see that the end of their meal together is near. She places her cutlery on her plate, her napkin on top, and stands up.

§

Francine has been watching her father, aware of the fine line they have both crossed. Her father glances at his watch. Oh, it's that time. Habitual and predictable. A measured moment to allow him time at home for a short nap before his next shift.

This lunch didn't go well. Why does she have to act like this when he's around? She wanted to tell him about Tim Johnson. Instead, she was her usual blabbing, nervous kid-like self, not the adult she wants to be for her dad. Tim Johnson's important to her, and she always shares her important stuff with her dad. She smiles at him as he rises.

'Here, Dad,' she says as she holds out a twenty-dollar note. 'Thanks for giving up your time. For having lunch with me. I appreciate it.'

'That's okay, Honeybun. Nah, keep your money. My pleasure. Here, give me a hug instead.'

'Term break's coming up, soon. Hope we can get to spend time together then.'

'Sounds good, sweetie. Mum would love to see you too, and Grandma. They miss not having you at home.'

'We've Uncle Daniel's birthday coming up.'

'Oh, yeah, don't forget to bring your apron. You know how Grandma loves to get us all cooking. Tra-dish-on-al. New Guinea-style.' She can tell by the sound of her father's laughter, he's not happy either about the way today's lunch has gone. But he continues his enthusiastic projection for the next family get-together. 'How about you and I team up? Think of something we can do, something different. Leave the fried rice and the chicken to the others. We'll surprise them all. Even Gran.'

She works hard to maintain a smile as she leans in to hug her dad. Tim Johnson. Dad would have loved to hear about last week's visit to the gallery, planned since the moment she heard Tim's exhibition was coming to Brisbane.

§

An early start. Through her kitchen window, the sky is cloudless. Thank goodness. It's a long walk to the gallery. Too long for walking in the rain. But if the sky's clear, there's a chance there'll be only low humidity. So maybe she'll get there without her clothes clinging to her. Across the street and through an access way and she's on the pedestrian path that runs along the river, passes under the bridge, and meets South Bank near its man-made Streets Beach. Several pieces of fruit rattle in a plastic container she has placed in the larger section of her backpack and a bottle of water is beating a rhythm against the outside of the bag as it hangs from a clip. Inside is her visual diary and her pencil pack.

Young mothers in exercise gear pushing strollers fly past her in convoy. She imagines them still sitting at the Streets Beach café by the time she gets there, rocking their babies and sipping lattes. An elderly couple, hand in hand, give her tight smiles and nod their heads. She feels her face stretch and return their smiles, adding interest to the deposit, as her dad always jokes, by making hers wider and brighter. There's a continuous stream of walkers and runners, some coming towards her, others passing her. She's reached the southern end of South Bank, at last, and as predicted the 'yuppy' young mothers have corralled a tumble of strollers near the café entrance. She can't stifle a self-congratulatory smile. Ah, ha. Gotcha, ladies. The gallery is at the far end, the northern end, of South Bank, almost to Kurilpa Bridge. She's underestimated the distance and decides on rest and an early lunch within sight of the gallery's distinctive building. Early lunch. Definitely. It's only eleven. Visions of Tim Johnson's work fill her head. She has spent hours scouring books and searching the web. Now an urgency to be there takes over her. She reseals her lunch box, returns it to her backpack, and continues northward, no longer able to contain her excitement.

Just outside the roped-off area in front of Tim's exhibit, she sits, legs crossed. Other visitors block her view every now and again, as they pause and contemplate the multiple elements of Tim's collaborative installation: three paintings, a plaster figure, a computer on which a CD ROM is playing, a glass sphere and an eighteenth-century Tibetan banner depicting Mt Meru. She's researched it. Mt Meru resides in both Hindu and Buddhist mythologies. In Sanskrit it is called Sumeru and in Pali, Sineru. It's a golden mountain that's the centre of the universe around which the axis of the world turns. It reaches down below the ground into the nether regions as far as it extends into the heavens, thus representing both Heaven and Hell. All the principal deities have their own celestial kingdoms on or near the mountain, and at different levels. Their devotees reside with them after death awaiting their next reincarnation. Perhaps for Buddhists these levels translate to the many planes of existence? She doesn't pretend to understand but she's left with a sense that Tim is visually expressing his interpretation of the depth and variety of human experience far beyond every day practicalities and values.

She's just far enough away that others can view the work but close enough for her to watch responses and study the installation. Her diary's in her lap, backpack on the floor beside her, and pencil in her hand. Mesmerised. Meditating. Fascinated. Time passes. So much detail; so many iconic elements. What's it telling her? Many voices speak to her from the work, many stories, but she senses they're all meant to come together, while directing viewers' sights to look beyond the work, into their own souls. If art's intended to evoke emotions and reflection, Tim's is succeeding. Layer upon layer of meaning. She thinks any understanding depends on all these layers being woven together. Is this a personal contemplation by the artist, a means for him to explore his own place in the world? Or is it an attempt to encourage someone caught by his installation? When viewers stop and turn and examine his work, Tim is inviting them to glimpse the complexities of the world we all inhabit. Then the decision to consider or not the layers on offer or to accept the artwork for its aesthetics alone is each individual's choice.

She sketches. She maps out Tim's various elements, something to which she can turn later, as an aid to jog her visual memory once she leaves the gallery, something that might bring her back to this moment. Tim's work has an emotional grip on her for reasons that are unclear. As though she is sorting through a storeroom of relics, each one familiar but their connections to each other ambiguous and beyond her reach. To make sense of the work, for her to draw meaning from it, it is imperative she spends time in front.

'Excuse me, miss. Half an hour to closing.'

Where's the day gone? Snapped out of her reverie she realises how hungry, she's become. She nods to the gallery volunteer, returns her diary and pencil pack to her backpack, and moves outside.

Her ambition: to create art that, like Tim's, moves viewers to feel something beyond the medium of the artwork, something that might arrest a tendency to skim the surface. Dual emotions overtake her: a fear she doesn't have the skills that wrestles with her need to articulate a vision. She has a plan. Every decision made since High School has been another step forward. Her will is strong. Nothing can get in the way. Work hard, as her grandmother would tell her, keep focused, and she will get there. Graduation, then into art practice.

Up the river, cloud banks are rolling in. It'll already be raining in Ipswich to the west of the city. She catches a ferry down-river to the jetty near her apartment rather than walk.

§

If only she hadn't been so adolescent. Her father's gone, and she's lost her chance. Maybe next time. But, as her grandmother says, the key to life is not to let opportunities pass you by.

'Nogat come again, Francie. Gutpela luck emi fly past. Yu nogat kissim em, na mebe any gut luck gone forever.'

Her grandmother loves to make grand statements like this in Pisin, as though she believes that using this language to express her ideas adds more meaning. Problem is that while some of the family can roughly understand the spoken words, less of them can converse in Pisin to reply. Of course, the whole family have adopted certain quaint phrases that are inserted into daily life and, yes, this kind of makes them feel a tenuous connection to the place that once was the family's homeland but they are meaningless. One used often because anything to do with food is important to her mob, is 'kissim kaikai' or 'dinner's ready'.

Gran's point is well-made today. Francine can see her father, representing today's 'lost opportunity', walking away from her towards Central Station. She watches him until he turns the corner. She could promise herself that next time – but that's Gran's point, you don't get a 'next time'. There will always be some other distraction, something more pressing and it will never be the right moment to do or say whatever you failed to do. She lingers at the table, smiles at the waiter, finishes the rest of her water and watches the crowd, wishing she could shop instead of attending her afternoon lecture. For the last few minutes before she rises, she lets her mind go back to Tim Johnson.

Some of Tim's installations cross between south-east Asian and Aboriginal art. His palette: soft pastels. Not like her style of bold colours. Tim's incorporates icons, bits of many religions or cultures, which float over a background that bears a similarity to the dots and lines of Aboriginal art. Each work stands somewhere between culture and spirituality. And though she struggles with understanding the work's profound effect on her, there's one significant aspect she recognises: its serendipitous entry into her awareness made more poignant by one of Tim's interviews. In it, he suggested that nothing happens without reason; that powerful but unseen events influence lives. Yin-yang. For her it seems right that his work represents not differences and likenesses, but many things influencing each other. She likes that. She contemplates how she might incorporate Tim's ideas into her big graduation exhibition due at the end of next year.

Today, she has lost the moment of sharing – her father's gone. She stands up, gives a casual wave to the waiter, and heads back down Edward Street towards the ferry terminal, looking forward to a relaxing journey upriver to the Queensland University's jetty.

4

WEST END RESTAURANT DISTRICT, BRISBANE
Approx. 3 am December 5, 2009

The early morning air has an unusual chill about it for this time of year. It's only in winter on those rare days of low or no humidity that Brisbane comes anywhere close to feeling cold. As she shivers, dressed as she is for the daylight hours when the temperature reached 34 degrees, she reminds herself that, years ago, long before she was born, her family had migrated from New Guinea. What was it like for them, transitioning from a tropical zone to a sub-tropical one? All – Mum, Dad, uncles and aunt, and especially her grandparents, Ah Ma Maria and Yeh Yeh Patrick – had never lived in any other zone before. Rarely does she acknowledge her family's other life. Here in Brisbane is where they all live. A good life. Everyone is happy. What more can there be to know?

Most days when she works, she doesn't leave as late at 3 am. This is an exception. Punishment Miss Francine, she snipes at herself, for letting her accounts work at Cezanne's get behind, 'just so you could finish your uni assignments.' Work, or the restaurant Cezanne's, is in West End, and it's not so easy to find transport at this hour, a time she'd 'guesstimated' she must work to if she was to catch up, so she's on a promise. She hopes her friend isn't too late.

'So, you can leave your ivory tower. Does that mean you aren't a princess after all?'

'Michael Cosgrove. What are you doing here so late?'

'Could ask the same of you. You're gone long before we floor people get to leave. Only proves Fate moves in mysterious ways, Miss Seeto. I'm very, very pleased that, on this late, late working evening, I can meet in person the legend of Cezanne's. I can see for myself you're not just a ghostly presence that hovers on the mezzanine above us mere mortals who are slaving away at floor level.'

He has a wicked, lopsided smile.

'What? A legend? Why on earth?'

It's easy to ascertain he has a weird humour. Despite his words she is not offended or put off-balance. His voice, maybe? Not mocking. Soft.

'The girl who sits and watches.'

'Oh, I didn't realise you floor plebs discussed my hobby. Just my coffee break recreation. Caught out, I guess. Anyway, I do nothing that can harm – just me imagining the floor of the restaurant as part of Renoir's 'The Boating Party', wishing I could be elsewhere, and splashing paint to recreate the scene. Gets me through a day of numbers and paper.'

'Oh arty, are you?'

She drops her head in mock-shyness.

'Oh, oh. Let that slip, didn't I? Put it down to weariness. Look, I'm too tired for social chit-chat. Can I just cut this conversation short by saying that's for me to know and that's where it should end?'

She braces herself to the challenge of staring back into his blue eyes. She can't deny she hasn't noticed him working below from the mezzanine, hadn't been tempted to catch the blueness of his glance, and she fears her eyes might reveal her weakness, but she needs to meet his challenge. There is laughter in his reciprocal gaze.

'Well, I'm going to ignore your snippiness. These moments don't come often and I do not intend to waste my lottery-win. I'd say you are both arty and serious. And I should issue a warning here, right up front. I've got a thing for serious women.'

'Bit late in the evening – sorry, too early in the morning – for you to be making a move on me there, Cosgrove. Besides, there's a no fraternising with fellow-employees rule, you know.'

'Shall I call you Seeto so we can maintain our professional distance? Well, Seeto, I'm "serious". I do have a thing for serious women. I admire women who know what they want and work at it and, because I am also observant, I have noticed that in you. Rare quality, these days. Most young women are flippy and more into current trends and getting by. Seriousness is definitely not a common trait among us Gen Ys. My dad says, in his opinion, most Millennial girls are busy trying to be a Kardashian or a Taylor Swift. Generalisations, I know, but most of us are pretty darn self-focused, aren't we, our generation? According to him, we all expect to be a princess or a president and for the world to be served to us on a plate. Slightly denigrating, and definitely drawing on stereotypes, but he might have a point.'

'You are sounding a bit like a Social Science student, studying the downfall of society. Do you go to uni? No. Don't answer. I don't want to know. So, I am going to assume you are putting the act on for my benefit. Don't bother. Plus, how could you know what kind of person I am? Or for that matter if I am indeed a Millennial? Actually, it's rather rude of you to make those kinds of assumptions, don't you think?' She softens this with a smile and a wink. He returns the smile. Lopsided. Cute.

'Well, as I said, I'm observant – and a quick learner.'

'Boy oh boy Cosgrove, you are playing with fire. And I believed you when you said you admired serious women. A true admirer wouldn't tease a serious woman about her seriousness.'

'Aha. And you said I don't know you. All I can say is, you've underestimated my superhuman powers of deduction. I know you: you're a girl who'll stand up for herself – like you are doing right now. Listen to yourself. You won't let me mow you down, will you?'

'Well, I think you've got a high opinion of yourself. It'd be safe for me to say modesty's not on your CV. Look, Michael. I am not interested in whatever it is you are selling, so this is a futile conversation. How about we let it end now, before there's tears? Yours, not mine. And for God's sake, where's my lift? Flatmates. Just can't rely on some people to keep their promises.'

She's humbled him. Or, as her dad would say 'taken the wind out of his sails.' And she feels bad but she's not going to show it. Never. But, relieved, she notices he has picked himself up. He does what she wasn't willing to do.

'Sorry if I've made you uncomfortable – oh, oh, and there you go – looks like the wait's over. Those headlights shining down the street, reckon they can only be your lift. No one else would be out and about this early. Or this late.'

'Gail. Where the heck? You promised to be here on the dot. I could do with some sleep, you know. Got numbers swimming in front of my eyes. Get me out of here, please. Pronto.'

'Frank, you're always so impatient.'

'Yeah well, if you hadn't been partying – s'pose I should ask, was it a good party?'

'Yeah, party was great. Got great goss to share. But if you're not up to it, it can wait till tomorrow. And hi there, sexy Michael, my boy. Frank, you don't mind, do you? Michael's place is on our way home.'

'You know Michael? Why didn't I realise you'd know Michael? You know everyone.'

'Yeah, well, coffee last week with my workmates, and Michael was the best waiter ever. Come on, boy-oh. Don't let old sourpuss put you off. Climb aboard.'

'Ta, Gail. Even if she's not, I'm up for the goss, if you're sharing. And this gal is Frank? Not Francine? Wow. Frank, the spy.'

'Don't you dare call me Frank. Only my friends call me Frank.'

'Oh, you two gotta be friends already. Only "friends" get that telling off, Michael. Could well be a 'Clash of the Titans' friendship, but I'm gonna enjoy watching you two battle it out.'

§

Text messages between Francine and her friend Elisa (December 6)

sooo Frank, wot's this about the
new guy at work????? Gail blabbed.
u got the hots,eh, babe? Lol

> prob covered in Southern
> Cross tattoos 4 all I know.
> u think im bogan-bait?

nah, I saw the bod, Frank. went
for coffee this arvo. Simon Baker.

> uni, uni, art, art. u can have
> him. urs, come get him.

2 white 4u Frank lol?

> ur racist. live with u don't I
> white bitch? btw u coming to
> our staff party? ur my date.

free booze? am cheap drunk.
cu soon Frankie girl :)

5

BRISBANE'S BOTANICAL GARDENS
Approx. 9.30 pm January 19, 2010

Francine's been suckered in. She rarely goes to something like this – the 'Big Day Out' Side Show – but this one, at the Riverstage, Brisbane's Botanical Garden, features Lily Allen.

On the main stage, the support act, Calvin Harris, is a dark silhouette that disappears and re-appears to the pulse of flame-red lighting. His version of house music is an epileptic's nightmare relieved by triumphant jets of steam blasting upward from front stage, as if Calvin needs to emphasise his claim to the words 'I Am Not Alone.' The frenzied electronic rhythm speeds up just as Elisa turns to face her companions. She lifts her arms high to halt their raggedy conga-line. Elisa's smile is a declaration she's sure she's fulfilled her promise of finding the 'perfect' location. No longer driven to move forward, the cluster of five protect each other from the bouncing and gyrating majority. As if an answer to the question 'What's next?' has come to them, Elisa, Gail and Gail's new boy, Nedzy, jump up and down and sway, like everyone else. Until this moment, Michael's light grip of her hand has guided her through the crowd, but he too seems to have received the same message and, in his need to bounce, he's let go of her hand. Abandoned, unprotected, and cooling, her hand dangles. Grief sweeps through her. Seconds pass before she realises, she is the only one not moving. She looks at the mass of bouncing and waving bodies and then Nedzy bobbles into her vision, his arms swaying above her head like a tree in a cyclone.

Her body moves up and down, up and down. It feels as if she's been doing this for hours, but Calvin has yet to finish his set. Then there's warmth and weight on her shoulders. She stops moving and turns. As she does, Michael drops his hands. Already she misses them. His face is ablaze with a smile as he moves closer. His eyes stare into hers. That stupid smile hangs around his mouth. She finds it impossible to drag her eyes from his blue ones. There is no escape. His face moves even closer to hers. Is their first kiss going to happen here, amidst this bedlam? Her breath fails to leave her lungs. Her body is waiting. His face passes hers and there's a flutter of air across her earlobe. He breathes his words into her ear.

'Want a drink?'

She isn't able to respond. It's as if his words don't belong in this slow-moving fantastical dream she's experiencing: pumping music, pulsing lights, moshers jumping and slugging and crashing around her, and Michael's lips on her ear. Denial is her only choice. She closes her eyes and waves and sways as though this is her music. Warm fingertips caress her cheeks. Palms cover her ears and turn her face forward. She opens her eyes. Michael's face is again in front of hers. His head tilts to one side, that same lopsided smile exaggerating the tilt, and she remembers a question needs an answer. His lips are moving, repeating his question.

'Can I get you a drink?'

She feels herself weaken. It requires only air exhaled into her ear and the feathery touch of his fingers to defeat her.

§

On that same evening, heading towards the 'Big Day Out' licensed area he's doing his job as drinks purveyor for the girl he's hanging out with. 'Now, Michael, remember, you can't say "girlfriend",' he jibes himself.

Tall and strong as he is, he has difficulty pushing through the gyrating mob. Buffeted this way and that by the feverish dancers, he uses the orange glow of the bar lights to guide him. He looks back at Francine. She gives him that strange half-smile she's good at, and then looks away, as if she's watching the performance. Calvin Harris will be disappointed if he expects to earn bucks from Francine through iTunes purchases. Calvin doesn't flick his switch either, but he'll do anything to spend time with this mystery of a girl. Whenever he thinks he's breaking down the barriers to learn more about her, she closes the gates. She seems to like him. She encourages him. Then she drops him cold, dismisses him, acts like he's not there. Someone else might take the hint, but he can't. It feels to him that the right place to be is in her life, no matter how small a role she might permit him. And he will take every opportunity to be where she is, even if it's putting up with this inane punkish noise.

When he's closer to the bar, he turns again. Her thumb is on her lip as if the digit remembers a childhood habit of being sucked. He's seen this happen before. When she's deep in thought. When, it seems to him, she believes no one will notice. His fingers ache to stroke that troubled brow. He'd give the world for permission to hear her speak of her fears and hopes. But the door between them opens only a crack before it's slammed shut again. Doesn't she feel about him the same as he does about her? Be patient, he recites to himself. Win her trust. She only needs time to see you are genuine. But there's a dark voice in his head, a voice of fear, that threatens by suggesting whatever it is between them can be only temporary. A fist grips his heart. She's only been in his life a short time, but he can't imagine how he'd cope if she was no longer in it. He's never felt this way before about anyone.

§

Francine's Facebook. Next morning.

got sore bones and weary head. Lily Allen was sooo great. Must be getting old, cant hack the mosh pit.

FrankieJHyde. Today, January 22,2010. 9.45 am.

did the sun rise today? I hit the sack at dawn and slept until evening. Oooooh my mum thinks I am doomed.

Elisa Simson. Today. January 22, 2010. 8.03 pm.

FrankieJHyde receives a friend request from Michael Cee.

FrankieJHyde accepts.

Later, same day.

Francine is hiding in her bedroom in the apartment she shares with her friends Gail and Elisa. She can't believe she has done this. Must be the hangover. She would normally take ages to even look at any friend requests on Facebook. And rarely does she accept them. All the people she wants to network with are already her friends.

Did she hesitate for a second – before she clicked the Accept button and did the deed? She can't remember. She saw the request flash, and the name, and after that she was on automatic. In that moment, she knew the risks of indiscriminate friending. Without thinking, she's pushed out of her consciousness her 'perfect' plan: no romance, work hard, and save lots of money to invest in her future Art Practice after she graduates at the end of this year.

6

CEZANNE'S RESTAURANT, WEST END, BRISBANE
April 2010

'Hola, pretty lady.'

Matias has been working at Cezanne's on a six-month work visa. He flashes his smile her way as she stands above him outside the door to her mezzanine office. Like many of Cezanne's employees, he's spent time and shared meals with her family, even shared a Broncos' game on TV with her dad. Behind Matias, the rest of the wait staff file in one by one, each waving, turning and smiling, or bowing to Francine as they pass below. No Michael yet. From Carl, the manager, she receives a half salute, done without turning or looking up, as he strides past the various stations in the restaurant, barking orders to each staff member as he goes. And finally, Michael's distinctive blond curls. He stops, turns, looks up and smiles at her. In her chest something is doing cartwheels. She lifts one hand, and moves it slightly in a restrained gesture, rolls her eyes, and turns away, as if heading for her office. But she goes no further than the entry. Against the wall, away from the rail, she hopes she is out of sight of those on the restaurant floor below.

She watches Michael's broad back as he bends to extract cutlery from the drawer beneath his workstation and then follows his body as it twists upward so he can reach for glassware. She could stand there all day.

She still hasn't invited Michael home to meet her family.

7

BRISBANE
May, 2010

That Michael's parents live on the other side of Brisbane from her family is a revelation. It shouldn't be. As she turns into their street, she notices the houses are different. This street is lined with restored Queenslanders raised high on their stumps, making them appear to float above the tropical gardens at their feet. One or two have closed in the space below the main floor. Gabled high-pitched roofs and wide verandahs suggest an area in which to relax and catch whatever breeze is available. She suspects that in this area the site alone, with its views of the city, is out of the average person's reach but, as she draws in a deep breath of appreciation, she recognises what these houses add to land values. They're not mansions, but they're rare, homes from a bygone era, still loved and well cared for, and representing a Queensland style of living. She imagines who might live here, because of the suburb's proximity to city and river: university professors, doctors, airline pilots, and Michael's parents. Add to the mix Michael, as she sees him: his fairness, quiet conservatism, a way of speaking that displays an old-fashioned politeness, suggesting perhaps he's the son of older parents. She imagines them silver-haired and respectable; his father an ex-banker, posh, organised and polite; his mother president of some organisation, like the hospital auxiliary, efficient and practical. The house, the imagined residents, and her assumption of wealth alien to the world she knows, on the 'other side' of Brisbane.

Carl broke his own rules to let her know about Michael's cousin's suicide. Only after she'd noticed and asked about Michael's absence. Carl's eyes betrayed his doubts, likely to be the same ones she has: why hadn't she been the first one Michael would tell? But a sleepless night has convinced her:

friend, lover, or just the charming user she pretends he is, she can't ignore how she feels. She must be with Michael. She can't bear to think of his pain and not be with him. With Michael is where she must be, welcome or not.

At the front door, through the flywire screen door, she can see daylight streaming in from the far end of what seems to be a central hall. She knocks. A large body moving down the corridor eclipses the brightness.

'Hello, there. Sorry to disturb. I'm looking for Michael Cosgrove.' The enormous significance of the moment, the certainty she's invading the privacy of Michael's family, compels her to add, 'I'm a friend.'

The man stares at her through the screen. For a moment her nervousness makes her feel as if he'll refuse her entry, but then without a word he half turns away and bellows back into the house, 'Muk. Muk. A pal.' And now he opens the screen and nods towards the sofa on the verandah. 'Muk needs a pal today. Not a good time. Sit. I'll bring youse a cuppa.'

A wide verandah wraps around the house. Filling it are several comfy sofas, furnished in the way she imagines those cool coffee houses at Noosa would be. Multi-coloured throws litter each sofa, nothing coordinated, nothing matching, as if each one individually picked up from second-hand shops or donated by someone who has had the pleasure of spending time here. Fitting their name of 'throws' is their casual and seemingly unplanned placement, which she decides is likely to be the polar opposite, each carefully and artfully disbursed. Spending time in this space would be a pleasure. Side-tables carrying quaint art objects sit here and there. This space has one purpose: to provide sanctuary and tranquillity. She imagines whispers of conversations, vibrations of spiritual connections, and communal anticipation of sharing. The vastness of this area alone suggests the potential of spaciousness for the rest of the house. The compactness of the homes she's known seem impoverished. At first, she's envious, but then she corrects herself. They're just different, that's all. Not better.

From inside, Francine can hear voices. Sounds like a crowd. Panicking, her mind scrolls through strategies for retreat before she recognises a silhouette in the space beyond the screen door. Michael comes towards her, back bowed. He collides with the screen as if it's an old enemy. She wants to back away. The door slams back against the stop and Michael lurches through the open space towards her. She studies his face and gasps. His fair face is a bloom of red and white blotches, his eyes red-rimmed and bloodshot. Her chest tightens. She's now frightened less by Michael than by the emotions flooding through her, and yet she lifts her arms towards him and steps forward. He stops and scowls. Neither of them speaks. The silence is palpable. Without warning, he falls towards her, tears streaming down his face, an oversized boy whose mouth is spewing out strange noises. His arms wrap around her. His head drops. Dead weight. Streaming tears wet her left shoulder. Over Michael's shoulder, she can see the big man is at the screen door. He's carrying a tray. Should she help? Michael has her anchored to the spot. She looks at the man and blinks. He nods and strides past them.

'Muk, some tea, lad. Have some tea. Get him to drink, will you, please?'

Michael's grip on her loosens. He pulls himself upright, looking normal again. Free from his embrace, she can stretch out her right hand to reach the man.

'Francine,' she says. 'I work with Michael.'

The man is tall and athletic. The singlet and work shorts he wears reminds her this is his home and his space. He pauses, as if processing what she has told him, and then he steps forward, takes a warm but firm grip of her hand. She notices a small movement to the corner of his mouth. Is he holding back a smile? Or is he questioning her tactlessness, her inappropriate timing, if she's a workmate of his son?

'Muk's dad. Jeremy. You're welcome, Francine. Tea,' he says pointing to the pot and cups on the tray. 'Drink.' He heads back towards the screen door and disappears. Behind him, there's a thunk and a click, as the door closes and latches.

Not silver-haired, nor anything like her imagination had painted him. And never, in her imagined stereotype, a New Zealander. Perhaps still a banker? How wrong could she be? How wrong might she be about Michael, about his mother, about his life? What basis does she have to claim she knows him? Dare she even think that thought, that reason why she thinks she knows him? That she knows him... because she loves him? She's here to be where he is but she can't admit to the possibility of the very emotion she's been denying. Instead, she lays the blame for her assumptions on insufficient evidence.

She eases Michael down into the sofa. Great shudders shake his body. She can see he's struggling to get them under control. The trembling subsides, and she can feel his body relaxing under her hand. He leans back into the sofa. He's Michael again.

'Sorry,' he says, the word still wet around its edges, as if he's fighting for normal speech. What makes him feel a need to apologise? The belief that she's an interloper? She should know more about what this death means to him but she doesn't. With a deep sigh, he reaches for the teapot.

'Tea? Tea fixes everything in this house.' He attempts a weak laugh that fails. 'Was doing okay until I saw you.'

'Oh sorry, sorry, Michael. I'm sticking my nose in where it shouldn't be.'

'No, no. Happy, thankful, relieved, that you are here.' And then he looks into her eyes, as if, through the clouds of grief, it has dawned on him. 'So, so happy. How did you know where my father lives?'

'Carl told me.' She feels the inadequacy of her answer, weighted down as it is by the questions she has running around in her own head. Why didn't Michael tell her about his cousin's suicide before he called Carl? There are many explanations but whatever the reason, this omission of his creates doubt about how he sees their relationship. She has reviewed her own behaviour. For her, there's a certainty: her erratic behaviour and resistance is connected to her fear she won't achieve her goals, but her heart is speaking louder than her brain. She covers her nervousness by arranging the mugs on the tray, and this reminds Michael that something had interrupted him as he was about to serve tea. He pours the tea, and she adds the milk. He picks up one mug and hands it to her and takes the other for himself. They've both gripped their tea mugs as if their hands need warming, as if they are somewhere colder, somewhere other than in Brisbane, and they lean back into the sofa together, shoulders touching, as if sitting on this sofa, drinking tea, is something they do every other day. Had that day been any other day, they might have turned to each other and spoken about the magnificence of the view of Brisbane in front, or the luxury of a house such as this, commanding such a view. But this was not that day.

8

COSGROVES' HOME, BRISBANE
May 2010

It's twilight. Seated on the Cosgroves' verandah, Francine can see Brisbane as a montage of diamond lights diminishing as the minutes tick by. She pictures children being tucked in, stories being read, garbage bins being wheeled onto verges as families prepare to turn in. She left Michael and his father washing dishes to come to the front for one last look. This family – and with a shock she realises that, despite her prejudgments, a family not so dissimilar to her own – have spent today comforting each other, reminiscing, planning, eating, crying and laughing, and including her as if she is one of them, as if she's in mourning too for the loss of Jake, some-one she knows and cares for, instead of Jake the stranger. She's elated and disconsolate. Happy to be embraced, happy that she can measure how she stands with Michael by his family's responses, but disappointed in her own preconceptions and more than ever aware of the wall she had built, despite her feelings for Michael.

All she might have known had she not kept Michael at arm's length, she has learnt today. His mother died of breast cancer when he was young. Each time she allows herself to consider that loss, empathetic grief floods her. She can only imagine the sorrow Michael might have felt. How can she know what it might feel like to lose a mother unless she projects herself into a similar situation? The thought of losing her mother at a young age is unbearable. Her mother is a constant presence, not physical but a solid, reli-able resource, ready if a need arises. A beacon that radiates love; someone who knows her daughter; someone who watches from afar, emitting signals of trust, signalling that she sees her child as capable and reliable. A mother's constant presence and support invites an offspring to aim high. It's different for a father. He's important but with your mother on your side, the world's your oyster. If that space is empty, what then?

A double blow for Michael: not only the loss of his mother at a young age but now also the suicide of a cousin. Just a while earlier, this cousin was anonymous to her. Now she knows he was like a brother to Michael. A devastating loss. Throughout the day the family have told the stories and retold them. They have recreated Jake through a library of memories. Jake, as dark as Michael is fair. Jake whose own mother died in a car accident and whose father had returned to New Zealand and then further away, into a hidden life from which he is yet to emerge. The depth of the family's pain takes her breath away. She berates her tendency to see only the Michael that suited her: the blond, beautiful man who made her heart tremble. Too beautiful to be hers. Remorse and reflection are permitting her to whip herself. The need to feel pain and regret overwhelms her. As if she should be repenting something, anything, to return her to the real.

She wanders back to the rear courtyard where the crowd has dwindled. Airbeds, folding cots, and sleeping bags are filling the floor space; some have draped their bodies on sofas. At last the house is falling into silence.

Michael hands his father the tea towel he's been using and comes to her. 'I'll call you a cab.'

He'd asked her earlier. Leaving was a strong possibility, then. But now, to leave doesn't feel right. Michael has assumed her answer and has taken the first step towards the telephone when she touches his arm and shakes her head. She can't look him in the eye. To do so would reveal to him the emotional battle she's working hard to contain. It's a puritan guilt thing, she knows. Her family have raised her to be chaste, but she lives in a world where the boundaries have changed. She's surprising herself that she's not as modern as she believes herself to be. Still, it would be dishonest if she didn't admit there's some covert anticipation that excites her, despite an underlying sense of inappropriateness. She lifts her eyes to his half-turned face. Is it her imagination or is he also struggling with containing emotions? Maybe, she forces herself to consider the possibility, he'd prefer her to leave? As she ponders the possibility, he turns back to her and draws in close. His mouth moves to her ear, kisses it and he whispers, his voice loaded with emotion, 'Thanks. Means a lot to have you here, with my family, tonight. You can have my bed and I'll sleep out here with my cousins.'

That's all it takes to do her in. She has surprised herself. She followed her gut not her logic. And this time it's total capitulation. Until now she has fought only minor skirmishes, those battles won or lost, but this time she has lost the war. The plan for graduation, art practice and no romance, is out the window. Come what may.

§

Michael looks over at his father. Father and son work on the opposite side of the large kitchen table. John Butler's rock lyrics of 'Zebra' are coming from somewhere in the centre of the house. A CD is spinning somewhere, belting it out or someone's iTunes.

> *'I could be loud man, I could be silent*
> *I could be young man or I could be old*
> *I could be a gentleman, I could be violent*
> *I could turn hot man or I could be cold...'*

He's resisting its seduction, yet wants to maintain the frenzy. For him, that's difficult. His natural tendency is towards mellowness, so he fights it, because it doesn't seem right that Jake's death should follow the usual path of grieving. Butler's rendition of 'Zebra' echoes the energy he wants to put into his grief. There should be fireworks and rage. He can feel the anger boiling away just below the surface of the normality this household has worked hard to achieve in the last week – that's his instinctual path, too – keeping his emotions under control, not doing anything that might upset someone else or make them feel worse than they already do, but it doesn't seem right not to be angry. And hell yes, he is angry. If Jake hadn't committed suicide, his 'twin' would punch him in the centre of that selfish, cheeky, lovable and loved face.

Jake, Jake, Jake. You and I, brother, shared everything. Well, we did until now. And there was a plan. Like 'twins', remember? Birthdays so close we had one party. Your mum looked after me when my mum died, and your sisters and my dad looked after us both when that maniac drove head-on into your mum. So why didn't you tell me? What could have been so bad you couldn't share?

Must have been bad. Must have. Too painful for Jake to bear, with death more appealing than life. He can imagine nothing that bad, but what's driving him crazy is the question: how did he miss seeing that pain in Jake? His mind flips back over the past few months: Francie. She's preoccupied him. But that's no excuse.

Jake, of all people, knows what death means: the ones who suffer are the living. Been through it at ten and fifteen, both mothers gone.

He slams the knife he's been using down on the kitchen bench. Damn, shouldn't have done that, because now Jeremy has a worried look flickering in his eyes. Don't want to get his dad upset again. Must pull himself back to appearing almost normal.

'Sorry. Knife slipped.'

It doesn't convince Dad, and yet he does return to cracking eggs into a bowl.

See? That's the problem. There's Dad, and there are your sisters, pal. Didn't you think of anyone else? The family has been through death double-up and now, God, buddy, there's a huge hole here.

In his mind, he re-lives this past week or two. The shock, first, of having to face the truth: Jake topped himself. The invasion by the coroner, the service, the cremation. Jake's life can't just end as an urn of ashes and a plaque on a stone wall. Too dull for Jake even if he's dead. Jake is or, he reminds himself, was a person who always had people around him, the life of the party, the daredevil, the sun that shone on everyone's life. A shudder passes through him. Had this happened a few days ago rather than now, if he wasn't drained of tears, it would have ended up with him in a wet shuddering mess. His anger now is running along a different track, a diversion, that what-comes-after death path and its shortfalls. A metal tag on a wall can't be the only mark left to remind them of Jake. Sure, his tag's not alone – there are hundreds on that wall. Maybe in death Jake's needs to be among the crowd, except these tags are anonymous: names, dates, a few words that say nothing about who they once were or what they meant to those left behind. Like the crowd at an AC/DC gig, all dressed in black so it's impossible to tell who's the biker, the thug, the lawyer, the politician or the average Joe. Only one thing unites these tags: the gig they're at is death. And the finality of that union weighs Michael down again. Will he ever not feel the wastefulness of this death? Mum – well, breast cancer is in God's league. Who gets it, who survives and who doesn't seem beyond human intervention. Same applies for Aunty Bess' car accident. Off on a weekend with friends, waving goodbye and then wham-o, God again. But suicide?

Can that be God-driven, or is it just human frailty?

Is this an event he has to learn from, he and Jake being so close, not only cousins, but more? So what lesson are you leaving me, Jake? Is it: don't piss your family and friends off by doing something stupid? Or, tell someone close to you if you are in trouble? And, brother, what a low deed, to leave your sisters and your bestie wondering what they might have done to stop this from happening.

'What's happening, there, son? French toast doesn't cook itself.'

He's stalled, knife mid-air, and Dad's right. Nothing's happening. Letting down his part of the production line. His dad is proving his point by whisking another batch of eggs in a huge bowl. The grin on his face from the other side of the bench lights up the kitchen, but his expression is empty. He can find proof of this in his father's eyes. They are pools of worry. Swirling around in them are his own list of questions, not only about Jake. This activity, a dual engagement, doing 'their-thing', which is making French toast when there are visitors in the house, is his way of distracting his son.

'You're not supposed to beat the eggs to death, Dad. Any recipe would say "whisk" not "trash".'

'Well, the eggs and I have grown weary waiting for you to come back into the real world. The patrons will be up and hungry. You finish this off and I will get the coffee going. Brutal egg-beater or not, we make a brilliant breakfast team, you and I.'

After his mother died, his dad did what he thought a single parent should do: fill the role of both parents. That was when his 'brilliance' shone through: packing lunches, cooking meals, washing and cleaning. But without his wife, he had nothing to talk about. For a while there, it seemed as if Jeremy had gone too. Maybe not to the same place as his mum, but almost as unreachable. These days, his dad's there for him, no matter what.

'That girl of yours, she's smarter than you, I reckon.'

'You'd say everyone's smarter than me.'

'You're right. But your girl, well I reckon she's got a lot more going on up here,' his father taps his head, leaving a smudge of egg on his hairline, 'a lot more than any of us will ever know.'

'You're not saying anything, son. Don't you agree?'

'Yeah, Dad, I agree, but I hope to hell that I fit somewhere into whatever's going on up there. I like her, Dad.'

'Damn obvious, son. She'd be blind, deaf and dumb not to notice, too.'

Jeremy moves off to the coffee maker and leaves his son to contemplate the workings of Francine's mind as he continues to fry the French toast and stack the toast slices on a tray for warming in the oven.

'Those patrons had better get rise and shine, Dad. Or there will be no resuscitating the French toast.'

Jeremy picks up an empty tray and a wooden spoon and calls the house guests to breakfast.

Jake never cracked when his mum died. Maybe that was his problem?

Jake's real dad had shot through when Jake was only two. Didn't miss him, Jake would say, but truth to tell Jake didn't remember him. Jake idolised Jeremy. Followed him around. Tried to please him. When you saw them side by side, Jake could have been mistaken for Jeremy's son: same dark complexion and hair, same thick body type, same straightforward manner of speaking. It might be said by some that it was him, Michael, who was the alien in this family, with his fair hair and skinny body. Maybe he looks like his mother. He can't remember her well enough to say. After Aunty Bess passed, he and Jake inherited substitute mothers: three of them. Jake's sisters were twenty-four, twenty-one and nineteen. Yet, the absences of mothers for both he and Jake never faded. They didn't talk about it, but a look shared between them when someone made a crack involving a mother, said to one another more than any words could say. That's the point. Jake should have remembered how the loss felt. He should have cared enough not to dump another death onto his family. Why, man? Why? Your sisters did not give up on you. Even on that first day, the day after you did the dirtiest of deeds, they were still fighting for you, Jake. His mind slips back.

§

Next to him on his left at their large dining table is Francine. More like a conference table than anything else, and for the first time in his memory it is fulfilling its purpose. His dad is on his right and raises his left hand to give his son a reassuring pat on the shoulder. Spread around the table, on an odd assortment of chairs scrounged from every room in their home, are the privileged members of the immediate family. The rest are in the background, either standing behind those seated or leaning against the walls and doorframes. Waiting. He senses Francine's restlessness, her sense of not belonging, but he needs her to stay, so he grips her hand and rests it on his thigh. Its heat reassures him he can get through this terrible day. Still waiting. Waiting for Jeremy, the head of the family, to start a conversation. Jeremy's still shuffling papers, writing notes, or perhaps delaying the inevitable.

Opposite him, at the other end of the table, Allanah, Myka and Bella form a tight group. Big sister responsibilities are weighing down Allanah, the eldest. He hopes she's not blaming herself. 'No, please Allanah, this is all Jake's doing, or the family's,' he wants to tell her. He fights an urge to get up and go to her. The timing's not right. There's a small hand towel folded on the table in front of Allanah into which she has buried her face. On either side of her, their arms wrapped around her like tentacles, their faces turned away from everyone else, are her two sisters. He recognises one from the other by the backs of heads he knows and loves – one head of beautiful dark curls and the other of short spikes. He imagines the intensity of their gaze whenever their eyes meet Allanah's. They'll be attempting to inject her with their own courage, to boost her, so she can cope. A knot of sisterhood. He's aware of how silent the room has grown, as if, en masse, the rest of the family is holding its breath. The only sounds are the sisters' breathing, snuffling and wet whispers. Everyone is waiting. Who will begin: Jeremy or Allanah?

It's Jeremy.

Strange, under the circumstances, but he feels elated by how his dad begins.

'This is Muk's friend Francie.'

He moves to stand behind Francine and rests his hands on her shoulders. A tremor passes through Francine's hand, the shock and, he hopes, also the pleasure of inclusion. The gathered family members are beyond doing more than to nod and offer a wan smile, but there's no doubt his lady is being welcomed. He hears her whisper 'Francie?' and sees the glance she throws towards him. He only uses that name for her when he talks to his father. To date, he has always used the name 'Francine' when he is talking to her or her friends, despite his perception of its formality, unwilling to risk disapproval, or of being seen to overstep his position with her. She always makes a point to not allow him to use 'Frank' as her other friends do, only to use 'Francine' in his company. He's wondered why, thinking perhaps it's keeping him at a distance, but, as always, he can swallow whatever she dishes out to him. He's a beggar for punishment if it means he has her permission to hang around, and it's only a name.

He studies her. Her left hand is resting on the table and it seems to have her full attention. Maybe she's noticing her nails. He smiles. Each is a different colour. So Francie. He imagines her mind churning over thoughts like, 'What will these people think of me?' or thrashing herself. She thinks he doesn't know her but he does. He knows what she'll be hearing in her head is her grandmother's voice scolding her. 'No respect.' He's heard her stories about the way her family 'show respect' through conservative dressing and modest behaviour. He has an inappropriate urge to make a joke with her about it, when his cousin Carole halts his train of thought by speaking to Francine. Carole is sitting next to Francine. There's no need for her to lean forward, but he's alerted to her purpose. She wants him to hear what she will say.

'Hi, Francie. I'm Carole. Welcome to the madhouse. Heard about you from Michael.'

Oh, no. There's that 'Francie' again. Francine looks shocked. Is it because someone is speaking to her, or because Carole has used the name 'Francie' again? That means she knows who's been talking. Oh shit, he's in trouble. Francine looks at him and then turns back to Carole. His cheeks burn, and then his face stiffens, spoiling his weak attempt to smile. Digging the hole that he's in deeper, Carole reaches over and pats his hand, the one sitting on top of Francine's and says, 'She is exquisite, Mike, just as lovely as you described her.'

'Nice one, Carole. Can always rely on you to put me in it.' And he gives Francine's hand a little squeeze. Around the table, everyone is smiling. Carole has broken the ice, price paid by him and Francine. Now Jeremy shuffles in his chair. He looks up, runs his gaze around the room, catching each and everyone's attention, and clears his throat.

'Okay, everyone, a sad, sad day. We must draw strength from being a family. We each might see things in different ways, but as a strong family, I know we will work through this. What we need to achieve is to agree as a family how we can see our boy off. We will need patience and sensitivity, but I know you all feel the same way. Each of us can have a say. Allanah, as his big sister, you get first say.'

Everyone looks towards Allanah. She lifts her head and wrings the towel between her hands, and places it on the table in front of her, as though it's fragile. Allanah. Gorgeous as ever. Despite the grief spilling out of her large dark eyes. His heart wrenches. So like Jake. That side of the family, the beautiful ones. After much throat-clearing and snuffling, Allanah's first attempt to speak ends in a sodden moan. Defeated, her face droops. Her sisters both look around in protest, as if their sister's failure is everyone else's fault, and one folds an arm around Allanah's right shoulder and leans forward to bury her face between Allanah's cheek and ear. She must have whispered encouragement. Allanah glances at her, nods, then straightens her back, clears her throat, gulps, and speaks in a voice that's scratchy and low. Her supporters sit upright. As smooth as synchronised swimmers, as one they spin around to face the group.

'Well, Uncle Jerry, we three want none of us to act as if Jacob's done something wrong. We know he has,' she stops as her body shudders and tears roll down her cheek. 'He's left us behind, but we reckon we might have helped him to feel he couldn't stay, though God knows why he had to do that to us… why?' Sob.

His dad nods and waits for Allanah to regain control. After a few minutes that feel closer to an hour, Allanah continues and now her voice has grown strong.

'We want full respect for Jacob.' As she says those words, she lifts her chin, looks around the table and then her gaze settles on Uncle and Aunty to her right. Her gaze is not hostile, but resilient, but Uncle and Aunty's expressions show she has hit the mark. He guesses there has been an earlier discussion that Allanah and her sisters are railing against.

Uncle looks uncomfortable. His eyes dart around, almost apologetic, and his head drops. He looks sad. But Aunty's head lifts, as if she's prepared for a fight.

Allanah nods her head towards them and says, 'Uncle Norm, Aunty Mabel…'

'But the Church says…'

His dad intervenes. 'We understand Mabel, but I rang the local Catholic diocese this morning, and I am assured that the Church has taken a new view. Do you think you might… what if… can I ask the local guy to come along and talk to us, discuss the implications, before we reject the idea altogether?'

'I don't believe the Church has changed its view, don't believe it at all,' Mabel says as she clenches her fists and looks close to tears, 'Don't believe this is so. "Thou cannot commit murder" applies to killing oneself. Sorry Allanah, Jacob was a beautiful but troubled boy, and more is our shame we could do nothing to help him before he reached this point of despair, but love him as we might, love's no justification for his burial in sanctified earth. It's not right.'

Loud upsetting noises, sounds of air being sucked in, followed by indecipherable muttering from Jake's three substitute mothers. Around the room, groups are forming and whispering, though he can't work out which side each individual is taking. It's disturbing to see this wedge being driven. He's distracted. There's movement at his end of the table. Past Francine, he can see Carole shoving her fist into her mouth. She glares back at him, and it looks to him as if she's biting into her own flesh. Her eyes are bulging with tears. His dad's back is stiff and straight. He's silent. On purpose. He can recognise his father's modus operandi. His core philosophy is that everyone needs time to work through things. Give them the time they need, and they will reach a solution. In his head, Michael can hear the lectures: 'Remember, son, everyone has a different perspective and while we may not agree with other's views and may not wish to go along with those views, each one is valid and each one has a right to speak. Listen and respond.' Proof he's an excellent negotiator.

Once more Jeremy rises. He raises his hands, pats the air, palms down, to settle the group, as if he is saying 'Not over yet, trust me.'

Norm pats his wife's arm. 'Perhaps we should talk to the priest, dear.'

'He's not our priest, Norm.' Mabel's lip quivers.

'No, he's not. But we should talk.' And Norm looks at Jeremy and nods.

Jeremy stands and walks to the phone, dials, and everyone waits and listens.

'Father Brian, Jeremy Cosgrove here. Yup, yup, if you can spare the time, be a great help. No, right now is fine. If it's okay with you. No, we're here and ready to talk and listen. Thanks.'

Then his dad turns, nods to Norm and Mabel, and says: 'Thanks Norm, Mabel. If you don't mind, we will continue along the path as though this is not an issue – even though it still is. If we can't break through this impasse, it won't matter, but I hope we can, in which case as a family we need to find a solution. We need to agree on what we should do and how. As a family, come on; let's try to resolve our differences. Okay, first, let's discuss what we want if it's okay with the Church and then, second, if it's not. Okay? So, first, Allanah, Myka and Bella, what are your ideas? What do you want for your brother?'

And so it goes for the rest of the day, a dance around the sensitive issues at play, and all the while he's wishing his mind would stop its internal interrogation. He's constipated by questions without answers. If he ignores them, they become like neon signs, flashing and demanding attention, burning into the back of his retinas. Why did Jake have to choose this? Like it or not, he had to concede it must have taken a lot of guts. Was this about Jake trying to be his hard-nosed self? What could have been so big a hurt that it squeezed out other stuff, like how much everyone cared for him? The idiot boys, Jake's sisters called the pair, linked in everything they did, and now Jake's proved himself to be the bigger idiot of the two. There aren't any answers, only more questions. The question hammering his brain is, was Jake's toughness just an act? And the biggest one of all: if tough, cool Jake can't handle life, what hope has his 'twin' got? His chest cramps when he imagines that dark place Jake must have reached. Jake's suicide can only have come out of some internal pain. What caused such deep pain? His thoughts slide across to Francie. Are his feelings for her so deep he might not survive them?

9

COSGROVES' HOME
Mid-June 2010

For Francine, there's a faint sense of guilty pleasure in the mornings in the house in which she has taken up temporary residence. She looks around Michael's room. This place, alien at first, is now home.

After that first night, with the home full of family and friends bunking down, conversing in small groups well into the small hours, she'd stayed. She'd made an instinctive decision. A humanitarian choice, she persuades herself in hindsight. Michael needed her and she needed to be there. When the opportunity to leave presented itself again on the next day, she shocked herself. Again she'd dipped her head to hide what her eyes might reveal. But she couldn't shut out the whispered accusations in her head, her own voice reiterating her harsh criticism of friends' behaviours that follow the contemporary trend of sexual freedom. It's not that she had anything substantial to support her disapproval. Perhaps at the core it emerged out of her deep-seated if often lapsing Catholicism or a lingering of her conservative upbringing. But something inside her made it distasteful to hear of friends going to parties and hooking up for a one-night-stand with someone who had been a stranger before the event. She reprimands herself. 'How's theirs any different to yours?' Except, this feels different to her.

She struggles to justify her actions. Not a desire, she tells herself, because that infers indulgence, but a sense of necessity. As if to drag herself away from him would wound her. She leaves that thought stranded, its complexities too much to handle.

She's hearing footsteps in the hall. Jeremy. A voice from the kitchen. Allanah. So comfortable now, she doesn't feel embarrassed to still be in Michael's bed, snuggling under the doona long after Michael has risen.

She loves this room. They have extended the old Queenslander from its original form. One half frames this side of the back garden, another the other side. Halfway down this extension, a hallway runs past a bathroom towards Michael's room, and on the outer wall there's large French windows that fold in to themselves and open the hallway onto the garden. When the bedroom door is open into the hallway as it is today, it's as if Michael's bed is in the garden, too. This morning the sunlight dances across the ceiling, an ever-changing pattern of light and shadow. The breeze is rustling the fern trees in the garden. Whispered secrets. Across the garden, there's another extension with a similar bank of glass doors that open the kitchen onto the garden. The doors must be open over there, too. Now, it's no longer Allanah, but men's voices amidst the clatter of what she imagines to be metal pans, crockery, and cutlery. She would need to concentrate to identify whose voices or what they are talking about, and her mind isn't willing to do that today. She pictures Michael and Jeremy in the kitchen making coffee and French toast together, as they have done each morning. In the background, behind the everyday noises of a household waking up and getting on with the day, there's soft tinkling. This, she knows, is coming from the chimes that hang from one branch of the Moreton Bay Fig tree in the far corner of the garden.

She stretches, and lets her eyes traverse the room, once again. This has been her morning habit since she's been staying here. Men don't tell you much about themselves but this room is revealing. Two cricket trophies need dusting, but she's already checked the engraving: Michael Cosgrove, First Eleven. From school. A framed Queensland State of Origin poster signed by King Wally. Another poster, this time the movie, 'Night of the Living Dead'. This makes her smile. Are guys so predictable? Her brother has the same poster. And there's another poster, radical and unexpected, of Merzbow, the Japanese noise musician. Merzbow appeals to a minority. Michael? The poster's tatty, so perhaps Michael has pulled it off a wall or a post, and now she knows more about Jake, she can picture Michael and Jake together laughing and wanting that poster, its removal becoming a fixation for them, and Michael the one who ended up with it. Did Merzbow mean more to him than Jake or was it a prize for a challenge that Michael won, or only of value because it was something Michael did with Jake? There's a certificate of graduation plus another that names Michael Cosgrove as a high school valedictorian and a strange collection of books, stacked with spines out as if Michael believes books deserve reverence. Tolkien's 'Lord of the Ring'; a Clive Barker horror, 'The Thief of Always'; and the surprises, a biography of Brian Eno, and Bukowski's 'Factotum'. Over this past month, she has learnt so much. About Michael – the real Michael.

The strangest thing is what she has learnt about herself in this sojourn. Ridiculous notion, the idea that being away from familiar spaces brings insight, because she doesn't live at home. She shares a flat with her best friends. So, already for her, there's been some separation for her from her childhood home. She decides it's not about separation, but about observation. Being the audience, so to speak, in the theatre of Michael's family's lowest ebb has magnified her recognition of relationships within her own family. As if she's sitting on the moon and looking down, she can see herself and her family as they sit within the rest of her world. In normal life – and this is as far from normal as she can measure at this moment – her perspective is they're Mum and Dad, brother Luke, Gran, Uncle Dan and Aunty Anna, cousins Jonas and Nathaniel and Uncle Gabriel. A tiny family compared to Michael's. She doesn't measure them or make judgments about them as others might, people who only see their outward appearance, which she recognises from her spot on the moon, is invisible to her. But others might wonder about their history, their stories, what influences might have shaped them. She takes her family for granted. She ignores their uniqueness, even her own peculiarities. Happy in her Australian identity, she rarely reflects on the circumstances that brought her family to Australia. Nor does she consider the cost to them of such a move. Is this, she asks herself, perhaps the moment she has become a grown-up?

The kid she was a second ago has been so wrapped up in her feelings for Michael, hiding in Michael's need for his family. She had momentarily forgotten that her own family care about her. She has without thought pushed aside the firm knowledge that her well-being is ever in their minds. Her life and theirs, so entangled, so entwined, and yet these past weeks, she has had only the barest of contact with them. And the marvel is that they have respected her choice. Did they? Perhaps what they are doing is waiting for her to be the person they know her to be, to be the adult who will consider others. Does she do the same for them?

Within this mood of critical awareness, she sees herself as selfish, self-centred, and oblivious to others' needs. Though that's not true. She knows this is coming out of the guilt she's feeling for her out-of-character behaviour of late. The creepy Catholicism remorse is warning her there will be a price to pay for her indulgences, regardless that they began out of concern for Michael in his bereavement. In her imagination she sees herself as the Disney Princess, idolised and flattered by every family member who each go out of his or her way to confirm the certainty of her success. She's letting herself and them down by this fall in standards. Despite her self-loathing, she can't help letting out a little snicker – her dad would die if he only knew what she's been up to.

This is her, Francine Seeto, going through a transformation but this new, emerging Francine is not yet ready to announce herself. Not yet ready to go public, not yet ready to share. She uses any excuse that might delay her emergence, no matter how guilty she feels. As sure as the old Francine has always been about herself, this one hasn't properly found her wings. She's an eaglet who has just discovered she can fly, waiting until the moment she can soar to new heights all the while expecting a drop in the wind that will send her plummeting. She credits her reformation to Michael. With him she's becoming whole, but so new is this awareness, she can't express herself, doesn't trust herself to distinguish emotion from reality, and can find no words that might express herself, explain herself, not only to herself and to her family, but especially not to Michael. No, she's not ready yet.

10

BRISBANE
Late June 2010

Finally, Francine has found herself able pull away and has been back home in her shared apartment for a few weeks. Tonight she has something on her mind. She's in her bedroom, pretending she's watching television, pretending she's not ignoring her pals, and pretending her world is not in a mess.

Television images are flicking across the screen, the volume muted. Nothing so far has caught her attention. Then something does. She raises the volume to listen to what is being said. On the screen, there she is, Ms Julia Gillard. Look at her. Bold as brass. Not one red hair out of place, her face as white as can be, like a Geisha's face, painted, expressionless, and her eyes fixed straight ahead almost as if she's trying to ignore those men behind her, as if she's aware they are holding sharp knives behind their backs, ready to use should she present them with an opportunity. Gillard knows what she's done to put herself in this place. She knows what's ahead. She took her chance. Australia's first woman Prime Minister. Francine's detached and simultaneously invested, making her own subjective comment without giving much thought to her judgment. Never thought we'd see the day. But should we women be proud of her or concerned about how she reached her ultimate goal? Not that we know how that occurred. Only in some future, after the limitations of restricted disclosure have lapsed, when no one cares about the past, will we understand. But in this present, how might her methods be used to credit or discredit women ambitious for positions of power? Oh, and look at 'poor Kevin' or 'K-Rudd', as the media have labelled him. Quivering lips, tears pooling in his eyes, not yet spilling down his cheeks but threatening. Can't help but feel sorry for the poor bugger.

Francine's own lips quiver. She recognises herself as an amalgam of Julia and Kevin. Like Julia she knows what she wants, thinks she has the courage to grab her chance, but likewise she can recognise the reason for Kevin's quivering lips because, like him, she's spoilt her chance for success through her own doing. Julia's a clever woman. Julia would never have done what she has. Julia would have kept her eyes on the goal ahead. The problem for her is, while still grieving the loss of a planned future, she is not ready or able to see what might be celebrated within any alternative path she will be compelled to take.

§

Facebook

wtf's going on with our girl. Lights are on but no one's home.

Elisa Simson. Today. June 27, 2010. 1.38 pm

Hangover? PMT?

Gail Cerny. Today. June 27, 2010. 1.40 pm

3-way share is not the same when only two are chatting.

Elisa Simson. Today. June 27, 2010. 1.41 pm

Cut the air with a knife is what.

Gail Cerny. Today. June 27, 2010. 1.43 pm

§

Later, when sounds of movement emanate from the third bedroom, Gail looks up from her phone. Elisa is on the sofa with her iPad in one hand. Both girls stop tapping and shrug their shoulders. The front door of the apartment slams shut.

§

Is Francine going to put up a fight or flee? She does have a plan. A flimsy one, a temporary one. After slamming out of the apartment, she heads to West End.

Max Ferguson looks at her, gazes around Cezanne's as if his restaurant is foreign to him and shrugs his shoulders.

'Girl, I don't want to lose you. Look, what say I try to do a swap – just temporary, like – with my mate Gil over the river at Milton. The Boat Shed. Gives you some space. When you have things sorted, you come back, you hear?'

Show no weakness. Remember, this is about leaving on your own terms, in your own way, and under your control. She can't explain needing to change her place of employment because she still hasn't accepted it herself, so she lacks a plausible reason to offer to her boss. Vagueness is part of her strategy to get by even if it is likely someone else might pay the cost. There's a good chance Max might draw his own conclusion, regardless what she says. He might decide that she has had a falling-out with Michael. It'd be terrible if this wrong assumption affects his high opinion of Michael. But to explain is beyond her. Instead, she attempts a big sell.

'Max, Cezanne's needs someone with more hours than I can give. I am heading toward my graduation at uni. There's a lot of work.'

To say those words are too close to the truth and she feels an enormous sorrow wash over her. But Max doesn't seem convinced. Perhaps what he heard was her own fears that the circumstances she is about to face will mean she won't reach the final year. But how flattering is it that Max Ferguson wants her back? And a surprise and a relief to discover that leaving doesn't mean no job? She will need money, that's for certain. Tears seep from the corners of her eyes. No matter how she tries to control them they seem to have a will of their own. She blinks, gives the smallest nod of agreement and a weak smile, an attempt to show him he's been more than obliging, in reality, been generous and gracious. Her now former boss hugs her.

Two hundred metres from Cezanne's, near the ferry terminus, her tear ducts win the battle, overflowing down her cheeks. There's a crowd on the wharf. As passengers disembark, she breaks the traveller's protocol by not waiting for the last one to leave and squeezes past on the narrow boardwalk, bumping elbows and being hit by bags and cases. Several individuals give her sideways glances, marking her down on crowd etiquette, but she's oblivious to their criticism. She doesn't hide her face or dry it. She continues up the ramp, head held high, and strides towards the stairwell. Experience tells her the open upper deck will have fewer passengers for the short run over to the city. Maybe the breeze off the river will clear her mind. She's Jean Grey-Summers in 'X-Men'; Phoenix is holding off a storm.

§

The day has ended at her parents' suburban home. She uses her key and walks in. Her dad is staring at her with what he'd call his 'blank Chinaman face', the one he thinks gets him out of trouble but that, instead, sinks him deeper into it. Mum's wide-eyed, lips quivering in her attempt not to say a word wrong, and succeeds by remaining silent. Freaky. Nor has she offered them any explanations. She's just turned up at their house, let herself in, and has been all cheer and jokes since. Going against habit makes her parents wary. They would think: 'What's up? She never comes here midweek. Coming this late must mean she's staying overnight. A joy and a worry.' They haven't received the good news yet. She can't voice her intentions to them, that this might be more than an overnight stay, because she hasn't fully admitted it to herself. Nor is she willing to concede she takes advantage of her family's love. All she could see was the safety of her parents' home and the absolute certainty that they will allow her to do what she needs to put things right. Not that they will leave it to lie unresolved. They will trust that when s he's ready, she will talk. She knows how precious is the assuredness of knowing their house will always be her home wherever it might be, always her sanctuary, no matter what her crimes or failings. This gift exceeds all value.

Secure in her childhood home, at last she's able to recognise how tight her grip on herself has been. Don't let the girls know that something's up; don't show weakness at work or at uni; and always there's Michael. Don't shatter Michael. Don't destroy him. It's not his fault. Wait, she advocates to her planning mind; wait until she can assess the full damage; wait until she has a plan, then talk.

She remembers as a kid reading the notes affixed to the back of a door in one of the highway-motels they'd stay in on a family road trip. When examined, the motel's 'In Case of Fire' instructions only tell you what to do within the first half-hour of hearing the fire alarm, just as the plans she has in her head will only get her through the next few days. First, go and see a free uni counsellor. Done. Next, act like normal in an abnormal situation. Tomorrow morning, she will be out there, in Mum's kitchen, acting as if all is okay, chatting as usual, cutting off the questions. She knows she will take herself off to work at her new job at The Boat Shed in Milton, not Cezanne's, which she had to chuck to avoid Michael. Mum and Dad will think she's had a falling-out with Gail and Elisa, who will think she has broken up with Michael, and God only knows how Michael will see it. Michael's her weakness. Michael's that thread that sticks out from a knitted pullover, the one you mustn't pull or else the whole thing will unravel.

Snuggled under her pink childhood doona, she is muttering to herself. Might as well sort the wood and forget the trees – counsellor's words, not hers. 'Understanding your own thought process is a start', the counsellor said, 'to regaining control of your life.' Point by point: assess your priorities and then act.

Her parents have tried their usual problem-solving techniques, bringing to her bedroom door her favourite food and drinks like crispy chicken and Milo and leaving her alone. Her father's finding the second one difficult. She has recognised his footsteps in the corridor, imagines him tiptoeing, listening, hoping someone asks for his help, and her mum frowning at him like he's a naughty child. He's such a darling. On the floor, discarded, is an A4 notebook she purchased in the city on her way from the apartment. She's been working hard to convince herself she would follow the counsellor's instructions, even if one part of her is not at all convinced. Time to act. Her hand, the pencil, the gripping fingers, all hover above the page, yet she cannot find the words she needs.

11

MICHAEL'S APARTMENT
NEAR WEST END, BRISBANE
July 15, 2010

Two weeks since Francine just up and left, without a word, the bottom has fallen out of his world and Michael's convinced he's done it to himself. Became too sure of everything. He'd pictured old age with this woman. Saw her as the yin to his yang. He's scoured his memories. Nothing stands out. But he must have done something wrong, something to upset her. And it must be huge. Must have been massive. Nothing else explains her coolness and her absences. If it's not him, then it's something radical like her family or uni. What is also worrying for him, perhaps more so than other notable concerns, is the question: why hasn't she talked to him about it? He'd be there for her and she'd know that by now. Or perhaps that's the problem? What if she doesn't know this? Perhaps he wasn't explicit enough? Maybe those doubts that kept her distant when they first met have resurfaced? He should have talked these issues out with her, not hidden his concerns, but he was relieved it seemed over and done with. What a fool he was. In realistic terms, as regrettable as it may be, this means he doesn't deserve her, because he didn't do his due diligence, because he took the lazy way, the coward's way of not facing up to any problems. Her unwillingness to invite him to meet her family might have been a clue. Why didn't he insist? Or at least ask?

He can't let himself think she's just been using him, playing with him. He can't be that wrong in his judgment of her character. Or the electricity he senses running between them. The emotions feel real; the connection seems genuine. He can accept nothing less than his belief she feels for him as he does for her. No. He can accept no other perspective. But he can't deny she's not talking. No one's talking. Not her friends. Not Max Ferguson.

Not Carl. He'd concede anything, even the blame, because then he'd know what to do to put it right, if not for himself but at least for her. And the final straw: she's stopped working at Cezanne's, so he can't even see her at work. The boss knows who has caused him to lose his best-ever accounts girl because whenever he's asked about Francine he scowls and grumbles to himself. He won't say whether he knows Francine is okay, or whether she has another job. Why won't anyone help him? It's like his guts are being eaten from the inside out. Life without her is meaningless. There has to be a way to put this right.

His mobile in his hand, Michael's thumb selects Contacts, scrolls down to Francine's entry and presses 'Call'. He's lost count of how often he's done this. It's become automatic: Contacts, 'S', scroll down to 'Seeto', select, and press 'Call'. Maybe just once she'll turn on her phone and he'll catch her unawares. This shutting out is no accident. Oh, how he regrets more than ever no invitations to her parents' home – at least he'd know where they lived, and there's a hundred Seetos in the phone book – the damn girls have clammed up too, thinking it's all his fault. Is it?

The pain of her absence is intolerable.

12

MARIA SEETO'S HOME, BRISBANE
July 24, 2010

Around Ah Ma Maria's kitchen table, many a Seeto family problem has been teased out, analysed, argued over, and resolved. Today, Francine is hoping she can find a solution to her problem without revealing too much.

Ah Ma's the sole Judge and Jury, here. She could also be the Prosecutor and Lawyer representing the Defendant.

It's around 9.30 am, a time selected because Francine knows the other occupants of the house will have gone, Uncle Daniel and Aunty Anna to their employment and the boys to school. Ah Ma is standing in the kitchen at the sink, tidying up the remnants of breakfast. Francine has come in through the back door and the laundry, and as she enters, Ah Ma looks at her, begins to smile, then walks to fetch the kettle and put it on. She takes two mugs from the overhead cupboard and begins making tea. Neither has spoken a word, not even in greeting. Francine watches her grandmother's busy-ness, transfixed. She has not moved any further into the kitchen than when her grandmother's activities began. Tea made, two steaming cups placed on the green pretend-marble kitchen table and Ah Ma has pulled out one chair and is indicating with a crooked finger for her granddaughter to take the other. Robot-like Francine does as beckoned.

Grandmother and granddaughter look at each other through the steam rising from the mugs. Francine notes her grandmother might have made a great poker player. It's apparent she has already decided that today's a day for deep and meaningful conversations, but her face does not show any glint of curiosity. Only patience.

'Drink,' Ah Ma says, and picks up her cup to take a sip, setting an example.

Put out by Ah Ma's quick assessment of the situation, Francine behaves like a churlish child and stares back at her grandmother. Ah Ma smiles and points again to the mug. Minutes tick by, her grandmother sips her tea and smiles each time she puts the mug back on the table while Francine is sullen, with hands tightly clasped in her lap.

'Ridiculous,' she chides herself. 'You set yourself a goal, now deliver it.' She's terrified of saying the words she needs to begin the conversation. The pressure inside her is escalating and she fears she might have a break down. She's already debated with herself about whether to return to the counsellor or do the Seeto thing. Gran won out because, instinctively she believes she has solutions but her resistance to adopt them has something to do with family or Gran and maybe that's pride and embarrassment. Whatever it is, it has her by the throat and she's not sure she can hold out much longer. It's the fear that does what her own words can't. She begins in what her father would describe as the 'outfield', using one of his baseball terms. He draws on these to indicate where someone stands in relation to an issue. Ah Ma's the pitcher. He's the catcher. Her mother Kathy is the first baseman and so it goes. In other words, she's starting nowhere near the subject about which she needs help.

'Ah Ma, do you miss Grandpa Patrick? Don't you feel lonely without him?'

'Six years now since your Yeh Yeh Patrick went to God. You haven't mentioned Yeh Yeh for a long time, Francie. What's made you think about him now?'

'I feel lonely, Grandma. I feel as if I'm standing in a crowd but I'm alone. So, I… I wondered if you feel lonely too?'

'What can make a lovely young woman feel alone? I don't believe.'

'Oh, not alone, Ah Ma. Lonely. Don't you miss Yeh Yeh?'

'I was lonely like how you toktok when your grandfather was still here. I understand lonely.'

'What do you mean, Ah Ma? Weren't you happy with Yeh Yeh?'

'Oh, Yeh Yeh not a bad husband. But he isn't the one I love. You savy, Francie? Sometimes you love but cannot have. That's me. Me no tell Yeh Yeh; me no tell anyone so, yes, me too, not alone, but lonely.'

'Oohwah, Ah Ma. You've got secrets. Yeh Yeh wasn't the man of your dreams? Oh, that's sad. Poor Ah Ma. So, who's your secret love, Ah Ma?'

'Francie, me tingting you got a secret, too.'

'Oh, mine's a different secret, Ah Ma.'

'All secrets same-same, Francie.'

'Well, Ah Ma, tell me please, what do you do if you keep a secret because you must keep it. Because if it's no longer a secret, it'll hurt someone or many people you care for?'

'Ah Francie, all secrets hurt someone. People you love are the ones secrets hurt. Me tingting that's why we keep secrets in first place: because we don't want to hurt the people we love, or want to protect ourselves from hurting. But there's no way to avoid pain.'

'How do you keep a secret long enough to discover what is the right thing and do it in a way where you don't hurt everyone including yourself in the meantime?'

'I know this kind of secret, Francie. He hard to live with, this kind. But me tingting, if you no can tell all of truth, tell some only. Bits and pieces. Then mebe it makes sense when secret comes out. No easy way – you no can stop this trouble, olegeta ways always he kissim trabil. It will come.'

When Ah Ma drops her good English for Pisin, the talk is serious. Francine hopes this grim conversation will help her, not add another heavy load on her pile. There's too many words and thoughts in her head to see any clarity. Perhaps she's needs some time for it to settle.

What she knows is this is the first time she has ever kept a secret from her grandmother.

§

Wise Ah Ma doesn't push too hard and the conversation moves to less troublesome topics, and they finish the tea. Francine is on her way elsewhere. Time now for Maria to examine what they have shared from every perspective. Her conclusion is that she has failed her granddaughter.

'You a fine one to give advice about keeping secrets and hurting others, especially those you love. What would Francie think if she knew what you have been doing for a good part of your adult life? And, now, you missed your moment. The big question is what could possibly be worrying this girl? More than loneliness, that's for sure, but what? Handled better, you might have got it out of her. But no, this lapun grandmother can't do that. Why? Because all the time she's thinking in her own head about the secrets she's keeping and the lies she's told to keep her secrets hidden. The result is an inadequate response to a cry for help. Worried more about your own secrets than helping your granddaughter. You have the perfect answer. You could have told her don't let your secret stay hidden until you are old because then it will be too late to tell, and too late to put right, and that will hurt those you love even more than telling the secret at the beginning. Because you know from personal experience what damage it does to both the secret keeper and those the secret is being kept from. But, no, this selfish Ah Ma has squandered a perfect chance, and what advice has she given to her grandchildren? Opportunities make no second appearance. Grab them while they are on offer. Can't even follow your own wisdom.'

She definitely should punish herself. Her mind picks away at her failings, her inability to share her secrets, when her experiences of life might have eased her granddaughter's pain. What can be the problem? Everything about this girl's life seems perfect. But who can tell? What does anyone know about another? What might one grandmother know about a granddaughter, and what might a granddaughter not know about her grandmother? The desire to penalise herself provokes more guilt. But as always, justified or not, the pain behind her silences leads her to divert the blame onto her dead husband.

'Patrick, Patrick. Alive, you made my life difficult. And now dead all these years and you are still doing so. Your lie has become my lie. All those lies have become a brick wall that hides the real me from my family. Perhaps it wasn't your fault, Patrick. You were not to know what was at stake. Me, I blame the man who sold you the dream. Seeto Wei. My uncaring, self-seeking father. Or if not him, then the man who used him as a puppet, Loi Fook. Both deserve the blame for stealing a life and stealing your wife. Me. Bad luck for you, Tak Tam, that the wife you got was nothing more than a ghost. Maybe you deserved more. Maybe you didn't. But we don't get what we deserve. And never, in my experience of life, do we get what we hope for. So, now, the world has turned and the daughter of that son who was your reward for taking a less than perfect wife comes and asks questions. The only answers are more lies.'

She clenches her gnarled fists together. If only there could be room for honesty. If only this was the time to speak the truth. Then the answer should have been: 'No Francine. Me do not miss the man you call Yeh Yeh but me lonely for your grandfather, your real grandfather.'

Stephen. This begins with Stephen. Lies about grandpa, lies about feeling lonely. The truth begins and ends with Stephen. Stephen is the only one she misses. Stephen. And her little brother Henry. But these words will remain unspoken. Secrets are such heavy weights. Silences are rocks that anchor the truth to the bottom of the ocean.

§

Francine's feet have taken control. They march her from Grandma's kitchen, down the path, and out onto the street. They turn her left, lead her up and over the hill, so she is following the footpath that runs along the suburban streets. The words 'Secrets, bring trouble' scroll through her subconscious, hijacking her awareness. She's sleepwalking. At No. 64, she is blind and deaf to the rowdy Islander children playing 'Touch' on the front lawn. 'No, Isaiah. Stop. Aaagh. That hurt. Mum, Mum, he's punching me. He won't let me have the ball.'

Pedestrians pass her, their eyes downcast. Are they worrying about their own lives? They don't notice when she doesn't make eye contact.

'Lonely.' The word contemplated by both her and her grandmother, which for her means the way she has been feeling since she cut out everyone, those who might have been able to help her. And whose fault is that? As she passes No. 102 where the Bikies live, her mind is too busy scrolling through her dilemma for her to hear their crude calls. Still preoccupied, she continues. Left and right, along tidy pavements or unkempt verges, on an arbitrary path. Later, when she looks back on her journey, she can't remember checking for traffic on the busy road she knows she must have crossed. She ends up at the Transport Terminus, a destination she can't remember planning for.

Buses queue but she passes them one by one, dodging the buses' would-be passengers who are heading in the opposite direction to hers but clearly driven by a sense of purpose – which bus they need and where it is waiting for them. For her, the next bus is not the one, nor the next, or the next, until she finds herself inside one empty vehicle, its route unknown. It's fortunate she has her transit pass with her. She tags on and walks the length of the vehicle to a seat at the rear. The bus fills. Although the driver's arrival is casual, making it seem to be impromptu, there's a part of her brain that recognises it's not. Months ago, a departure time would have been predetermined and displayed in timetable black-and-white, then printed and posted under Perspex on a pole or many, or on a website. The female driver drops her lunch pail into a spot beside the driver's seat, a daily habit, then wriggles herself into her zone, closes the cage, and makes a final check of her cargo, before pressing the button to start the engine. She engages the gears and leaves it to the last second to close the doors. The bus beeps its intention to pull out and soon it and its passengers are rolling along at a steady speed. With only trivia to engage it, Francine's mind permits her to make a pragmatic diagnosis, not about her personal predicament but about the bus she's on. It's only picking up. Its destination must be a place the majority knows about. She's not curious where that might be and yet she can't stop herself from examining each new arrival. Perhaps it's instinctive, a self-preserving response, but concentrating on every entry, young or old, male or female, provides her momentary distraction from her inner turbulence. In one pause, a bubble rises, like carbon dioxide in lemonade. A tiny piece of clarity pops to the surface.

Her mind issues orders. 'You must attend to the shared apartment. It's not fair on Elisa and Gail.' But its brilliance doesn't extend to telling her what she might do to rectify the situation.

At the next stop, an elderly grey-haired woman takes what seems like forever to haul herself up the steps and shuffle forward on the landing, even more time to dig into her handbag and bring out her travel card. The driver smiles, nods and waits for this new client to move towards the nearest empty seat, which is the one that requires her to step up. After a few stalled attempts, she settles. The driver is in no hurry to move the bus. She wants this passenger seated: a benevolence noted by Francine.

Next stop, a mother with three young children boards. The mother works her children as if she were a farmer's kelpie heading off a mob of sheep. First her right hand shoots out then her left. The children zigzag their way up the aisle, ogling their 'fans' because it seems impossible for those they pass not to smile or say hello, even the pimple-faced earphone-bedecked teenager in the second row who, Francine censures, should offer his seat to the family. The mother negotiates with the driver over the paying of fares. No travel pass, Francine notes, so not a frequent traveller and who could blame her? Meanwhile, the two older children, girls, have broken free and are clambering up on the seat in front of Francine. She can see these two small humans are hoping to make friends. Rather than sitting, they both pull themselves up by the seat back, and turn to stare. Faced with two sets of innocent eyes and broad smiles, Francine battles her tendency to be social. She orders her eyes to look to the side window to the anonymous blur of passing traffic. The mother drags the third child along, plops him down on the seat across the aisle from her other two, and spends several minutes fighting with him to keep him seated by pulling his legs down, not once but multiple times. He gives in. Mum reaches across the aisle to pat the girls into a seating position. Their heads are bobbing nonstop.

But, again, a benefit comes out of these distractions, an 'oh yeah' moment, when she recognises something else that needs prioritising. She's not over-joyed by these enlightenments because, until now, everything has been a mess of fear and panic. And hiding herself in the confusion has afforded her a strange relief. Avoidance, maybe. Or denial. This new revelation concerns Michael. If she doesn't explain the situation, it will seem to him to be a chastisement, or a rebuff. What would she do if he chose to no longer be in her life? Nothing could be worse than that. Yes, she needs to speak with him, but to do that, first she must stop avoiding him.

The bus doesn't travel far before it swings into a wide circle, a movement that causes its standing passengers to cling to the hanging straps. Some groan. The seated ones gather belongings. There's a whoosh of the air brakes and they come to a standstill next to an impressive, art-embellished bus stand. Through the bus's windscreen a glassed entrance portico towers, the front door to a grand shopping mall, one that's unfamiliar to Francine. Without enthusiasm, she looks for a sign that might hint at the name of the suburb they are in, but gives up, distracted by the outpouring of passengers, including the mother and her charges, who no longer need guiding in their eagerness to uncover the next adventure. Looks like it will be a big day for those kids.

She's a lone traveller, in her rear seat. Her surrounding space expands. She relishes the temporary stillness and silence. But, outside, there's a queue at the bus stand. Individuals are shuffling forward, eager to embark. Many of these have spent their money and are taking the goodies home. Big shopping bags mark each owner's progress. Thwack, thwack, thwack. One bundle strikes Francine on the head. She offers a steely glare, more at the disturbance than because of any pain. The bag carrier mumbles an obligatory 'sorry' that lacks passion. Now the bus is full. The ritual begins again: doors close, beeping happens, engine roars and they lurch out from the bus stand, into the traffic.

During the next phase of her journey, she takes less notice of the passengers' comings and goings, and no longer registers the irregular heavy breath of the bus's air brakes and the passing vista. Not once does she consider where she is being taken. Because of the ins and outs of pickups and drop-offs, the need to obey traffic lights and to dodge other vehicles, and the sudden braking, the bus motion, though erratic, is meditative. Her scrutiny turns inward. For the first time she can view her self-imposed and troublesome situation with less emotion. There are secrets, hers and her grandmother's. What's not under scrutiny is not whether her grandmother realises her usually truthful granddaughter has lied but rather that Francine can't deny she may have destroyed something she values. The relationship between her and her grandmother is special and she has weakened it. Sure, Ah Ma did testify today she too has kept secrets, but that doesn't seem as damning as Francine's own failure to be honest. She doesn't like this person she has become, the one who responds to unexpected and difficult situations by panicking and lying, a person who can no longer pride herself on clear thoughts and controlled behaviour. This mood she's in is all about her failure to maintain her own personal high standards.

Yes, Ah Ma's hint of another life unknown to her granddaughter has shaken her. Until recently, she had felt smug about 'knowing' herself, being sure of what she'd be willing to do or how she might behave, especially sure of her right to be proud of being strong and directed and clever. How she perceives herself is shored up by her family reaffirming her right to be proud. But Ah Ma's revelation has diminished her confidence in her ability to predict family members' behaviours and be certain of their reliability because she 'knows' them. But is it 'knowing'? No one 'knows' anyone; no one knows themselves. If she's honest, she'd admit she has only ever been interested in what applies to her – the history that includes her – and that's only in Australia. Ah Ma's secret, well, that probably comes from a prior history, things she hasn't questioned or paid attention to, or maybe has never been told. But that's not an excuse. She's an Aussie first. A blended racial heritage just adds an exotic touch to her perception of herself. Sure, she acknowledges, she'd be naïve to ignore the larger stories. But she has done so. She never begged for those stories, did she? What might have discouraged her father and uncles from talking? The only story she has heard is the romance story Dad rolls out every year. Is it only once a year? Somehow it seems more often. The Mum romance story is mainly about how lucky he is. It doesn't speak about the social balances, or imbalances, that her ancestors may have endured, if the history in other similar colonial places is any measure. She's educated, so she should understand about the shifts of power, the hierarchies of dominance, and that it's negligent of her not to recognise that her own family's story might provide a chapter in a larger history. Has it been self-centredness on her part that has stopped her listening or asking? As a modern girl, has she devalued those former lives, seeing herself as having moved beyond that past?

She's known, almost from the moment she became aware her life was about to change, what she needed to work on but the funk she'd dropped into was like a childhood 'woobie' blanket, a comforter to suck on and feel, to hide under, a mask for her denial, and an excuse to avoid facing the hard realities. The weight of being the 'clever' girl everyone believes her to be compelled her to overwork the problems and crowd the possibilities of solutions. She couldn't find a way through the intellectual maze so found it easier to withdraw. Today's journey has acted like the stander ladder she had seen on the Amazon website. She's been fascinated by it, such a practical but barely talked about idea that she believes would make the lives of many easier, a way to tackle the most fundamental of all needs in daily life. The stander is a rope ladder that hooks onto a bed base or any other sturdy support and allows any prone person to pull themselves upright rung by rung. Sitting in that bus, glimpsing fragments of others' lives, none connected to hers, has lurched her upright. Head clear, and yet with no real solutions apparent, a short list of priorities shines a light towards forward progress. Step by step, rung by rung, she has empowered herself to solve one issue then move to the next.

Hours later, her bus discharges passengers at a railway station. She astonishes herself by standing and walking towards the door. She's left it late. The door is already closing but the driver, diligent as ever, sees her move and reopens it. Released, Francine follows the others towards the station entrance. Something's changed inside her. Her feet seem to know where they should go. She's following a plan she can't yet articulate. Take the rail to the city, then a ferry across the river to her former residence, and engage in an overdue conversation with her besties. She has not the slightest doubt that resuming her place in the apartment is impossible, given the mess she has got herself into, but she knows Elisa and Gail can't afford to pay more than the third of the rent they'd all agreed to pay when they signed the lease. Knowing the facts and persuading them to take in another person will be the challenge. More lies required, no doubt. More guilt, as she's the one who sold Elisa and Gail on the plan to live near the city. Her dream. Her plan. And, sure, it had been a perfect plan. For her, sharing the apartment, earning money working at Cezanne's while studying, was phase one. It suited the other two for different reasons. Phase two for her would come after graduating. She'll build an art practice of her own. If she abandons her friends, as she must to survive, they will be paying the penalty for her failure but as for her own situation, such is her confidence in her family, she knows that once she shares her problem, she will find a solution for her. Support will come and while she may need to make compromises, somehow, it'll work. It might mean needing to rent a room with mum and dad plus careful spending. What arguments can she offer her friends so that they aren't impacted? She flicks away her guilt, one of the elements that have stalled her to date, and reminds herself to take one step at a time.

The largest hurdle will be finding not only the courage but a way to explain to Michael. Her friends, her family, well, that's all practical problems and there's always a solution for those, even if they are sometimes hard to digest. But Michael? Well, if she can't work something out about Michael, then does anything matter? First there's some repairs and apologies needed, and then a way forward needs to be worked through with him, a way that ensures he won't be victim of his own good and generous nature. Again, because most of the issues are hers, not his. The one thing that is his, she's certain will be okay, one way or the other.

13

MARIA'S HOME, BRISBANE
September 16, an anniversary of PNG Independence

Maria converses with herself, ticking off why this event is happening, justifying it to herself because she knows for some in her family there's been criticism.

Yes, it's a Thursday, not a weekend when most of their family get-togethers happen, but it is the actual day of the thirty-fifth anniversary of PNG's Independence. Although this might sound like a winning argument for insisting on holding her party on a weekday, she's can't ignore that this valid-sounding excuse arrived late to her, well after she'd made the original decision. Permitting herself to fall into the sentimentality of the national event is odd, especially when in retrospect she reminds herself that the anniversary of PNG Independence is not a day in which she usually invests. Oh yes, they've had their parties every year but that's for the benefit of others, not because it's Independence Day. Any excuse for a party to bring her family and friends together is good. Too many ill-feelings and reminders rise out of this historic moment for her personally but she is able to push them aside just to give a name to a gathering of the people she loves. Aware that her behaviour is out of the ordinary, she's wary. Is her inner self betraying her? Is her conscience finally forcing her to do something about her procrastinations?

Whatever motivated her choice, today's the day. Daniel and his family are all out there, doing what they do – work and school – and she's left to do one chore. She must prepare her specialty dish for tonight's feast. For a body no longer as energetic as it once was, there's a need to begin the day's preparations with a motivational speech to herself.

'Remember, Maria, your good habits: rise early, work hard, be frugal.'

She hopes Nenek's oft-recited and wise words will goad her reluctant body into action. For her relatives, back in earlier times, as in-betweeners in a colonial state, this chant had pulled them through difficult periods of restrictions or limitations placed on their community as neither indigenous or expatriate or when facing other circumstances beyond their influence. For Maria, the most difficult period was immediately after the war. Before the Japanese arrived in 1942, there had been five sharing Nenek's house with a verandah: Nenek, Maria's mother Josefina, her stepfather Daddy-George, her brother Henry and Maria. By 1945, when the Japanese surrendered, there were only two left. Two were dead, and the other one refused to return. Other former residents of Rabaul had a rough time, even those who had spent the war years in camps away from the town. For Maria and her grandmother, because of who they were, there had been no choice but to ride it out within the viper's nest of the garrison town of Rabaul. Consequently, they had not received the aid from Red Cross and such forth that had been offered to the camp dwellers. For the years that follow the two of them needed good frugal and diligent habits to survive. As the Japanese left and the Americans arrived, there were fewer supplies for the non-white locals. The constant American bombing had destroyed most of the buildings taking with them what might have otherwise been scavenged. Their good life habits around hard work and perseverance had them digging in the rubble, scrounging for war scraps to rebuild, doing whatever was necessary to make do, like everyone else. The scavengers were classless. Supplies were short even for the Australian officials charged with restoration. Former army barracks became the homes of these officials and damaged and abandoned US jeeps and trucks their transport. Converting military detritus into useful peacetime objects was a goal shared regardless of social status or standing. Of course, this was short-lived. Once a sense of normality had been restored and delivery of supplies more certain, the former hierarchies also reappeared. Some months later, Stephen emerged from the jungle. Before then, Maria and Nenek had needed to take care of themselves, as they had done throughout the war.

And there's that time, after Nenek passed, a different deprivation was faced by Maria. Drawing from Nenek's practices helped her through.

She often hears her own voice delivering Nenek's wisdom to her family. Maybe they hear them but think 'just old woman words.' These days, the world is different. New rules in play: just take it easy, do things when you feel like it. But it doesn't matter what they think. If she never begins with the phrase 'my grandmother said…' it's not because she's wants to claim the wisdom as her own but, because… well… she can't acknowledge Nenek and her wisdom without explaining… and that's too much. But she does need to hear herself reciting Nenek's maxims. They reassure her, take her back to a time when she felt safe and loved in Nenek's care. And yes, she reminds herself as she glances around her bedroom from her motionless position on her bed, Nenek's words brought her and her family to this house – with its verandah – and, after thirty-five years, it's still the centre of her family, as today's event will show.

'So much to do. Use Nenek's ideals to invigorate yourself,' she recites. 'Lift yourself, forget your weary, aching bones.'

She's started as she intended, waking early – but she hasn't moved. Using the excuse of 'organising her thoughts' she's remained prone for a little longer than would meet Nenek's standards. In her head, where she's still a young and able person, she's already flying through the chores of the day, and checking off her mental list, picturing herself picking up, cutting, stirring, preparing and placing the finished dish on a rack in the fridge. But nothing is being done, not even rising and dressing. A reminder of wasted time comes through the voice of her bedside clock – tick-tock, tick-tock, tick-tock – as it notes the passing seconds and minutes. An hour has disappeared. She's still not out of bed.

'You'll be running out of time, silly woman,' she chides herself. 'Come on. Move.'

She works hard to roll her body into a better position. Her ribs ache with the effort. She knows she must concentrate. 'Breathe, press your fists into the mattress, and push.' Success. Or partial success. Her upper torso free falls towards one side and then remains stooped. She takes another breath, and gives a final almighty twist to move her heavy frame. Now most of her upper body is upright and her legs swing over the side of the bed.

'Not so easy,' she gives herself a pat for effort. And yet she's only halfway there. More deep breaths, followed by a quiet few minutes to settle her head, to stop it spinning, before the final hurrah, an almighty heave-ho. She's standing. Once upright, she takes a second or two to steady herself before she moves to her wardrobe to begin the slow, almost painful, process of dressing.

§

Maria has reached the kitchen.

Earlier, family members have assembled the ingredients for her. The aibika plants, dark green and peppery, stands in a bucket of cold water in the sink. The coconuts are on a tray on the draining board, split in half by Andy on his way to work this morning. In the fridge, there are a number of fish chosen by Anna who took delivery of them an hour ago before she left the house. Maria nods approval. Anna has a good New Guinea eye for gutpela abus, so when she shops, she delivers only the choicest, freshest pieces of meat or fish to their home.

First things first. Before beginning her preparations, she looks to Jesus Christ who's gazing, not down at her but, towards the ceiling. No meal's prepared in this kitchen without the Lord looking away, as if he cannot bear to see the food spread upon the table below. Sometimes she feels she should replace this image for one where His eyes look down, but the Bridegroom one, with Jesus in his glorious red gown and the bright gold of his halo, appeals to her. It's the red of the Lord's gown that keeps the image from being changed. Red for good fortune, she smiles to herself. Excellent outcome. Chinese beliefs crossing over into her Catholicism works for her. Double good fortune, she tells herself. And, as if to show a little more respect to religion than the less weighty benefits of Chinese luck, she says a silent prayer before she reaches out one hand for the aibika, shakes off the water, and wraps it in a damp tea towel. The aibika's now ready for when she requires it later.

She reaches over to turn on her portable radio. A little music always helps. This transistor has travelled the long distance from Rabaul. Bought from Chong's too, like her mirror, but unlike the mirror, the transistor still works. No mould on its red case. Can't buy radios of this style nowadays, and not in her favourite colour, which is red. Only as big as a small box of Roses, it has a small antenna at one end. Andrew's boy, Lucas, tells her she should have an iPod, but she ignores him. Too much trouble. And who wants to do that fiddling? What does he call it? Loading down or something. She moves the dial to tune into easy listening. Charley Pride is playing, and his rich voice moves her. His voice is familiar and comforting, been listening to it for decades. 'Ramblin' Rose' or 'Danny Boy' are her favourites. This time it's 'I Love You Because'. Almost as good.

She rinses her hands once again, in case. Outside she can see her neighbour Pavle is working in his garden. Pavle is a Serbian from Yugoslavia, he says, and Pavle means Paul in English, but she calls him Pavle, not Paul, because she thinks she understands it might be important for him to hear his name in his language. Language carries you back to your homeland, to people left behind. Reminds you of home. He would have heard the name Pavle throughout the years he was growing up. That's how she feels about preparing traditional meals. Reminds you of who you are. Something else she should credit Nenek for. Remembering who you are. But she doesn't let this linger. It's loaded with guilt. However, she does validate the value to her of traditional food by permitting her eyes to sweep around her kitchen and take in the particular ingredients awaiting her attention – New Guinea-style – thus disengaging herself from her neighbour's activities. She often watches him as he goes about his routine, but today she has wasted enough time.

She removes the aibika from the tea towel and smiles at the exposed plant, as though seeing an old friend for one more time. Ah, aibika, its peppery aroma, its deep green leaves. makes us ex-PNG people feel homesick. For her, it's the contrast between the sweet pepper of the young leaves and bitter bite of the old. As in life, there are sweet times and bitter times and you need to know only how to makes the most of what you have.

After hearing her constant praise of the plant, her grandson google-d it. What he read made his eyes open wide.

'Ah Ma, did you know aibika has twelve times the beta-carotene content, twenty times the folate content and five times the vitamin C content of tomato?'

She didn't know those details. In fact, she didn't know anything about beta-carotene or folate, impressed her grandson did, but she was happy to hear that the computer agreed with generations of New Guinea cooks. Eating it is good for everyone. She nods to herself. Good for pregnant women. Not that there are any pregnant women in her family.

Anna buys the aibika for the family from a local market. The leaves must be washed well. If not, traces of sand and soil will remain. She spends several minutes washing her selection of younger leaves under cold running water. Already she can smell the faint peppery aroma of the aibika. She shakes the excess water off the leaves, then turns towards the table and places them on her chopping board. Now the sink is behind her, the table and board in front, all part of a well-rehearsed dance – repeated over many years – where she swings from sink to table as she cooks.

As she moves the aibika leaves from the board into a bowl, she looks around her kitchen and into her dining room. She smiles, and nods her head, though there's no one to see her act of approval. She feels good about these freshly painted rooms. Ah, yes, she loves the way her home looks now. This is evidence of her win over her youngest, Daniel. She needed Daniel to do the work, but he could not see the urgency. Nor did she have the heart to say to him what was in her own head: 'Me like this done before me dai pinis. Me like spend my lapun days in a house that looks good.' Those words would have frightened her son. He doesn't want to think about his mother dying soon. It would destroy him if she said those words. She can imagine what he'd say. 'You talk stupid, Mum. Got plenty of years.' And if he had been granted an opportunity to deliver this excuse, she might have been persuaded not to pursue her goal. Thank goodness, he has given in to his mother's nagging. She fears she is running out of time. She can feel it in her bones, the aging, the weariness, and the state she fears most, the inability to raise enthusiasm for anything. She doesn't want to become a woman who sits and stares all day, who can do nothing for herself, but she doesn't know how she can halt her regression. Maybe she should take herself off to a nursing home before she becomes too senile, and in this way take the decision out of her sons' hands. A brief notion of an up-side to these dire predictions is the forgetfulness that accompanies dementia. The past won't be able to haunt her any more. Or maybe, she smiles to herself, when she has lost her marbles, she will only remember the expression on Daniel's face when she asked him to help her. Now, that was hilarious. She wanted to say to him, but didn't, 'Bad luck, Daniel. You can't help who your father is.' Sometimes, Daniel displays small bits of Patrick in his character or how he behaves. However, the painting of the house was no such moments. Patrick, he no likim work around the house. Different reason for not doing than why Daniel doesn't like to paint. Daniel is lazy, but he's also nervous about big challenges as he probably perceived the painting of the house to be. He would be afraid of failing. But his daddy, Patrick, think emi too good to do these kinds of things. Too many years of giving orders and having a New Guinea worker do it for him.

She reaches for another bowl, rummages in the cutlery drawer for the scraper she always uses for this next task and turns back to the sink and to the already split coconuts Andy left for her. With one half of one coconut in her hands, she turns again, back to the bench and places the half coconut on her board. With her hands poised, her fingers grip the handmade special-purpose scraper, made in Rabaul and brought down to Australia and she applies pressure to the inside of the coconut. The goal: to grate the coconut meat into a bowl. After the first one or two pushes, she pinches a little meat between her fingertips and tastes it.

Sweet. Nice. Good coconut.

She continues scraping. Sweat pops out on her forehead. She struggles to breathe. Getting too ancient to keep doing this. Shame. Because in her heart, she loves the effort required to prepare traditional meals. She encourages her family to invest their time and energy in the same way, rather than always go the modern way, the quick takeaway or the Aussie meals, which are fine, but just not all the time, and not for special occasions.

Once the shell of one half of the coconut no longer contains any meat, she turns to repeat the process with the other. The effort is taking its toll, but she must continue.

'Dish won't taste right with only half the coconut milk she needs,' she encourages herself.

When she completes that task, she rinses and dries her board, returns it to the table, and from the second drawer down, she takes out of a sealed plastic bag a length of muslin fabric. She spreads the gauze over her board. She empties the coconut meat into the centre of the gauze, and gathers in the corners and edges, then knots them together. This task she has done so often it's automatic. She places the bowl, empty of the coconut meat, on the board, and into it returns the gauze bag of meat. The next task is to squeeze the juice from the coconut meat and this requires her to use her weight to press down on it. She pauses briefly, gives the gauze bag a shake and then presses down again. In each pause, she pours off any milk extracted into a jug. It takes time to press the milk from the meat, and as she continues to shake and squeeze, she contemplates what this house means to her: home for more than just her and Patrick. Andrew, Kathy and their family lived under its roof for over twenty years of their marriage, and Daniel, Anna and the boys are still here. Gabriel drops in and out as suits him. At one time, when Andrew lived here, his kids Francine and Lucas had shared the main bedroom with her and Patrick. She'd called the bedroom 'the kids' room' and they'd call it 'Ah Ma and Yeh Yeh's room'. For her, it had been a comfort to listen to their breathing. It was the only time her bedroom had been a place she wanted to be in. In the room that should be the heart of a marriage, Patrick's presence had always been hard to tolerate.

Tonight's for talking, laughing, eating and family; a time to push aside dark thoughts, lusim bad tingting. Her family will come together to share the cooking and eating. Oh, so special, and tonight her little house will sing with family, love, and good food. New Guinea kaikai, familii – make tispela haus special. All good medicine for an old lady.

And now another coconut. When finished, she puts aside the coconut milk, unties the gauze bag and discards the coconut meat into her bin. First, she rinses then washes the board, but leaves the gauze crumpled up on the draining board of the sink to wash later.

Now the fish. She takes a tray from the fridge and examines each fish. Anna bought them from the local fish market. The flesh looks good. She draws out her favourite knife from the rack, and one by one cuts the fish into bite-sized pieces, which she places into an empty bowl. She reaches over her head to take down the large pot she hangs from a ceiling hook and places the pot on her table. Then she tips into the pan the fish, the coconut milk, and the last item, the aibika. She carries the pot to the cooker, turns the gas burner to high, positions the pot over it and reaches for the salt. After seasoning, she turns the heat right down low, and stirs the contents, then watches. This takes only about seven minutes to cook. Good to have this done early. Once the others come, she will forget to watch, too busy listening to what everyone's talking about, and then the milk will boil. Too easy to spoil this by not keeping her mind on the job.

The kitchen fills with the peppery, sweet aroma of the dish. What dishes will her family cook tonight? What other smells will fill her house?

§

They are here.

Andy's choice is his specialty, chop suey, using the New Guinea ingredients he'd used in Rabaul as a teenager. No partner to help him chop the ingredients because Francine, who had promised to help, hasn't arrived yet. He doesn't seem perturbed. This dish is distinctive and delicious. Kathy is making chow mien and fried rice. They tease her – for an Australian she cooks Chinese food well. Gabriel's helping his mother prepare crispy deep-fried chicken, sweet and sour cucumber and dried mushrooms braised in soy sauce. Andrew's helping Anna cook her New Guinea mumu pig on the spit outside, though it's not a whole pig because that would take too long, and already this been turning since early this afternoon. Daniel has picked banana leaves from a neighbour's tree and he will cook another New Guinean dish of taro, banana, aibika, and coconut milk. Tonight, he's cooking it in Maria's oven instead of a pit.

This is true 'New Guinea' style; family, our style food, lots of talking and laughing. Though some might say we're not New Guinean if that means the tribal people. But there's no name for us. We're migrants who moved to Australia, but what name can we give to our cultural heritage? She sighs. The kitchen rings with the metallic song of the knife as she sharpens it with wide, confident, determined sweeps. Bowls and pots of many shapes and sizes and many ingredients scrounged from Sunnybank's markets and Asian stores crowd the bench. Someone makes space for her chopping board by moving one or two items. Around her, members of her family sit on stools or stand. Flashing knives, reflecting the fluorescent light, wave, crush, and dice. Aromas of ginger, five spices and chilli explode and collide. No one looks away from what they are working on. As they immerse themselves in their preparations, no one speaks.

She takes up her position in front of the chopping board. Beyond her, her kingdom. Her grandsons, still playing the video game, cooperating, laughing and the adults working together in the kitchen. Andy is challenging the others. 'Who will get gold stars from Mum tonight, eh? Me and Francie, I reckon.' He winks at his mother. His cooking partner still hasn't arrived. Maria worries. Francine is still not herself.

Daniel replies to his brother.

'Maski, brus. The battle's over before it begins so you can forget any hope of scoring. Anna's the best chef ever with New Guinea kaikai. And, besides, Mum l-erv-s Anna: Anna emi lukim me tru, she says. You tupela nogat a chance. You two can give up now.'

Anna diverts the conversation.

'Oh, did you see the new Asian Food Supermarket opened in Sunnybank? Taking Mum there on Thursday. She will be so darn excited.' She gives Maria a wink.

Now it's Gabriel.

'Hey, guys, did any of you hear about Joseph Chung? Saw his brother-in-law in the city last weekend. Story is, Joseph is going back to PNG. Doesn't like it here. Wife and kids aren't going.'

And Andy, comes in with a classic closer.

'He's onto a winner, there. Gets himself a new meri who will do all his cooking. Fresh start. Ow. Don't punch so hard, Kathy. Being all skin, bones, and no muscle makes a man vulnerable.'

'You're too skinny, man. You need to eat more,' Gabe advises.

'Oh, don't tell him that,' says Andy's wife, flipping her fine blond hair away from her eyes with a sharp twist of her head. 'He already eats plenty and, damn him, it disappears. Makes me sick.'

Andy pretends he's offended.

Maria's face shows only concentration at the task at hand. Inside she's feeling warm and frothy. As soon as the food is ready, they will move outside. This means the boys will need to leave the computer. What can be predicted are frowns and scowls which will discarded once the food is served. And next the neighbours and friends will arrive. 'Food for everyone,' Maria congratulates herself. 'Altogeta kaikai.' But where is her special girl?

14

IT'S AH MA'S INDEPENDENCE DAY PARTY

Despite Francine's resolution to be her calm, cheerful self, a mask she hopes will fool her family, her gut is tight. She feels nauseous. This isn't like her. Had to park in the next street because Gran's street is already littered with an excessive number of parked cars. There are vehicles on the verge and one is straddling the footpath. Someone's willing to risk a scratch along one side. Pedestrians in this suburb can be short on social graces and patience. Holy cow. That's Uncle Gabriel's car. Ho, ho. Of course. He would be the one to test the mob. Now, there's a turn-up for the books. She can't help a smile spreading across her face. Uncle Gabriel is fun. Everyone loves him. She feels old tonight so she will welcome a good dose of Uncle Gabriel. Never does she feel grown-up around him; he always makes her feel like she's still a kid. She had never quite got why Gran called him 'her Harry Belafonte' until a rather beat-up Belafonte album turned in one of the market stalls a few years back. But there he was, a more handsome version of Uncle Gabriel's face, a beautiful face, an open face, one that when you recall it, you've no choice but to smile in memory of the good times spent with him.

Uncle Gabriel being here tonight is a double blessing for her. He's fun but his strong presence means the spotlight will be off her. She can't believe how apprehensive she is about seeing her family and yet, when she considers that phrase – her family – she can't contain a smile. Her family. Her safety zone. Her safe space. Often, she asks Gail and Elisa to family parties. Tonight, Gail has a date and Elisa has dinner with her family on the Gold Coast. Their absence has meant there's nothing to distract Michael from asking the hard question, like, what's been going on with her, and she's scared, right to her core, he will see right through her delaying tactics, compelling her to do what she should have done earlier, before she's ready. All this nervousness and she has divulged nothing to him yet, nor to anyone, stupid person she is. Not sure when she will, either. Seems a step too far. Still searching for that elusive perfect plan. She's on her own and lost. Strange. Never been in this place before. She's always had tonnes of support. Now, when she's facing her biggest problem ever, she has no one to be there with her. There's a wrenching inside her, and again the accusation, 'And whose fault is that?' She can't shut it out. Because it's true. Can't see Michael's car out front. Maybe she should wait on the porch for him to arrive.

She pauses before taking the three steps up onto the porch. This was once her home, still is the heart of the family. Feels good to come here. Home. Already wafting through the screen door are tantalising aromas and a mash of voices. It's a chook pen, with hens and roosters clucking and crowing. Her father. She can hear him laughing. She guesses he's laughing at something Uncle Gabe has said, and without reason she laughs too. She twirls herself around, arms lifted high, then plops her body down on the top step, elbows on her knees and face cupped within her hands. This is the world as she knows it. And in recognising that, everything feels right. She feels certain she can solve any problem, and there's nothing that needs explaining or justifying.

Everyone's in the kitchen, food is being prepared, those she loves are arguing, teasing each other, laughing, talking and working together. Strange that she never remembers her grandfather Patrick in the good old times. Well, not so strange. He was the grumpy old man on the sofa, growling at the young ones who wanted to watch TV, complaining about the noise, telling them to get their feet off the sofa, and never joining in the banter. Until Gran would come and stand over him. She would not say a word. The look on her face alone would make her point. He'd skulk off to his bedroom until the food was ready then eat in silence. She rises off the step, turns around, reaches for the latch of the screen door and enters.

'Well, look-ee here who's arrived. Running a little late, missy. We needed you about an hour ago to chop vegies, your favourite job,' her mum laughs.

'And where's this friend of yours? Still coming? Plenty to do. We need an extra hand, or two or four,' remarks her dad.

'And what's your contribution to the meal, Miss Francie? Hope you don't think you are sponging off your family, young lady,' says Uncle Gabriel.

'Nah. Picking up Kentucky Fried. Very traditional.'

'Yum,' says Uncle Daniel. 'That's my kind of tradition.'

Gran gives him a wallop on the shoulder. 'Lazy boy.'

She looks around at the laughing faces of her family and remembers that it was in primary school she first learnt that caterpillars go through a transition. First, they weave cocoons, and then they become fat grubs before bursting into the world as butterflies. She remembers thinking what great stories those butterflies would have to tell about the many worlds they'd seen: inside a cocoon, the outside world through fat-grub eyes and then, if only for a day, soaring above the trees and bushes. Which story might each butterfly tell? Tonight, for the first time, she sees her family as transitive beings, no longer as Uncle Daniel, Uncle Gabriel, Aunty Anna, Gran, Mum and Dad. This is what Michael will see tonight when he's meeting them for the first time. She wonders what stories a stranger like Michael might read from each of their different faces, stories so familiar, too often unspoken, so that not even the family understands them any longer. Faced with the certainty of a barrage of questions from Michael, it hits her: how will she answer? There's so much about her family she doesn't know. The only sure thing is that they are her family; they love her, and she loves them. Maybe that's all she needs to know.

§

Michael is here, at the Seetos. He's still getting over the fact she's included him. He's watching and learning and liking what he sees.

And there's his girl. Well, is she his girl? Feels as though she is, but he's still not sure of anything. There's that one digit, her thumb again, curled up near her mouth. Cute. But he knows that look. Means something's on her mind. Like, yeah. No one believes the unconvincing story she's handed out about her interstellar visit to another planet, nor her explanation for throwing in the job she loved and every other strange thing she's done. But to be back here in the inner circle makes him happy. Patience will be his motto. He knows what it feels like to be outside and he doesn't want to be there ever again.

What a strange but lovely creature she is. She's sitting next to her mother who's animated as she talks, wagging a finger, pointing to individuals, laughing, and he's watching the star of the show from where he's sitting, across the garden. Francie gives her mum a weak smile, lacking her sparkle and engagement. To him, that confirms her behaviour is bogus, this 'the world is great' impression she's been delivering. For whose sake? His? Or the family? Or for herself? Wonder if her mother knows she's not listening. Probably does. Probably, as it is clear to everyone and to especially him, Mum's not willing to push too hard, not willing to risk losing her again. He's thankful for the opportunity to meet her family. At last. They're how he imagined them to be. Bits of Francie appearing and disappearing in them, in different shapes and forms: beautiful, welcoming, and they share his kind of humour, so he feels right at home. It's great they haven't kicked him out yet. They might have blamed him for Francie's… what? Weeks of weirdness? Her un-Francie-like behaviour? There's tonnes of food. Francie's grandmother's the best. Got eyes sharp as a hawk. Surprising blue eyes that miss nothing. Bet she's got Francie's number, or is close to discovering it. Maybe it is just to do with uni, graduation coming up, pressure, and so on, like she says. Nah. It's not.

What he sees with a clarity that almost surprises him is the many shades of the girl he knows he loves. All those separate pieces of her, each biting into his heart, have come together within the collective that is her family. This is her world and this is the real Francie, not the modern universal woman she displays outside of this place. He's seeing the parts of her that, until now, he couldn't comprehend and yet burned to know shining in pure brilliance. The mystery of her is making sense to him. And out of the insights the night has brought him comes certainty. This is his one true love, regardless of how she feels about him. She's spoilt him. For him, she has set a standard too high for anyone else to measure up to, should she discard him and should he be doing the one thing he cannot imagine he would wish to do, and that is to be looking for a replacement. As that daunting possibility passes through his consciousness, a chill of dread and fear runs down his spine. Been there, done that. Not again. Please. His eyes lift to the sky, as if he is appealing to some higher authority.

15

MARIA'S HOME
Late in the evening, 16th September

Maria sinks into an armchair. Leftovers have been cling-wrapped and refrigerated. Chicken bones gnawed bare and globs of rice scraped from plates into waste bins. Dishes washed and dried. Kitchen restored. Everyone moves to the television. There's a scheduled documentary about the path to Independence. It's the habit of those with any links whatsoever to PNG, familiar or otherwise with the history, to watch anything about the region. An immigrant thing, perhaps. Something that promotes an almost fraudulent sense of national pride. Probably the Vietnamese migrants watch or read anything about their former homeland, or the British about the Royals and the United Kingdom, and the Greeks about their burgeoning debt crisis. Her family despite the mix of their racial ancestry can only turn to PNG to explain their identity as migrant Australians, and that's a fragile connection because their ancestors were always only temporary residents even if some families' ancestors had been living in New Guinea for almost a century. As hers have.

The documentary has begun. First, the usual: the touted Leahy Brothers and gold mining; next news footage of a western dignitary visiting the Mount Hagen Cultural Show. The man wanders from one feathered and painted group to the next, then the dancing begins. Gabriel copies the singsing dancers by tucking a tea towel into the waist of his jeans and bouncing across the room, two feet thumping the floor, his mouth chanting 'whoa whoa whoa'. The children laugh at his foolery. Maria worries what the enthusiastic dancer may break. Then, modern trekkers reliving Kokoda, their adventures in colour interspersed with black and white footage of wounded Aussie diggers, knee-deep in mud with frequent mention of the

'Fuzzy-wuzzy Angels', footage of Rabaul, the ABC's coverage of the 1994 eruption, with before-and-after shots of Chinatown, the part of town buried the deepest, archival shots of trade stores, of people leaning in doorways, of the dancing Chinese dragons. Familiar images. Andy darts forward to the screen and back to the sofa, his finger instructing. He's the self-proclaimed expert, the one who remembers, but he's neither.

'See. See. Chinatown. Where Mum and Dad lived.'

Andy recognises a face. 'Oh, lukim yupela, see, it's Julius. My mistake, Sir Julius. Sori-tu-much-ia. Mi should toktok ex-Mr-Prime-Minister, Sir Julius Chan. Before, he was only a pencil-pusher for Treasury Department, a baseball player, someone's friend. Em tasol.'

Nathaniel looks over at his grandmother and says, 'Uncle Andrew doesn't know Sir Julius, does he Grandma?' She lifts her eyebrows and gives him a smile that is conspiratorial, yet non-committal. 'Aww, come on Uncle, you don't.' She knows that for Andy it's not 'knowing' Sir Julius Chan that's important to Andrew. His connection, remote as it may be is the knowledge that Sir Julius has a Chinese father and had lived in Rabaul. Similar history to Andrew's. That makes them kin in Andrew's perspective.

Through the drone of the television commentary she can hear her family's 'oohs' and 'aahs'. These are the tales reiterated year in, year out, as though the ones here had lived them, reactions that Maria might find comforting, as if her family are attempting to remain connected, but this evening they sound hollow. They remind Maria that she has failed. As she sinks into her self-loathing, the phone rings. It sounds far away, almost in a different world to the one she's in. Her head is buzzing. She looks at her family sitting on sofas or curled up on cushions on the floor, their eyes intent on the screen. They're unaware of how false this is.

'Oh Maria, you have forgotten your grandmama's wisdom. She toktok yu: always remember. You and your secrets. Now see what happens? Your boys. You couldn't bear to discuss the past. Now they only know this same-old Aussie history, this television history, the one that everyone knows. Not your history, not their history. Not your ancestors, not how we came to belong in Rabaul, how we became us. Kokoda is Australia being proud. Their soldiers, so brave. But when do we learn why they evacuated the Australians from Rabaul before the Japanese invaded and occupied Rabaul, and how they left us there? There's the history of New Guinea tribes' transition to self-government and Australia's part. But where are we? We need to hear our stories. But who is the person who hasn't told them?'

Her gut twists. Regret drags on her. She imagines her grandmother's stories left in the gutter of a Rabaul street, abandoned, a consequence of her granddaughter's neglect. The stories she should have retold, the ones to which she should have added, washed away in a tropical downpour and trodden into the earth by the footsteps of others with louder and more important stories to tell. These, on the screen. She slips back into her childhood. Nenek is whispering, 'Always remember Ria.'

A hand grips her shoulder. Is it Nenek? No. No. It's Andy.

'Are you okay, Mum? You don't look well.'

'Just dozing, son. If I was as wise as I like to pretend I am, I would have taken myself to bed. Before now.'

Andy holds the phone out towards her.

'First you have to take this call. Big surprise. It's PNG. It's Uncle Henry.'

§

For Francine, it has been a long evening, yet as tired as she is, she's adamant the dreaded conversation with Michael will happen before he leaves. If she doesn't do it tonight, soon it will be too late. The issue will be irretrievable. How could she explain taking so long about something like this?

He is ready to leave. This is it. She walks out through the front door and, on Ah Ma's beloved verandah they stop, side by side. She sits down on the step, looks up at Michael and pats the floor, and he folds up his long legs so he can sit beside her. There are centimetres of space between them, and yet she can feel heat radiating from his body. At first, he hesitates, seems nervous, but an assuredness seeps out of him and he turns towards her, holds her gaze and places his right hand over her left hand as it cups her knee. The world is as it should be, and her earlier edginess is calmed. He turns to the front, and they both gaze out into the darkness of Ah Ma's front garden.

Cars drive up and down the street, their headlights temporarily interrupting early morning dimness. Faint voices of the few that remain inside the house waft in and out. Probably still talking about the surprise phone call. Or not even that. Probably just dealing out trivia, as is the norm. She clears her throat and turns towards him. He looks to her, smiles, and then turns back into the nothingness ahead of them. She feels his uneasiness return. As if he fears her intention. Minutes drag, and she tries again. This time neither looks at the other, the words she has to say are just thrown out there, for anyone to hear.

'Michael. Thanks for being patient with me. I know I've been a bitch.'

'You a bitch? No never.' He tries to laugh but it comes out sounding weird.

Inside, a chair scrapes on the floor as if someone is pushing it back to stand. Michael half turns, looks to the door, and then says, 'Hey, it's late. I should go.'

'No, please, Michael. Stay.' She nods towards the interior and say 'They'll be there for ages. They've forgotten they have work tomorrow.'

'Oh, okay. If you are sure?'

'Well, actually, Michael. I have something I need to tell you.'

His expression freezes. She tells herself she truly is a bitch. It's cruel to make him suffer, wondering what the heck is going on. He's half standing, still bowed over. She reaches up and takes his hand, staring into his face.

'Please, sit, stay.'

He eases himself back down beside her, his face overwritten with uncertainty. She strokes his hands and looks deep into his eyes. Even in the limited light their blueness and kindness is apparent. But she can see the pain she's caused him. He's uncertain of her, uncertain of where he stands, doesn't know how to react. She has to tell him so he can find his way, too, like she found hers.

He's not as close as before, as if he's preparing himself for separation. She wants, no, she needs to feel his warmth once more. As if he has sensed her desire, or perhaps because he needs the same closeness, he bends his head towards her, and she feels the weight of his arm around her shoulder as he shuffles his bottom closer to her on the step, never once breaking their gaze. This time his left hand crosses her body to enclose her right one. She's wrapped within his two arms.

'Take your time. I'm here. I can wait until you are ready.'

This is her Michael. To her it sounds as though he's saying, 'I can take whatever it is you will say, painful or otherwise. I am ready.'

She looks down at their interlocked hands on her lap, the sight of his fingers entwined with hers reassures her. They are bound. He'll not disappoint her.

'I was a bitch, Michael., even if you are polite and say I wasn't. Worse,

I lied to you when I said it was uni pressures. Poor excuse. You would have seen through me. You probably did but had no other explanation unless I offered you one. And I didn't. This has nothing to do with working at Cezanne's or Elisa and Gail or you. The truth is, it's me who's wrong. And I am wrong purely because of the kind of person I am and how I deal with things. I'm stupid; I'm a reactionary; I'm a control-freak – you name the flaw and more than likely I can claim it. I try to be perfect. Too perfect. I want my life to follow a textbook path, to be able to make a plan and stick to it and can't handle when something changes. I need to learn to be flexible. And I measure myself by how close I am to the strategies I have worked out and thrash myself when I miss the goal. You know all this about me.'

She searches his face for a reaction, but it is calm Michael, reassuring Michael, that looks back and yet there is a small wrinkle across his forehead that shows despite his patience, he is anxious.

She continues. 'Yet you put up with me. I also struggle to take others' help. There's only one way for me and that's being independent and solving everything in my head. So something has happened that blew my plans out of the water. Not necessarily a bad thing but because I am who I am I didn't deal with it appropriately. The truth is I now realise I need others' help. I've always had it but took it for granted. And what I have learnt about myself, despite my outward act, I can't bear being alone and independent, not really. I probably, if the truth's known, always need an audience.'

She smiles, hoping he sees the comedy of this, though it's serious.

'I see how much I need others and how worthwhile it is to involve others. I'm just late to mature. I do need others. I need you. I really need you. Without you, I am nothing.' Her right hand reaches over and pats him on the chest and then she twist so she can bury her head into his shoulder. And from that location comes the muffled reinforcement of her declaration. 'I can't do anything without you. I am stupid and insensitive.'

'So, is this the big news? Because,' he says, smiling back at her. 'I already know this.'

She punches him with her free hand and he feigns injury.

Her serious mask is now back on. She has to do it. Must do it. Now. No delays. But rehearsing the phrase in her head makes it sound harsh, tainted, and the words refuse to come out. Uttering that phrase is going to begin the writing of a whole new life for both her and for Michael, together or apart. Can she say what she has to tell him just using those three short words in one abrupt but indisputable sentence? No cushioning, no preamble? Straight out there, as blunt as it comes? Is that method too cruel? She can see no other way. Messing around might be even more cruel. Whichever way she does the job, it will be a shock. And then, there it is. The phrase.

'I'm pregnant.'

Her eyes search his face. They aren't calm blue ones but frantic, questioning ones. She can read them clearly. Why is she telling him this now, so late? What does she want back from him? What can he do; how can he do what's needed? What's the right thing to do?

She counsels herself. She has had time to take this in. He hasn't. Don't expect the perfect response. Give him time. And even if he were to respond in a way that to her might be measured as perfect, what would that be? She doesn't know what she wants from him and yet she does. What if he just smiles? No. That would feel as if he's trivialising or play-acting or struck dumb. Then what? Neither can she predict how she will react to any or all kinds of responses. Maybe nothing he does will please her. Will she resort to anger? Or resignation? Will she, conceding her own mismanagement, accept whatever happens as inevitable?

The only thing she is sure about is that she's terrified. She fears her mismanagement is going to cost her something precious. She knows she can find a way through having a baby whether with him or not. That's just practical or economic considerations. But to lose him? Because she was stupid?

She sees the shock rippling across his face. He's working hard to not make the wrong move, not to say the wrong thing, as he takes in what she's said. But she can see he thinks he's failing. Will he say, 'That's it, we're done, this isn't what I want. I didn't sign up for this.'?

She hears air exhaled, a sigh deeper than normal. She's shocked when he lets her hand go and withdraws his arm from her shoulder. Is this it? His hands move to the sides of his head. She can't speak. Even if she knew what she might say. The waiting is intolerable. But wait is what she knows she must do. To be fair to him. She wants to cry but acknowledges that would not be the right thing to do, so she cries inwardly, cries for the potential loss she fears is minutes away. Then he lifts his head and turns towards her. She searches his face and sees only calmness and a tiny smile that he's failing to keep under control, but also tears on his cheeks. He's crying, undisguised, free-flowing streams of water, crying no less than he did on the day she turned up at his father's home after Jake's suicide, and the weight of the likely loss of him becomes heavier. This is the man she loves. Is this to him a tragedy of equal proportions to that of Jake's suicide? She hears him swallow, sounding almost as if he's drowning. He turns away, wipes his face with the back of his hands, and when he turns back, he's smiling again. There's not a frown on his forehead or a tightness to his mouth, and when he speaks, his voice although croaky and rough, like before when he joked earlier about her bitchiness, is softer and sure.

'Oh shit, this explains a lot. But Francie, so sorry, everything you planned down shit creek, all your dreams, and my fault.'

Is that it? Is it over between them?

He gets up from the step and she thinks he's going to leave. A spurt of anger fires off in her head. Before she lets loose, he turns around to face her and kneels on a step below hers as he takes hold of both her hands and lifts them up to his lips, like some scene out of a romance movie. His eyes lock into her eyes. She thinks they are searching for answers. No. That's not what he's doing. He drops his eyes, searching on the step on which he's kneeling for the words he needs. She holds her breath, preparing herself for the worst. His words tumble out.

'How do you feel, I mean, oh hell? What can I say? I don't know what's right to say. Except, God, I thought it would be something far worse, like you were kicking me out. Oh God. I am doing a rotten job here because I shouldn't be saying there might be something worse. Hell, for you, this might be the worst thing you could face, ever. The end of your dreams. I am not the one whose body is pregnant so how can I judge what's worse or what's better? Yeah, I am involved – well, I am, aren't I?' He spits out a weak giggle. 'But all the shit will come your way. No avoiding that.' Another nervous twitter. 'Uni, parents, baby or…?'

He grabs her with force, pulls her to standing position, steps in close and locks his arms around her. Once he has her inside his embrace, he pulls her face to his chest. Over her shoulder, his breathing is irregular, as if he's holding it and then letting it out in a rush. Tremors move through his body. Is he crying? She is. She surprises herself by something that feels like anger rising up from her stomach. Why is she angry? Is it with him or with herself? She can't understand why he's crying. Does he feel trapped? Or is he panicking? Wild assumptions flood her, none flattering to Michael even though she knows they are coming out of her own fears not his actions. This is a reaction to the releasing of pent-up emotions. She's angry, relieved, frustrated, fearful, and strangely in some small way elated. Nothing is rational. Her body relaxes. She's done what she needed to do, which was tell him, and now, for better or worse, whether a sad or happy ending, or together or apart, they just have to work on solutions. Her practical self is back in balance.

As she waits for him to come to the same conclusion, she returns to worrying about losing him. That's something over which she has little control. That's the price she might have to pay. Already she is grieving his loss. As a huge wave of sadness for that empty future wells up within her, she hears his voice from over her shoulder. It's throaty, as if he has to wrench his words out of his mouth.

'Is it wrong for me to feel happy? This is our baby, yours and mine, and that can't be wrong? It can't be, can it?'

Now it's her turn to find speaking difficult, so she says nothing and the silence grows between them, first in an awkward way as though he has assumed she doesn't like what he said, and then as she relaxes into him, letting her body do her talking, they grip each other and do not move. As if they are glued together, or, as it feels to her, they have become one. Inside her is a huge traffic jam of words and feelings wanting to rush out. Which one first? Minutes tick by. Again, in an alien voice devoid of expression, as if he's saying what he needs to say but they're scripted lines and he's not sure how they will be received, wanting them to be heard but scared of the wrong kind of reception.

'Should I be asking if you want to do something, like, ah, an abortion?' The words rush out followed by an almighty gasp. He unwinds himself, places his hands on her face and holds it in front of his, sufficiently far away to allow him to look into her eyes. She sees his pain. She convinces herself she can't interpret what his thoughts might be. Perhaps, she asks herself, you're afraid to discover. He's kissing her forehead, her cheeks, and at last he finds her lips.

'Please, no,' he whispers.

Tears pour from her eyes and his. She can taste their blended saltiness on her lips, her tears and his.

'An abortion?' He repeats in a normal voice, holding her out again to see her face. Allowing her to choose. Again, she can't answer. She's numb. Does he mean this? Oh, she'd never have predicted this. His face crumbles, his head drops, and now, again, it's him crying.

'Please, if you need, yes, but… Our baby, Francie. Our baby. Can't we make this work? Can't we find a way so it's not all on you? Our families, I know they will help. I am sure we can do this. I want to if you do. And you can graduate and do everything you planned… we can do it, but it's your call. Absolutely.'

Oh, yes, he is who she thought he was. He's still holding her face, still staring into her eyes.

'I mean it. Your decision. You tell me, and that's what we will do.'

The fear has gone. They can do this.

16

SOUTH-EAST SUBURBS OF BRISBANE
October 28, 2010

Andy's in his backyard. It's a beautiful Brisbane Saturday. Been up since six, doing chores. His body is thin and supple for fifty-odd. It bends easily at the waist as he reaches to pick up timber short ends a piece at a time and tosses them into a neat pile in a corner between the house and shed. Timber upon timber sounds musical and vaguely familiar to his ears, like an echo of something he once knew, echoes of his life before Australia. Of New Guineans playing Lucky, risking their tobacco issue on a 'lucky' fall of the cards. Always someone playing a guitar and another beating out percussion on a peculiar cross of timber with metal bottle tops nailed on it. Everything feels right as he builds a rhythm, picking up and tossing, and he keeps the music in his head going on and on. He's feeling good, productive, and a smile is trying not to show itself.

He sees Kathy come out of the house, waving her arms and her mouth is moving. He's off his rhythm, now, as he tries to understand his wife.

'Gabe's on the phone. Mum's missing.'

Gabriel? What the hell? Mum can't be missing. She's always there.

§

Francine is rattling around in her grandmother's bedroom. Earlier, when her father called, she had been watching a doco that follows the path of the new Australian government sworn in during August, something she had missed because during that month she was living only in her own head. She knew it had happened, but didn't have enough interest in the outside world to take in the details. On screen, as she watched the retrospective news, she saw the new PM, the redheaded female one, being introduced, followed by the Governor General's swearing in. Though Julia Gillard has secured an electoral mandate in her own right, will she survive as Prime Minister? A violent takeover makes her future shaky. Those men standing behind her with tight smiles are not her friends. Are they holding the swords that will decapitate her when they are ready and able to grab power?

There's a lot of shakiness going around lately. Who would have thought solid, reliable Ah Ma could become shaky? Left her home, the place she said she's never leaving except in a box. No one wants to consider their mortality and yet, when you think about it, it's the only certainty we all share. Gran's packed a bag, taken her passport, and headed to PNG. Everyone's as stunned as they were when Julia kicked out Kevin. Today, in her real life, not the one that involves politics and television, it's her job to find clues. About that disappearance.

Feels strange, no, weird, to enter the inner sanctum of Gran's bedroom, though it was once hers to share with her grandparents.

A whiff of sandalwood. Or is it camphor? Sheets of paper scattered, white and cream autumn leaves that whisper 'No one is here.' Where are you Grandma? Under her fingertips, the soft ridge of the nearly threadbare chenille bedspread settles her momentarily. This has been on her grandmother's bed for as long as she can remember. Six again, and Ah Ma's and Yeh Yeh's bodies are bumps beneath its pale greenness. She has the top bunk and her brother the lower one and their bunk is at the foot of her grandparents' double bed. She's a bird looking down, an angel from on high, watching those bumps slowly, methodically, rise and fall, rise and fall. She's safe. Surrounded by love. Other kids are proud of having a bedroom of their own. But they don't know what they are missing: the privilege, the comfort, the security, of sharing a bedroom with your grandparents and a brother.

Today the bed is empty.

'You found something, Francine?'

'A mess is what I've found, an un-Grandma-like mess.'

'Got to be a break-in. Some crook's taken her with him.'

'How's he getting a big woman like Mum out of this house, Andrew mate? You'd need a crane and a hefty chain. And if she didn't want to go… man there'd be blood everywhere. Use your brains. She's gone somewhere on her own two wobbly legs. Must have been looking for something, couldn't find it and now gone elsewhere to find it, or found it and taken it with her in a hurry.'

As certain as her father is this walkout has come out of Henry's phone call on Independence Day, he's confused because the one certain thing he knows is that his mother has not had contact with her brother Henry not even when they were children. His biggest question is, why didn't his mother tell everyone? Why didn't she tell him? It doesn't seem right somehow.

'But why, Gabe? Why would she return to PNG? What could Henry have said that made her want to go?'

Francine intervenes.

'Dad, please, calm down. There must be a clue in all this mess. For a start, Gran must have been in a big hurry judging by this mess. Sooo not her. I'll look for clues. You and Uncle Gabe go ring around and see what you can find. Someone in the ex-New Guinea mob will know. They know everything. Even before it happens.'

And, to herself she vows, 'I will get this room back to how Gran likes it.'

No clues are to be found. This chaos is upsetting in its unexpectedness. Knots coil tighter in her gut. Oh Gran, what does this mean? Please be safe.

There are other notable absences in this house: those who are always here, the ones always here, so much so she hasn't considered non-appearances as significant. Has anyone? Has everyone been so caught up with a missing mother/grandmother they haven't noticed a missing family?

She shouts from Gran's bedroom, 'Dad, has anyone called Uncle Daniel?'

Aunty Anna and Uncle Daniel's first holiday ever, first time away from home, which also means Gran's first time alone in this house, and she's done this. Not good. Aunt and Uncle will blame themselves. Or everyone else will blame them.

And then there are her own emotions, not what she might expect of herself. What about you, smug young lady? How about some guilt on your part? Sure, you are afraid for your grandma, but admit it, deep down there's that tiny snickering, sniffling, sense of relief. The one that gives you an almost valid-sounding excuse: to do what she had intended to do today would be wrong. Only Gran's location and safety is important. Another day or two won't hurt. No need to tell them yet. No need to add to their worries. She has Michael. Michael is her rock. But these declarations have lost their resonance because the reality in which all that had felt stable has shown itself to be untrue, dependent as they are on Gran being always here, her family remaining intact and readily available to her nearby, with the outside world of chaos beyond them. Now she wonders if she has based her assumptions on part truths, and the truth is nothing has ever been consistent and secure. Gran's disappearance has opened the door to glimpse into the world she had not been aware of or had always ignored. Now, as she stands outside the door looking from outside in, she feels as if she's an alien in that once secure world, and the group of people she loves, and who she's always known to love her back, have transformed into individuals whose different histories are now clear. There's no way to hide from the reality that these histories are beyond her reach, these strange and unspoken histories and yet, she realises with clarity those pasts, whether known or unknown, are certain to influence her perception of each of those she loves, of herself, and theirs of her and of her lived world. Without her usual unshakable confidence in who they are and who she is, she has become unsure of everything.

Francine's trembling. 'Ah Ma, you have shaken my world.'

PART 4
PAPUA NEW GUINEA

1

HENRY SEETO'S HOME, VUNATAGIA, EAST NEW BRITAIN, PNG
August 2010

Maria. His sister. He's not uttered that name or thought about that relationship for a long time. Some might say, for too many years. But it's his choice she's been taboo. Of late though he can't stop thinking about her. Should be expected, he guesses, as everything about him is falling apart. Why wouldn't his control over his subconscious also break down? And it is. Strange notions pop into his thinking at the oddest of times. If things were normal, he'd never allow even a tiny contemplation of his sister or any of that other family to squeeze in unless it was accompanied by anger. But lately, when there's nothing else to think about, there's Maria, and as much, as he wants to deny it, these flashes invite in him a sense of nostalgia. This Maria is the child Maria. And, he argues with himself, of course this would be the one he sees because he has a lot of questions to ask her. He's had them all his life. But because he wouldn't allow himself to give any time to Maria, then, of course, there's no one to which he can direct the questions. And he's avoiding the pain that he anticipates will come by asking them, or hearing the answers, which he thinks he knows but dreads. He slams the slightly opened door shut with the declaration they, especially Maria, are the enemy.

There's one unavoidable question that rolls around, rattling him. Must have worn a groove inside his head, he reckons, he's heard it so many times. 'Why, Maria, were you allowed to stay with mumma Josefina and Daddy-George but I had to leave?'

Perhaps he's dying. That might explain everything. Especially the breaking down of his barrier around Maria. He's heard dying people become delusional and their bodies do weird things and that's him at the moment. Not only does he have these rogue thoughts but also his body sweats too much, he's lost a taste for food he's always loved, even fish and he's survived on fish most of his life, and he has a too frequent need for the toilet. Even his Tolai friends notice this last one.

'Ah Henry, yu sick.'

It feels like he's been betrayed by a friend, an amalgam of his body and mind. He counsels himself that maybe this is something he needs to accept. He's no longer a pikinini. Only a few of his friends have lived to 73, like he has. Can't go on forever. But it's depressing to give up like that.

His son's diagnosis: 'Papa, you can't sleep at night because you are a lazy man all day.'

True, true. Ling's right. Most days he does little. But it's not the lack of sleep that worries him. It's the dreams.

If Ling's worried, he's petrified. If he's dying soon, he doesn't want to spend eternity as he's lived his life. And that's where Maria comes in. If he's changing the pattern of his afterlife, then Maria is a roadblock he must deal with. She holds the key, the one that might open a peaceful afterlife for him.

That's a far too rocky road to tread so he goes back to contemplating Ling's theory. Perhaps Ling is right on the money. He dozes too much during the day and then doesn't sleep so well at night. Or if he sleeps, it's too deep, and he wakes in terror, trembling and clawing his way out of a mad, violent dream. There's always a faceless woman in them. She's facing him and he, her, with a void between them. No clues as to where they are or what they are doing. When he wakes, even if he can't remember the actions being played out, what remains is a sense of two certainties: one, of emotional weariness, and two, that the woman is without doubt Maria, as illogical as these convictions seem in his waking state. Another conflict within these certainties is that when he recalls his dream, Maria is childlike in her actions and yet an adult in body. A tall thin dark woman with jet black hair streaming out behind her and deep black eyes. The regularity and consistency of this dream disturbs him, and for a good part of the day that follows he tries to rationalise it. Unfinished business. That's how he defines it. Forget all this symbolism rubbish. It's clear cut. He's thinking too much about the past, still blames Maria, and needs these matters resolved before he dies. He sees childlike behaviour because he doesn't know the adult woman Maria. And when it comes right down to it, as she's older than him though he's not sure by how much, there's a good chance she's already passed and that means he has no chance of working things out, so he might as well accustom himself to being tortured throughout eternity. Maybe this dream is a means for the spirits to tell him exactly that. Maria is dead and you, man, are doomed.

He distrusts the dream. He can rationalise the bit about Maria but there's another part that doesn't work for him. In his dream, he's an angry, violent man. The dream makes him believe what he's seeing is real but that's not the man he knows himself to be. It goes against his ideas of himself to dream he's that kind of man. He asked Ling what he thought about interpreting dreams. Ling, whose education is much better than his father's, says, 'Don't forget Dad that dreams are only the subconscious grabbing fragments of significant memory to tease out the nagging whispers we try to suppress.' In his own teasing out of this dream, his analysis is that it's illogical: the angry man of his dream can't be him. But he's not sure because while he doesn't show his anger, he knows that there's something rattling away inside. But this dream-man's anger is repugnant. It's fiery, and seeing that makes Henry feel uncomfortable. Anger is what he saw in his father. He was scared of it. How could someone be so brutal to someone else? When he gets angry, he works hard to suppress it. As he tells himself, 'I'd rather eat my anger than show it.' Had he been another man, the dream-man or his father, a man who wants badly to resolve whatever anger issues he holds, the crate that's still at the foot of his bed, six years on from when it arrived, is the perfect tool for him. It's hers. Maria's. He could send it on, or he could open it. And claim it as compensation. Either way he's done nothing, neither use it as an excuse to face his sister or to be vindictive. Either choice would mean that at least he would be taking action. But what's he do? Nothing.

2

VUNTAGIA, EAST NEW BRITAIN (ENB), PNG
Six years earlier, August 2004

It's 2004 and PNG is competing in the summer Olympics in Athens. Over the past few weeks Ling and his grand kids have been coming to Henry's home to watch television. Today, the kids are with their mum and Henry and his son are giving the television a rest. They are watching what he likes to call his own beachfront private big screen: the real life one that looks out over the harbour.

'Man, pops, hate to say it but it's such a luxury to sit here in peace. I mean, kids are great but, man, can they talk a lot? Too many things to argue about.'

He's about to agree when they hear someone calling from the roadside.

'Eh, masta, you savy some pela nam bilong em Seeto Wei?'

Ling looks at his father. Neither of them moves or speaks, unsure if announcing any relationship with a man called Seeto Wei will bring anything but bad outcomes. The voice continues.

'Excuse me, masta, I bin told to come here for Seeto Wei.'

Ling sucks in his breath, unable to ignore the call, and pulls himself out of the deckchair. He saunters across the lawn and around the side of the house. After disappearing for a few seconds, his face appears once more, looking back at his father with a quizzical stare.

Hoping for some support, Henry decides. But he'll let his boy work this out. Good chance it'll end in tears, and trouble's not his thing.

Ling takes longer than expected to return. Henry clucks his tongue, reprimanding himself for not going with him, though in all honesty he didn't want to. Or he should have been firmer, ordering his son not to respond. Too late now.

He follows the path his son took. When he turns the corner beyond which Ling had disappeared from sight, he hears Ling talking, and someone else replying. Nothing discernible, but at least it doesn't sound aggressive. No shouting. That's a relief. He creeps along the path until he comes to the next corner, pauses, and pokes his head around. Childish behaviour, he chides himself. There's Ling with a woman. Looks like she might be Tolai, so possibly, he deciphers, a local woman. She has bleached her hair, as these village women like to do for a reason he can't fathom. His wife Rachel used to do it too and she bleached their daughter's hair as well. The woman's dress suggests this visit isn't official. Her clothes look well-worn or are working clothes. He judges her. 'Not displaying suitable respect, coming to his home dressed like that.' His ears tell him Ling and the woman are conversing in Kuanua. Yes. He's right: she's Tolai. She's pointing her finger and waving her hand. Talking a lot. As the village women like to do when they converse. He watches as she and Ling walk towards the road, and the woman gestures. Is someone waiting a little farther along the road? Next, she points to his home. Together Ling and the woman walk back towards the house, still talking.

Ling notices him.

'Oi Dad, come here. Do you know someone called Seeto Chun Yuen, or Uncle Stephen? Yeh Yeh's little brother. I didn't know Grandpa had a little brother, or that I even had an uncle except the step-uncles like Solomon and his brothers.'

What the...? Where did this come from? He obeys his son's finger gestures and joins the pair. He doesn't permit his eyes to meet with the woman's, hoping perhaps this – inconvenience? –will disappear if he can't see her, yet he's somewhat curious, all the same.

'This meri—sori tumuchia, wonem nam bilong yu? – oh, that's right, it's Sara. Sara She didn't want Yeh Yeh at all. She wanted Seeto Wei's son. You. Sara, here, is haus meri for this man Stephen Seeto, and he is sending you a crate.' Ling waves his arm as a beat-up rusty truck rumbles its way off Kokopo Road towards Henry's home. 'According to Sara, her masta wants you to ship this to your sister. What's inside belongs to her.'

'Diu.' He's even shocked himself by using this Cantonese swearword. And yet he repeats it under his breath in English, 'Fuck.'. What the hell is happening here? What makes this Stephen, who isn't unknown to him but who is someone he doesn't 'know', think just because he's her brother, that he has any knowledge of his sister? Or what makes him think he has any desire to do anything for her or him, especially not any favours?

His son's face tells him Ling knows some Cantonese.

'Are you swearing, Dad? This is getting interesting by the minute.'

'Sorry. I don't get it. What's this got to do with me?'

'Well, Sara says she has plenty of money to give you so you can send this crate to your sister. She says the crate is protecting something precious that belongs to your sister and her masta says it is time for your sister to have this returned to her. She also has your sister's contact details in Brisbane. Her masta has told her what to say. Her words: "He knows you are a man of the world who knows who can do this for you." He's up-to-date, knows I work in shipping, Dad. Look, I can do it for you. No problems. But first we have to take this crate off the truck and store it. The paperwork can come later. Before it can be shipped, we'll need to know what's inside, for Aussie Customs. Okay, Dad? Crate inside, and the rest later.'

Ling's face is lit up like a schoolboy given the day off to go fishing.

'This is great. I forgot all about our Australian family. We got an address now,' he says waving the notepaper Sara had given him. 'We can get in touch. Oh, this is fantastic.'

Henry's struck dumb and unable to respond. His brain has become lost somewhere between, only moments ago, when he'd been enjoying the peace, and now, here, at the front of his home, where his world has turned upside down. For a start, who wants to get in touch? And he doesn't want to get caught up with this, this, complication. No way.

Ling takes charge. Several men, who had been relaxing on the tray of the truck around the edge of the crate, clearly awaiting their instructions, respond to Sara's finger. Some jump to the ground, others remain on the tray. There's a lot of noise as they move the crate closer to one side of the tray so that it's in a better position for lifting from the truck. The grunting and moaning become louder as those on the ground take the fully weight and wait for the others to clamber down and share the burden. With all six now able to heft the crate upwards to their shoulders, like pallbearers they head to Henry's front door. This invasion flabbergasts Henry. This thing is entering his home.

At least the woman's clothing makes sense now. She wasn't being disrespectful. They are working clothes.

'Come on Dad, show us where you want this stashed.'

Somehow, a rectangular, rough-timber crate now makes its home in precious floor space at the foot of his bed.

Meanwhile, Ling's getting Sara and the men drinks and food as he continues to chat with Sara. Ling has a thousand questions for her but is gaining no real information.

'Masta he lapun tru,' says Sara. 'He toktok he brother long your grandpa.'

Henry finds his tongue. 'Not a brother. They come from the same village in China.'

He doesn't want to talk about his father, so he snatches the mug of tea Ling offers him before sitting, and attempts to look as if he's got no interest whatsoever in Sara's gossip.

'Masta Stephen, he enjoys drawing pictures. Oh, many pictures. He lives long Warangoi and now he gives you this, he moving long Kavieng.'

As he listens to Sara's and Ling's conversation, he looks back towards his bedroom, and stares at the tomb that now resides there. Why? Why did he let this happen? That's the stupid man he is. Never protests. Just lets this… thing. Into his home. With all its associated complications and obligations. His head's bursting with unappealing possibilities.

In an internal show of resistance, he makes a private declaration. Might not send this to Maria. Why should she get this? Looks like it's something important, so it begs the question, how come Stephen has something that belongs to Maria? What's his connection to Maria? What does he know about his sister? And one obvious question: why hasn't he sent it to Maria himself?

Before she leaves, Sara says to him: 'Oh, me lusim. Masta, he tok me, not to forget. Masta belong me toktok this belong your sister.' She waves a scroll of yellow paper. 'He thinks if you are the one sending it to her, masta shakes his finger when he toktok, "she gets two good things in one." Me no savy long what he toktok but he tell me this.'

Ling raises his eyebrows as if he's thinking 'Interesting.' The smirk spreading across his face means this business with Sara has converted him into a detective. He'll be looking for clues and trying to decide if his father knows more than he's telling. There will be no peace. He'll dig and dig until he winkles something out of all this.

Later he says to his father, 'Well, what's this all about? Are we opening it or sending it?'

'Don't want to talk. Let it go for now. Just leave it where it is.'

'Hey, yeah, sure pops. But it's taking a big chunk out of your bedroom. You don't want to leave it too long. Let me know what you want, and I will do it. And, hey, here's your wad of cash and the details. Omigod, there's got to be a huge story here. We will have to open it sometime because we will have to sign a customs declaration which we can't do if we don't know its contents.' Ling's smile broadens. 'Wonder what the hell's inside. If it contains old Chinese gold, the Aussie Customs will have a field day. Ha.'

Ling is still sparking with this new focus when he leaves to go to his own home.

3

VUNATAGIA, ENB
August 2010

Ling asks every year: 'When are we shipping it, Dad?' The crate has yet to be opened. And Henry's made it quite clear that Ling is not to make contact until a decision about the crate is made. Ling has a strong opinion on this, but he won't go against his father. Henry's depending on this. Otherwise, matters could get well out of hand.

Is it spite that stops him sending it? Does he think what's inside should be his, a reward for his life of deprivation, compensation for his losses? Or is he afraid that this will be a Pandora's box? He's recognising this crate is one of the many obstacles stopping his smooth transition into the other life. Maria and this crate are weighing him down. He lacks the guts to either open it or to say to Ling, 'Yes, son, ship it.' Let Ling look inside and write out the declaration, if he must, and then he will be distanced from it. And the issue has grown larger as now Stephen's dead. Died towards the end of 2008. Where did those years go, between 2004 when the crate arrived, and 2008 when Stephen died, and now it's 2010 and still no action? Stephen's another ghost that will haunt him in the afterlife. 'Why didn't you do as you promised, Henry? Why?' Well, he didn't promise. He had the crate foisted on him. If anyone 'promised' it was Ling. He does try to summon the courage to open it, urging himself with the fact that sometime he's got make the final choice: open it and not send it or do the right thing. At this moment he's never sending it, is he? But in a minute or two that'll change. The money and the details are inside a shoe box that he's left sitting on top of the crate. There's the inconvenience as well, and this emphasises his stubbornness. He has to walk around the crate and the shoe box whenever he's in his bedroom. And why hasn't he opened the box? It has to be opened sometime, if only to do the customs declaration. As Ling says, they have to make a list of its contents. Or does he want to be spiteful? He doesn't comprehend his own behaviour. What's stopping him from letting Ling ship it? Maria means nothing to him. A stranger's crate left by another stranger, well almost a stranger. And that's a lie too. Both statements are lies to some degree. More weight to take into the afterlife. But still he does nothing. He neither satisfies his need to hit back nor rids himself of the cause of his resentment.

The rattle of metal and the drum of rubber on bitumen break through his rumination. He looks up and just above the hibiscus hedge that separates his property from Kokopo Road, a glimpse of the upper section of a rusty truck cab, then the tops of many heads, all curly-haired and swaying. A village truck. Several pass his home throughout the day. Despite the frequency, each passing surprises him. A hundred metres from his home to the right Kokopo Road bursts out from behind an embankment and then disappears around another corner two hundred metres to the left. From either direction, one minute there's no vehicle visible, no sound, then a flash of one and a roar, and then, once more, nothing. Nothing to see or hear but the wind in the palms. He'd always imagined that since the big eruption of 1994 there would be less traffic, considering there's only one place to go, to Rabaul, and he's convinced that place is only pretending to still be a town. But the traffic continues so others must see a different Rabaul to the one he sees. People still have somewhere to go or somewhere to come back from. Human resilience. Meanwhile, he sits and waits to die. The trucks and their noise are examples of how large or small events always surprise him. He can't understand why this is so. What others seem to understand is never clear to him. All his life he's been waiting for the fog to clear, for life to have meaning, for a feeling that there's a purpose to it and he has his role in it. But the news still hasn't reached him.

He's thinking about fishing again. Fishing and life go hand in hand for him. Until these past few years since he found it difficult to get in and out of the lakatoi, he would have fished at least once a day. Oh, there must have been days when fishing was impossible – weather, illness, somewhere else to go and other things to do – but none come to mind. The last time he saw his father involved fishing. Strange. As a kid he didn't think about its strangeness but now, in retrospect, it stands out large. Oh yeah, he attempts to emphasise the point. Everything stands out large. He's more and more convinced Death is preparing him ready to go to the next life.

4

HENRY'S STEP-MOTHER'S VILLAGE, VUNATAGIA, ENB, TPNG 1950

Brigid, Henry's Tolai step-mother, has known Henry and Henry's father, Seeto Wei, for eight years. Brigid was eighteen when her life became entangled with Seeto Wei in the early stages of the Japanese occupation of the Peninsula. Brigid had been caught away from her home village on the coast when the invasion began, and asked for help in a nearby inland village that by chance happened to be the same village Henry and his father were sheltering in after their escape from Rabaul. One thing led to another until after the war, when Seeto Wei went on his way and left Brigid with a baby conceived by him and a stepson of nine years, who had already decided that Brigid must be his real mother because of the way she seemed to love him. Over the years, Seeto Wei 'drops in' now and again and nine months later another child is born and his son Henry is again left behind along with his other children and their mother. Brigid doesn't want to go with Seeto Wei. She's happy in her village. She loves her children. Besides, she has a Tolai husband with whom she has children.

Now it's 1950 and Henry is thirteen years of age. His youngest step-sister Beka is eighteen months old and is meeting her father for the first time. Brigid's friends and family have private jokes that as Brigid is only twenty -six, she has many more child-bearing years ahead of her. The Chinaman is here and the only question is whether the next one will be a boy or a girl. Henry's heard the jokes, sees them as cruel but also suspects the witticisms mask the anger of Bridget's friend. It's Brigid's choice, but it's not right.

Henry loves his little sister Beka. He envies Beka. The Tolai way means that there are always people to love and care for you. A child belongs to a Tolai village, regardless of who your father is, or if your mother is a sole parent, or if you have no parents. All children. Even a foreign child, like he is to them; even an adopted, or an abandoned one.

Seeto Wei always arrives unannounced but expects full hospitality. His son sees this as disrespectful to the people of the village and more so to Brigid. He's heard rumours that Brigid and this village are not the first or will not be the last to suffer from Seeto Wei's demands and that he's left his gifts of abandoned children elsewhere. It has also not escaped Henry's attention that during this visit Brigid is avoiding being alone with his father, a strategy that others are showing support by way of covert actions. On the surface, there's nothing changed from any other of Seeto Wei's visits. But subtle manipulation of events are keeping Seeto Wei busy or placing Brigid elsewhere.

Henry's not sure how old his father is but he can see the signs on his body of neglect. Too much shao jiu rice wine, and hum bao steamed rice flour buns stuffed with barbecued pork, he conjectures, naming the only two items Henry can remember from his childhood. His papa is sluggish and disinterested in just about everything. However, as is always the custom, and the respectful and honourable thing to do, Brigid's brother Solomon is ready to take the visitor out on the harbour for some fishing. Truth is, it's always and only Solomon who fishes, and not his father who, Henry has observed, always stretches himself out and relaxes. It's a wonder his snoring doesn't keep the fish away, he's joked to himself. He imagines his father asleep and Solomon doing whatever he does, but he can't say for sure, because no one has ever included him on these excursions.

And as is the recurring theme during his father's visits, the son sits and watches and waits, hoping for recognition and in the meanwhile brooding, certain things are going to be as always. He hungers for compensation in any form. If only someone might say 'young man, you have had your life stolen from you and it's not your fault.' That might ease his suffering. But they don't and he will continue to suffer his abandonment.

As he sits on a fallen palm trunk, he's torn between wanting to take part in whatever is happening and needing to mark his anger by withdrawing his emotions, constantly swinging between the two extremes. Both ashamed and inflamed, he attempts to disguise his turmoil by stabbing a stick into the sandy space between his two feet, as if he's sketching. Except he isn't looking at his so-called sketch. His eyes keep flickering from the ground to across to where the men are preparing for their fishing outing.

When he makes this last check, he's surprised. His father is looking directly at him, actually looking at him, which means he isn't invisible, which also means that his actions might have been noted and probably are being criticized. He scrambles for containment, shuffling his bare feet to obliterate his scribbles and discarding the stick as if it means nothing to him. He looks away and then turns back. His father is still looking at him, and now he's crooking his finger and wriggling it, the sign that means 'come'. This can't be what his father intends. Can't be. He must be meaning something else. The last time his father included him in anything was when he was four, when his father took his hand and led him into the jungle. After which Brigid came into his life.

Common sense is returning to him: his father does want him to come. Without doubt. But all that means, he's convinced, is that his father needs something doing, a chore, and who better to do it than a lazy son. Yes, that's it. He jumps to his feet and scampers over, and despite the negative connotations, he's keen to please, even if it is only to carry out a menial task. Someone has noticed his presence. His father then points to the canoe. What? He feels a light push on the shoulder and when he turns around, there's Brigid, a broad smile across her face. She knows everything, understands his hunger, feels his pain. Henry clambers in and clings to the sides of the lakatoi while Solomon pushes it into deeper water. He takes a position in the nose. The paddles slice into the deeper water and the lakatoi feels alive. This is when Henry decides this will be the best day of his life.

5

HENRY'S HOME
Back to the present, late August 2010

The practice of fishing in all its forms has become meditative for Henry. That one afternoon with Seeto Wei asleep and Solomon with his fishing spear had created a template. In retrospect, there were many other afternoons of fishing that had proved more pleasurable than that last one with his father. That day, like many things about which expectations are high, had turned out to be a definite let-down as far as father and son relationships go but in other ways it was monumental. Recalling it always settles him.

Sitting in his deckchair, today, he's doing that very thing, thinking about fishing, recalling the sensation, the pleasure, its calming effect. The pleasure rippling through his body as his line plops into the harbour's lukewarm water; a sense of satisfaction when he feels a gentle tug, then after pulling in the line, the thrashing and wriggling of the fish's death struggle that ends on the floor of the canoe, a final flip and a flop before stillness. A grand catch a measure of success. The sensation of floating is his addiction. Drifting in comparative silence. Oh, there's always the soft slap of the waves on the hull, or from the shoreline the distant rustle of wind-blown trees, or even the faint sound of children laughing and playing, but in the bubble of space around him as he sits or sometimes lies prone within his vessel, there's a muffled silence in which he can lose himself. Despite its other failures, he'll concede this addiction began that afternoon spent with Solomon and his father.

On that afternoon in 1950, when the pleasure triggered his obsession, he could not take his eyes off Solomon. Again and again, Solomon's body would lift from his boat's crude seat to stand tall, raising high the one arm that held his spear, followed by a thrusting of the spear and then dragging it in with a flapping fish on the end. For each repeat, Henry would hold his breath as Solomon paused, muscles flexed, before thrusting. Then, he'd stare at the spot where the spear entered the water. There wasn't a ripple on the surface, as if nothing had happened, nor was the sleeping Chinaman disturbed. In those moments, as their eyes met after each thrust, a mature man and a boy on the threshold of adulthood forged a lifelong bond over the act of fishing.

Fish are a staple diet for the Tolai and fishing a necessity. But for him, it's more than just hunting for food. On the water, he becomes a different man. His body relaxes, his anger and frustrations dissipate, and he is at peace with the world. And so it has been for decades. Put him in sight of a lakatoi, and his muscles will twitch, convinced he's not in his seventies and they are still fit and capable, raring to go, and in his mind he's once again one of those strong men pushing a lakatoi down the sandy beach and out onto the water of the harbour. He pictures himself as one of a group of men laughing and shouting, high stepping as the level of the sea water rises, laplaps soaked to groin level. Following this boisterousness comes the final grunt of effort as each man lifts his body from the sea floor and into the vessel. Then only the gentle sucking in and out of the water as paddles dig in and lift out. He feels the breeze caressing his face, his legs and hands registering a trembling vibration, almost imperceptible, as water resists wood, as the lakatoi moves forward, a lunge interrupted and repeated, interrupted and repeated, as the vessel's nose kisses incoming waves. And afterwards, on the beach, the catch cooked and devoured, the sun dropping below the horizon, the deep black of a tropical evening providing a blanket over the fishing party. Only the stars and the dull red glow of the coals in a dying fire provide light. No one speaks, but someone, always one, has a ukulele and is strumming. The calmness that comes with those rare evenings washes over him, and for a moment he forgets his sweating body, pounding heart, his lack of appetite, his sister's questions, and his fears. If all he does is think about fishing, it's the same.

'Aiyah, Pops. Where do you go these days? Body here, but where does your thinking go? Been talking to you and you not listening.'

Ling rolls his eyes and strides off towards the house. Has his son given up on his father and gone home? He feels guilty. As he should. Lost in his reverie, he'd forgotten his son. Lost in a past moment, forgetting the preciousness of the present. Another thing for Ling to worry about: now he will think his father is losing his mind. And has he gone home angry?

But Ling is back, carrying a tray.

'Here, Dad, a meal for you.'

Fish and rice and tea, ginseng tea. This, he discovers when he lifts the mug to his nose. He nods his gratitude, and notes Ling has no food. Studying his son's face it is clear his son's purpose is not only to bring a meal. Ling wants to talk. Oh, no good can come out of this. He tries to stall, lingers over every mouthful. Down to the last few grains of rice. Can't delay any longer. This is it. Ling notices and pulls his wicker chair closer. As soon as he's taken the last mouthful of rice and the last sip of tea, Ling removes the bowl and the cup from his hands, stacks them, one inside the other, and places them together on the grass between the two chairs.

'Dad, I am worried. Things are not right with you. You seem so sad. I think maybe you should see a doctor. Just to check. Eh? Will you do that for me? I've been a good son, done what a good son should for his father. Now I'm asking you to be a good father for his son. Please, go to see the doctor who's visiting Kokopo next week. Please. You're booked in to see this doc next Tuesday, 1.30 pm. If you don't go that's okay. I know what a stubborn lapun you can be so I'll pay the doctor for the appointment you don't keep. But for your family, your grandchildren, your great-grandchildren, who all love you, please see him, even if you tell him lies. Maybe he will see past them. I hope so. You aren't well. Please.'

Wow. Not what he'd been expecting. He examines his son's face and for the first time sees Ling, not as an eight- or nine-year-old but as a man not so young himself, well into his middle age. Ling's life's so different from his because Ling's a different person from what he is and was as a younger man. Ling takes on responsibilities far beyond anything he'd ever accepted. Guess his wife Rachel's easy-going Tolai nature and his own slackness have shaped Ling to be like this. Too often the adult of the family had to be Ling. Aged before his time. Nor can he compare his life to Ling's. At Ling's age – what's he now? He can't think, must be in his fifties – he had no father, no mother, no wife, and no responsibilities. His children all off elsewhere, taking care of themselves. He was free as a bird. But Ling, he worries about his own children and their children, and he worries about his father. A twinge of guilt. He knows his own faults. These days he can see them. Not always though. Ling's like his mother. He is, and she was, a person who worries about others. Rachel did all the work in their home. And yet while he's thinking these kind thoughts about his son, the spiky claws of bitterness grab hold of that benevolence. Sure, well, it's okay for Ling. He has a father to worry over and make him feel like a good person because he does what a good son should do. But Seeto Wei never allowed him to be a good son and in so doing, be enabled to feel good. The childhood pain is as fresh as if he's six or seven again. Twice rejected. Nobody wanted him. The first time a blue-eyed mother sent him away, and the man she sent him away with never wanted him either. And now his bitterness moves on to that earlier pain.

'Get a grip, you stupid fool. This's not about you, your father or your mother,' he tells himself. How can he say no to such a request? Out of love he nods his head as if agreeing with Ling to visit this doctor. Ling's face lightens.

'Shall I come and pick you up, Dad? Or is that being too pushy, eh? I've left the name and appointment time near your telephone.'

Ling picks up the bowl and mug and then rises from the chair. He notices that Ling hesitates before he walks, showing the stiffness of age-weary knees, a slight bow to his shoulders, and a clear inclination not to stride it out across his father's lawn, as he once would have. New awareness of his son's aging settles over him. Another weight on the scales to confirm that he himself is aging. Death will be next. He must not let Ling see his fear. He forces himself out of the chair and takes the bowl and mug from Ling's hand.

'Still able to wash the dishes, son.'

These words must do instead of 'Thank you for caring' or 'I love you', phrases not shared between him and his children. Never has he been that other kind of man. A man must always maintain his respect, despite approaching decline, and this makes such expressions no longer important. He knows it's not the right way to be and sometimes he wonders, is it because he never heard those words from his father? For the Tolai, words are unnecessary. Actions speak, and everything Brigid and his Tolai family did showed how loved he was. And he's right back to that place again, where he questions his own motives. Is it approaching death that has softened him, so he almost said those words to Ling? Is it approaching death taking him back into places he would have never gone when he was young and strong? Is it approaching death that makes him want to grab hold of his aging son and hug him, though if he did so, he's certain Ling would not wait until next Tuesday when the doctor from Australia will arrive. He'd have him at the door of the hospital's Emergency Ward in a flash. The image of such a fictional event makes him laugh. Ling looks around in shock, eyebrows lifted.

'Just thinking about the many years that have passed since I last went to the doctor's surgery. Too long ago for me to remember.'

Ling turns, shrugs his shoulders, and walks towards the house and to his car.

'Well, there you go, old man. Time's right for a visit if only to see a new face. See you on Tuesday.'

§

At 1.30 pm on the following Tuesday when his father does not arrive at the hospital for his appointment with the Australian doctor, Ling apologises to the receptionist, his wife's cousin, and goes in search. It's surprising to find his father's car is still in the garage. Although Henry doesn't drive very far these days, he would have had to get a lift to the hospital. His father's antisocial. If he was doing the right thing, trying to get to the doctor's, then that would have been sufficient motivation for him to drive himself to the hospital. But Henry's home is empty. His father is a stay-at-home. An empty house is cause for panic. He runs to the nearby village. He knows everyone there because they are the family of his grandmother, Brigid. Someone there will know where his father has gone. Several villagers offer suggestions and have opinions on where his father might be. Nothing definite. But after about half an hour, it's established that the last person who spoke to Henry was the cripple, To Vole. Every evening, To Vole, aided by a long pole, takes a stroll along the beach past Henry's house. To Vole hobbles in to join the discussion. He's uncertain if it was last evening or the evening before that he spoke to Henry. Henry was talking about fishing, the good old days.

To Vole cackles. 'The good old days, masta say, the good old days. Now he's lapun and all days are old, nogat good.' His chortle echoed along the beach. On some other day, Ling might have enjoyed the irony of the old guy's humour around aging but not today.

Ling and men from the village go back towards Henry's house to trace him. Someone notices the dinghy's missing, but everyone agrees it has been years since Henry has taken the dinghy out. They agree Henry would have trouble getting the boat into the water. Ling calls the police at Kokopo.

The police tell Ling, with evening approaching, it is pointless searching for Henry until the morning. Ling phones his wife and tells her he's sleeping the night at his father's home. Was it because he made that damn doctor's appointment that this has happened? His father can be very stubborn. He replays his conversation with his father on the last day he saw him. Has he overlooked any clues?

The morning arrives and so do the policemen, and with them many more villagers. People begin the search, along the beach and through the coconut plantation on the other side of the main road. Someone tells Ling to stay at the house in case his father returns but Ling prowls the beach. To Vole, who has seated himself on some driftwood and is watching Ling pace calls out to Ling to tell him he same-same muruk. Cassowaries bend their heads and take long strides with their legs. Ling scowls at To Vole. Not the time for jokes. He continues to pace back and forth along the beach, angry with himself.

About three in the afternoon, one of the New Guinea policemen calls to him. 'Found your father, sir. Along the beach. You come.'

Ling runs towards the constable. To Vole cackles. He has no fears for masta Henry. Ling passes the constable and heads in the direction showed. He runs and runs. Around a point. Along another stretch of beach. In the distance he can see a group of people. His legs push him faster, his chest hurts, his mind warns of the risk of having a heart attack because it's been years since he has pushed his body like this, and the possibility grows in his mind as he struggles for oxygen. There, in the shallows, he sees an upturned dinghy. On the beach in front of the dinghy he sees someone with a red laplap over his shoulders. Dad? A constable is holding a bottle of water to the man's mouth. Yes, it's his father. Closer now, he sees his father's eyes are closed, his mouth open enough to take in the offered water. Someone's moaning. It's him. Ling. He's shocked himself. Tears are rolling down his face. Free-flowing. A grown man, crying for his daddy. At last he's there, and he falls upon the sand beside his father.

'Papa belong me, you no die finish. Please, Papa.'

Henry opens his eyes. Tears well in his eye sockets, and a strange whimpering sound leaks from his mouth. Ling has never seen his father cry. The shock of this new experience makes the fear that his father is dead redundant. His moan grows louder. Father and son, moaning and blubbering in unison, cling to each other.

Henry's wailing evolves into words. 'Thought I was going fishing with my father. Stupid, ah?'

Ling stops moaning, hugs his father, and buries his face in his father's shoulder, as Henry manages a weak cackle, like To Vole's earlier. Old men. Laughing is hard come by. Ling gets to his feet, thanks the constable who points to the vehicle on the road and nods towards Henry.

'Come on Dad. We need a lift back home.' Behind his father, he sees the villagers pulling the dinghy up safe above the tidal line and waves thanks to them. He helps his father get to his feet and together the two stumble their way towards the police vehicle.

Henry knows he hasn't escaped the Australian doctor.

The constable asks; 'Where are you going, masta Ling?'

Ling taps his forehead, rolls his eyes, and grins at the constable.

'Papa belong me maybe a little longlong. Too much fishing.'

The constable cackles as if he knows how Ling's father can be. Perhaps he thinks all fathers are a burden.

Ling says, 'We go long hospital. Check-up.'

The constable puts his foot down on the accelerator, in the way of PNG drivers, and before long they're in front of the hospital.

After the constable has helped him out of the police vehicle, Henry feels on his shoulder blades the soft but determined pressure of his son's hands.

'Long this way, Papa.'

'Ah, Mr. Seeto. You found your father. Still got time. Let's go in here.'

Ling knows things are heading in the right direction when he hears his father's complaints.

'How many ways can they tap and prick, prod and examine, a man's body? The Aussie doctor says: "Results will be back in a few weeks. Will be in touch." But he's not so smart for two reasons. First, the results will come back and say, "advanced age". A waste of time, this poking. Second, what's this rubbish he and the doctor talked about? "Yes Mr Seeto, you might find the partaking of ginseng helpful in some circumstances, but intake of excessive amounts also causes problems." Knows nothing, this man. He's talking rubbish when he suggests that too much ginseng could explain his insomnia, his irregular heartbeat, his low sugar levels and his stomach issues. Can anyone partake too much ginseng?'

Situation normal, Ling sighs.

6

HENRY'S HOME
35th anniversary of Independence, September 2010

Henry holds his breath, drops the phone back onto the cradle and stares at it. Well, who would have thought? The shock of his actions ripples through him. He jokes at his own nervousness. 'Better be careful, shock can kill an old man like you.'

Her son answered. Andrew, her eldest, he'd said. Said he went to school with Ling who, he thought, might be a little older than he. He hadn't realised she'd had a son so close to his own. Probably shut it out of his mind. When he presses himself to remember, he has to admit, yeah, yeah, Ling said he'd been to school with his cousins. Overtaken by unexpected twinges of conscience, he knows he hadn't taken in Ling's gossip over the years, did not hear everything and anything about that family. Never even tried to tell his sister when their father passed. He'd had moments of guilt but had convinced himself there was no need to feel bad about cutting her out. What they'd done to him... Well, truth was, he'd never identified his father as her father. The son said the family was watching a documentary about PNG on television. Anniversary of Independence. At least talking to the son had settled his nerves. When she spoke, he was less frantic.

She's got three boys, she told him, easy, friendly, just as you would speak to someone close to you – like a brother – like it was only yesterday she'd last conversed with him. But had he told her about his own family? He can't remember what he'd said to her in that phone call.

He can't picture her face, as it might be now. Can't imagine a face to go with her voice. Round or dark, thin or light? It surprises him when he calculates: she must have been only a child, just two years older than he, when he last saw her. Madness, fear of dying, or whatever, he's broken the

180

long silence. What will come from this bold move? His head is buzzing; he jokes to himself, scoffing at the Aussie doctor: too much ginseng.

Stumbling through his home to the back door, across the grassed area towards the beach, he falls into his chair and sighs. Relief sweeps over him. At last, he can immerse himself into what lies before him. This is his sanctuary, this wide magnificent view. Tall coconut palms wave their fronds in the gentle offshore breeze. A lakatoi, left discarded since his last canoeing trip, the disastrous one, and a woven fish trap resting side by side against the wall of a small thatched hut nearby. Paradise, he thinks. Simpson Harbour and across there, Rabaul, despite the dark grey bursts of ash and rocks. He's accustomed to the volcanoes' temper tantrums. He prefers to be mesmerised by the soft regular waves rolling across the bay before making a silent run up the short but steep beach.

He runs his hand over his balding head, its smoothness comforting, familiar. Maria's not familiar. She's a stranger. Even Stephen would qualify as part of his family before she would. Thinking of Stephen makes him remember how, when he'd heard Stephen was sick, dying, he'd gone to Kavieng. Like a good son might do for a dying father. He doesn't know why. Maybe he had been trying to fulfil the son's duties that his father had not permitted him to carry out. Too complicated for him to figure out his own motives. Afterwards, he recognised that somehow Stephen could have replaced his father. They shared common values, they could talk on many subjects, and the lives they had lived were similar. Every bit of information he hears about Maria is new. His phone call, for example. He tells himself he made this on a whim but that wasn't so. Nor can he deny he's been heading towards contacting her for a long time. Since 2004. When Sara delivered Stephen's crate to his house. He's felt a subconscious pressure building within him to make the call. Perhaps even before Stephen sent his crate. He can trace his drive to make the call back to his recent obsession with dying and his desire to clear his path into afterlife. Stephen had hurried along the motivations for action that he had resisted. To care for Stephen in his dying weeks, hearing Stephen's perspectives, his resistance to reconnecting with his sister had been softened. Even so he had surprised himself when he actually did it.

The deed done, and Henry has moved back sixty years, reverting to the Henry he was born to be, not the Henry he has lived his life as. He doesn't recognise this former Henry. Who is this person? But that other Henry is taking over and he's finding the changes sweeping through him difficult. Over the hours after the call his armour of anger, denial, and hostility to those he believes didn't love him are being stripped away. He's feeling vulnerable again, as he had as a child, a young boy waiting for his sister, a microscopic flicker of anticipation building. Is it hope? Could this be possible? He expected nothing from anyone, so there was nothing to hope for. Is it also eagerness? A window into the moment he might at last be free of the burdens he has piled upon himself. And surprise? Perhaps astonishment? That is the emotions he had felt during the call. Those feelings hitting him from behind, unprepared and naïve as to the purpose and expected outcome of his call.

'Ridiculous for a man of my age. Life should be a home run now, a jog or a toddle to the finishing line. There should be no hurdles, no second thoughts and no revisions.'

The surprise for him was the lack of awkwardness between them, despite their sixty years of estrangement. As if the two were picking up a conversation put aside when last they were together. Impossible. But yes, he decides. That's how it felt.

The common greeting of 'Halo', in Pisin, flowing between them without impediment. He expected the rest of the conversation would be jagged and halting, like two strangers trying to find a mutual interest, so the speed with which it had converted to a brother-sister conversation took him aback. Maria sounded as if she'd been waiting for his call, as if it had been only yesterday that they had talked. Stephen knew this. He knew Maria was waiting. He knew this was how it would be. An unrelated man who, known only by name until a few years ago, proved how well he understood Henry's sister, and showed Henry the falseness of his belief that she was a stranger to him.

He digs his toes into the soil underfoot, not white or golden post-card-type sand, but coarse grey aggregate: pumice from the local volcanoes. He lets the water wash over his feet. Ah, this beach. He can almost smell the Chinese spices he and Solomon chose when they cooked their catch in banana leaves. It was to this spot he'd brought Rachel and his young kids, when he was thinking of leasing the land from Brigid's village. Decades later, and it's his backyard. No longer is there Rachel or their kids, except Ling's mob, to share with, but still, he lets his eyes mark out his terrain, as a dog's nose will do, from the beach up through the tree-like hibiscus bushes and blossom-laden bougainvillea to the modest home he built for himself with some help. Facing the beach now, he looks out towards the township.

Reclaiming a sister takes him elsewhere, towards reclaiming his home, this land, and that covenant reminds him of the privileges that arrived via his mother Brigid. Yet contacting Maria brings him to thoughts about her mother who, deny it as he might, was once his mother. Only known to him as Mumma Josefina or Mama now a faceless mother because for too long the anguish, anger and guilt surrounding his loss of her has crowded out whatever fragments of memories he might have kept. He hears words in Pisin that say to him, 'See, brown skin from my mother, kinky hair from my grandfather's mother, and blue eyes from my grandfather's father.' These words, he thinks, were spoken by his mother. And always he sees blue eyes, blue eyes against a dark face, and this face atop a silhouette, waving. He feels his younger self looking backwards, and seeing, there, visible at the far end of Malaguna Road, his mummy still waving.

He announces, as if saying the words out loud will confirm that it's really happening.

'She's coming. His sister's coming.'

She'll soon be here and already the wall he'd built is crumbling. He no longer has a reason to hide. Soon he will tell her, face-to-face, how angry he has felt because they left him behind but they didn't leave her. He trembles at that thought. Accumulating in his gut, awaiting release, are all his pent-up emotions.

But the other memories, the ones he had blocked, because they were too painful to recall or re-live, are also tumbling forth. He cannot suppress them. His four-year-old world is rushing in. Daddy-George is wrapping him in his arms, so tight he can't breathe. Over Daddy-George's shoulder Nenek's face is looking at him, her hands fluttering, as if she's trying to take hold of the air. She isn't crying. Daddy-George's hands are under his arms. He's feels as if he's flying. He thinks Daddy-George and Mama are playing a game with him, like they do sometimes. Mama takes his hand and they walk out of their house. Maybe he and Mama are going to the market. They are walking along the same street as they do when they go to the bung. A man is there. Mama says: 'Emi numbawan papa belong yu. Yu savy? This is your true papa who is taking you on a holiday.'

Is Daddy-George not his true papa?

'Yu are a brave pikinini. Remember, me lukim yu soon. I will come get you soon, my son.'

He's looking back. He sees Mama. She is standing at the end of the road. He remembers her blue eyes. Mama.

7

MARIA'S HOME IN BRISBANE
After that call on the evening of September 16

Sister and brother are a pair again. Tupela.

After that phone call, Maria's mind has been crawling back into her memories of her brother. Last time she had Henry for a brother, Henry was so tiny. She can only remember that day as a sad one: she is staring at Henry's hand, watching as it leaves Mama's hand. Her eyes follow it as the hand of the man Mama calls 'numbawan papa' clasps the tiny fingers she loves, not Daddy-George's. He's their stepfather, their numbatu papa. That's the last time she saw Henry's hand. Its tiny fingers, its chubby palms. Even hands can look sad.

Papa's straight back, his dark hair. This is a father who is almost a stranger to her. She only saw him when she was young, when he told her she was his beautiful Chinese daughter, but he did not come back. Henry knows this papa even less than she does. She imagines what is happening in Henry's head. This stranger his mama calls 'papa'. And now this man has hold of Henry's baby hand and they are walking, walking, walking. Her eyes walk, too. They walk from Papa's head across his right shoulder, down his arm, to his hand where Henry begins. And at this place, Papa's big hand swallows Henry's tiny one. Papa's body is straight like a bamboo pole. Henry's is twisting and turning, like a fish on a line. His little head turns to look over his right shoulder, then over his left shoulder. Each time he turns, his legs are no longer steady. Each time he turns and wobbles, Papa shakes him. For a short while after each shake, Henry's body is straight, like his papa's. But then he turns again. And they go, two together, until they are just two small dots disappearing along Malaguna Road, heading out of town.

Each time Henry turns, she pictures his baby face. She imagines she can see his straight fine black hair flicking back and forth, like it does when he runs and plays with her. She imagines his little lips quivering, but she knows that seeing his baby face can only happen in her imagination. Henry and Papa are too far away. Each time he turns, she cries 'Henry. Yu stap. Please stay, Henry. Liklik brus, my baby brother, you are mine. You cannot go.' Her face is wet. In her mind she's travelling with Henry. Her eyes are his eyes. When he looks down at the road and turns back to look at a sister and a mama, she sees what he sees. Henry. Henry.

Like the soldiers about to fill their town, the tall trees along Malaguna Road stand guard either side of Papa and Henry's exit.

Her mama's hand is still reaching out for her boy, as it was when Papa took Henry's hand from hers. Mama's mouth is open, like she wants to say something, but she is silent.

She stands beside her mama, holding her body still, like her mama holds hers, still and stiff, and together they watch Papa and Henry until there is nothing to see but quivering dots. Her mama eyes can look nowhere else but to the place where Henry once was, as if she's forgotten there's someone standing at her side, still holding her hand. Is her Ox brother frightened? He doesn't even know this papa. All his life he has had only one papa, and that is Daddy-George.

Poor brother. He nogat a mama. Nogat a sister. Nogat a numbatu papa Daddy-George. Nogat a nenek. Only got tispela stret-back no-smile numbawan papa, a stiff man who never smiles, who never checks on his son, who knows nothing about this little boy, not what he's afraid of, not his quiet sense of humour, not his loving ways.

In Brisbane, she brings her mind back to the present and shocks herself by calculating it's sixty-eight years since Henry left. All those years ago and yet still she remembers him as a frightened little boy though she has never forgotten how old he really is. Every year she remembers his birthday, lights a candle for him, and whispers 'Happy birthday, brother of mine.' She doesn't expect that Henry has done the same for her on her birthdays. She reminds herself that he and she lived on the same peninsula, on the same island, those many years after the war and before she migrated, but he kept to himself, she suspects in a local village. A brother nearby but lost. He has his reasons. She excused him, though it wounded her to do so. For her, no reason should separate a family. None.

She was two when Henry was born. She's a Dog person, and she's proud of her Dog-like qualities: a man's best friend, faithful, courageous, smart and warm-hearted. A keeper of secrets. That's who she is. She has doubts about whether Henry fits the traits of an Ox person. In some ways he is but in others he's not. What she remembers of him. What she imagines he's like. But sixty-eight years is a long time. How can she be sure? Ox people are honest, industrious, patient and cautious, but they are also obstinate, and poor at communication, according to her book about Chinese astrology. He must be an Ox. Otherwise he would have remembered his sister and spoken to her before now. Yet another secret she's been keeping from her family is her wish to see Henry once more.

The burden of her many secrets is weighing her down; it becomes heavier every year.

8

TOKUA AIRPORT, GAZELLE PENINSULA, ENB, PNG
October 28

On the day Maria arrives, Henry wears what his Tolai half-brothers call his 'kong kong' face, using their Pisin word for Chinaman. He hides his darkest and most turbulent emotions behind this face. His brothers, always carefree and laughing, their faces bright with their broad white grins, have spent a lifetime mocking his sombre control. Just like his father. He can't remember when his father had ever shown emotion, let alone smiled. Not even the day the Japanese had searched the village, screaming abuse at the villagers, upturning everything, taking away stored food, and missing him and his father as they lay hidden only a few feet away in the tall kunai grass. Henry had felt the warmth of his pee as he wet himself in fear, but not a muscle had moved on his father's face. Nor did he comfort his trembling son or wipe his tears away. Henry had spent a lifetime mastering that self-control. On this day, when he will greet his sister for the first time in decades, he needs self-control more than ever.

He'd taken her return phone call, feigned surprise when she told him she would come to visit, though he had always hoped that what's on his bedroom floor would seal the deal. Although it's what he wants, the certainty of a visit had precipitated a minor panic attack. Never had a visitor in his home before. A list of the expected demands upon him is growing. From that, he moves to the terror of their conversations. To allow himself to vent his anger is the only thing he planned to do. Never did he think through the next step where his sister might have her own points of view that would require responses from him. With the visit imminent, he can no longer ignore the potential. He reminds himself: she's family and, as a true Chinese gentleman, it's his duty to offer her hospitality. The casual slip between being a New Guinean and being Chinese goes unnoticed. Habit of a lifetime.

He gathers up an air of controlled indifference to accompany him to the airport. As insurance he squashes down any curiosity about what she'll look like or why she needs to come home. As he watches the passengers enter the terminal, all too young or white or male to be his sister, he appears calm. When one passenger shouts and runs towards a waiting person, he averts his eyes. The only female is the last passenger to descend from the aircraft. Her tallness reminds Henry of his lack. She's large, tall and brown; he's tiny, short, and bald. For a second, he isn't sure but, when no one else disembarks, he's convinced. Yes, it must be his sister. She looks nothing like the Maria of his imagination.

Her skin is golden brown. She has short tight wiry curls. She picks her way towards the terminal, keeping her head low as if her life depends on seeing what is underfoot. He feels his body gravitating towards the entrance doors as if drawn to this unfamiliar person. When they are less than three metres apart, his sister lifts her head as though she's sensed he's near. Her eyes are wide. He's certain she hasn't blinked. He's in shock. Maybe she is too. He doesn't know if he's excited or frightened or happy or disappointed. Whatever it is he's feeling, he's not sure he can keep it under control even though he is an expert at containment.

Her eyes are blue.

All these years of thinking his mother had been waving him goodbye. His memory has betrayed him. Now he remembers not only his mother but also Maria and a tall, thin and dignified grandmother watching him as he left with his father. What else has he misremembered?

A hairline crack works down his 'kong kong' mask but the need to gather luggage aids his control.

He appreciates that she, like him, has not a lot to say, though he finds one thing she says a bit odd.

'I thought, now, it would feel different. But it doesn't. Just soil. Just a place.'

He doesn't understand, but he accepts her words. They seem like something he might say had he been away for over thirty years.

His sister's here, he breathes in that thought with amazement. He's sharing coffee with his sister. Then they will drive to his home.

'You got blue eyes.'

'Oh please, don't start that again.'

'What you mean? Don't start that again?'

'You tease, oletaim, about blue eyes. Everyone else got brown eyes or black eyes, you toktok. You always make me cry. Oletaim.'

'But what about Mama? Weren't Mama's eyes blue?'

His sister's eyes cloud. He feels an urge to say something, if only to break the tension, but before he can, she is shaking her head.

'Nogat. Mama eyes black. Yu lusim – you forget your mama?'

She looks like she has a toothache. Her hand plunges into her clothing, and draws out a stiff brown envelope which she plops onto the table. She pushes the envelope towards him. The look on her face is one of suppressed glee. When he doesn't take it, she slips her fingers inside the envelope and pulls the contents out.

'I brought these for you from Brisbane. This one, and this.'

Two photographs. Her fingers manipulate each one until she's happy with their placement on the table in front of her, side-by-side, upside down, then she slides them across to his side. Daddy-George, the hairy face of his memories, stares up at him. An Aussie. He sees past the stiff and prim pose of the formal photograph and remembers. A flood of love fills him. And the dam has broken. He's embarrassed to be crying in public. The other face: the dark one. His numbawan mumma. Eyes like dark pools. Not blue. He lifts his gaze from the photographs into the sad blue eyes of his sister. He wants to ask that question, the one he has suppressed since the war ended. Maria already has an answer. She whispers: 'Mumma, Daddy-George, the war he kaikai em, ate them up. They left with no goodbyes.'

Tears roll down her brown face.

9

HENRY'S HOME
October 29

Equatorial days arrive early. First morning, Maria's up with the dawn. Aaah, home. And Henry's home feels so… so what a home should feel like. Like something she has dreamt of for a long time, something remembered from childhood.

She takes an early morning stroll along the beach, breathing in the place. How lucky for Henry to live here. Perfect. Quiet. Peaceful. She sighs. Never thought she'd be back. Now too late, far too late. Stephen is no longer waiting for her.

She clutches her stomach. The pain is always sharp.

When she returns, she falls into Henry's cane chair.

Later, she senses Henry emerging from his home. She doesn't turn. He doesn't speak or come to where she is sitting. Is he shy with me? Perhaps he needs time to become used to a stranger in his home. After several minutes Henry places another chair beside hers. Oh, this is his chair. She feels a little embarrassed, but Henry says nothing. When she turns to see, he's staring across the harbour. Her eyes follow his gaze. Oh yes, there it is, Rabaul.

Yes, maybe silence is right for now. She too gazes across the water, not seeing anything but feeling the soft breeze blowing in across the harbour. It's almost as if she has never left. Yes, this feels right.

Later, after they've been silent for hours, Maria notices Henry's making small movements. He turns to her.

'Like im tea?'

Instead of answering, she rises. Henry does too. Together they stroll towards Henry's house, glancing towards each other every few steps. In his kitchen, Henry is efficient. He fills a kettle, ignites the gas, and places the kettle on the gas ring. It whispers as the metal heats. He reaches for mugs, a teapot and a sealed container of tea leaves.

She smiles. 'Oh, that's something I had forgotten. You need to seal everything. Mildew.'

Henry's smile hints there might be more she's forgotten. Maybe, she tells herself, that's not what his smile is saying. Maybe he's trying to make her feel welcome. How can she tell? She can see the boy in the man, but the man is still a stranger. Henry reaches for another sealed container. This time, it's sweet cakes, which he places on a platter. She watches as Henry prepares the tea, places the teapot, mugs, and platter onto a tray and notices a jar of creamer, not milk. Oh, yes: milk doesn't keep. Strange, how some little things you forget but others are as real as ever.

'Sugar?' he asks, and grins when she shakes her head. 'Me too. Diabetic.' Then his eyes drop to the sweet cakes and he laughs out loud. She grins back. Good sense of humour, she decides.

As Henry is giving full attention to making tea, she can examine his face uninhibited. His loneliness is palpable. Is it because his wife has passed away? He has several children. Why aren't they filling his life? She decides perhaps he's always been a loner, hard to get to know. Her brother. And yet in so many ways, a stranger to her. Sixty or more years of a life she knows nothing about. Sadness washes over her. How stupid they both have been.

Back on the beach, together they gaze out across Simpson Harbour as they eat and drink.

She finds the courage to ask a question: 'Henry, you told me you have many children. Tell me about them.'

He does, and she responds.

For him, a wife gone to the afterlife and many children, all adults, some with their own children, scattered around. Most he doesn't see often. He admits, with a little humility, this is because he was a grumpy papa. But Ling and his kids, yes. He gives no details, nothing to help her imagine them. Does he miss those he doesn't see? Is he lonely without his wife? But she doesn't ask those questions either. Only nods her head as he gives what he's willing to give.

Now it's time for Maria to talk.

'You spoke to Andrew. He's my eldest. He has a daughter and a son. Lives near me. All my children live near me. Then there's Gabriel. A bachelor. And Daniel, with two sons. Daniel's family live with me. And nearby, lots of PNG people, people you know.'

Henry nods but it's clear he doesn't believe he would know anyone who lives in Australia. She takes this as disapproval of her husband's choice to leave.

'I didn't want to leave Rabaul, Henry. My husband thought it was the right thing to do. I still don't know. And I miss the smells, the weather, everything.'

'Oh, it's not all good here, Maria. Changing. Nothing stays the same.'

'Well I guess I have spent too many years thinking about how much it hurt to leave and not enough time, Henry, to admit there's much to like in Brisbane for us PNG people. Come and visit, Henry. We can have mumu party. Sunnybank is a big shopping mall filled with many stores of eastern and Asian foods. Yum Cha every day. Other stores, similar to Chong's.'

'Sister, Chong's, he gone long Rabaul. Gone. Eruption.'

And now they have another topic to talk through.

'Glad I wasn't here for that. Saw it on television. So sad to see the familiar places destroyed or covered in ash. What was it like, being here, Henry?' And she looks out to the perpetual cloud visible on the edge of the horizon.

Her brother takes a deep breath, and begins: 'Rabaul always have tremors, gurias. You know that. But they were getting worse and then, a few weeks before that last day, gurias, one after another, plenty, earth shaking, but me, and others, we pretend it's not serious.' His voice quivers. 'Everyone's homes, businesses, gone. Most got no insurance. Everything buried. Hard to get our stuff out. And help did arrive, but at the usual casual pace. Never hurry. Government disorganised. Set up camps – Kokopo. And you know how people are. Practical. They make do, get by, do what they need to survive. Not complain, put up with the chaos, the mess, the indecision, and after a time, everything settles down. You have seen it before. You can't have forgotten how it is.' He sighs. 'Lucky only a few died. All of us so, so lucky. Could have been disastrous.'

Henry's story seems familiar to Maria. But how can that be? So authentic does the memory feel, inside her there's a knot of anxiety, as though she too had been trapped in her home, as if she too had felt the ash raining down, and as if she had worried about hers and everyone else's future. Out of the fog of the past comes a recall of a glass of milk handed to her, a blanket wrapped around her legs, and a mat spread on the ground. Daddy-George is there. There's no clarity, but she knows it's real. And as it grows in strength, she can give these fragments a label. An earlier eruption. Before Henry was born. She recalls the smell the fear that seeped out of everyone. Not that she could give it a name at the time. Only that nothing was normal. All that she as a five-year-old had always depended upon was missing. Only rock-solid Daddy-George. She tries to tell Henry about that time, but she has nothing tangible upon which to build her tale.

In this way they spend her first day back Home; and the next day, more of the same; talking, filling the gaps, remembering. On the second evening, hiding her face in the folds of the evening's blanket of darkness, she asks Henry about Stephen.

She still hasn't called Brisbane.

§

Did she come back because he made contact? Or did she come back because he mentioned Stephen and the crate? What's inside the crate? What could it be, to bring her home? Look at her. She's old, too. Not easy for her to travel this long way.

And now she's asked the question, his emotions are getting the better of him. Her question requires him to talk about Stephen, and that's hard because his experience with Stephen is precious. He doesn't want to share it. But how can he answer her without revealing this late-in-life connection? He falls back to Pisin to mask his emotions. He can't look at her.

'Like me toktok, he die pinis already. He died in 2008. Sara, his haus meri come here to tell me he was dying. I go long Kavieng to see him. Sara, she had been here before, another time, earlier.'

He tells her about the 2004 visit and the arrival of the chest. That's easy, that telling.

'In 2004, Sara, she gives me this letter.'

He's been carrying the scrolls in his pocket since his sister arrived, expecting the topic of Stephen to arise sooner or later. He holds it out toward her. She doesn't shift her glance from his face. Nor does she respond. He shakes the scroll gently, and looks down at it, hoping she will follow his example.

'You can see. It looks old, yellow, but me think – um – maybe just that the paper been lying around a long time. Red characters. Cantonese, maybe. Red for good fortune. Ha ha. Could be Japanese. Me, I wouldn't know. Understand some Cantonese, I understand when listening, but not reading.' His sister still doesn't take the paper from his hand. Her facial expressions are blank. Nothing there for him to interpret, nothing to salve his curiosity.

'Sara tells me, "For masta Seeto's daughter."' He looks over at his sister. 'That's you. Why you? Do you know Uncle Stephen?'

She ignores his question. Instead, she enquires. 'And did you see Stephen? Do you know Stephen?'

Two can play this game. He withholds his story momentarily.

'Stephen's a mystery man. As a kid, only saw him when he and my papa got together.. Didn't get on, those two.'

He can't tell what's going on in her head. Now, her eyes are keeping themselves busy by studying her own hand, as if they are detached from the rest of her body. She folds them and unfolds them in her lap. All her attention is focused on her hands. Maybe, Henry wonders, she doesn't want her eyes to fly off, out of control, and spill her secrets. He remembers his earlier suspicions she knows more about Uncle Stephen than he does and challenging that somehow has become a one-sided competition for him.

'Not my father's brother you know. Sorry. Our father's brother. Papa's story was different but Stephen told me he was only an orphan or a street boy who had bad fortune, a stranger to papa. Someone made the mistake of thinking them as brothers – same surname. Made things easier for Stephen. Too young to stay if he'd migrated on his own. No one knew that they weren't brothers – this mistake, made by so many, amused Papa. He'd say,' and Henry let his voice change, attempting to mimic his father's voice: '"Shows how foolish Westerners are."'

Discarding his imitation of his father, he continues.

'Loved to tell me about how he and Stephen journeyed on the same ship. Told me, over and,' again he imitates his father. '"All I had when I leave the village, fifteen silver dollars from a married sister."' Again, he returns to his own voice. 'Said, "Dollars to pay fare." He'd hold his hands out and shrug. "Where to? Wherever... That's where I stop. Work. Earn money for the family in China." He'd tap his head and smile. "Smart. Cost nothing along the road to the port. Work for food. One whole year. It took me. Then, lucky, a ship coming to New Guinea needed a cook. Very lucky. Free passage for cooking. Silver dollars still in pocket."'

She nods her head, but it's unconvincing. Is she encouraging him to tell her more? Why then is there a strange look on her face, like something is bursting to come out? Maybe she doesn't believe his lie, his stories made-up to show her she might have had their mumma and grandmother, but he'd had their dad. There's a doubt rattling away in his head. What about that time he saw Maria and their father together in a Chinatown trade store? Maybe she's the one who knows or rather knew their father, not him and if she knew him only a little, it wouldn't take much to see through his stories.

'Papa never liked to discuss his own life.,' he confesses. 'Ask too many questions, and he'd shout "tambu. Forbidden territory." I'm not being honest. What he used to shout in Cantonese was "sei hoi", which means "fuck off". My apologies if you find that offensive. But "tambu" sounds too tame, and doesn't show the real man. The real man was like a vicious dog.'

No dog for this son. Only a silent cruel dictator, who could smash his offspring with only a lift of an eyebrow or a twist of his lips. Does Maria know? Was papa the same with Maria? A leopard doesn't change his spots. Truth is, Papa was elsewhere most of the time. Inaccessible. A blessing and a curse.

Futile as it may be, illogical perhaps and, he convinces himself, also contrary to his present state of mind, his customary bitterness is showing itself. It causes him to cast a disparaging glance in his sister's direction, as internally he is once again his four-year-old self, railing against injustices, searching for signs of gloating or, worse, disrespect from her, because she knows he's talking rubbish and is making a fool of himself. But those blue eyes speak of something else. Pain? Sadness? Should he ask her about that time, why she and their father were together in that trade store? Clear the air? No, he counsels himself. Don't let your stupidness win. You have your sister here, now, and she is listening. Don't spoil things. Don't let those old angers get the better of you. He puffs himself up, back to where he's the son loved by their father, a son who had shared a life with their father, if only to convince himself.

'Papa gave me one silver coin. Never give me anything so precious. And at the time gave me instructions.' Henry points towards the house. He leans over, showing his willingness to share. 'Must show you later.' Again, she nods.

'Papa told me "You don't lose this, this tell you to work hard, and never let those white bosses win."'

He takes a deep breath, his head drops a little, knowing the lie of his claim, but he covers his momentary lapse well. 'Did me no good. I stand up for nothing.'

He's nearly knocked off his feet when his sister rises and wraps her arms around him. So strange to have physical contact with her. She whispers, 'Oh Henry. Why are you so sad?'

His sister sees her brother's sadness? No one except Bridget has ever said they see that. Even Rachel his wife could not tell how he was feeling, because he was the master of disguise, wore his mask so well – but his sister sees. This revelation causes him to unravel. Should he tell her the truth of the silver dollar? The silver dollar, yes, his father waved it in his face and, yes, he ended up with it, but not in the loving fatherly way he's making it sound. He chooses not to spoil the moment with the truth. She throws herself back down in her chair and he follows suit. After a moment's silence, he loses control. He's babbling now.

'Know so little about papa's life in China. Like most Rabaul Chinese, for him better to be a silent grumbler who ate his resentment. Except he told me he had a wife back in the old country. Did you know that?'

Maria shakes her head. Her eyes search his. There's sorrow in them. But he's too carried away with his story to question why.

'Well, he said he wanted to bring her out. Against regulations – according to him, authorities didn't want us to increase in numbers.' He wants to joke but isn't sure how Maria will take it. He smiles at her and tries his luck. 'It didn't work. Papa just made plenty multicoloured babies.'

When he sees a smile growing on his sister's face, he laughs out loud. And she laughs too. Her laughter grows and grows until it's full-bodied. The sound takes him by surprise.

He begins again, but this time he can't keep the truth inside.

'After war, papa and me hide in the bush. He didn't stay, left me with Brigid, Tolai lady who come from this village.' Henry waves his arm to indicate this space around them is his. He belongs here. 'I only see Papa now and then, years apart sometimes. Not know him well. I gaimin. Make up my stories. Sorry. Same as lying.'

She doesn't respond. What does he expect? He's at the point where he is thinking they need other subjects to converse about when she speaks.

'I can't lie to you either, Henry.'

Her hands have her attention once more. She's staring at them. What is she going to tell him? The silence between them lingers and then is broken by her softly spoken words.

'I don't like our papa very much. He was older when I knew him. Maybe he was different when he was young.'

The minutes tick by. His sister doesn't move her eyes from her hands for a long time. Then they flash to his face. As she stares into his eyes, it's like she's boring into his mind, reaching the heart and soul of who he is. He's waiting, but she doesn't explain her statement, only fixes upon him with her piercing glare.

Another start. 'Ah....'

But then....

'I hated him, Henry. With a passion. He is a terrible man. Mumma told me this, and so did Nenek. Never trust him, they toktok long mi. They have no choice but to give you over to his care. At start of The War. But later, after Nenek go On High, I couldn't get free of him. He held my life in a fist-like grip, and he made sure I knew that, and he ruined it. The man cares for no one but himself.'

She's permitting herself to let loose. She's sobbing, gasping for air, swallowing and yet holding herself as stiff as a board. He doesn't know what to do. He's seated like a ramrod in his chair, worrying that if he wriggles or stretches, she might read any movement as disrespectful. Seated as she is beside him, she's scrunched herself down, shoulders turning inward to her chest, arms clutching her stomach, and head down as low as it will bend. She's barely moving. Amazing effort, he notes, given her size. Her suppressed sobs fill the space between them. Sometime later, she ceases weeping. He'd wished her to stop earlier, the sound and the emotions that came with it was agonising. He had nothing he could do or say to help. Just had to sit and wait. Now he wishes she hadn't stopped. The silence is too raw. He still doesn't know what to do or say and desperately and awkwardly lands on the subject that had held her interest earlier.

'Back to Stephen.' His voice sounds strained even to himself but he forces himself to continue. 'Now this meri Sara tells me that once the crate, your crate, was safe in my bedroom, the "little brother" Stephen needed me. The truck and its crew went back to where they came from and I drove Sara back to Stephen's home. Long drive. Along the coast to Warangoi, then way, way inland. Hours of driving, driving, driving. Up a rough track. Thick bush, not cleared much. Then we come long hut. Lopsided. Rusted truck at front. Furniture that looked like it had had better days. I figured Stephen hasn't much money, but it's not a bad house, just bits and pieces. Haus meri, she cries out, and I wasn't sure if she was crying tears of sadness, or of joy to be home, or of worry for her masta. "There," she says. "There's masta Stephen. In the tree's shade. He sits there and reads." I think now maybe she was just pleased to get back and see he was still alive. Sure enough, there he was. All skin and bone, long-haired.'

He stops talking. His sister's face has turned from him, as if she's looking at the scenery or anywhere but in his direction. At least she's stopped sobbing, but he can see from the stiffness of her body it's an effort for her to stop, and the shine on her cheeks tells him the tears are still spilling out. It's a relief not to hear her weeping. The air shimmers between them; he compares the tenseness of her body to the tautness of the strings of a pipa. Ah, yes, the strings of a pipa. He recalls the time his father had 'acquired' a pipa, playing mah jong. Some poor loser had brought this treasured musical instrument all the way from China. His father couldn't play it. The few times the pipa had surfaced, he'd felt sad. When so few items might be chosen to accompany someone on a long journey, that poor loser must have really loved to play his pipa, so a win by a man who appreciated nothing meant that that other had lost more than a game but also the possibility of making lovely music. The day his father returned home carrying the pipa, Henry said nothing because he knew what his father would reply if he'd asked about the instrument. 'Foolish man for gambling.' As if his papa could point the finger at others. Papa's life was a gamble every way you looked at it. No doubt his father would have laughed long and hard at the expense of the pipa player. But, given any thought, it's easy to recognise the pipa player must have reached the bottom of his particular well. His only option for survival was to gamble his most precious possession. As it did then, this insight sits heavy inside Henry's heart. He'd wondered over and over what Fate had delivered to the former pipa owner.

Well, if his sister doesn't want to talk, it's okay. But there's a sharp edge of guilt attached to this concession. He's caught between wanting to comfort and not knowing how. With no other option presenting itself, his mind permits words to tumble out to fill the space of awkwardness.

'I thought Stephen was skinny because he was sick. But I discovered later that that's who he is, a thin man.' She is nodding. 'And he was old. What'd he be in 2004? In his eighties, maybe?'

'Eighty-seven,' she whispers.

She is listening. At last, a word. A victory. This means she does know more than she admits about Stephen

'Oh. That old? Anyway. It surprised me how agile he was. When I put my hand out to shake his, his hand shot out, like, boom.' Awkward. While outwardly his sister doesn't seem to be taking much notice, there's a sense she'll sit there and take in anything and everything he has to say about Stephen.

'I stayed a month, and he told me his life story. What I hadn't known before about the Chinese and Mixed Race of Rabaul I soon learnt. Slow learner, me. Live my whole life in it and noticed nothing. I resented being in the bush all those years, thinking it as a kind of banishment, when being there kept me away from the lunacy and politics of town. Well,' he continues, while examining his sister's face, 'Maybe not everything. He told me the history but not the reason for this letter, nor why he so openly included me into his life.'

He flaps it again and waits, amazed she still hasn't taken it from him. Not a ripple of expression. Bored with his tale? No, he can feel her hunger for news of Stephen. He's managed to hold close to himself any insight into what caring for a dying Stephen a few years later did for him. Does he think opening up makes him appear weak? No. He likes the person he became in Kavieng with the dying Uncle, and he's afraid sharing the memory might weaken it for him.

He flaps the letter again, then puts it down. This is only to stall for time. He has an urge to be honest, which he's trying to resist and yet failing. Already failed. He justifies the failure by telling himself it's time to take a risk. With a sigh, he admits to his sister, 'A big education for me, spending time with Stephen. I went to his home in Kavieng. Later. He was dying.'

Is that the sound of weeping again?

'Me, I lived a life of letting things slip. My policy has always been to question nothing if my reward was likely only to bring trouble to myself. Or I let my anger get the better of me. That's why I couldn't go back home, after the war, too angry. I didn't feel wanted.'

He couldn't say the word he meant to say. 'Loved.' A horrible noise comes from his sister's mouth but he behaves as if he's heard nothing.

She flashes a quick but startled look at him and then turns away again.

'Since meeting Uncle Stephen, I have realised that way's not living a life. Did you know Uncle Stephen reads everything? He knows histories most of us don't even bother about. Like how we aren't just interlopers. He toktok me that our ancestors, well, somebody's ancestors but Chinese at any rate, were here where Rabaul was, before even the Germans. They built ships. Had a shipyard out on Matupit Island. They traded with the tribes. Then the Germans made this area a colony, brought in more of us and called our ancestors "non-indigenous natives" using them to do the mid-level jobs: build German houses and stores and workshops, build German tramways and German wharves. Some even maintained German business books. New Guineans were the labourers and the ones who'd come from elsewhere were the craftsmen, the artisans, the tailors, the chefs, the ones who took care of money – all the important stuff. Later, when the Australians were in charge, people like papa's boss established their own commercial enterprises. They acquired land such as plantations, blocks in town, anything they could get their hands on, by any means available. Under the laws of the Territory, we weren't permitted land ownership. Stephen told me that while the power was in the hands of administrators, Germany first and then Australia, the wealth ended up in our community.' He's slipping again, from him identifying as New Guinean to Chinese. Immersed in his story as he is, slippage is the last thing on his mind.

'Stephen said Europeans were the high-level clerks and managers, acting for whoever was in charge of the region, and in between them and the labourers, in the positions that earned all the money, that was us. Yet we are told we don't belong. That New Guinea was all about the tribes becoming a nation and the expats helping them get there. But we in-betweeners were and still are stubborn. Having travelled a long way from homelands like southern China, or Indonesia or Samoa, or Malaya, or Japan and elsewhere, knowing they had to work hard to survive, to succeed, they did just that. Invisible. But successful. Stephen teach me this.'

'Papa told me nothing and yet he worked for one of the wealthiest businessmen of the town. Papa's focus was only on himself. A boaster. Thought of himself as big power-wise but in truth he was a small man in every way, and never one of those Stephen said were the cornerstone of Rabaul. Stephen was a detail man. Given other opportunities, he could have been one of those successful ones. You know this too. You must know, if he can write you a letter. Yes?'

He glances, still hoping she will rise to his bait. A tight smile is all she offers.

'I didn't want to know that stuff before. Everything made me angry. Too much for one man to take in. Thought it didn't concern me. But,' he said, looking skyward with respect, 'someone wanted me to learn something. At first, when I saw him at the Warangoi, I saw my future self in Stephen. Could end up just like him, old in a hut somewhere and dying, if I wasn't careful, with everything and everyone gone.' Henry sighed. 'What I had assumed about Stephen was wrong. Yes, his hut at Warangoi was primitive, but he hadn't lost who he was. I am well down that track. Never cared enough to find myself.'

He lifts his head, feels pride flood back in when he thinks of what he did for Stephen.

'He told me that since he had taken care of the crate, he was moving to Kavieng, That's the place he wanted to die in. What he meant was, since he had given me the crate to send to you, he could move on. And me being me, I never admitted I hadn't sent it, not even when he was on his death bed. Sorry again, but that shows you what a stupid man I am. Helping him pack in 2004 and staying with him in 2008 made me think for once I might have been a good son, if my papa had given me a chance. But, as always, I turned the good into bad by lying about not doing what I said I would. Shipping the crate, I mean.'

He lets the impact of lapsing time sink into his own psyche. He can no longer deny his part in a larger story. The repercussions of his procrastination have become real and measurable, ensuring he recognises this story stretches beyond him and his issues. Should have… but he didn't. That's the story of his life.

'Sorry Maria. I take a long time to tell you about the crate he left for you.'

She flinches. Is she sick of hearing him apologise? He flaps the letter once more. Despite his guilt, he feels lighter, even permits himself to pat Maria on the shoulder. He waits until she turns to see why he has stopped talking, her face open, as if she thinks he has something more to say. What does she want? He's convinced she wouldn't have expected to hear the things he's been telling her. How could she?

'Hah. Uncle Stephen knew your address when your brother did not. Could have just sent the crate to you himself. Why didn't he?'

Her expression fills him with shame. She knows the reason. He is just too dumb to get why and it's too hard for her to tell him. Her face is awash with emotions. He can only guess what they might be: sadness, acceptance, hopelessness, fear, guilt, or maybe even resignation. But he doesn't understand.

It's he who got to know Stephen, not her; she's been in Australia for too many years, so how could Stephen mean so much to her? Maybe he should have responded earlier. Maybe. Again, he says, 'So sorry. I'm slack. Selfish. Did not realise the crate's importance.' Another lie. He always suspected. But his anger got in the way. He wanted revenge. What good did it do him? He sees himself as his father's son. Abhorrent.

His sister drops her head, sucks in a wet breath, but doesn't explain. She doesn't look Chinese, but she behaves like all the Chinese he has known. Gives nothing away, keeps everything private. Curiosity eats at him.

One thing he knows: he admits he's ready to like his sister after all these years of hating her, of allowing his resentment to govern his actions, and of insistence on carrying this negativity throughout his life. He pauses, takes a deep breath and plunges into the truth of it – ready to admit to himself he has always loved her, always missed her, even when he wouldn't speak her name. They spent only a few years of childhood together, so long ago; how could they know each other, miss each other? But this person knows him, this person understands him.

He hands her the yellowed letter. 'Here. Please take this. Stephen wrote this to you.'

10

HENRY'S HOME
October 30

Now he's truly her brother again, Maria admits to herself that Henry deserves to know what Stephen means to her. He doesn't understand, can't understand, why Stephen did not send her the chest himself instead of asking Henry. Only Stephen knew she wanted to reconnect with Henry. Only Stephen would consider the bigger picture and see a way to put right what was wrong. And he waited until Patrick had died. Nor does Henry understand why she isn't rushing to open the crate or why she isn't curious about what's inside. She can't tell him yet, because that would mean she'd have to tell him the whole story, that she already knows what's inside. If he did know the rest of the story, she might be able to say to him, 'Henry, I had this crate made, years ago, to protect Nenek's chest so I could send it to Stephen.' Knowing that makes sense of everything else; knowing that answers all his questions. Without doubt she knows that Stephen would have left the contents of Nenek's chest as they were when she sent it to him. He may have added to it, as he has done on many occasions in earlier years. As much as she'd love to see what he might have added, to learn what those items might be will have to wait. Nenek's chest and its contents represent every lost part of her life. She knows that to open it will rip open the stitches of an almost fatal wound. She's not ready yet. Soon. Anyway, she needs Ling's help to open the crate without damaging its exterior. She has a plan.

She's been here in Henry's home for less than seventy-two hours. The barriers erected over sixty years of separation are melting away, a brother and a sister connecting through talking about Stephen. And yet so little spoken. Not anywhere near what could or should be. Perhaps it's time for her to talk, and perhaps the perfect listener if it can't be Stephen is her rediscovered brother.

As he sits beside her, Henry appears calm. She finds this comforting and reassuring. She wraps the sense of their bond around her and, in doing so, permits light to fall upon the parts of herself she has kept hidden in darkness for too long. Freed at last, words flutter out of her, the ones that speak from her standpoint: leaving Rabaul, making a life in Brisbane; her jealousy of those like him who could stay back home; her garden in Brisbane; a little about Patrick. Not facts or events, but emotions. Twisted in with all this chatter and talk that she can't seem to stop or control, she can hear herself telling Henry of the emptiness, the disconnection, and the invisibility she feels. Several times she's used the word 'Home' to describe Rabaul. Home.

As she talks, running in the background is another awareness, one set in her deep sadness for her brother and a wish to weep for him, or, if only it were possible, to weep with him. She understands his need: it's the same one that's embedded in her too. It's an emptiness that is insatiable, despite the reassurances she knows are there for her, of being loved by many. She even understands his desire to claim Seeto Wei as his own father, and not hers, regardless of the man he knows him to be. By speaking as though he knew papa better than she, such a claim shores up the notion that someone cared for him. But, 'Oh,' she is wont to say. 'How well I know that man.' Too well. Would it help, or only be cruel, for Henry to know their father's lies begin with his story about how he found himself in Rabaul? That gloating voice she so often heard would have delivered to his son false tales of grandeur, all lies. The truth is their father, Seeto Wei, David Seeto, was first a beggar and a thief, then a servant, and a gambler and a bully, plucked from the streets of Kaiping by a grieving traveller who elevated him to the role of his adopted son. A thief who stole that other man's story to lie to his son and make himself feel grander than he was. No wife, no sister to give him silver coins. For a moment she wonders if Seeto Wei's lies allude to his own unfilled dreams. But she pushes that aside within seconds. In Rabaul, he had a wife and he had a family which he chose to disregard. She snatches back her empathy.

David's saviour was Loi Fook. Had Maria not once been one of his slaves, she might have felt empathy for Loi. His story was indeed a sad one. He left his village in southern China early in the twentieth century. His only goal was to escape poverty by finding an outpost in which he could build sufficient wealth to support the wife and son he had left behind. He ended up in a German colony, a hard place for a Chinaman to make any headway. It took years, too many, for him to accumulate the wealth he needed, but in the early 1930s, he returned to Kaiping, only to find his family had perished years earlier in the 1917 influenza epidemic that hit Guangzhou. The same catastrophic epidemic that the well-read Stephen had told her became known as the 'Spanish flu' taken to Europe by the thousands of Chinese migrant labourers of that era. Stephen also told her that, devastated by the loss of his family, Loi had stumbled through his village, bereft of any motive to live. What point was there now in building wealth? He had no one to share the rewards of his labour. A young thief had tried to steal from Loi. Loi had taken this accidental meeting as a sign from his gods. 'I could mould this young man to become a son, my successor. He has no life here in China. Why would he object to travelling to another country?' On the eve of their departure from China, the thief also had his own epiphany – while begging and stealing might be a hard and not very lucrative career choice, would a role as a servant be a step up or down? On that evening, he too had an accidental encounter with a younger lad, whose circumstances were far worse than his. The lad had the same surname as his: Seeto. Without the boy's consent, he introduced him to his new master as his younger brother. Thus, the thief no longer stood on the bottom rung.

Earlier, as she had poured out her emotions, Henry had not interrupted. She couldn't stop her words but she wondered how Henry might have heard them. She'd watched for signs that might reveal his thoughts. She assessed that as she talked and talked, Henry's potential judgments became less and less relevant. She was expelling the emotions of decades. In the guise of talking to her brother, she discovered that she was speaking to herself.

The sense of freedom from hearing her own perspectives was exhilarating. To express her emotions and insights without fear is becoming addictive. On and on she is waffling. And in those moments of release she realises that the last time she had felt so liberated was during those rare but glorious days spent with Stephen. That revelation is her undoing. Throughout most of Henry's storytelling about the decline of Stephen and his own dereliction of duty she had distanced herself, visualising this man with the name Stephen as a stranger, a character in Henry's story. Yet the wall could not stand forever and remembering the crate brought her to recall the contents and the reason Stephen had it. The reality of Stephen's life post-1959 has evolved in her mind. She can no longer push to the side the truth that Stephen is dead. The tiny flame of hope that has flickered in her since 1959 is at last extinguished. The reappearance of her one-time property had temporarily reignited the flame and, yes, she dreamt of a reunion, but her practical side had conceded it was unlikely, nothing more than a wish. If examined by some distant observer, it might be read as a coping mechanism, one she had perfected during the long waits between Stephen's visits in the trade store days. In those hours, days, months and years of waiting, somewhere inside her a tiny vibration had offered proof of continued life. It had provided her with reassurance that Stephen's life elsewhere was running in parallel with hers, that both of them were continuing as they must, until that moment when they could break geometric conventions and converge on the one location. Conceding his death is like slipping into a living death herself. With nothing on the horizon, what point is there in living? She is grieving for Stephen, and she grieves for herself, as she also grieves for an unfulfilled promise.

In Henry's garden, now, grief is contorting into anger. The ability to express it after years, decades, of repression makes it volatile. It needs a focus. There's no one else but Henry here, so he becomes her anger's target. Look at him. Blank-faced. Is he yet another person who won't or can't comfort her, acknowledge her, or see her as she is? Is everything only about him and how he's hurting? Can't he see what he's done to her? First, leaving her to live a life without the other half of herself when he was as a child. Then ignoring her. And now, too late, teasing her with a late hint of a reunion. No, no, no. As always, she's alone. Alone and hurting. Henry, like everyone else except Stephen is a waste of effort. And if only he had told her earlier about the crate. The time chosen by Stephen to return the chest to her was the year her husband had died. She wistfully counts. Had she returned soon after, she would have had at least three years with Stephen.

As she is thinking these malicious thoughts, Henry jumps to his feet, body tight and shoulders hunched, like a boxer entering the ring. A short, bald-headed, and angry boxer. Nothing but noise and grand postures. Henry wastes none of his intensity on his sister. His anger is real. Has there been a symbiotic transfer of her volcanic anger to him?

However, his action are so comical to observe, she can't maintain her rage. As hers diminishes, Henry's escalates, translating into weird poses and actions. From her viewpoint, it's an hilarious pantomime. She struggles to contain her mirth, aware of how disrespectful it would be to laugh at a man experiencing extreme emotions. It's a battle to keep a straight face. She watches as Henry strides towards a palm tree, gives it a karate kick then takes up a position facing away from her, arms folded; then he charges towards her. She braces herself for impact. There's no need. Half a metre short, he halts, places his hands on his hips and glares at her, eyes wide and challenging, a bull whose face is bright red and blotchy. Is this the real Henry, the one who seems can only hate her for ever? Was his keenness to reconcile a sham? What is behind this anger? Some imagined hurt she has inflicted on him? She can't remember anything that might deserve this violent response.

Brother and sister stare at each other, both too overwhelmed by each other's outbursts to say a word. Henry seems as surprised by his own actions as she is. Seconds drag into minutes. She can't ignore Henry's distorted face, his rigid jaw, his clenched hands. She watches in agony and then his body slumps, as though he's expended all available energy. His face crumbles. Is he crying? Words are struggling from his mouth. One word, pause, and then another, pause. Only as they fall from his mouth does his face return to normal. Angry words. So angry they stick in his throat on their way out.

'Home?'

'You call this. "Home"?'

'No. We. Only. Tenants.'

'No one. Ever. Says. We belong. Never. And never will. Never say. "You guys are. Part of this country". Why are they like that? Hate us. Hate our skin. Hate the way we speak. Planned for us to just die out. Or go elsewhere. Tolerated is all. Unless we forget our traditions and adopt theirs.'

She can read his face. Though he says these things, even he knows they're lies. But he's too invested in his anger to be honest. He's not ready for that, not yet.

He slams his hand onto the back of a nearby chair. 'Don't know what to do with us, they don't. And you guys,' he shakes his finger at her. 'You guys made it easy for them. They got rid of you. Sent you to Australia. Solved their problem. But me, I stay.'

He sighs. To her ears his sigh has come from the bottom of his soul, a last great vent of emotional steam. Because, at last, his shoulders have relaxed, and his limbs are still.

'For what I stay?' he shrugs his shoulders. 'Me, I got Tolai brothers.

They're kind and love me. Act like I belong.' Shoulders sag. 'But, no, no, no. They savy true. Me savy. Everyone knows what is going on here. We, you and me, we belong nowhere. Who are we? Might love New Guinea, but we not New Guinean. We might speak Cantonese...' He looks at her with a half-question in his eyes, as if he's not sure if she speaks Cantonese. Is he wondering if he can include her in his 'we'? He spits out an answer to his own question. 'But we. Not Chinese. We. In between. We nothing. Got no name. No home. No nation. Nothing. Invisible.'

His words hit her hard. Yes, it's anger. Maybe fear. She recognises the emotions. Is this part of her anger, too? She recalls as a seven-year-old, noticing how the Japanese mistreated prisoners 'just because they were Chinese', knowing that part of her was Chinese, and how she felt 'less than', or odd. And that part of her still not being seen as Chinese, because of her skin colour or her frizzy hair or her blue eyes, and being excluded at school or her opinions discounted as someone who could speak about Chinese subjects. Experiencing the subtle exclusion based on birthplace or ancestry. As an adult, reading much more into those exclusions. Judging herself as deficient or not belonging, as she'd felt judged by others, yet thinking, why? Yes. I'm angry.

She looks at Henry. He's staring back at her. Are her feelings showing on her face as his did? Inside her, a mountain stream is racing through rapids. It's almost as though she can hear a familiar voice. Grandmother's. Nenek's. She can feel the drumbeat of fingers tapping on her chest. And it all seems clear. It has taken all these years to make sense. She turns and wraps her arms around her brother. His body tenses, but he does not move away.

'Oh Henry, it is home. Not the town. But what it is and has been. No one can tell us who we are and who we aren't. Someone, anyone, saying we don't belong does not make it so. If we see this as Home, then it is Home, no matter who we are or where we come from. No one can erase a past written inside us. That past has shaped us. Even if we don't see it, it's there. And it comes out through our eyes and mouth, in what we like to eat, by how we do things, what and how we understand, and even though our kids don't know it, we have passed it on to them. It's in our DNA. Doesn't matter where we live, what our passports call us. We know who we are. If we have done anything wrong – I know I have – it's forgetting. Nenek used to tell me, when there was just her and me after The War, know yourself. Remember who you are. And....' Now she is shaking, tears welling in her eyes. She's losing control. In her animated speech to her brother, she reaffirms her own failures. Only her grip around Henry is keeping her upright. 'Oh, my little brother, I think it's too late for me.'

Beneath her embrace, she feels Henry's body crumbling and moulding itself into hers. He's little Henry again. The one who left her on Malaguna Road. She waits until her brother leans away from her to follow his lead. They both return to staring across the now pitch-black harbour, the silence that stretches out between them a comfort, this time not the wordlessness of strangers but a warm quietness and contemplation. The minutes stretch. It's impossible to gauge the actual span of time, and then Henry's voice, pained, thin, breaks the spell.

'Maria, what happened to our mother?'

She knows Henry needs an answer, knows she must drag those words from the dark recesses in which she hid them long ago. Their foulness works its way to her mouth, and its sharp edges cut into her, until it takes solid form and become undeniably real in the brutal form of articulated fact.

'Forced to become Japanese "comfort woman". Executed.'

She can't tell him all she knows: the betrayal Mumma suffered, via a local lad who was at risk of being put to the sword, or the manner of her execution. Hands bound behind her back, lumbered onto a Japanese harbour vessel. Those on the wharf watched it speed out leaving a trail of white water behind it. It was last seen heading beyond the Beehive rock formations. Later, word came that the same vessel picked up passengers in Kavieng, perhaps POWs, but when it returned to the wharf there were no passengers. A Tolai crew member whispered what he had witnessed and the news spread like wildfire.

'Young missus Pereira, she lusim head. Big Japanese boss cut it off and throw it in the sea then push the rest of the missus in too. Same-same Aussie soldiers.'

Maria discovered years later, that not only had their mother died but also a yet-to-be-born brother or sister. Nor can she provide a description of Daddy-George's fate. Possibly their step-father suffered a similar fate to their beloved mother. No one knows what happened to the prisoners on board the 'Montevideo Maru'. Did they go down with the ship or were they, as many speculated, executed on New Guinea soil before the vessel set sail for Japan? Either way, he never returned. Already, with only such a small part of their history told, she can hear the sucking in of air. She's uncertain whether it is her own breath or Henry's.

Now they are silent. A strange but familiar habit, she notes to herself. Did we learn it as children? This locking inside of our hurt and pain? A tool for survival? And now the moment has come when being silent no longer works. One question from Henry has given her a thump on the back. How many other questions requiring answers lie within the silences of the years? Maybe he wants to fill the gaps – as she does – all the bits and pieces that their separate and separated lives hunger for. How will she know if he's ready, as she is?

'Henry, do you remember our grandmother?'

He shakes his head. His blank face gives nothing away, but she reads the slight turn of his head to mean he's not opposed to hearing whatever she has to say.

'Henry, how about we get something to eat, a good long drink, make ourselves comfortable and let me tell you grandmother's stories. I am so sorry you weren't there to hear them with me. I missed you, Henry. My little brus. Missed you so much.'

§

Maria's eyes are caressing the rough blond timbers of the crate. She has to wait until seven-thirty. That's when Ling will come to open it for her. Now the moment is near, the waiting has become an agony. This box has brought her home. This, and the promise it offered. That call. The one she never dreamt would happen. Her brother's words during that call. A sentence she reflected upon for hours after the call. Henry had said: 'Uncle Stephen has asked me to make sure you receive this crate.'

She can't erase Henry's turn of phrase and the assumptions she drew from it. Again, and again, those words. She can only hear those words, 'Uncle Stephen has asked', as telling her 'Stephen is alive.' Yet she wasn't brave enough then to have this notion confirmed, to ask Henry the question, afraid the answer might not be the one she wants to hear. And willing to pretend that her version is the truth, because only that version could propel her beyond her everyday Brisbane life to do what was necessary to go home, despite her fear of what that trip might bring, or cost her, and despite knowing how such a trip might compromise her already fragile health. That sentence had fertilised hope, which had blossomed. Ahead she could see only Stephen, a younger Stephen, there in front of her younger self. By focusing on that after Henry's call, she could bypass a strange emotion that had accompanied the hope, a degree of angry suspicion that had spoilt her elation over at last hearing from her brother. When something you have longed for is delivered, it is natural to have doubts and questions that need answers. Especially when deep down you never believed this could happen, when for decades there was no communication, no replies to letters sent, no casual dropping in when in town. The wounds of rejection are too deep to plaster over. Until 1975 they'd lived in the same, not so very large town. She'd see him from across a street, or in the market, and her hopes would rise, only to have them dashed by a furtive turn away, a failure to make eye contact. For what reason? Why had he refused to return to the family as he should have once the war was over? She pushed past her doubts and rode a cloud of belief that only the best outcome could come from accepting Henry's invitation. She applied for a visa, bought an air ticket and that was it. Decision made. Let the chips fall where they might, she counselled herself.

When Henry told her about the crate in his bedroom, it was a shock. She had never considered Grandma's chest as lost. Once hers and given to Stephen, she never expected it to come back to her. The last time she had seen the crate and the chest it contained was in 1959 – she'll never forget the year, for many reasons – and it was swinging across the wharf, high above her car, heading for the hold of a local supply vessel. When the cargo was delivered to Loi's island plantation, and when Stephen opened it, did he discover her heart inside, as she intended him to do?

She slumps onto Henry's bed and lets her mind go back to 1959, to the moment she has fought to keep secret ever since.

11

CHINATOWN RABAUL, ENE, TPNG
1959

She's listening to Radio Australia. Errol Flynn has passed away. He died in Canada. A long way from New Guinea, where he once belonged, where once he owned businesses that failed. She likes the connection that comes through Errol, between Rabaul and places like Canada and the US and the UK.

Hum bao are steaming on the cooker.

Had it been someone other than Stephen interrupting her listening, she might have been cross. Patrick informed her yesterday that Stephen was in town, otherwise she might not have known. Since they had given up hope of living their dream, Stephen has tried to keep his distance, not always succeeding. But it's been four or five months since she last met him. Feels like it's been forever and, under the circumstances, she should know exactly how long, except she doesn't want to give that knowledge any substance. He's asked her to meet him at the Small Ships Wharf.

Patrick also reported that her father, David, had ordered Stephen to pay him a visit. Her father's not the 'ordering' kind of person, especially when dealing with someone who also works for his own employer, Loi, as Stephen does. If things need to happen, they do, such is the hold that Loi has over his so-called employees. She recognises this must be one of Patrick's exaggerations.

For Stephen, she worries. Exaggeration or not, this might be a bad sign. Patrick's exact words were: 'Stephen kam long store na toktok important samting long papa belong yu.' Is it Stephen who has requested the important meeting, not her father?

She too has business with Stephen, but her business is best conducted without a face-to-face meeting. It's been in a storage room at the wharf, awaiting the next shipment to the plantation. As much as she fears the pain of seeing Stephen again, now he's asked her to come, how can she say no? Face-to-face will be hard. Stephen's the only person with whom she has ever shared her most private thoughts, and he used to read them without her speaking. Today, though, she must keep those thoughts locked inside her. If he knew her secret, it would rip him apart. Although it is her nature always to be honest, something her Nenek had taught her, honesty here might be fatal for Stephen.

She suspects only bad possibilities for what her father and Loi might have in mind for Stephen. Nothing can make Stephen's and her own futures better. She and Stephen are pawns in the two men's games. Loi's plans, whatever they might be, always come at a cost to Stephen and through Stephen, to her. Bottom line, for Stephen and for her, there's no getting around the reality: he's married to Mei Yee and she to Mei Yee's brother. Patrick's the only beneficiary of these arrangements.

As she drives along the Small Ships Wharf, she can see him standing at the far end, waiting for her. This is as good a place as any for their meeting if for no other reason than because it's far from Chinatown, far from family and friends. The wharf could do with some maintenance, considering the myriad of vessels that use it to take on supplies for outlying plantations, missions and communities. It's a sad place for her. From here, Stephen far too often boarded a vessel and left her behind. She's convinced this will be their final farewell.

The regular afternoon downpour has left puddles along the uneven surface of the wharf. As she drives towards Stephen, water splashes up on the side windows and the windscreen: like the tears she cannot allow herself to shed. There are trucks and wharf workers everywhere. Her eyes are watchful. A crane towers overhead, dangling a blond-wooded crate. She stops the car and looks. Yes, that is her crate. Is this a sign?

No, she tells herself. If it is an omen, it's not a good one. Since the day her father announced her forthcoming marriage to Patrick, she has contemplated how to find a means of reassuring Stephen of her enduring love, despite the way things have turned out. She knows he'll read her message from the crate, and all she can read from seeing it pass overhead is that it's on its way to his plantation. In New Guinea talk, this could be 'long gutpela payback.' Once the decision was made, to crate Nenek's chest was the easy part. She's aware how few opportunities she will have to send it to Stephen. This current visit to Rabaul provides her that window of opportunity.

She stops the car a short distance from Stephen. He has only eyes for the boy in his arms. Once she's out of her car, and walking towards him, he turns at last to face her. Only a short walk, but each step feels heavy, like her body is aging with each one, and finally, standing in front of him, she feels much older than her twenty-four years.

Maybe this is the act of a kind God, this slowing of time.

Last look. Goodbye, my love.

This is the first time she has seen his son. The boy is a baby version of Stephen. He plays with his father's hair. Her own fingers ache with longing. The boy looks at her and smiles.

It's as if she, Stephen and the boy are in a space separate from the hustle and bustle: the ship being loaded and the trucks coming and going. She hears the drone of an engine. Her body feels a vibration running through the wharf. There's a smell of copra and diesel. She feels ill, tastes bile in her throat. But she knows these symptoms are not to do with the wharf or the moment, as large as this is. She works hard to hide them.

Behind Stephen, high on the ship's bridge, a man is watching them. The captain. She recognises him. What's-his-name? Someone from schooldays. His grin suggests he might suspect something unusual is happening right before his eyes, something about which he can spin a yarn the next time he's having beers at the Ambonese Club. Contributing to the Rabaul gossip machine. Maybe he's thinking: why is this unlikely duo meeting here, at this stinking place? He's right. It's odd. Only wharfies frequent the dock unless some soul's boarding or disembarking.

Stephen must have a reason for choosing this place. Maybe it allows him a quick escape. He and the boy can board when she and Stephen finish their business. Maybe Stephen's trying to avoid prying eyes.

Stephen must know the captain's there, but he doesn't turn. His dark eyes, his tense jaw, his rigid body all announce that he's here to do what he needs to do. The effort required is noticeable, writ across a face so familiar to her.

The boy's tapping his father's face. This makes her smile and seeing that, the boy tucks his head into his father's neck. Again, desire washes through her.

In Cantonese, Stephen speaks to her: 'You know Mei Yee can't stay. No Australian passport. Time's up, got to go back to China. Leaving next week.

I'll be back at the plantation by then.' She doesn't trust herself to reply. The silence grows.

He adds: 'Besides, she wants to go. Hates it here.'

One quick look at his boy before he lifts the baby towards her. She feels his pain, swallows a gasp, and reaches for the child.

In Cantonese again, he speaks to her: 'Here. He's your son.'

How wrong were her suspicions about the business between Stephen, Patrick and David? But she was right about one thing: today has been at a cost to Stephen and to Mei Yee, and their son. And for what?

Without protest the boy moves from Stephen's arms into hers. Once in her embrace, he curls his body and burrows his head into her chest. She kisses his forehead, draws in the aroma of his body, wraps his pale skin in her brown arms, and bone-on-bone, skin-on-skin, she feels his heartbeat. His tiny hands reach up into her curls. From this moment he becomes her son, not Stephen's. From this day forward, she will be his mother. She's unable to look into Stephen's eyes. Nor is he looking at her. She watches as his eyes walk along the body of his baby son, follow the boy's fingers as they creep into her hair, and wander down to his toes. She notices how the muscles of his jaw ripple like the taut ropes tethering the ship behind them to the wharf. And then, as if having memorised every part of the child's body, he's able to move away. Only then does he turn and face the vessel.

Later that evening, she wonders how they managed the exchange without a single touch. The imagined possibilities of a touch that never happened begin a continuous loop in her mind during her drive home, perpetuated as a sensory background to a life that no longer delivers any promise for her except through this child.

But earlier, still on the wharf, still not parted from him, she hears the captain's voice float down from the bridge: 'Work pinis long wharf, Masta Seeto. We're sailing in an hour.'

Patrick's waiting for her when she reaches home. He takes the boy from her, laughing and lifting him high, proud of his new Chinese son. There's a strange expression on his face. Is he waiting to see her reaction?

'Stephen never coming long Rabaul, never. Loi nogat want him leave plantation. Just order supplies and supplies go long liklik ships. Stephen he gat nuting. Stephen nogat Chinese wife. Only kissim New Guinea meri long plantation. Soon Stephen he olesam papa belong yu: kissim plenti New Guinea pikinini.'

She senses he's waiting to deliver his punchline

'Baby's mother sold her son to your papa for a fare back to China. This boy my reward for marrying you.'

The term 'Baby's mother' removes Patrick from the biological connection that the mother is also his sister, and this boy, Chao Liu but now Maria's son Andrew, is also Patrick's nephew. Does her husband have no emotional depth?

However, that announcement almost makes everything clear beyond any wheeling and dealing between Patrick and her father. As she had seen a need to send a final message to Stephen by way of the contents of the crate, Stephen, again in a lose-lose situation, has ensured he still has an influence over the future of his son. To comfort herself, she sees Stephen's gesture as his way of saying to her: 'If anyone should have my son, it should be you,' a gift to her in compensation for the promises neither one of them could fulfil. She doesn't dare let her emotions show.

A losing gambler her father may be, but in this one risky venture, he has shown himself to be a winner. Oh, how she hates him. And her husband.

Patrick's satisfied. He has his Chinese son. He doesn't seem to mind he's not the father of the boy, only that the boy looks Chinese. Nor does he show any concern that his sister will soon go back to China, leaving her son behind. A Chinese son presents him a face of respectability in this town. Does a Chinese son compensate him for his not-so-Chinese wife? In face of Patrick's celebration, another question flutters through her head. How Chinese might Chao Liu's half brother or sister look when he or she arrives in five months' time?

As Fate has it, Gabriel is not-so-Chinese looking. His face and body show a little of his father, Stephen, and much more of his mother. He too is New Guinean, on the outside.

12

Maria is crashing, crumbling, collapsing. Oh, Chun Yuen – she uses Stephen's Chinese name for more intimacy with him – Fate did not smile on us. The image of the wooden crate sitting in Henry's bedroom all these years burns into her heart. A missed opportunity. Her desire battles her logic. But for what? She feels ill.

Her legs do not want to carry her body. She wills the tremors of her arms to cease. She's aware it's not the climate that's causing her to sweat. Even her eyes are betraying her. Diabetes has been her companion for far too long not to recognise the warning signs. Her anger is turning to fear and fear into recognition. This is not going to end well. She's dying, soon, if not right at this moment, and more than likely she will die without her family nearby. Yes, yes, Henry and Ling are family. But they are not her sons and her grandchildren. And that falls upon her own head. If she had not been secretive, Andrew could have travelled with her. But all she could see was Chun Yuen, the two of them together again. Her and her stupid, stupid wish. The impossible wish.

Through the fog that has overtaken her she recognises she must make plans. Must prepare herself for the worst. She berates herself. Andy's not here to help, nor Francine, nor Kathy and Anna, nor Gabriel and Daniel – because you were a stupid woman who left your family behind, in more ways than one – and worse, you didn't tell them anything. They must imagine many things. And how could they ever know what she was thinking about, rushing here without warning? They'd think she'd gone longlong, mad, senile. And all so close – because who'd ever think a level-headed, sane woman would take such a gamble? And what are they going to believe when all the dust settles, and the reality hits them: mum in PNG, dead, because of a stupid chest and a brother who could have visited his sister in Brisbane rather than drag her up there, in her condition.

She takes up a pen and some paper, and fighting against her trembling body, she heads outside to the lawn that leads to the beachfront of her brother's home, hoping the cooling breezes off the harbour will allow her clarity.

Time is short. There's no doubt in her mind about that. She needs to make a plan now and stick to it. Perhaps what was meant to happen, always, was for Stephen and her to be together but not in life. Henry said Stephen's grave is in the Kavieng cemetery. To travel to Kavieng might require a miracle. She cracks a small joke to herself. 'Well, if everyone gets a miracle in their life, then I must be due for one. No miracles so far for me.'

What to do about Nenek's chest is the next issue. It's a family heirloom. She already had a plan to ship it to Brisbane. Yet that involves more than arranging its consignment. Shipping's the easy part. Ling's in the shipping business. Easy solved. Yes, she will enlist the help of Ling, and maybe he can help with the follow-on problem. In her original plan, she would have been there to tell Nenek's stories as each item came out of the chest. But she knows without doubt that will not be happening. Together, maybe, Ling and Francie can work together to fill the gaps, recreate the stories. If Death comes earlier than expected, she will record her instructions.

Less panicky, she closes her eyes and imagines the chest on its way to Brisbane and being opened by her granddaughter. She pictures Francine, wide-eyed and intrigued, plucking each item out of the chest. Curious, is her Francine, and she'll follow through. But what will each item say to her?

Oh, and there it is, the evidence of her failure. What can these precious objects say when there have been no stories attached? And whose fault is that?

Her secrets will float out of that chest like moths. Vampire moths, she amends to acknowledge the label her young grandsons might add to the likely damage wrought by the escaping insects on her loved ones. Questions without explanations; perceived truths turning into definite lies. Words of love disintegrating into deceitful fabrications. Multiple thrashings by whip would be less painful than this self-punishment. She can no longer push aside the full impact of her neglect. It's real and damaging. Her heart is emulating the pain her sons will experience when they learn what she has hidden from them. Andrew will learn he's not her son, nor Patrick his father, that he's not the person he has spent his life believing himself to be. Gabriel, too, half a lie. And Daniel. What will Daniel take from learning he is the only true son from the marriage of Maria and Patrick? Will this destroy his relationship with his brothers? Will he look at their age differences and wonder? Then, there's Francine, her one and only and adored granddaughter. The one who has heard throughout her life how like her Ah Ma she is. Will her pretend grandmother's secrets destroy her? All this damage because of a selfish woman, afraid that the truth would take her sons from her. Not wanting to risk losing her eldest. They will only remember her as a liar.

Her heart is breaking. In every way, she's failed; she's let everyone she loves down. There's no one left who can tell Nenek's stories. They are too new to Henry for him to remember them. She's slipping back to those special evenings on Nenek's verandah. She's there, opening the chest, choosing an item and waiting for Nenek to tell the story. Perhaps Nenek's chest offers hope. Perhaps Francine can create stories, not the original ones, from what's inside the chest. Nobody can tell her story, hers and Chun Yuen's. She aches to hug one more time Chao Liu, her special son Andy, and to be with him when he discovers he's an orphan so she can reassure him.

'Andrew, my son, please remember that the woman who said she's your mother has loved you as if she had given birth to you. More so'.

No one to tell Gabriel about his father, that he was born out of love, nor to reassure Daniel that the son Patrick gave his wife was as precious to her as her other two sons. Will they hate each other? Will her secrets destroy her family?

A breaking heart can do no good for a woman suffering from diabetic shock. But a brother can. The house lights silhouette Henry's body. In one hand he grips a cup, in the other a bowl.

'Tea, plenty of sugar, and some egg tarts. Make you feel better, sister.'

And yet the ghosts of the past linger. The guilt of her failure is the chain that drags their former existence into oblivion. The simple truth of her situation is apparent. She will die soon, here, not with one part of her family, and her death is likely to precipitate the destruction of her Australian family.

PART 5
THE INACCESSIBLE

A hotel in Kavieng, New Ireland Province, PNG, November 2010

Still there, waiting, in her plain room, dying Maria is calm, semi-conscious, yet drawing ever closer to where she wants to be. The voices from elsewhere have grown stronger. They are speaking to her of key moments and events that, had they been known to her, may have aided Maria in her search for identity and connection, the inaccessible stories of her ancestors.

I
Maria Seeto's grandmother Koti Pereira (deceased), 2010

Ria, this is your nenek, Koti Pereira, from On High. Ria, my precious grand-daughter, my Rabaul woman, I am watching and waiting. I know how you beat yourself up for the secrets you have kept. Too late, I hear you cry. You believe it's too late to remember who you are. It only seems so. Is it ever too late? Transcribed into our bodies and embedded in our thoughts are our identities. The past is our inheritance. Over the centuries, from our earliest ancestors, one human has joined with another and created another. Each generation before us has passed on traits, perspectives, beliefs and influences. We are our secrets. That which comes in our genes are the unrecognisable and yet intrinsic particles of our inher-ited personas; they sculpture our bodies; they translate events and provide our understanding of the world and how we fit within it. Their whispered messages guide us, as they will continue to guide all future generations.

You are so close. Soon you will be here, with me. That is why I can share these stories. Perhaps hearing these will reassure you that our secrets never disappear. They live within our silences, within our bodies, within our habits, and advise us what to value and what to discard.

I am waiting for you, Ria.

II
Maria Seeto's grandmother, Koti Pereira (deceased) in the home of Herr Heinrich Schultz, Rabaul, Neupommern (New Britain), Deutsch-Neuguinea (German New Guinea) 1913

Masta Schultz's company has done well since it moved from the mainland to Rabaul. The masta's so proud of himself that he tells his haus maid, her, Koti, frequently about how much money the company sends back to Germany. The house, it's so big. Many, many rooms. Many people working to keep everything perfect. Powerful man. Boss of everything. If you must do hard work, why not for a man everyone respects? That's what she thought until tonight. After this, when everyone toktok, what they say won't be good. There will be no work because if he's someone important then she is worth less than the dirt under his feet. No one will listen to her.

For several hours she has remained as the son left her, willing herself not to panic, not to do something she might regret; imagining herself through the eyes of the gecko watching her from his lizard spot on the ceiling.

Gecko he tingting how this tall meri look so small and why she curled in a ball on her bed? Koti, Koti, Koti. Nogat lusim. Don't let yourself unravel even if you know no one will believe you. You'll find a way around this problem. Move. Tell yourself: if yu nogat move, then manki masta Heinrich, that young man will win, big time. Big masta will never tingting Koti toktru. Masta Schultz senior will toktok everyone Koti, you tell a fib. Masta only believe pikinini belong em, his son. Son's word always carries more weight than a servant's, and masta Schultz too powerful to fight.

She wants to run away from this place, from these people. But run where? This town, Rabaul, is on an island, and even the other town, Kokopo, is on the same island. Everyone knows everyone. Rabaul gossip would make sure everyone knows something bad has happened. For someone like her, whose job is to care for a masta and his missus, there will be no job. She must be clever.

And, besides, her belongings are precious to her. She can't afford to leave them behind. She will not leave her marriage chest behind. Never. But she can't tuck it under her arms and carry it out.

Make a plan, Koti. Think, Koti. Tingting smart.

She has until dawn. By dawn, all those who work for masta Schultz will have begun their day's work and will notice if she isn't at her usual tasks.

Masta Schultz's workers, oli man na meri, will wonder: Koti, emi sick? We look and see Koti nogat kissim work, nogat wasim laplap, nogat kukim kai, nogat brumin floor. Wonem? Something must be wrong.

She guesses there can only be about two or three hours before sunrise. She has to get herself moving and find a way that will work for her, not against her.

Lifting her head and her shoulders, she brings her upper body to its full height. Her legs are curled beneath her on her bed, a kapok palliasse. She lifts her chin.

Yes, Koti, yu savy bigpela, think hard, and you will find a way around this problem. Move.

Her sleep-out is only walled to rail height, so she can watch the main house across the garden. There have been no lights in that building for some time. No movement or lights in the male servants' quarters behind the main house on one side of the garden, either. But she knows no one ever sleeps well. The nights are too hot and sticky. She cringes at the possibility of meeting anyone, although habit tells her those meetings are always silent: pass a man or meri in the night and no one looks at the other, no one speaks. Just pass and walk to wherever the sleep deprived wander.

She worries that written on her body is the young masta's crime for everyone to read. She sniffs the air and, yes, she nods, her body stinks – his stink, a foul stench that causes her to gag in disgust. The only way to rid herself of his dirty boy stink is to wash. Wash-haus kallim long Koti – a laundry room song: Koti, come long me, me gat water na soap.

She spends half her day in the laundry, and its everyday sounds and smells sing to her, familiar and comforting: to her ear, the sound of water hitting the bottom of the concrete tubs; to her nose, the aroma of freshly laundered clothes and soap. The desire for the feel of water and lathered soap on her body becomes an obsession. And masta Schultz's wash-haus is a place like no other she knows of in this town of open doors and windows. This wash-haus has hatches that can be closed. Drop the hatches, close the door, and she shuts the world out. At this moment, this privacy, if only for minutes, seems most precious.

Her sleeping room backs onto the wash-haus, so she knows how short the walk will be: out of one door and into another. On other days, she could do that walk several times and be invisible. But tonight, her height and the circumstances make her feel as if everyone can see her. She drops to her hands and knees and crawls towards the door of her sleep-out, out through the doorway, around the corner, down the path and into the wash-haus. Once inside, she takes a moment to catch her breath and then gives the door a gentle push and makes certain it's closed by applying light pressure with her fingers. At last, in what seems her only haven, she allows her body to relax, but it's short-lived because she knows she shouldn't forget the consequences of tonight's event for more than a second. She's very weary. She has to fight a desire to curl herself up once more, to not move. Despite the sweet aromas of the laundry, she can't escape the scent of the young masta that rises up from her body, clogs her nostrils – and that's all she needs to spur her on.

Must waswas. Must wash away her shame.

The darkness of the wash-haus is no hindrance. She knows this space so well she can feel her way across to the window. Once there, she stretches her long arms in front of her, allowing her fingers to feel for familiar shapes and work their way outwards and upwards towards the hatch. Ah yes, there it is. She stands. Feeling exposed, her eyes do a quick scan outside the laundry as her hands seek the end of the hatch's brace. If a storm blew up, she'd grab this, drop it to the floor, and let the hatch bang, wood on wood, against the sill. Not tonight. She wants no one to hear anything. One of her hands takes the weight of the hatch cover and pushes out while with the other she lifts out the brace so she can rest the cover and it can be eased against the sill with only the slightest 'oomph'. Only then does she bend down and place the brace on the concrete floor.

At last she can breathe.

She's invisible to the outside world. Olegeta man na meri no ken lookim long Koti.

For some minutes she sits, secure in the pitch-black room, but the voice in her head won't give her peace. The night's drawing to an end. She must have a plan in place before dawn. And she's feeling the effects of the hatch being closed. There is no breeze to blow away the humidity. The wash-haus is a hotbox. Sweat pools over her body, the reek of her own body even more repugnant. This body's no longer hers, changed forever by the young masta. She dry-retches.

Waswas gutpela. Koti waswas strong. Scrub that boy's scent away.

Much as she fears light, she can't do without it. Masta Heinrich Senior keeps emergency supplies stored in the wash-haus, in a cupboard beside the door. There'll be two battery-operated flashlights. That's because the threat of an eruption worries masta Heinrich. He believes it essential to keep these torches ready for any emergency.

She wriggles across the floor, feeling her way, until her fingers curl around the wooden knob of the door to the storage cupboard. Inside the cupboard, her fingers creep around, feeling for the smooth leather of the torch grips. At last, she finds one. She uses her forefinger to slide the metal latch, and a glorious beam of yellow light fills the storage cupboard. She brings the torch out into the larger space, closes the door, and focuses the beam on herself.

Until this moment, her thirty-three-year-old body has served her well. But at this moment, in the torchlight, she can only feel disgust for it.

Pikinini masta only a sixteen-year-old. Only a boy with a man's body. Why he do this?

Though it's hard to admit, one thing he has done to her tonight is worse than the other. What he did to her body is bad enough, but the other, to her mind, has crippled her. Through his absolute disregard for her, he has crushed something precious. He had been like a son to her until tonight. She had aided his mother during his birth, and since that birth, she's been with his family like a second mother to him, and his brothers and sisters. Now, two times over on this night he has shown how he sees her, shown her he thinks of her as someone with no voice, no power: a nothing person. He has also shown his self-assurance, that he's aware of the security and power of his own position. He has shown her he knows that whatever she says, even if people believe her, no one will do anything. They'll pretend it's not important. His papa's company owns this town. She knows he's right to see it this way, for that's how it is. She also knows she has to find a way through this without seeking justice for herself, or punishment for him. Like an insect, she must hide in a corner if she's saving herself. She swallows to stop the bile rising up her throat.

She can find ways past the dirtiness of his act, and her anger at being treated as nothing, but can she retrieve the most important thing that tonight has damaged: her belief in herself? Leaving home at fifteen, losing a husband, being left without home or money so young, all had to be faced with courage. She has always believed that if she gives something sufficient effort, she can find a way through. She has never seen problems, only a need to find solutions, supported by a belief that as hard as those solutions might be to find, if she wants them, she can find them. The young masta has stolen that. He has shown her who she is: shown her that all her efforts have been for nothing.

Mummmum

Her mantra.

Her arms wrap across her chest and her hands grip her shoulders.

For him, no cost.

Koti will lose everything: pride, the job, a place to live. Hunnnnunnn. Koti. Koti. Koti. Stop now, Koti. No more of this. She can only allow herself a short burst of self-pity. She must move.

Anger gives her the will to lift herself from the floor and stand at the tub. She grabs the tap's brass wheel and wrenches it round, as if it's the young masta. The effort has her complete concentration. Round and round, round and round, until it's open. As the water pressure increases, the tap creaks, the pipe whistles and groans in protest. The rush of water lifts her beyond this evening. She forgets her fear of someone hearing and wondering at the oddity of such a noise at this hour. The great waterfall strikes the bottom of the tub, and then flies back up at her face and her shoulders, drenching her upper body. The breeze created by the rushing water refreshes her. She forces a stopper into the drain and waits for the water to rise, and to continue rising, then plunges her head into the tub, down, down, down, as deep as she can go, as deep as the limits of her bended body will allow her to go; until she can submerge her head and shoulders. She thanks the gods for her tallness that permits her to bend so low. She works hard to resist an urge to remove her clothes and climb in to rid her body of the smell of his sweat that had pooled and slurped between them when he assaulted her. For a moment her awareness of the rest of the world returns, and she lifts her head. What if someone finds her here? How would she explain? But she squashes that voice and again submerges her head and shoulders. Listening to the sound of the water falling, the bubbles rising through it as she plunges in, before coming up for air. The excess water pours down over her smock. The few minutes of submersion have made the wash-haus her own fragile but private space. In that space, she can shut out the sounds of a Rabaul night: the rustle of leaves as the breeze buffets the vegetation; feet plodding along the nearby road as the Tolai carry out their endless nocturnal wanderings; and not least the buzz and click of insects, and the tut-tutting of geckos on the ceilings. Shutting out those sounds makes her feel removed from Rabaul, safe and without fear.

Anger's never too far away. She pounds her fists on her chest. The scrubbing brush sitting on the bench beside the tub dares her. She snatches it up, releases the water from the tub, but leaves the tap running. Into the running water she dips the brush and scrubs her arms, chest, and her legs. But – not that place. Can't touch herself there. Not yet. Dirty. Filthy. No tears, though. The scrubbing, the pain of the brush on her skin, releases her, brings back her resolve.

Tingting, Koti. Pindim way, Koti. Yes, Koti, yes. Like yu tingting before. Be clever.

She reaches over to the pile of freshly laundered towels, takes one, dips it under the running water then lathers it with laundry soap and lifts it up and under her smock. Using force, she scrubs between her legs, around her breasts and her backside and as far as she can reach up her back, every part of her body that the dirty child has invaded. She can't stop scrubbing and rubbing and rinsing, but her internal clock warns it's time to turn off the tap and dry her body. On the shelf, a pile of clean laundry, and one of the house-staff has left a clean smock behind. She removes her drenched and soiled one and dons the clean one. Now she must face that terrible room. Standing proud and tall, she leaves the wash-haus and enters her sleep-out. She grabs one end of the coarse mattress covering and pulls it, gagging and retching at the stink of semen and sweat steaming in the night's heat. She throws the cover outside. Weariness overtakes her. She turns the mattress over. Her body falls onto its bare surface and there she remains, in a crumpled bundle.

Sleep comes and goes, interrupted only by delirious dreams. She's back in Hollandia and begging for a berth on a cargo ship heading for Friedrich Wilhelmshafen, the town on the mainland where her husband of less than a year has gone to work on the tobacco plantations. 'Josef, Josef', she cries in her half-sleep. In her dream, she does not complete that journey, does not reach the place in which he died only months after arriving. Died with so many other tobacco plantation workers. She cries. Josef, Josef. You died alone. Those men died alone. Families will never know of their death. If it wasn't for those deaths, perhaps she might never have come to Rabaul, for it was the fear of the swamps that brought the Germans from Friedrich Wilhelmshafen to Kokopo, and then to Rabaul. As is the way of dreams, she moves from one sea voyage to another, this one with several other people – young men and women – dark and tall like her. They are calling out to each other, encouraging each other. They speak her father's language as they bend their backs and lift their arms, driving forward their large canoe through the waves.

She wakes in panic. Has dawn come and gone? Her dream is still with her, as fresh as any memory. She thinks back to the time before Friedrich Wilhelmshafen, to her island home, west of New Guinea. Then she was a stupid young girl with too much courage, influenced by tall tales of foreign sailors.

Mebe this why trabil has found her. Koti too sure of herself, she forgets who she is, forget she's just a brown girl who works for masta and missis. Maybe Koti make it seem she think herself as good as missus na masta, that anything is possible and masta na missus not like meri tingting this way.

She reimagines her father's shame over a disobedient, wilful daughter. So much time has passed, so much has she changed, she cannot gauge what her father's response to her leaving might have been. Or how the community might have judged him. Yet, she admits, the tales the sailors told were in the main true enough: the escapees found jobs and a whole new world. What none of the escaping youths had expected was the cost of that new life. They had lost a homeland, the companionship of people who saw the world as they did, and a daily life in which they could hear their own language spoken. Since leaving, she hasn't heard her own language, and she feels its loss. The sailors didn't warn of these things, just as they made no big deal of the risks of dying or of being swept off course. Yet the six rebels had paddled from island to island and for the last, far longer journey, the prevailing winds pushed them towards Hollandia, as the sailors had said the winds of a certain season would do. The rowers should have been afraid. Their journey was a risky one. The possibility of death by drowning was high. But she doesn't remember being afraid, and she was brave too after Josef's death. She needs courage today.

Yes, Koti, you ready for this day. You can be strong.

She lets her thoughts linger on her father. If she could see him once more, would she tell him that the pain she caused was for nothing? How, instead of washing, cleaning and cooking for a husband he'd have chosen for her, she did those chores for someone else's husband, someone else's children. She tries to think in Malay, but it doesn't come easy. Malay words get mixed with Tok Pisin and the few words of English and German she speaks every day. What comes to her is that her papa's name for a house was rumah. He used the term tanah airku to refer to the place where the heart resides and that fits her perspective of a 'home', where love and shelter come together. House and home. She has only ever had a house – a place in which to sleep and eat, to work – never her own home, never a place in which she could feel secure, surrounded by things she holds dear. 'Tanah airku' is a luxury out of her reach. For so many years she has worked for the German masta Heinrich and his New Guinea missus. The German word for Henrich's house is the same as the Pidgin word haus, which means two things: first, a building or shelter to keep rain and wind off the body and, second, a home that belongs to you. In German, there's another word for home. This is heim. She sighs. No home for her, and a house just means work. Masta Heinrich Senior once invited her to make his haus her heim. She snorts. Words come easy. Doesn't mean they are true.

She knows, and so does masta Heinrich, she's a hauskeeper, and all she's given is space at the back of the laundry. Em tasol.

First chore of the day is to take the soiled linen into the wash-haus to boil in the copper, and next, to fit a fresh cover to her palliasse. Must make it look like nothing happened. Need to make the young masta's act invisible. This necessity brings back her anger. She fights to control it, reminding herself that the invisibility is for her own good, not his, but she loses the battle. The Schultzs have been like her family She'd witnessed the birth of all the Schultz children… so she makes a pledge to herself. If she runs from this place, good or bad, rough or smooth as it might be, never again will she forget the important lessons learnt this night.

Past sunset and after filling the day with her usual habits of work, she has a plan. For once Heinrich the father has kept Heinrich the son busy throughout the day. That's part of young Heinrich's problem. Too much idle time, too much drinking, too many New Guinea women to make trouble with. At this moment, the other haus meris are in the kitchen cleaning up after the evening meal. Which means, if the Schultzs have finished their evening meal, as is their habit, the two Heinrichs would have taken to their wicker lounges on the verandah. Such verandahs are for the lucky people. Verandahs turn a haus into a heim. She dreams of a verandah of her own. She peeks through the bushes in the garden. Ah, yes. In the deep blue of the evening sky, she can see the clouds of cigar smoke, and hear their laughter.

They will have glasses in their hands and a bottle or two on the table beside them. Their life is going on as it always does. Last night's events would not trouble young Henrich. Other women have suffered invasions of their bodies too, she has now convinced herself, and as she reaches this conclusion, murderous thoughts fill her head. This surprises her. Never has she felt this way about others; never has she despised anyone to the point of wishing them dead.

Koti, tingting stret. She must think none of those rubbish-ideas: like adding poison to young masta's glass. If he gets sick or dies, Koti doesn't win. Koti's troubles only grow larger.

She carries those black thoughts with her as she heads behind the high vegetation at the rear of the property and walks along the path towards the back gate. She's taking the long way to town. It's a humid night. Loi Fook's house in Chinatown is quite a distance. Sweat bubbles on her forehead and down her arms, making her ebony skin glisten. The New Guineans she passes know her as black and do not mumble their usual greeting of 'Good evening missus', as they would for a European missus or even a Chinese missus. Instead, the men snicker. Mosquitoes eat her. She's thirsty. She ignores everything. The town is quiet. The offices of the German New Guinea Company and Hernsheim and Company are closed, their people same-same masta Schultz senior have gone home to their families. Trams are in their sheds. She tramps along the dusty Rabaul streets, rehearsing her plan in her head. Past the unevenly low and high timber buildings of Chinatown. At last she's striding down a lane. The soft glow of a kerosene lamp filters out of an open window. She's reached Loi Fook's humble hut. She takes a deep breath and knocks.

Loi works for masta Schultz as a handyman. He will do anything he's asked to do, because he doesn't work for the German to earn money, but for something more important. She wonders if masta Schultz realises how clever Loi is. While he acts like a humble servant, he uses every opportunity to learn so he can put that learning to use for his own benefit. She sees his businesses growing. One day he will be more powerful, far richer, than all the German mastas of Rabaul put together. She has heard from Schultz's New Guinea gardener that Loi's about to open a trade store. She hopes she's correct. If it suits his purposes to continue working with the Germans so he can learn from them, keep abreast of events, he might see the value of someone running his trade store, a reliable person like Koti Pereira.

A woman. Controllable. She has to be that person. She has no other options. A flutter of fear passes through her. Is she selling her soul to the devil? Loi, she can see, cares for no one but Loi.

III

Grandmother Koti Pereira (deceased)
in the house with the verandah under a Mango tree,
Rabaul under Australian Military Administration
1914

War is happening.

Koti lukim. She sees the Australian army come. They take everything off Germans. Loi Fook, he's laughing. The government says Chinaman can't buy property but Loi, he pays white men to buy property for him. Loi has plenty plantations. Too clever. Loi, he's a silent danger for everyone. He's like an octopus. His tentacles reach into everyone's business. He can destroy lives. And she has put herself into this position with him. She knows she must be very careful.

Though the danger is still there, she's glad she didn't poison the drinks of those two Heinrichs as they sat on their verandah on that dreadful night. On her behalf, Fate has stepped in. War comes and war says it's the Germans in Rabaul who are 'nothing people', just as young masta Heinrich had made her feel she was of no account. Some Germans have remained in Rabaul, saying this is their home, but they no longer have their big houses or their powerful jobs. The big war is in another country but a little war happened here at Bita Paka, between the Germans and the Australian Navy. But that's over now. The Australian Government has taken over the German-owned plantations and their houses. Both the Heinrichs went, but they left behind Mrs Schultz. She's New Guinea-born and her home's in the town of Friedrich Wilhelmshafen, a long way from Rabaul. She cry, cry, cry for the son she knows she'll never see again. This father and son have treated their wife and mother worse than they treated their servants. This abandoned mother has no money, but she needs to feed and care for the younger children, all brown children that the father wants no more. Father only wants almost white son Heinrich. The New Guinea mother could live in her village near Friedrich Wilhelmshafen if she had money to pay their fares. One good thing has happened, though. The new administration has changed the long name of that town to 'Madang'. Nice and short now.

And Koti cry too, but this is a happy cry. Now that the two Heinrichs have gone she need not worry about her baby girl, a gift from young Heinrich, one he might want back some time. Gift-child only one-and-a-bit-years old, but so beautiful. Dark same long her mama and dark like her husband Josef, so much like him her mumma pretends pikinini comes from him. Not from dirty bad boy Heinrich. She calls this baby Josefina. Josefina Pereira. But she reminds herself, it's because of Heinrich junior that she has Loi Fook to worry about. When Loi Fook shook her hand on that bleak night, he told her: 'Koti, you can live in one of my houses on condition you give me help when I need it. Sometimes I might ask, Koti, you talk to someone on my behalf, or do something, nothing big, just help me.' A cold shiver ran down her spine. A warning. There'll be a cost for such an alliance. But she had no choice. Still has no choice. She doesn't fear for herself but for her sweet daughter. What price might she pay for her mother's cowardice? Never trust Loi. So far, all he has asked is to deliver paperwork to the administration office on his behalf. He wants no clear path to his door, doesn't want people to know how rich he has become. That's why he still lives in his little hut in Chinatown.

She need not put this statement before the Tolai village judges, the 'tena vakurai', to be certain it's valid. Her future will bring with it trouble. There will be no avoiding it. If it's not via her own current project, a little enterprise that began with masta George Brown who asked her to cater for officials visiting from Australia, it'll be another. Contact with administration personnel is what Loi would see as an opportunity for him to manipulate and from which to benefit. Putting Loi's ambitions aside, this little enterprise of hers makes her happy. Oh, and she is so proud of her achievement. They love her food, they love her. Oh, at last Koti. You aren't a nothing meri any more.

IV
Maria Seeto's father, Seeto Wei or David Seeto (deceased)
Rabaul part of the Australian administrated League of Nations
Mandated Territory of New Guinea
1934

Seeto Wei has recognised how things must be. Here in this English-speaking town he calls himself David Seeto, not Seeto Wei as in China. China's a long way from here. Through the Kuomintang, the Chinese Nationalist Party, he's tried to keep pace with news from the homeland about the Red Army marching through China. But how does this affect him? Well, he's never going back. Can't. Nothing to go back for or to. He lets himself ponder how his village might be now. If Loi Fook hadn't recruited him to come to this remote place, how might his life have gone? He reminds himself of the desperate position he was in when Loi stumbled across him. Starving. Homeless. No family. Such is Fate. He might not have lived much longer if Fate hadn't brought this foreign Chinaman to pass his way. But the present is what's important. Today his future is heading on a new path. He's doing what his benefactor has directed him to do. No emotion involved. No high expectation. Only obedience.

He first met Josefina Pereira the day he arrived in Rabaul. 'Raw-bowel,' his master pronounced it. She was serving customers in the master's trade store when they arrived there. Young. He knows now she was about eighteen then. Tall. Dark. On first sight, he'd assumed she was a Tolai, the original people of Rabaul, because that's how his master had described them on that first day – tall and proud. He didn't notice at the time there was something about her that differed from the usual Tolai looks. Darker. Straight black hair, not tight curls. Her black eyes missed nothing and yet had looked right past him. This alone was reason enough to make him dislike her. She said little. But he could see that while she played at obedience, there was a hint of defiance. Even pressed against her will, there would be limits on how obedient she might be. It was clear she had strong thoughts of her own. In his own opinion, this was an attitude way beyond her standing as an indentured labourer, one that would cause problems for her or someone else. Again, in his opinion, she needed reining in. But he'd noted that the old man did not appear ruffled by her brusqueness or her high estimation of herself. The master must know he has a hold over her.

Meeting his future wife for the first time is not dissimilar to his first encounter with Rabaul. Both require unravelling their mysteries.

Their ship had docked at dawn, the cargo unloaded. At last dry land, albeit foreign. They had left the boy Chun Yuen with the cargo on the wharf and already, before they had left, he was off in his dreams, scratching with charcoal on whatever flat surface was handy. David wondered, having observed the boy during the voyage, had it been a mistake to grab whatever homeless boy had been nearby and name him as a younger brother? Impulse.

He had sat on the bottom rung of the hierarchical ladder for too long. With a 'younger brother' he would be the one in the middle for a change. Receive orders – pass them down. Brother to adopted brother, two fates locked. Seeto Wei and Seeto Chun Yuen. Lucky the boy had the same surname. But had Loi Fook believed his lie? As they'd walked away from the cargo and the boy, he had lifted his eyes to see if the master had shown any reaction to the boy and his charcoal scratchings. His mentor seems set on other matters. Not leaving his cargo too long at the docks, for one. What did it matter? The boy's here, in Rabaul, and how he uses the boy is up to him.

His first day in this strange town had been remarkable. Fresh-eyed, open-minded, he'd taken everything in. He had told himself: knowledge is necessary if a man is to survive. He had learnt that lesson well on the streets of Kaiping.

There's a Chinese saying that when Fate decides your path, that is what it will be. Should you stray from it, Fate will still bring you back to that path. Today, years after their first unfavourable encounter, Josefina Pereira is his wife. Not the wife he'd wanted. He was ambitious – wanted a Chinese wife – but Loi Fook, always the realist, had pointed out there were only a few unmarried Chinese women in Rabaul and these few therefore were worth more to their fathers if offered to any richer families seeking brides for their sons. Those families would already have established allegiances. Loi in his wisdom had also advised that a businessman with no wife lacks credibility. Loi Fook may have learnt from his own experience. He has no wife here in Rabaul. His Chinese wife and son in Kaiping died in the influenza epidemic. That perverse twist of Fate and Loi's loss to a disease has been this one-time beggar's gain.

But, he concedes, having no wife or family allows his master Loi to become invisible. That is the way Loi prefers and regularly utilises to his advantage. However, Loi insists that the person who represents him, the one he chose in Kaiping to take the role of his 'son', must present an appropriate and acceptable face to their community. He needs a wife. Besides, as Loi has pointed out, a wife and children are cheap assets. They cost little, they are obedient and can work long hours for no pay. Deal done between his boss Loi and the bride's mother, Koti Pereira, and Josefina Pereira, as his wife, will become an obedient servant and the mother of his future son. He'll make certain of that.

V

Koti Pereira (deceased)
in the house under the Mango tree, Rabaul,
in the Mandated Territory of New Guinea
1937

The earth shakes again. The air is thick. Vulcan, the cone on one side of the harbour, is growling and spewing. It's difficult to walk, but keep walking Koti must. Walking, walking, walking. To Josefina. Her clenched fists drum a marching beat on her thighs.

Where husband to lookim long Josefina and pikinini meri?

Josefina's husband is absent. Safe on some other island, he doesn't worry about his wife and baby girl, whether they may eat volcano dust or be crushed under the dirt and rubble. It seems to this mumma, should David's wife and daughter die, it might even please him. Ah, yes, this is the man that Josefina married; this is the price Josefina pays for her mother's security. Their first child not a son. As soon as Josefina gave birth to a girl, he lost interest.

David he lookim long pikinini and he toktok: 'Ah, tispela pikinini meri tasol. Where my Chinese son?'

But this baby girl's so beautiful. Josefina calls her Maria. Maria has a brown face, not black like her grandmother's and mother's, and not Chinese like her father's. But she has blue eyes. These blue eyes cause her so much trouble. No one expects blue eyes to be on a brown face. Her grandmother, if she were an honest woman, might explain where those blue eyes originated. A little German has shown itself. Strange how babies turn out. At birth, Josefina could have been a Malay child, not the daughter of a Malay woman and a part-white/part-brown blue-eyed, stupid boy. This grandmother lied about who Josefina's papa was, and now has to live with that lie by pretending her granddaughter's blue eyes are God's blessing, something that makes Maria extraordinary. Maria's blue eyes frighten her poor papa. He doesn't like the brown face either. Too much New Guinean and not enough Chinese. But the blue eyes terrify him. As if they are the eyes of a spirit come to judge him. He's a man with many reasons to worry about ghostly judgments and likely harsh punishments, from what she knows of him. And God only knows what sins he left behind in China.

Doesn't matter how his daughter looks. David's smart enough to look to the future. He knows that a daughter with a Chinese father is worth money in Rabaul. There are too many Chinese men and not enough Chinese women. It doesn't matter whether she looks Chinese if she shows herself as Chinese by her habits and beliefs. A part-Chinese daughter provides her father with good bargaining power. Maria's papa tells her every time he sees her, which isn't often, that she is a beautiful Chinese daughter. To know that it pleases her father for her to be Chinese also makes Maria happy. He goes back to his plantation counting the dollars he will receive when she is sixteen. So happy is Maria to be Chinese, she wants no Malay grandmother but a Chinese one instead.

'Nenek, papa thinks I am a Chinese girl. Me so happy. I think I will stop calling you Nenek and call you Po Po instead, my mother's mother.'

'Me come from Malay island. Nenek is the name for a grandmother, not Ah Poh. I am not a Chinese grandmother; my daughter is not Chinese.'

But this papa, he pretends his daughter is special, all the while averting his eyes from her face. He's the stupid one. Maria is a special meri. No matter what her papa thinks, it's of no consequence. Papa is always somewhere else. He has many wives in many places. He only comes from his plantation to make trouble in town both for his family and in Chinatown gambling dens, and then he goes back to his New Guinea meri on his plantation. Last time David was in Rabaul, he made a new baby inside his wife's belly. But Josefina does not tell him he will soon be a papa again. This is her way of showing him he doesn't control her. It's easy to see that Josefina is strong – much stronger than her mumma. Josefina says she hopes this baby is a boy with a Chinese face if only so she can keep him for herself. She knows a son is all he wants.

But now, the volcano will blow and there is nowhere for Josefina, Maria and the unborn baby to go. No one besides Josefina's mother to take care of them. This eruption is punishment because Josefina's mother Koti Pereira is such a bad person. This is the price for the lies she has uttered and for selling her soul to that devil Loi.

Koti cries. There is no one to hear her.

Oh wah, please mama earth, do not eat Josefina and her pikinini. me. Please, mama earth, kaikai me, eat me. Me nothing.

VI

George Brown (deceased),
Australian Administrative Officer, Rabaul,
Territory of New Guinea
1937

Well, Mr George Brown, he tells himself, your young life has been full of indulgences and now you might be paying the price. Part of that life was to travel to Europe, and he once viewed John Martin's 'Pandemonium' in the Louvre. Inspired by Milton's 'Paradise Lost', it's red and chaotic. Today, the artwork is coming to life before him. But, thank God, the good residents of Rabaul have ceased their denial. Almost daily, the citizens experience earth tremors so gurias have become a way of life. This makes it tempting for them to ignore the seriousness of today's event. Now there's a scramble to leave this space. It's his job to round up whatever stragglers missed the first evacuation.

He's overseeing the loading of the last evacuation vessel.

What oh, is that Koti Pereira? Who is that with her? A pregnant woman and a child. Why weren't they included in the first evacuation? He tries to prevent his mind from supplying the obvious answer. Malays. But now he's worrying about matters within his jurisdiction – milk for the child. And care for the expectant mother.

'Oh, ho, there, Koti. Is this your family?'

'Masta Brown, yes, my daughter Josefina.'

'Come on, let's get you ladies settled. You wait here and I will be back.'

He uses his authority to have the ship's crew find seating for the mother and blankets and then goes to the galley for some milk and fruit. He's taking a risk here. There are many people to get on board in a short time, and no doubt they all have particular circumstances that could do with some help. He can't afford to be too generous only with some. But he likes Koti, respects her having witnessed her dealings through the Administration Mess. And though he attempts not to show it, what he's interpreting as racial bias is upsetting him. Koti's pregnant daughter and child should have been on the vessel that left yesterday for Lae, all kitted up for mothers and children. He glances over at the woman. Yes, Malay. Dark. Like Koti. Therefore, both will have only a tiny voice within Rabaul's hierarchy. Their darkness labels them. Bloody business, colonialism.

Back on deck, he watches as the lifeboats go to the beach empty except for the crew and return full. Time's running out. To fit more on each lifeboat, the crew have been encouraging evacuees to stand, a precarious venture. But how much time do they have? Should one vessel to capsize, this evacuation will turn into a disaster. He dreads having to decide in favour of the majority, perhaps having to face a need to abandon the few because time has run out. He shudders. Oh God, please let us finish this job, and go.

VII
Maria's step-father, Daddy-George or George Brown (deceased)
Rabaul, East New Britain
1941

George's eyes sweep around the room, holding tight in their gaze what's precious to him. He's eternally grateful for the past four years. Before that he was a man whose life comprised a bed in single-men's quarters, work, and evenings in the club. Since the eruption, this has been his family. A family he loves.

Koti Pereira's home's a small, very modest space: a verandah, two rooms, and a bathroom. One room contains a kitchen and living space and in the far corner there are two beds, one for Koti and the other shared by her grandchildren Maria and Henry. He and Josefina have the only bedroom. But space means nothing. It's what's in that space that's important. Here, the luxury is family, and it's all about loving and being loved. Others have loved him: women, his parents in Melbourne, friends. But this is different. This is not just sexual love for Josefina, or mother-love for Koti, but an all-encompassing, interdependent love. He senses that its loss would cause him to shrivel and die. He never knew how lonely he had always been until he was no longer alone. His eyes take in the sight of the children's sleeping bodies: Henry on his back, arms reaching above his head, and Maria as always protecting her brother, on her side, one arm across Henry's waist, her head bent towards his head. Maria, unselfish as always, takes up as little space as possible for herself on the shared single bed. Not his children by blood and yet, he tells himself, his for many other reasons, despite the existence of their real, albeit ever-absent, father. He's filled with an urge to run over and wrap them in his protective arms, but he allows the warmth of love simmering inside him to spread across the room. He's a man torn between a longing to show his love and his old habit of containing his emotions within himself. Still, tonight the magnitude of his love threatens to burst out of his skin as it faces what's ahead. And larger still is his ever-growing fear of impending loss. It's impossible for him to keep his fear at bay.

He drags his eyes away from the sleeping pair until they settle on Koti and Josefina, at the other end of the table. For a moment, his eyes lock onto Josefina's. He tries to mask his inner fears but she can always read him, so he prays she's too distracted to detect his interior unravelling, while accusing himself of self-pity, of narrowing the problem they're all facing down to being his problem, his potential loss, and his fear. This is not the moment for such indulgences. Tonight, he needs to be the person he has trained to be, the one the Admin pay him to be: a solution finder. But while he tries to resist the sense of futility and his anger over administrative unfairness, what's beating him is the bad timing of everything. Just as he has reached a point where he has all he ever needs, there's nothing he can do to keep that life safe, with the people he loves.

He reins in his melancholy and looks again to the women. He sees that Koti's sitting bolt upright, her hands resting in her lap, her body tense, belying any calmness suggested by her folded hands. Josephina's appearance offers no such masking pretence. Anxiety crumples her face, her eyes are wide and, in her agitation, she wrings and releases her hands again and again. Her anxiety increases his own. Yet, despite this reminder of their situation, he can't prevent his love for her washing over him, his love of those dark-pool eyes, her smooth ebony skin, her long, slender fingers that carry with them a memory of their exploration of his body. But tonight, there's no escaping reality. All of those heart-stopping moments are being snatched from him. Yes, fear is what they are dining on tonight.

Josefina can wait no longer.

'Well?'

'Patience, girl. Steady, steady. Emi tok when he's ready.'

Josefina turns to her mother.

'Mumma, you know so many of the Australian women and children have already gone because the volcano's erupting again. Everyone knows the Japanese will pick a place like Rabaul to make a base. It's obvious. Now, think about what happened at Pearl Harbour, only worse, because unlike Pearl Harbour there's no one here to defend us. We're on our own.'

'Australia he kissim boat na...'

'Oh yeah, mumma, that boat will only evacuate the few remaining Australian women and children. But you can't think they will worry about us. Our only hope is if they take the Chinese children. They should do this, as China and Japan are already at war. Maybe then they'll also take our pikininis too. But I should know better. It will not happen. Look what happened in 1937 when the volcano went up. Who did they leave behind then? It's up to us to think of something… something… for the pikininis… but what?'

Her voice breaks, she wipes tears from her cheeks with the back of her hand and turns to look at George for a response.

All three look down at the floor for a solution. And there's none there either.

He knows Josefina is right. In 1937, not included on any evacuation list of women and children was a very pregnant Josefina and her two-year-old daughter. Not that anyone spoke the words, but he's certain their exclusion came about because, as neither European nor Chinese/Chinese Mixed Race, they weren't on any list. Malays are at the bottom of Rabaul's ranks of power. That should not have been reason enough to leave them behind, but when some official was ticking off the list, Malays would not have appeared. Invisible people would not have warranted any questioning of their omission. He cringes. It wasn't him, even though his job was to coordinate evacuations, but he's aware that the man he had been in 1937 and earlier could have committed the same oversight without even raising an eyebrow. It's a guilt of which he can't rid himself. And he knows that the Administration has nothing planned for evacuating the citizens who remain. This includes a handful of persistent Europeans and the Chinese, Ambonese, the category into which Koti and Josefina fit, and other people of mixed ancestries. They haven't even warned the Tolai. Rumour has it that the impression Canberra wants to give any Japanese informants, and they know there are some in Rabaul, is that no one suspects a threat. But the Chinese-Mixed Race community is making its own plans, splitting into two camps: Catholics and Methodists. He's aware that the Australian defence authorities have a strategy they're operating under – it's hinted at in every command the Administration receives – but they aren't telling anyone what it is, not even the administrative employees who have to set things in place. Locking this knowledge in his head only makes his sense of guilt heavier, makes him feel complicit in this discriminatory distribution of aid and information, though he concedes he's a pawn in a bigger game.

He can stall no longer. They need to know what they're up against, if they are to protect the children. The decision of afar have doomed this five, in different ways perhaps, but many others too. There is no plan that can save anyone left and the odds are definitely not with them. Even the volcano Matupit recognises the hopelessness for all of us who remain here. She is once again spewing out her rocks and ash in protest.

VIII
Maria's mother, Josefina Pereira (deceased)
Rabaul, ENB, Territory of New Guinea
1942, prior to Japanese Military Occupation

Josefina knows she must be strong. Together the three – she, George and her mother – have decided on a plan, a questionable one, yes, but the only one possible. The hard part is making it happen. She has had to involve David, and he's only helping them because of his own desire for a safe passage. He arrived in Rabaul too late to join the Chinese Catholics at Ratongor. And he's well aware he's not liked by the Tolai. He will require their help if he wants to remain out of sight of the Japanese and he knows the Tolai will not turn the child away. As always, David's true to his nature as the man who uses others for his own benefit.

The moment has come. She's not ready for it. Already she can feel her heart being torn from her body. She watches as father and son leave her. They're walking away. They already seem like ghosts to her, fading off down Malaguna. Away from their home. Away from Rabaul. Away from her.

The truth is the safety of the larger one doesn't concern her. What is or is not between her and her husband is in the wind, and this has nothing to do with surviving in a war zone. But her baby – her little boy, her Henry. To care for her son, she must trust the man she finds most untrustworthy. Trust him to care for her baby. So trusting is he as he takes the hand of this stranger. He does so, because his mother says he must do this. His mother has told him he must go with this stranger who only yesterday his mother whispered to him 'This is your father'. So dutiful, her little boy. Yet she can feel his eyes, hear his thoughts, and she knows he blames her. She imagines his anger at her for staying in the place he calls home while she demands he must leave, but to explain would make him more fearful than he already is.

He's only a child – but does he not see her pain, does he not understand she does this only because she must? Because she loves him? It's only in her heart she can say goodbye, because she needs him to be strong, needs him to see a future she herself no longer sees.

And this man, this husband of hers – the one who should care most for Henry, should protect him with his life – about him and his actions she has no confidence. Because she knows this man too well, knows that to him what's paramount is his own survival. He has shown his weakness already in her life. He'll argue to himself that provided he lives, he can always take another wife, have another child who'll carry on his heritage. This knowledge, in other times, might not have troubled her; she might even welcome it. Go find yourself another wife. Go find another heir. Just leave me this child. My child. That man might have another son if he loses this one – but could she? There is no option but to leave her son in his care.

He's gone now, her Henry. Too late she remembers her gold cross, how she'd wanted him to wear it around his neck for protection. But cross or no cross, please God, protect him.

It's dark but still she can't leave. She can't stop watching the space where she last saw him. She thinks about Henry's face, that dear sweet face she might never see again, and in it she sees his father's face. That's the reason he must leave. They say the Japanese hate the Chinese, and Henry is too Chinese to stay. But still there's Maria, a Chinese girl too but one who can hide behind her other inherited features and stay with her mother and grandmother. Both innocents must trust those who love them to protect them and make their choices for them. The boy's in the care of his father. No choice. Maria has her grandmother and her mother. The two, mother and grandmother, in order to protect the child are denying a lifetime they have spent resenting their invisibility because of skin colour in the hope Maria can hide in plain sight as a Malay or New Guinean child.

§

For Josefina, it's not death at the hands of a Japanese soldier she fears, but death from the pain of separation from her younger child. Two days since she let her boy go, and now George has gone too. George is a volunteer rifleman. His group are defending the town from the jungle. Such a scraggly lot of barely trained but brave men are they. Soon, George, the love of her life, will face men with bayonets, no longer the creatures of nightmares but real and dangerous beings invading the space everyone has always seen as safe. Soon foreign soldiers will be everywhere, perhaps even in whichever village David has found to shelter their son.

Please God, let Henry and George survive. Let everyone survive. Even David.

IX
Commandant Tsukamoto, Commander-in-Chief, Japanese Occupied Rabaul, East New Britain
1942

Commandant Tsukamoto has been Commander-in-Chief of the Japanese forces in Rabaul long enough to hate his job. He'll never let that show. He sees it as a suicide mission, although that's not the reason he hates it. It's important to hold this place, a stepping stone to Australia. The cost will be great, but an important part of a total war strategy.

What he hates is the constant grime. He brushes the shoulders of his uniform. It's coated with fine pumice dust from the volcano, showering ash daily since his forces have been in Rabaul, turning the vegetation outside of his tent dull grey, so it becomes yet another disappointment for him, something else in this place that doesn't measure up to the sharp clean landscape of a homeland he's missing. Some pilots complain. Until other airstrips are ready, there's only this narrow dusty one available to them, against the backdrop of a nasty volcano looming metres into the air. Every few minutes the ground trembles and the volcano groans, then hurls out stones and thick, choking smoke. How can anyone survive this place?

He looks over to the officers' mess, a blaze of light tonight as he ordered, a brazen declaration of the Japanese military's possession of Rabaul intended to counter what Tsukamoto sees as losing face. Seeing Rabaul as a strategic location, he had expected its occupation to count as a great military event to add to his career record. This should have been another Pearl Harbour style victory. Instead, it became a mere ripple in the pond of war, not worthy of mention, except to say it ended as intended. Rabaul now belongs to Imperial Japan. The Australian defence was despicable: a small inexperienced force, dressed not for full combat but in commando-style shorts and singlets and armed with only light-bore rifles, requiring no subterfuge, subtlety or endurance to overcome. His landing forces faced little resistance, not through a deficit of commitment on the Australian side but because the Japanese forces outnumbered the Australians. No big military victory then, but more a herding together of angry, snapping dogs.

At the dining tables, his officers have taken their places according to rank, a protocol for which he's glad. He detests his men's fatuous small talk and lack of intelligence so this seating-by-rank arrangement ensures him some distance from the others. As he takes his designated place, his men stand and bow, but Tsukamoto averts his eyes, so that although he is sharing the mess with them, he continues his previous habit of dining alone. Instead, he watches the elderly Malay woman and her daughter as they serve his men. They're both dark, but somehow not quite the same as other Malays. They have other qualities. Perhaps they're mixed and their attractive blend of tallness and elegance is an inherited trait. He's forgotten that his men scrutinise his every move, that it's not fitting for an officer to display a desire for alien women, not a dark native woman such as the daughter. He allows himself the luxury of watching her as she moves around the room. This one's special. Exotic. He lifts his head, and the mother comes running to him. He continues to gaze at the younger one and notices a covert flash in her dark eyes. The mother's still there, before him. Head bowed and eyes hooded. Feigned. Can't fool me, you old hag are the words his eyes challenge her with. She dishes out a full serve and takes half a step away but returns to add more. As she does, her gaze meets his. For a second there's no barrier between him and her, but then she lowers her lids in a play of subservience. He keeps his face expressionless, as if he's playing her game, even as he's thinking, 'I've seen how clever you are, out there, just as now, giving me that extra ration, smiling as if it's your generosity that privileges me. You know your life is in my hands.'

The daughter passes by in the background, the challenge shattered, but then he recognises the senior woman's true intention is to keep him at a distance from the younger. A surge of rage invades him. A vicious desire to outsmart them both replaces his rage. His desire grows. He's more determined than ever to take that dark young woman by force or guile. She's his.

X

Koti Pereira (deceased)
in the house under the Mango tree
Rabaul, Australian Administrated UN Territories
of Papua and New Guinea
1946

Koti, you no can bury head in dirt.

Despite this pronouncement, she can't avoid the harsh realities of existence. However, she chooses not to utter them for two reasons. The first is to shield her granddaughter from the truth, the second is to make them less real for herself. She will break into a million pieces if she concedes to reality.

Only she and Maria are left. Loi's house has survived. Her chest, buried underneath the verandah, survived too. But the people? Henry and his father, no one savy long where those two have gone. Maybe the war kaikai them. The war has swallowed many people. No one knows where those they knew before the war have met their end. Josefina is dead. She lost her head, to a Japanese blade, my poor, poor girl, and then thrown from a boat. Also dead is George Brown's unborn baby. And George Brown gone, gone to Japan maybe, or he's dead. No one knows. The last time she saw George Brown, he was with Japanese soldier. Prisoner. She saw him boarding a Japanese ship. Many Australians go too. 'Montevideo Maru' the ship's name. She thought this was a good omen. Maybe George Brown going to be okay. Everyone whispers in Rabaul about heads being lost and men shot by the Japanese at Tol Plantation. Bad, bad place, that Tol. For so long, she'd pictured George Brown without a head. She was so relieved to see him go long ship. But now no one knows where that ship went, so maybe George Brown's dead anyway.

Thanks be to God, George not savy about Josefina. He didn't know she pregnant and he was missing when she died. If George's dead, he maybe died while still thinking his Josefina safe. Better he thinks this. Better he not learn the truth. The truth's too hard to bear. If George Brown know Josefina lose her head by Japanese knife, or worse things that happened before then, he'd have gone crazy. Better if he is dead that he went with good thoughts in his head.

Only me and Maria.

PART 6
FINALE

1

KOKOPO, ENB, PNG
November 2010

'Ling Seeto. Call for you from Kavieng."

Ling knows the announcement through his works' intercom can't be good news. He rushes back to his desk. When his aunty voiced her wish to visit Uncle Stephen's grave, she left no doubt she would brook no objection, showing she knew well what the perils were. As an alternative plan, Ling had attempted to take time off work to go to Kavieng with the aging, sickly pair but his boss would not oblige. 'Too busy,' he grumbled. Ling's been sweating blood since. Worrying about them. He never had any doubt there would be problems. Despite the fuss of getting them boarded – for Aunty's big body, a small aisle, small seat, and much puffing and sweating, and for Dad, panic and fear, protests about never liking to fly – he did get a call to say they got there okay. A small let off. They've been there several days. But Ling's still nervous, still arguing with himself about whether he's just being over-protective. He's resisting a strong need to call his father, to check in again, but the call from Kavieng has taken the decision out of his hands.

'Hello, hello. Dad. Dad. Is that you? What's up?'

Not a sound. There's something squeezing his chest. He feels a need to panic. Meanwhile he needs to fill the silence with nonsense.

'What's it like in Kavieng, Dad? Years since I was there. Aunty get to pay her respects? How's the hotel?'

The phone crackles. He takes a breath, ready to ramble again, when he realises it's not crackling, but snuffling.

'Son, son. I need your help.' His father sounds like one of his kids when they are in trouble. 'Please, son. You come. Aunty not well. Doctor, he says she can't leave.'

'Oh shit, Dad.'

He was right. He does need to panic. This outcome is worse than he had predicted. Aunty's Brisbane family will kill him for not taking good care.

Aside from the fear of Maria's family murdering him, his common sense tells him there's a strong possibility, given how she was when she boarded the aircraft, that Aunty won't make it to Rabaul, let alone home to Brisbane. He races through to the boss's office, opens the door by slamming it back against the wall and begs. The boss takes pity. He says his own elderly father causes him a lot of worry too, and tells him if he goes and sees a bloke about a business matter while he's there, the business will pay his airfare.

In the hotel room, he finds Aunty, and her appearance terrifies him. And yet, she's still firing on all cylinders, making jokes, giving orders. She has his father under her thumb.

'Henry, please sight-see. Go with your son. You can't make me better by sitting here. And you,' she said, addressing her nephew who had risked his job to come. 'Thought you were too busy to come on a holiday to Kavieng. Ever been here? Even sick lapun meri like me can see this is a nice town.'

He promises to do the touristy run with his father, if for no other reason than to clear the way to other issues. He settles his father back in his own room with a cup of tea and some sandwiches and returns to Maria's.

Before she left his father's home, she had only one focus. Uncle Stephen's grave. He asks her whether she's done what she needed to do, here, and she nods. But she has that look in her blue eyes again.

'God calling me.' She doesn't blink when she delivers this. He wonders if she's decided that's how it's destined to be. Or maybe the Kavieng doctor has warned her.

She waves money. 'Plenty here to pay hotel or hospital. No worry about me. Take your daddy back to his home.'

She hands him her air ticket. Two seats from Tokua to Brisbane. She must have paid big to ensure comfort for her big body. Her finger's in the air and wagging.

'Now you a man of influence. You go toktok long Air Niugini, tell them me go long heaven and you need to go to Australia to tell family. They do it.'

No asking can he, or will he? Just do it.

'Please. Yu toktok long my family. You tell them it my choice. I the one who want to stop here, long Kavieng. Important they understand. And, anyway, if you don't convince them, they might think you cheapskate family who doesn't want to pay for my body to go back to Brisbane. You speak. My granddaughter Francine, she's the one to speak to. She will work it out.'

He receives his instructions for shipping the chest.

'Use the money Stephen give your father, ship it to Francine, my granddaughter. Only extra from what was there before is some paper. Letters. Already put them in.

She makes him memorise everyone's name. The family he never knew except for Andrew and Gabriel. She told him about their strengths and their weakness. All he has to do is add a face to this and he might as well have known them all his life.

'Here, I already write on this paper telephone numbers and addresses. You promise? You ship my crate long my granddaughter Francine. Yu ship but yu no toktok I dying. You tell them afterwards. Otherwise they will waste money coming here to look after me and for no good reason. I am going to be okay,'

What could a nephew say to his aunty? He's already weeks or months ahead in his mind – thinking of how he will get his father on an aircraft to travel to Brisbane.

2

KAVIENG, NEW IRELAND PROVINCE, PNG
November 2010

The walls of the hotel room disappear. She no longer hears her brother's whimpering, sniffling and nose blowing, or Ling's consolatory words to his papa. They've come back from Rabaul because her doctor says any time now. No one can help her. Her final journey has begun. She's not alone. She has her brother and his son nearby.

No pain or discomfort now. She's floating and drifting through her life, slipping through the early years spent a boat trip away in Rabaul, slowing for the years with her family in Brisbane, and stopping and remembering the moment in Henry's bedroom when she's opening her grandmother's chest for the final time. Ling had put aside the rough timbers of the outside crate to await repackaging. He told her he had taken notes to prepare for the form-filling required by the Australian Customs. He says he can't help but admire the exposed carvings on the marriage chest. And then, after he'd left, she lifted the lid.

She's back there, seeing the chest opened one more time. Her senses react to the overpowering aroma of camphor oil that takes her back to her past when she had opened this chest and taken out an item so Nenek could create her stories. And one last time, she tells herself, for her to run her fingertips over the etched figures: men with back's bent as they toil. Was this the carver's recognition of the world he saw around him? Another story, she's certain. Inside, she can see the first layer of the chest's contents. She pictures a younger Stephen, the one who visited her at Loi's store, with shoulders bent and arms outstretched placing each one in a particular order, patting and tucking as he did, shifting one to the other end to ensure the perfect placement of each fragile item. He's boxed or wrapped in tissue every piece.

She imagines him gazing down and whispering: 'These are for you, Lizhen, my Chinese bride.' Lizhen? Not Maria. Lizhen because he knows she always sees herself as Chinese.

She takes out each piece one by one and lays it on the bed. Nenek's jewellery and belongings on the bottom, the well-fingered pieces imbued with Nenek's stories, then her cheongsam, Stephen's artwork and photos, her secret letters written to him over the years, and his to Andrew, a father's letter to the only son he knew he had, but still not sent. What a surprise that will be for Andrew... and for Francine and Lucas.

The real world drags her back. In her delirium, she whispers a plea for forgiveness, but Andrew will never hear it.

'Please forgive me, my precious son. I couldn't bear to share you. To tell you, Andrew, my little Chao Liu, of your real mother might mean I'd lose you. I couldn't bear that. And how could I explain to you that your birth mum sold you? How could I impress upon you how much you were loved by your mother, Seeto Mei Yee? Please understand that to leave you in your daddy's care was Mei Yee's only choice. You were my precious gift from your daddy. Was it selfish to want you to believe you were my son? You were his son, and you were the family he and I dreamt we would have. I am so sorry to have lied to you, but I couldn't risk losing you. You are my son. Mine.'

No letter here to Gabriel from his father. Stephen may have guessed if he had counted the months from their last time together, but he had never said. Patrick accepted his blessing of a biological son, because Andrew represented both a victory and recognition. Patrick's favourite has always been Andrew if only because he knew Andrew's parents were both Chinese, unlike Gabriel and Daniel whose mother is a person of multiple ancestry, a point he enjoyed making. Letters to both these sons can only come from their mother. Will she be able to write these letters to her sons before she dies? Sitting on her brother's bed, she has vowed to do so.

Unless. God takes her too soon. Or she hasn't the strength. Then all this will all go to the grave with her. A flurry of panic. 'Oh please God, give me that time.'

Her willpower gave her the strength and her many letters are there, on the top, leaving space for the last item to be placed inside the chest in Henry's bedroom, ready for Ling to ship to Francine.

In her room in the Kavieng hotel, that last item is still in her hand. She'll have to let it go soon, give it to Ling to include. It's a roll of parchment tied with red silk, her favourite colour, its Cantonese characters scrolling down:

Lizhen,
Today and forever my bride
Carry these words in your heart always.
The lotus root may be severed, but it still connects its fibered threads.
Seeto Chun Yuen

3

RABAUL, ENB, TPNG
1952

In the garden of Nenek's home, Lizhen the bride is in a blue embroidered cheongsam that mirrors the brilliance of her blue eyes, Seeto Chun Yuen the groom, immaculate in a white fine-linen suit, and the celebrant/witness Koti Pereira sets off a royal blue kebaya with a long string of artificial pearls and matching comb to catch up a snatch of grey hair.

Laughter is suddenly silenced as each head bows towards the others and three sets of hands gently grip each other's. Pledges are made by two in Cantonese and repeated in Tok Pisin, vows of never-ending love and enduring hope endorsed in optimism by the third and, finally, the passing from one hand to another of a scroll of paper, held in its tidy circle by a ribbon of brilliant red.

The ancient frangipani beneath which the words are exchanged is saddened by its privilege of knowledge. This love, like all loves represented by its blossoms, is fated to long periods of separation. Only in death will these lovers be able to fulfil their vows to each other. To compensate, the ageless tree offers the trio an abundance of yellow and white blooms, forming a canopy above and a carpet below.

And, so, in this way, with yellow and white blossoms, a string of pearls, and a blue cheongsam, a day is marked for ever in three memories and carried forward with them through the long years of estrangements and deprivations that follow.

4

BRISBANE, AUSTRALIA
January 2011

Sweat rolls down Francine's face. Outside, rain. And more rain. Flood warnings for Brisbane. Humidity and sweat. Bulging belly. Bending, puffing, panting, resting. Chaos and confusion spilling from a gaping chest. Scattered paper. Pearls. Silky smooth under fingertips. Beautiful blue cheongsam. Embroidered. Elegant. Infused with the aroma of camphor. Wrapped in tissue paper. Loved. Landscapes painted in watercolour. A long jetty stretching into blue water. Thatched huts. Charcoal drawings. Faces, faces, and more faces. The same faces. As if to remember this face, someone must draw it often. Drawings with names on the reverse side. One name is 'Lizhen', a woman dressed in a cheongsam, the one in the chest. Is this woman Grandma Maria? Does this tell a story? Who is Koti? Or Josefina? Who are these people? A parchment scrolled and tied with red inside a protective bubble wrap cone. Someone valued it. She is convinced they are Chinese characters. What do they say? Is it important? Can she find someone to translate?

Then, a bundle of letters. She unfolds one. From Maria. Another from this man called Chun Yuen. A reply from Maria that uses the name Stephen as well. Who is Chao Liu? She guesses this is her dad. But he never calls himself that name. Did he know that's his real name? Who is who? Words on cheap letterhead. Some in Grandma's handwriting. Hard to read. Shaky. A few words in, and she has to call her father. Has to. And there are two more. Newer. Again in Grandma's handwriting.

'Daddy, Daddy. You must come as soon as you can.'

'Wah... Is baby coming?'

'No, Dad. We're doing fine. Your mum has written a letter. OMG... many letters.'

She can't continue. The words she is reading are choking her. This is just too much. Oh, poor Daddy. He'll be destroyed.

'I'm on my way,' her father shouts, his voice tight as a violin string. It's clear he's not convinced she's okay. She knows he will be panicking that his daughter or the baby are in trouble. And because he's rattled, he won't take in what she says next. She tries to simplify the information she has now gained. But the words waiting to come out of her mouth are jumbled. Because nothing makes sense.

Calm down, she counsels herself. All she needs to tell her father is two simple sentences.

'Dad, go get Uncle Daniel and Uncle Gabriel. They should be here, too.'

She will have scared him. He'll be worrying why are his brothers needed at their mother's house? Why can't this wait until the weekend? What is upsetting his girl so much?

These letters are life-changing. They leave no doubt. Maria has lied to them.

Perhaps keeping secrets is a handed-down trait. How long did she keep her secret from those who would have wanted to know?

Francine uses her concern for her father to push aside what is now clear to her. She's not who she believes herself to be. But who is she?

And what about Maria? Is she still Ah Ma? Or is she a stranger with the name Maria Seeto who wore the mask of her beloved Ah Ma? And Grandfather, who is not Yeh Yeh Patrick Seeto, but someone else altogether.

The baby kicks.

'Ah Ma Maria, whoever you are, a blood relative or not, how I wish I could tell you about this one.' She massages her stomach.

What a mix-up. What confusion. What extraordinary revelations. Undecipherable information. But important, precious, and without a doubt, whether understood, each fragment life changing in large and small ways. She settles herself by the reassurance some sense will come. Surely it must.

She tries to bring everything back into balance. Fails. It's as if the reality of the chest's contents and the shock of their disclosures have broken her. The sound of her own laughter. Shocks her. It began as a gurgle and now it is full throat. And manic. She's rocking her head back and forward. The noise issuing from her is beyond her control. and escalating. Louder and louder, hysterical. Her whole body is shaking. She needs to grip her swollen belly. She fears she will wet herself. And then it's over. Done. The storm passed.

The room is silent.

Tremors runs down her body. Probably shock. Not something to cause her father concern.

Briefly, the hysteria returns then fades into silent tears. Her knees give away, and she's down on the floor, head bowed, and her arms wrapped around her girth. No longer attempting to understand what is being revealed, her resistance is broken.

'Maria Seeto, I don't care who you are. I miss you.'

Her baby kicks, as if it's reminding its mother of its investment in the outcome of this research, a jab to its mother about what it also loses. If her grandmother had returned, if she was still in this world, anywhere, in Brisbane or in Rabaul, there are so many things she would want to hear about: a baby, a wedding soon, and despite these speed-humps, plans in place to continue studies, and graduate, and begin her art practice, thanks to Michael and her mum and dad. A flashing image of Maria's face lighting up when she heard this news almost ruins her. Her most ardent supporter. Maria's belief in her success a constant motivator, no less for the knowledge that she's not Maria's biological granddaughter and the lie that Maria had perpetuated throughout Francine's life. Thinking about the twenty years of deception brings about a cyclone of emotions that lifts her up then crashes her down. She only feels love beyond the biology, beyond the truth, and she feels gifted. She wishes she could speak of this to the unrelated Maria Seeto, to say you are my grandmother regardless. But practical concerns are what's important here and now. She must get this under control, before her father and uncles arrive.

Legs folded, seated on the floor, surrounded by the chest's detritus, she settles into quietness. Time for reflection, regret, and also guilt. Finally, calmness. Only momentarily because the cycle is building once more. When it arrives, it's with a roar. Not of frustration or pain but of revelation.

'OMG. This is so aptly Seeto. It's a Chop Suey. Instead of the left-over vegetables going into a pan, it's fragments of significance appearing only slightly connected but thrown together by way of accumulation in this beautiful chest. How apt. How else might her family explain itself?'

And then there's clarity and release. Just like the way she feels when she's attempting to express herself in her art. She'll have the canvas ready, the media prepared, and then she'll wait and wait, immersing herself deep into her subconscious. Without warning, she'll move into automatic. She'll pick up brushes and choose shades. Strokes will appear and transform the canvas seemingly with no direction from her. She accepts this gift, knows it's her particular means of creativity, of accessing and liberating ideas and understandings that might otherwise be inaccessible. Once fluid, they offer her uninhibited paths of perception. What appears on the canvas, in her colourful style, will be her interpretation.

The strokes appearing on the canvas of her mind are revealing patterns the offer tiny glimmers of hope for her family. Perhaps biology isn't everything? Perhaps there are other things that might provide glue? She rationalises: there's so much we can never understand about anything or everything or anybody; we don't even know ourselves let alone another person, no matter how close they seem or how loved. And most of the time we don't even think about what we don't know. Until something like this happens. But does everything need an explanation? She's wondering if understanding might come down to giving in to intuition.

This brings her back to thinking about Tim Johnson and his Mt Meru installation. Is this what Tim was trying to convey in his compendium of icons? Was he suggesting a notion that individuals don't stand alone? That his symbolism represents the beautiful mess of Life, of human existence? Was Tim offering possibilities for contemplating the great existential mystery? Maybe for him the many levels surrounding Mt Meru represent infinite forms of human experience and beliefs, from the hellish to the heavenly, each symbolic of the human struggle to understand, each waiting for reincarnation to become part of the never-ending and perpetual transference of knowledge? She still doesn't quite get it, but she thinks she might 'feel' it, intuit it.

As if freed, at last, from the weight of all the new and confounding information, her mind is racing. Can emotional connections and a sense of belonging only be... ah, felt not justified? Maybe? It's not too hard to accept, not too far 'out there' to comprehend. And love? No one knows how they stumble across it. Not really. There are certainly some weird couplings that can't just be explained by clichés such as 'opposites attract'. Chemical reactions, some say, or is it a sense of trust? Can't be, because sometimes it seems people 'say' they love someone even if it's clear they don't trust that individual, and there are many examples of loving a little-known person. Plus, there's always those trusted and loved individuals who prove they are untrustworthy, the characters that moviemakers and book writers love to explore.

She shakes her head. Not Ah Ma. No. None of this applies to Maria. In her heart Francine knows that while Maria may have kept secrets and, yes, even lied, Maria is, or was, a person loved even if, as the family is now brutally aware, not ever fully known. She ponders if love of Maria might be reciprocal love. No one can doubt Maria loved her family, whether as they now have discovered they are biologically-linked or not, and how could anyone not love back the person who devoted every second of her life to her so-called 'family'?

Will the doubt and uncertainty that the chest brings destroy her family? It could. She's terrified it will. There's no doubt the until-now rock-solid foundation of 'family' has been weakened. Yet there's a sense growing inside her. As if she can see into the future. No one, not herself or her father or his brothers, is a different person than they were before they knew these things about Maria. No one thought much about their ancestors before all this, and these revelations have only spotlighted something they hadn't known. It doesn't change who they are, because they are who they have always been. This new knowledge only changes how they see themselves. Once the loud noise of anger and hurt rolls off into the distance, like the thunder of a passing storm, each one will come back and re-group. They mightn't be quite the same Seetos as they used to be, but still a family united by the same experiences and memories and, eventually they'll admit, also united by love. Maybe each of her family will see Maria as the bridge between two ancestries, and recognise that three generations have sheltered beneath that bridge. It's those experiences that provide the glue that will hold them together from this day forward. At least she hopes it will. But how long that will take is hard to say.

Maybe what lays before her, spilling out of her grandmother's chest, will give them something to build upon. Maybe they'll understand more about how they ended up in this place and maybe they won't. Perhaps they might understand more about what has shaped their beliefs and values or they might learn to trust their instincts, and keep following the habits passed down through generations, even if they have nothing to inform them of the origins. But she's certain that over time each one will forgive Maria. They'll come to concede they belong together and this woman kept them together, protected them and loved them. It won't matter whether she's remembered as Mum, Maria Seeto, Ah Ma, Grandmother or Lizhen. For her, Francine Seeto, and her child, this woman will always be loved, no matter who she is or was, and where her life took her. Francine admits to herself she'd like to know more but, as Ah Ma would say, you can't always get everything you want.

The End.

EXTRAS

TIMELIME
Partly fictionalised

1873   Johann Cesar Godeffroy and Sohn and Hersheim and Kompagnie establish trading posts in the Bismarck Archipelago, both on Matupit Island and at Friedrich Wilhelmshafen (Madang) on the mainland.

        Loi Fook arrives on Matupit Island near Rabaul.

1878   Submarine volcanic action causes the rising of Vulcan Island, producing vast amounts of pumice that blocks seaways.

1884   Under the auspices of the Deutsche Neuguinea-Compagnie (New Guinea Company) the German flag flew over Kaiser-Wilhelmsland (Bismarck Archipelago and the German Solomon Islands).

1893   Koti Pereira leaves Ambon and marries Josef Pereira in Hollandia or Numbay

1894   Josef Pereira travels to Friedrich Wilhelmshafen, German New Guinea, to work, and dies soon after of fever in the mosquito-ridden tobacco fields.

1899   The German Government takes over civil administration of the colony from unprofitable Neuguinea Kompagnie. Government headquarters are established at Herbertshöhe (Kokopo), New Britain; Koti Pereira arrives in Herbertshöhe (Kokopo) and is employed by the Schultz family as housekeeper

1905   Tramway constructed from wharf to various stores; Schultz family and employees move to Simpsonhafen (Rabaul), New Britain.

1914   Britain declares war on Germany; Battle of Bita Paka between the Australian Naval and Military Expeditionary Force and the German East Asiatic Squadron over a wireless station; Australian military administration of German New Guinea begins under the League of Nations; Heinrich Schultz junior returns to Germany.

1915   Planned uprising of the remaining New Guinea Germans uncovered.

1918   War ends.

1919   Germany signs the *Treaty of Versailles* and cedes all claim
to sovereignty over New Guinea; Australian government's seizure
of German properties, which enables individuals such as Loi Fook
to acquire plantations (using covert means and paying Australians
to act as their agents), despite restrictions imposed upon
non-indigenous natives (Chinese) regarding land ownership.

1920   Australia begins administration of Mandated Territory of New
Guinea (formerly German New Guinea) under the League of
Nations.

1930   Loi Fook travels to China and returns with Seeto Wei (David) and
Seeto Chun Yuen (Stephen).

1931   Japan invades Manchuria.

1937   Japan invades China; Chinese Communists and Nationalists
nominally unite to fight Japanese; volcanic eruption destroys
Rabaul; evacuation of civilians to Kokopo.

1939   A letter from Germany tells of Heinrich Schultz's death; Germany
marches into Czechoslovakia and Poland; Prime Minister of
Britain declares war.

1941   (December) Japan occupies Manila and attacks Pearl Harbour;
USA declares war on Japan; Rabaul identified as next target;
European women and children evacuated from Rabaul.

1942   (January 4) Japanese bombing of Rabaul begins; Chinese
community buries valuables and makes two camps outside of
Rabaul: Ratongor for the Catholics and Vunakambi for the
Methodists; (January 21) four enemy cruisers sighted near
Kavieng heading to Rabaul; Civilians instructed to 'carry on with
normal duties'; (January 23) the fall of Rabaul to Japanese
occupying forces; (February 8 to 15) Battle of Singapore; (June);
'Montevideo Maru' lost at sea with 845 POWs from Rabaul on
board supposedly en route to Japan.

1943   Aboard the vessel 'Azikazi' somewhere between the ports of
Kavieng and Rabaul, brutal executions of several civilian POWs
enacted, including a woman of Malay ancestry.

1945 (May) VE day (end of European war); (August) A-bombs dropped on Hiroshima and Nagasaki; Japan surrenders.

1946 Australia begins administration of two separate territories: Territory of Papua & Mandated Territory of New Guinea, under United Nations treaties.

1949 Communist Party takes over China; Nationalists flee to Taiwan; Chinese of Rabaul with Kuomintang allegiances no longer free to travel to homeland.

1957 Stephen's Chinese bride, Mei Yee, arrives from China accompanied by her brother Tak Tam; talk of independence grows; some Rabaul Chinese individuals are granted Australian passports.

1959 Maria marries Patrick; Mei Yee returns to China.

1975 (September) Papua New Guinea government begins its role of governing the new nation.

1994 Volcanic eruption covers Rabaul deep in ash.

FRANCINE'S FAMILY

```
┌─────────────────────────────────┐
│            SEETO                │
│         Southern China          │
└─────────────────────────────────┘
```

SEETO (PATRICK) TAK TAM
B 1926 Southern China
D 2003 Brisbane

& MARIA SEETO
B 26 Dec 1935 Rabaul
D 2010 Kavieng
M 1957 Rabaul

SEETO MEI YEE
B 1929 Southern China

& SEETO (STEPHEN) CHUN YUEN
B 1917
D 2008 Kavieng
M 1957

DANIEL SEETO
B 1970 Rabaul

& ANNA SMITH
B 1973 Lae
M 1990 Brisbane

ANDREW SEETO
B 1957 Rabaul

& KATHERINE CUNNINGHAM
B 1957 Sydney
M 1978 Brisbane

JONAS SEETO
B 1994 Brisbane

NATHANIEL SEETO
B 1995 Brisbane

FRANCINE SEETO
B 1989 Brisbane

& MICHAEL COSGROVE
B 1988 Brisbane
M Mar 2011 Brisbane

LUCAS SEETO
B 1991 Brisbane

AISHA MAREE COSGROVE
B Jan 2011 Brisbane

MARIA'S FAMILY

HEINRICH SCHULTZ & ASEA KITU

HEINRICH SCHULTZ JUNIOR
B 1897 Madang D 1939

& KOTI PEREIRA
B 1880 Ambon D 1954 CLW 1913 Rabaul

JOSEFINA PEREIRA
B 1913 D 1942 Waters off Rabaul

& SEETO (DAVID) WEI
B 1910 Southern China D 1988 M 1934 Rabaul

& GEORGE FRANCIS BROWN
B 1806 Melbourne D 1942 Montevideo Maru CLW 1937

GEORGE BROWN
Died in womb 1942

MARIA SEETO
B 1935
D 2010

& SEETO (PATRICK) TAK TAM
B 1926 Southern China
D 2003 Brisbane
M 1957 Rabaul

& SEETO (STEPHEN) CHUN YUEN
B 1917 Southern China
D 2008 Kavieng
CLW 1954 Rabaul

DANIEL SEETO
B 1970 Rabaul

& ANNA SMITH
B 1973 Lae M 1990 Brisbane

JONAS SEETO
B 1994 Brisbane

NATHANIEL SEETO
B 1995 Brisbane

GABRIEL SEETO
B Mar 1960

HENRY SEETO
B July 1937 Rabaul

& RACHEL AIMUN
M 1955

LING SEETO
B 1955 Rabaul

& BESS AITOLA
M 1975 Rabaul

GLOSSARY

abus	protein such as fish and meat	haus boi	male servant
		haus meri	female servant
aibika	native spinach	hum bao	steamed port buns (Cantonese)
altogeta kaikai	sharing food		
Ah Ma	father's mother (Cantonese)	in-betweener	outcasts
		kaikai	food, dishes, eat
Ah Poh	mother's mother (Cantonese)	kam	come
baju kurung	traditional Malay dress	kapok	fluffy white inside of the seed of a Ceiba pentandra tree used for stuffing mattresses
betel nut	seed of the areca palm that is stimulant drug		
bilong	belong	ken	can, able
bilums	woven string bags	kebaya	traditional blouse-dress (Indonesian, Malay)
bin	been		
brumin	sweeping	kiap	field officers
brus	brother	kissim	get, retrieve, carry, use, fetch
buai	betel nut		
bung	marketplace	kissim wok	do her job
congee	rice porridge	kissim kaikai	bring the food
dai pinis	dead	Kuanua	Language of the Tolai of New Britain
Datuk	grandfather (Malay)		
em tasol	only	kukim	cook
emi	will	kunai	tall native grass
familii	family	kundu	hour-glass shaped drum
gaimin	pretend or false	lakatoi	outrigger canoe
gat	got	laplap	waist or loincloth
geko	tiny lizard	lapun	old
givim	give it	lapun meri	old lady
go where	where?	laulaus	the fruit of the Malay apple
go-finish	gone for good		
guria	earth tremor	likim	like, like something, approve
gut	good		
gutpela	good job	liklik	little, tiny, small
gutpela ples	good, good spot	lo	short form of halo
halo	hello	long	at, in, near
hapcas	half caste	longlong	mad, crazy, upset
		longtaim	a long time
haus	house, home	lukim	see, watch, aware

lusim	forget	plenti moa	excessive
mah jong	Chinese tile-based game	polis	police
manki	male youth	samting	something
maski	forget it	samting nuting	insignificant, not worth noting
masta	master, man, boss		
Mataungans	The Mataungan Association is a Tolai political body	savy	know, understand
		shao jiu	rice wine
		singsing	ceremony
Mixed Race	a term that represents a culturally and racially blended social group	slack	careless, indifferent
		sori tumachia	very sorry
		stret	straight
missus	western woman	tabak	tobacco, usually straps of
meri	woman, girl	tena vakurai	Tolai advisory group
mi	me	tin pis	canned fish
moa	more	tingting	thinking
mumu	food cooked in a pit	tingting stret	think clearly
muruk	cassowary	tispela	this person
na	and	Tok Pisin/Pisin	One of the three official languages of Papua New Guinea
nam	name		
Nenek	grandmother (Malay)		
Niugini	New Guinea/PNG	toktok	talking, discussing, announcing
Niuginean	A citizen of Niugini PNG		
nogat, nogot	no, nothing, haven't got	toktru	speak truthfully
numbatu	second, number two, step-parent	tok stret	be honest
		Tolai	the people of the Gazelle Peninsula of New Britain
numbawan	first, number one, biological		
		tupela	two, couple
nuting	nothing	trabil	trouble
olegeta	everyone or everything	wah	commonly-used Cantonese expression of dismay
olesam	the same as		
oli	all/everyone		
Papa tru	biological father	wantoks	speakers of the same language
pela	fellow, person		
pipa	four stringed Chinese musical instrument	wash-haus	laundry
		wasim	wash
pipel	people	wasim laplap	do the washing
pikininis	babies and children	wonem	what (what name)
pindim	find, search, research	wonem tispela	what is this?
pisin	pidgin	Yeh Yeh	father's father (Cantonese)
ples	place		
plenti	plenty	yu or yupela	you, you (group)

ABOUT THE AUTHOR

WENDY GLASSBY once lived in the beautiful town of Rabaul in Papua New Guinea, the people and the experience of which she has never forgotten. Decades later, the unique history of Rabaul has influenced her research for a Creative Writing PhD and the writing of the novel 'Between', about the Seeto family who migrates to Australia after Papua New Guinea Independence. Wendy is a published writer, a passionate reader, and an obsessive collector of books. Her particular passion is centred on the importance and power of quality fiction to engage us completely while helping us make sense of our world. Drafts of this novel have been recognised by two Varuna, the National Writing House awards. She is published in short fiction and essays.

ACKNOWLEDGEMENTS

First I must extend my sincere gratitude and thanks to former ABC journalist for Papua New Guinea (PNG) Sean Dorney. His generosity of time to read my manuscript and then to write what is, for me, the most perfect Foreword. Whether intended as such only Sean can say, but read by me as an absolute endorsement that my words, sentences, paragraphs and chapters have been comprehended by at least one special reader familiar with the subject. Thanks also to PNG poet, Gwendolyn Kalupio, for her poem 'wai na yu go', about which Gwen is most modest but, for me, to have not been able to reproduce it here would have been a great loss as it captures a sense of loss that I hoped to portray in my writing.

Most importantly, I must express my absolute appreciation of the creative time and energy of my daughter Cathie who, as she struggles through Covid-19 isolation in her home in Melbourne, created this book's distinctive, flamboyant, and unique cover illustration and designed the typesetting of the content. Never have I been so proud and so grateful at once.

Along the creative journey I have had many unwavering supporters and contributors. Top of the list are my husband Arthur (the CEO of our partnership) and my family – Karen, Cathie, Danny and Rosée – whom I thank from the bottom of my heart. Patience, enthusiasm and encouragement are the gifts they granted me. I thank my readers Christine Nott, and Gerri Cox and my sisters, in particular Robin who not only shared her recipes and experiences but also endured the reading of many trial versions and yet still sweetly reassured me each one brought tears to her eyes. Whether out of truth or generosity, these words were a comfort to me amidst my writerly doubts. Siblings are great supporters, and I have many to thank who, despite my suspicions that, perhaps, because of the duration of the writing process, one or two might have had moments of doubt this would ever be finished, all of whom were sufficiently polite never to say so. That restraint is immeasurable in its worth to a writer's insecurities. A special thanks to my constant Territorian enthusiast Gordon, in my mind definitely my 'numbawan' fan, someone who knows the subject of Papua New Guinea sufficiently to assure me his opinions must carry weight and thus, intentionally or otherwise, encouraged me to persevere.

In the support of peers and like-minded friends we find our greatest strength. They know the industry, understand the demands and appreciate the effort required. I wholeheartedly thank my former academic supervisor and now friend Associate Professor Anne Surma, Academic Chair for the Creative Arts, Murdoch University, Perth, and Christine, Geraldine and Michelle.

I also thank Varuna, the National Writers' House and the Dark family for several opportunities of residential scholarships, which aided the development of early drafts and, for the final stage, my editor Ilsa Sharp, President of Editors Western Australia and a Professional Member of IPEd, Institute of Professional Editors, Ltd.

Contributing to the creation of this work has not only been personal observations but also considerable research. Should any reader be interested, a bibliography of research undertaken is appended to my PhD thesis 'As much as fits on an aibika leaf: Writing/reading fiction in a globalised world', Murdoch University, Perth, Western Australia.

www.ingramcontent.com/pod-product-compliance
Lightning Source LLC
Chambersburg PA
CBHW050033120726
47903CB00006B/2027